To Karen
July 10th 1995.
Happy Birthday
All my love
Hugs and kisses
Maddx xxxx

HERSELF

Book Five
in the sequence
Daughter of Tintagel

HERSELF

Book Five
in the sequence
Daughter of Tintagel

Fay Sampson

HEADLINE

First published in 1992
by HEADLINE BOOK PUBLISHING PLC

Reprinted in this edition in 1992
by HEADLINE BOOK PUBLISHING PLC

10 9 8 7 6 5 4 3 2 1

British Library Cataloguing in Publication Data

Sampson, Fay, 1935−
  Herself. (Daughter of Tintagel books)
  I. Title II. Series
  823.914 [F]

  ISBN 0−7472−0452−7

Typeset by Medcalf Type Ltd, Bicester, Oxon

Printed and bound in Great Britain by
Richard Clay Ltd, Bungay, Suffolk

HEADLINE BOOK PUBLISHING PLC
Headline House
79 Great Titchfield Street
London W1P 7FN

To Paul, Catherine and Jane

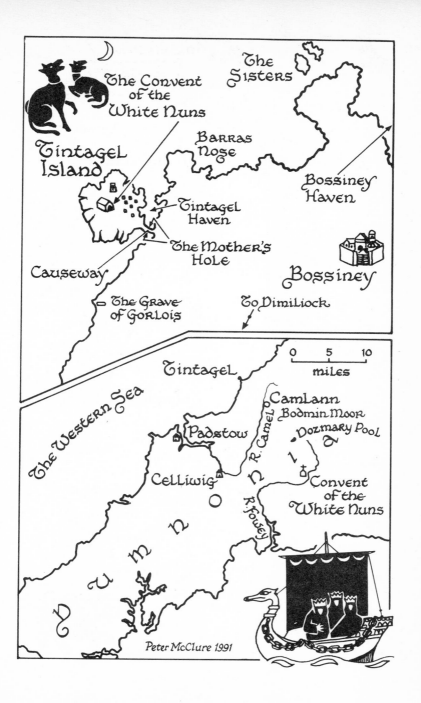

The Convent of the White Nuns

The Sisters

Barras Nose

Tintagel Island

Bossiney Haven

Tintagel Haven

The Mother's Hole

Bossiney

Causeway

The Grave of Gorlois

To Dimiliock

Tintagel

0 5 10 miles

The Western Sea

Camlann
Bodmin Moor
Dozmary Pool

Padstow

Celliwig

Convent of the White Nuns

R. Camel

R. Fowey

Cornwall

Peter McClure 1991

Author's Note

In physics, Dark Matter forms an unseen world that is the inverse of the matter we observe. The two were created to exist in equal proportions. Together they hold the universe in balance. But when they come into contact, the result is mutual destruction. Morgan's story is the Dark Matter of Britain.

But was it originally so?

I am indebted to a host of sources, translators and commentators. Some of these will be found listed on pages ix–x. But my greatest gratitude is to the late Lucy Paton for her *Studies in the Fairy Mythology of Arthurian Romance* in which she collected with love and learning all the Morgan material. Other scholars have added to and sometimes reinterpreted her work, but not replaced it.

Bibliography

Many of the older sources are available in a variety of editions and translations. I have listed here some of those I used.

Trioedd Ynys Pridein, The Welsh Triads edited by Rachel Bromwich. (University of Wales Press)
Arthurian Romances by Chrétien de Troyes. (Dent)
The History of the Kings of Britain by Geoffrey of Monmouth. (Folio Society)
Life of Merlin by Geoffrey of Monmouth. (University of Wales Press)
The Mabinogion translated by Lady Charlotte Guest. (Dent)
The Mabinogion translated by Gwyn Jones and Thomas Jones. (Dent)
Arthurian Literature in the Middle Ages by R. S. Loomis. (O.U.P.)
Celtic Myth and Arthurian Romance by R. S. Loomis. (Hashell House)
Wales and the Arthurian Legend by R. S. Loomis. (University of Wales Press)
Le Morte d'Arthur by Sir Thomas Malory. (Penguin)
British History and the Welsh Annals by Nennius. (Phillimore)
Studies in the Fairy Mythology of Arthurian Romance by Lucy Paton.
Taliesin Poems translated by Meirion Pennar. (Llanerch)
Four Ancient Books of Wales translated by W. F. Skene. (Edmonston and Douglas)
The Vulgate Version of the Arthurian Romances edited by Oskar Sommer. (Carnegie Institution of Washington)
Sir Gawain and the Green Knight translated by Brian Stone. (Penguin)
The Works of Tennyson. (Macmillan)
Arthurian Chronicles by Wace and Layamon. (Dent)

The Poems of Taliesin edited by Ifor Williams. (Dublin Institute for Advanced Studies)

I am grateful to Martin Myhill and his assistants at the University of Exeter Library for helping me to track down numerous articles and dissertations dealing with the figure of Morgan.

The modern novels referred to are:

The Mists of Avalon by Marion Bradley. (Michael Joseph/Sphere)
The Pendragon Cycle by Stephen Lawhead. (Lion)
The Merlin Trilogy by Mary Stewart. (Hodder and Stoughton)
The Wicked Day by Mary Stewart. (Hodder and Stoughton)
Sword at Sunset by Rosemary Sutcliffe. (Hodder and Stoughton)
The Coming of the King by Nikolai Tolstoy. (Bantam/Corgi)
The Once and Future King by T. H. White. (HarperCollins Publishers Ltd)

My thanks are due to the authors and publishers given above for permission to quote copyright material from Rachel Bromwich's edition of *The Welsh Triads* throughout (with some spellings changed), from Meirion Pennar's translation of the *Taliesin Poems* on pp. 64–5 (lines drawn from several poems), 66, 229, and from T. H. White's *The Once and Future King*, Rosemary Sutcliffe's *Sword at Sunset*, and Mary Stewart's *The Wicked Day* in chapter 72.

Prologue

I make no excuses. It matters less than nothing to me what you think. I know what others have said of me, even young Taliesin, though I was kind to him.

I am what I am.

I am eternal. I am the shape-shifter. I am Morgan the Fay.

Yes, you may recoil. If you have heard of me at all, it will be nothing to my credit. I am the half-sister of good King Arthur and his archenemy, am I not? The wicked witch, the embodiment of evil.

And yet . . .

Others call me Morgan the Goddess.

After the Battle of Camlann a silk-hung ship comes to fetch the mortally wounded king away to Avalon. I am the queen who takes Arthur in my arms for healing.

How could you understand?

You do not want to live with this ambiguity. Some editing of the story will clearly be necessary.

Chapter One

After Camlann. It is over now. All across Britain women are waiting for the heavy step that will bring the news they dread. In eastern halls the Saxons are laughing as they raise their drinking-horns. What need of invasion now, of armies of spears and battle-axes? We have torn the heart out of Britain ourselves and left a hollow bloodstained shell.

A cold dew covers the field. The ravens have flapped their heavy way to rest. The worms begin their work.

The great names are almost all dead. Gawain, Agravain, Gaheris, Gareth, Modred. Margawse's five sons, our younger generation. All your male lusty love of life, all our wise women's worship of the life-giving forces, seeps away with their blood into the earth.

And here in a lonely chapel in Cornwall the king is dying. A wind is rising in the west, beginning to spread the mourning rumour across Britain. The king is maimed. Plague starts to stalk the land.

It is not the fear of death in battle that appals you. That is how Arthur the soldier wished to go, on the field of glory. But the battle of Camlann is a day that should not be remembered. This is a warfare that should never have been fought.

The people of Britain have rejected Arthur. His queen is faithless. This king has killed his son.

The sad survivors search the field. They will find many sightless faces to make them weep. They will not find Arthur.

The druids howl for their dead and their lost opportunity. Britain will not be whole under Arthur or Modred.

The Christian priests are coming with book and bell. They kneel beside the fallen, grave, compassionate, setting some on the road to healing and committing others to heaven. They will not close Arthur's eyes.

3

The light is gone from Britain. What died on Camlann's field will never rise again.

Have I done this?

Tonight I stand again, as once in childhood we were parted, with the water between us. So small a pool. So great an ocean of misunderstanding.

I watch, as then, through hard-held tears, and you, as then, know nothing of my watching. You are helpless. Others have carried you to this place.

Tonight I am whole and you are wounded. That is not how it seems.

Chapter Two

I am the product of many fictions. I have few facts to offer you.

For the year 537 the Welsh Annals record only this:

'The Battle of Camlann, in which Arthur and Modred fell.'

It makes no judgment, claims no kinship between them, awards neither the victory. It does not say they fought on different sides. Dead, they are here accorded an equal honour.

The medieval Welsh Triads sound a more bitter note:

'Three Dishonoured Men who were in the Island of Britain: The third and worst was Modred, when Arthur left with him the government of Britain. He turned against Arthur. And then there took place the Battle of Camlann between Arthur and Modred. And Arthur slew Modred and was himself wounded to death.'

'Three Harmful Blows of the Island of Britain: The second Gwenhyvach struck upon Gwenhyvar: and for that cause there took place afterwards the Action of the Battle of Camlann.'

'Three Futile Battles of the Island of Britain: And the third was the worst: that was Camlann, which was brought about because of a quarrel between Gwenhyvar and Gwenhyvach.'

The bards' voices are heavy with the burden of this old grief. Women are dishonoured because they provoke this war. Men are dishonoured because they fight at Camlann. The war-band of Alan White-Ankle is dishonoured because they turn away from

5

him by night and do not go with him to Camlann, where he is slain.

'Save seven, none returned from Camlann.'

'There was a sad battle, provoked by wanton passion, Camlann through slaughter and pursuit; and fair Gwenhyvar, lively-nurtured, yellow-haired, brought it about.'

'You would go to battle, if you get a chance, to a more just fight than Camlann.'

Chapter Three

Darkness is here. The Battle of Camlann is finished. Arthur is dying.

No, do not weep. Do not shriek and keen. Do not tear at your faces. Stand silently and bear witness.

Far off now the battlefield by that little river. Out of hearing the bloodstained victors who hunt for their grievously wounded king. They will not find him now. His friends have brought him to the brink of the Otherworld.

They have come upon a holy place. A little chapel by a mere in the heart of Cornwall. The Wheel of Fortune has come full circle for him. We are back at our beginning.

His friends are few now. This war has been cruel. Lucan, who struggled to carry him here, is dead before him, killed by the clutch of his king on a wound of his own that he tried to disguise. Only Bedwyr is left tonight.

And a woman, standing unseen in the shadows across the water, watching.

How long have I been there?

Ever since Arthur was born. I have waited a lifetime, always in shadow, always this depth between us.

The wind troubles the trees. The moonlight slips from my goose-white face and finds it again. Will he see one, or three, or nine women under the shifting branches?

Too late to wonder. Blood dances the reel of death in front of Arthur's eyes. He never saw me clearly when the sun shone for him. How could he now?

One thing alone he grasps as though to let it go would be to surrender life itself. Even in darkness he can see it blazing in his soul through the touch of his practised fingers. The first and last reality for him: Caliburn, his sword. A hilt of doubled dragons, golden, tongued with flame. A blue steel blade marked with the runes of victory, its keen edge dulled by bitter blows, its brightness fouled tonight with a blood so dear he dare not name it.

But he has won. How could he not? While he holds Caliburn he cannot be defeated. This is the sword that gave him Mount Badon. This is the blade that turned the Anglo-Saxons back. This is the weapon that held the line for Christian Britain. Here is his immortal fame. Here is his justification for everything else. Hold it tight.

Why then does he groan from more than the agony of his wound?

Why is there no one to heal him?

I clench my fists so hard that the blood spurts from my palms and the forbidden tears creep down my cheeks like falling stars. But I will not move.

He holds his power yet, in the darkness and the pain and the smell of blood. He will not let it go. Beyond all reason his failing strength still grips Caliburn with an obstinate hope. He is Arthur. He cannot die.

But he is dying.

And I stand across the lake, clenching my healer's hands, motionless, waiting. For what?

A cloud wanders across the moon and the darkness swallows me, blots out the chapel where Arthur lies, smothers the lake. Will the world have changed when it lifts? How long have we waited for each other to move, we two? How can this water be bridged?

I, the woman, have power too in my empty hands, of another sort. I hold the gift of life.

Will he take it?

Why does he fear my love?

Chapter Four

I come from the shores of sunset.

In the British Isles the far south-west is always fairyland: Welsh Dyfed with its magic pigs; the kingdom of Meath in Ireland, famed for its sorcerers; Cornwall.

The legends are here, at Tintagel, Slaughterbridge, Dozmary Pool. Here our story begins and ends. Arthur and Morgan. He is, perhaps, history. North is masculine hero-country: Cuchulain of Ulster, Maelgwn of Gwynedd. Future historians will claim the soldier Arthur for Hadrian's Wall. No archaeologist will dig for evidence of Morgan the Fay. I am a legend. The west is where I belong.

In the very first story that links my name with Arthur's, I reign on the fortunate island of Avalon, in the farthest west of ocean.

Some find in Avalon the Island of Apples. Others say it is the country of Avallach, king of the Otherworld, my father.

Chapter Five

I did not know that, as a child. I only knew that the sea called me with a powerful voice. When the sun shone I raced down to Bossiney Cove from my parents' fort and felt the long grass whip my legs as if I were a champion mare in sight of the finishing mark. Barefoot over the sand and straight into the waves. Darkly green my skirt now, undulating round my knees like dulse, my toes sinking into fine sharp shells and sand. Far, far behind me the calls of my old nurse Gwennol, and I laughing and splashing spray in the sun. I knew even then that Gwennol's shouts to me were no more than fond cautions. She would squat in the sun, mending our clothes with her still-deft fingers, her wrinkles deepening as she smiled secretly to herself. She must have known the truth. She never truly feared for me when I scrambled on rock-stacks slick with green slime or waded to meet the crashing breakers breast high. No harm would come to me from the sea. Gwennol was a wise woman.

Yet it was Gorlois, Duke of Cornwall, I called Father, and loved him with all the passion of my eight-year-old heart. He was all the fairy king I ever wanted. Strong, as only a war-leader who clashed with his men every day on the practice-ground could be. He was no king, but battle-chief of the western tribes of Dumnonia. Black-haired as a chough's wing, with the flash of red lips below his moustache. Scarcely a strand of grey in that coarse black hair as I reached up to stroke it, though my two sisters, Elaine and Margawse, were growing marriageable. Only I, of the three, was dark like him, a matter for rejoicing. What did I care if my mother Ygerne called me an ugly little crow? Gorlois was dark and proud. And so he should be. So was I. Look at me, twining my arms round the bound leather of his legs.

'You're going to fight for Uther Pendragon? You're going

10

to lead the warriors of Cornwall to beat the Saxons? Take me too! We'll be fiercer than all the men of Devon and Dorset. The Cornish will be more victorious than the armies of Powys and Gwent put together.'

He threw back his great dark head and his white teeth laughed as he snatched me up on to his horse and hugged me strongly.

'Do you not think I can do all that without you?'

'Of course you can!' I cried at the top of my little voice so that all the war-band should hear me. 'You should be King of Britain, not Uther Pendragon. But you'll need this.'

And I slipped my charm over his head.

Gwennol had never taught me, though she was instructing my eldest sister Elaine. I was a knowing child. I saw that Gwennol might teach me too, whether she would or no. She had a reverence for the sacred things, Gwennol Far-Sight. She could not disguise it. I watched her hands hovering, heard her lips whispering, even when she avoided a holy flower or feather or stone. Playful as a puppy, I skipped out of the reach of her rheumaticky legs, through the gorse-bushes on the cliffs, or over the boulders on the beach, and crouched out of the wind, suddenly still. When she had passed, I would slip back to gather what she had seen and left.

How did I know the patterns to make from my secret store? A sense of rightness. The sacred shapes are there to be discovered, as the petals unfold, as the apple is cut, as the snake lies coiled. The words I sang came to me on the wind. I believed them effective.

Now my garland fell over Gorlois's armour. I grieved to see that the primrose flowers were bruised already by my too-eager hands. Never mind. There were darker, more lasting things in that pendant pouch. I heard the hiss of Gwennol's breath behind me.

'What do you think I am? The May King, to send me to fight with flowers?' Half jovial, half angry, my father blustered. A part of him was afraid to be shamed by a girl. But the hand that grabbed for the holy chain faltered. Gorlois claimed himself a Christian, but the old fears remained. Especially with Gwennol watching.

His arm released me and I slid to the ground. His last kiss was for my lovely mother. They were cantering off, three hundred warriors in a cloud of dust and a storm of cheering. It was a brave show; they could not keep that pace all the way to Winchester to join Uther Pendragon's army. But they would ride the last mile in the same way, with their jewellery jingling.

'What shall I bring you back, my little mermaid?' he shouted to me.

'The head of the Saxon chief to swing from the doorpost!' I shrieked back at him.

They were gone, but not so far I could not see him break my garland with his hand and let it blow away in the sea wind. His blood was up now, fear of the unknown crushed in the thunder of hooves and the feel of leather and metal round him. He thought his manhood was all he needed for this war.

I was a girl. I was not the son he wanted. When he turned his back on me I became nothing.

I spun round too, and felt the wind lash my face with a burst of vicious rain. Then I was running, straight for the high cliffs above Bossiney Cove.

'Stop her! She'll be soaked to the skin,' cried my mother Ygerne, shooing my sisters back under the thatch before the rain could spoil their fine clothes and the embroidered ribbons in their hair.

She always dressed herself and us most beautifully for a day of leavetaking. They said that Ygerne of Cornwall was the loveliest woman in Britain. Curling yellow her hair, as ripe corn when the wind ripples over it, and her fair face touched with pink like the wild rose petals in June. Yet even the richest jewel takes added fire in a silversmith's setting, and the ruby wine glows warmer in a golden cup. She made sure that Gorlois would remember her so. Very potent, my mother's spells of binding. She had others too.

Gwennol could not have caught me. Could not, and would not. She puffed and scolded, but she knew the space I needed. She understood what pertains to healing. She always followed me in my storms of temper, but she seldom interfered. Even then, I believe she feared my untaught power.

That morning my mother did not rely on Gwennol, for all her wisdom. It was Ewa she sent running after me. A black-toothed smelly slave, who caught me in her big wet arms and carried me struggling back.

I lay and wept, with the rain hammering on the walls, a rage beyond reason. I had lost the father I adored, twice over. I had lost his presence and lost his heart. He did not love me. He was my Fairy King, and he had shut me out of his Land of Joy. I patterned sharp thorns and pebbles against him. All day I would not speak or eat.

I woke in the night and the wind was still howling. Summer or not, I could hear the waves drum below the cliffs like the warning of Samain Eve. I was sure they were beating for me.

Thick darkness in the sleeping-hut. A mingled sound of breathing. Elaine and Margawse were asleep. Gwennol had gone. I sensed the emptiness even before I reached for the bed where she should have been guarding us. It was still warm, but untenanted. Wrapping myself in what clothes I could reach, I stole from the door into the damp silver of flying storm.

I was not afraid of the roaming yard dogs. One padded over, sniffed my outstretched hand and licked my bare feet. Beasts always recognise me. I blessed him with touch and word. Then 'Stay,' I commanded. He stood like a grey stone, a stray gold star reflected in his eyes as he gazed after me.

Nimble as a cat, I went over the slippery palisade, dropping on to sodden turf. Cold now, my wet skin taut, toes cramped. I welcomed the pain, accepted it into myself. It had no power to stop me. Gwennol's absence had left the prison door of my childhood open. I could escape from the bitterness of my life, where no one wanted me. It was not the first time my nurse had been missing in darkness, pointing a pathway into mystery for me. But tonight I was not curious about her. I was bound for my own final destination and my beginning. I would rejoin the sea.

Such a noble act could not be done just anywhere. Even when my dark-accustomed eyes showed me the scatter and tumult of the sea, still the last step into the void must not be yet. I paused only to cast stones over the edge and curse my father's name again. For Gorlois's rejected daughter, too short a leap would mock my towering anger. Only the highest and most jagged point was fitting. My mother's blood, if not my father's, was royal.

Westward then, towards the cliffs that faced Tintagel headland. Where else more high and holy, more deep and dangerous than that? I staggered up the slope of Barras Nose to be met by the full force of the wind and a startled shock. There were lights low on the rocks of Tintagel Cove that was the heart of this sacred place. On the ledges of the headland opposite, the convent slept in darkness. Below me, the beach was astir with a secret life. I had been wrong not to be curious about Gwennol. My childish fury was forgotten in excitement. Or no, perhaps these were the sea-folk, mermaids and giants and leviathans, rising from the waves to avenge me against Gorlois and invade his land. My kin? Strange that I did not fear them, even at the dead of night, alone.

The moving lights were gone now. Only a ruddy glow lingered and played on the walls of the deep cavern that wound right through the cliff under Tintagel convent. I do not remember that Gwennol had ever told me, and yet I knew well whose this cave was, though not yet why: the Hole of Her whose name we never spoke. I crouched and peered down into the darkness and the hint of flame.

The wind was dying, the sea settling, the tide still rising. I did not move. I held myself as still and sharp as slate. At last the fire was doused and in the sudden blackness there came cries that bellowed from that cavern. I felt my bowels, if not my conscious mind, catch their animality with an answering bound. The core of my body quickened with a hungry life. My death-wish was forgotten.

Shaken and strangely joyful, I witnessed shadows lurching from the cleft, splintering the water, men and women, some still clutching each other in a drunken stagger. Are these my people? I thought. Have they come for me? I watched them, frightened, fascinated. The thought of my death had disturbed me less.

I stole along the cliff to the top of the gully path that led up from the beach, and waited again. A few boats splashed softly away. Some white robes glimmered up the zigzag path towards the convent. Other darker-cloaked figures came my way. I recognised two of their shapes, even beneath the masks of fox and doe. I stalked Gwennol and my mother home in the darkness. I dimly understood already why Gorlois might not be my true father.

Chapter Six

If Avallach, Lord of Avalon, is my father, then you might say that Geoffrey of Monmouth was my godfather. No writer before him couples my name with Arthur's. His book: The Life of Merlin. *The year: 1148, or thereabouts. Before this Geoffrey has written his great* History of the Kings of Britain. *This is an imaginative chronicle that traces the foundation of Britain back to Trojan heroes. There is plenty about good King Arthur in it, the story of his life and deeds from his conception at Tintagel to his death at Camlann. It starts a whole new literary fashion. It makes no mention of me.*

But now in this second, more fantastical, volume, the legendary bard Taliesin is swapping stories with the enchanter Merlin.

He names me Morgen. I am one of nine excellent sisters who rule by a pleasing set of laws on the Fortunate Isle of Apples.

I am the eldest, I am the wisest, I am the healer.

I know all the arts. I have taught mathematics and astronomy to my sisters. I am beautiful beyond comparison with mortal women, loveliest of all the nine. I can fly through the air to France or Britain. I can change my shape. I am an eminent physician.

We are nine, yet we are three, each triads of ourselves. Geoffrey names us: Morgen, Moronoe, Mazoe, Gliten, Glitonea, Gliton, Thiten, Tyronoe, Thitis, correcting a slip of the scribe's pen, since the only copy that survived lists Thitis twice. Our earliest sources are not wholly trustworthy.

The Muses are nine, the Fates are three, the Earth is one. Nine maidens fan the fire for the Otherworld Cauldron of Annwn rimmed with pearls, which Arthur once set out to steal from the Fairy Fortress. Three are the Matronae, the Mothers of Europe. We must not be separated from our sister-selves. To the Greeks we are Kore, Demeter, Hecate. To the Hindus, Parvati, Derga, Kali. We are the Three-in-One. We are the Triple Goddess. Within each separate self we hold a triune being: Maiden, Mother, Crone.

15

We sisters wait with all our centuries of wisdom in our hands where the sea-girt land gives its abundance generously in every season. The earth yields for us grain and grapes without wearying labour, and the woods are sweet with the scent of apples. This is the western paradise of the Isles of the Blest.

I, Morgen, wait with all honour ready for the ship that is bringing the dying prince from Camlann. Arthur has fought his last battle. The wound is terrible.

His friends have summoned to pilot them the wise Barinthus, an ancient sea-god, messenger of the Otherworld, who also gives directions for Saint Brendan's miraculous voyage. He steers the grieving company over the ocean, guided by the starry heavens.

We nine receive great Arthur on that far, fair shore chanting our welcome. Take him up lovingly. Do not keen. With me there need be no grief, no mourning, no despair. My chamber is ready for him. Lay him down gently in my own golden bed.

My skilled hands search his honourable wound, while his friends hang on my verdict. My answer is all they hoped, what they trusted, why they have brought him so far to me. This cure will not be swift, it will not be easy, but if Arthur will trust himself to me for long enough, I can heal him. If they will leave him in my hands, he shall be made whole.

Other legends add that every year Arthur's wound bleeds afresh. Every year, the hurt must be mended again, with the water of the Tigris or the presence of the Grail.

. . . Do not be afraid, Arthur. I am here, I am eternal, there will always be healing . . .

Note, in this first story I am not Arthur's sister. I am not mortal. I have no husband.

I am dependable when all other help has failed. My plans are wise and effective. I am benevolent to those who trust me.

Geoffrey puts this first description of me into the mouth of Taliesin, who says he took Arthur to Avalon himself.

Geoffrey of Monmouth is notoriously unreliable.

Chapter Seven

And yet I grieved for Gorlois's death with a sharp anger. No one else should have robbed me of his love.

It was Merlyn's doing.

I saw how Gwennol trembled when King Uther's magician was mentioned. I saw the hunger in her eyes. Magic is power. When Uther Pendragon fell in love with my mother at his crown-wearing feast in London, Gorlois fled with her back to Cornwall, leaving the king's guards dead. There was consternation in Bossiney. Of course, Uther would have to come after my parents; we all knew that.

Bossiney rang with the blacksmith's hammer and whined with whetstones. The heavy gate was shut on us, even in the day. I was a prisoner. They would not let me run on the sand or swarm over the rocks or ride my pony after my father in the hunt. We were the hunted now. We cowered in our burrow.

'I'll fight them!' I cried, brandishing old Sulian's big sword. 'You beat Octa and all his Saxons at York. You can beat Uther.'

But my father knocked me aside without looking at me, so that I almost fell off the rampart walk.

I saw how my mother was flushed and nervous, and talking earnestly with Gorlois about his plans for defence. And it came to me slowly, like the knowledge that the tide has turned, that she hoped more from her own power than he did from his. At the age of eight I did not understand fully what our power was, but for the first time I, that had kilted my skirt like a boy and loved nothing better than to ride muddied in the hunt, found myself shortening my steps to match Ygerne's and copying the trail of her green and gold embroidered gown and the swing of the amber beads in her braided hair. I caught Gwennol watching us both knowingly.

17

And then he came. Not Uther. After days of waiting, three riders only crested the ridge. Two I disregarded. They were like any other men in leather kilts and metal breastplates, flashing their gold chains and tossing their curls, as though we hadn't prouder warriors in Cornwall. I was dragged from the palisade and flung into the women's bower with my mother and sisters, like a prize mare and her fillies when the horse-rustlers are abroad. The door was barred before they strode through the yard to give Uther's ultimatum to Gorlois. 'Return at once to the court, and bring Ygerne with you, or the Pendragon's army will be revenged on you.'

Sword-talk.

The greater threat remained outside our walls. I had seen him from the ramparts. Tall, mockingly strange. A rider on a white mare, dressed in a multitude of coloured rags, gaudier than the feathers of any bird that flew in Cornwall. A man who was not afraid of the sacred, who greeted the things of power like an old friend. I saw him reach out his hand and caress the great oak in Bossiney Meadow. Even at that distance I could have sworn I caught his smile.

While the warriors argued — you could not call it a parley — I climbed on a chest and peered towards the sea. Over the palisade I caught a glimpse of clifftop and a man on a white horse, like a standing stone, staring towards the headland of Tintagel.

And still we women fled to Tintagel, against my father's orders.

I remember the gates of Bossiney swinging wide. I remember Bryvyth the Abbess striding through on her bare feet. She was broad and wholesome as a barn, with two quiet nuns in white gowns attending her.

'You sent for me. Is your business so urgent that your man must come yelling at my gate while we're singing in chapel?' she challenged Gorlois.

'I've reason enough to rouse the whole of Cornwall. Uther wants my wife. When he hears my answer, I shall need a better fortress than this to fight from. There is one place, and one place only, that could hold out against such a war-host: Tintagel. Bryvyth Crook-Staff, for friendship's sake, give it back to me for a stronghold.'

'On your knees, godless man. Shame, that you should even

18

think of it. You gave the headland to us for prayer. You shall not have it back for war.'

'You traitress! Would you take sides with the Pendragon against me?'

'I serve no Lord but Christ, and him I'll fight for with all my strength. There's one way only Gorlois will come to Tintagel – when he brings his lady wife to me for sanctuary. No warrior passes our wall bearing weapons, nor ever shall. If Uther Pendragon comes, it will be Bryvyth Crook-Staff herself will meet him on the bridge. But Gorlois, war-lord of Cornwall, will have to fight his bloody battles somewhere else.'

He would have had her thrown out of the dun in a towering rage, but she grasped her staff and turned on her heel and marched back to her convent over the cliffs like a warrior-queen.

I watched her go, and felt the stirring of another power than Gwennol's.

Bereft of friends, like a wounded stag, my father drew his troops inland to Dimiliock to make his last stand. My mother was terrified when she understood his plan.

'You'd leave me *here*?'

'Three soldiers and a handful of servants. You won't need more. Here's the one place he'll never dream of finding you. He'll think the place is deserted when he hears I've gone. He's High King of Britain. He'll go where there's the strongest fort and the greatest war-host. You know that man's pride.'

'You're mad to leave us to his army! You defied him. His troops will burn every dun, every farm, before they reach Caer Dimiliock. What if some of them come here without the king?'

'I'll leave you a faithful guard. Sulian, Tudy, Coan. They'll know what to do if you're found.'

She gasped, and then she screamed at him, 'And what of your daughters? Would you have your men kill them too?'

I could not speak or move. This was my father, who had tossed me in his arms when I was small, who had lifted me on to his horse and laughed to see me strike my heels against its sides, who had taught me swordplay. My eyes were fastened on Sulian's weapon.

19

Only a week ago I had hefted that sword and sworn to fight the Pendragon. Did my father want me to bare my neck to this same blade to defend my mother's honour?

'At least,' Ygerne begged, 'send us somewhere safer than this. Let us go to the nuns on Tintagel Island as Bryvyth said. They'd give us sanctuary.'

'There's only one way I'll have you go to Tintagel now,' my father roared. 'If you hear that Gorlois is dead, then shear your hair and take off your gown, and go to Tintagel with my daughters and take your vows as nuns.'

He had serving-women swathed in cloaks to resemble Ygerne and Elaine and Margawse and me, and carried them off in chariots with him and his war-host. He left us alone in Bossiney with a tiny bodyguard. His wits had been bewitched.

Gwennol worked what she could. Margawse, my second sister, came rushing up to me, her red hair, black in the twilight, streaming behind her. She grabbed my hands and whirled me round.

'Morgan! Morgan! I'm to be taken into the circle tonight. I'll be the Maiden.'

'You haven't been maiden since cider-making four years ago.'

She gasped and dropped my hands. 'You little vixen-cub! If your eyes get much sharper they'll cut your nose off.'

I was not initiated. Gwennol feared to wake my power, even then. She made the circle without fire that night, with Ygerne and her waiting-woman Ruan and Elaine and Margawse, newly made wise. I was not summoned, but they could not stop me watching from the darkened hall, though Gwennol scowled and muttered in my direction. Elaine was white and frightened, Margawse hot and eager. And my mother Ygerne? She lifted her face to the east and the shaft of the rising moon. The words of protection slipped from her lips while she dreamed of the way by which Uther must come to her.

In the morning I looked east to the road from London and west to Bryvyth's convent. Which was really the way to power? I made my own childish patterns and hummed over them when Gwennol was out of earshot.

Even so, I was frightened when Uther's army passed us by on the road to Dimiliock, and a stray raiding party broke away from the rest towards Bossiney. We fled up the ladder to the store over the rafters.

Gwennol was last, save for that poor boy Keby. None of us missed him at the time. Too late we found he had stayed outside with his axe to fight them off singlehanded.

My nurse's gnarled old hands fumbled on the ladder sides. She hoisted her stiff knees up two steps and could get no further.

'Come on, Gwennol! Quickly!' I screamed at her.

'It's no good, my lover. I can't get up so high.'

I would have scrambled down to pull her with all my little strength, but Sulian had me by the waist and flung me into a corner under the drooping thatch. I lay with my face in cobwebs, hearing the panting of frightened people round me and the rustle of rats.

For a time Gwennol muttered and cursed in the hall below us. Then she fell silent, till the door burst open and the men broke in. For a terrifying long while they searched the hall. They did not see us, crouched on the rafters sheltered by the shadow of Gwennol's spell. But they soon found Gwennol.

I heard her cry out, 'Easy, now! For the love of the Mothers, can't you take it steady?' Then she was screeching without words and there were noises of a man like a bull and others cheering. It lasted a long time. There were eight of them.

When it was over, they looted as much of our home as they could carry and fired the thatch. The moment they had ridden off, we had to scurry down the ladder for our lives. I found Gwennol hanging over the well, retching. Keby's body was beside her. They had cut the boy's throat.

They left Bossiney blazing.

And so, weary and shocked and blackened with soot, we took our tattered dignity to Tintagel. Bryvyth gave us sanctuary. It was the first time I crossed that threshold. I felt the power of the place. I truly believe no warriors could have got across that causeway by force of arms. Hundreds of feet above white-topped breakers to the south and the still, shadowed cove to the north, a neck of rock links the mainland to Tintagel Head. Three men with swords could have kept that gateway. Bryvyth alone with her staff would have been a more formidable foe.

Her generous, honest faith was no defence against a devious sorcerer.

She let them in. Uther, Merlyn, Ulfin. At dead of night, in urgent haste, the names they whispered to the porter at the gate were Gorlois, Jordan, Britael. And so they seemed to be.

Except to Gwennol.

I woke and heard voices in the passageway outside. Ruan's, I recognised. One name brayed in my head like a war-horn. I thought I caught another voice, deeper. Terror entered the room. The door closed and Gwennol leaned against it, breathing fast. I sprang up on my bed.

'What is it? What did she say?'

'Hush, my lover. It's nothing. Go back to sleep.'

'No. Tell me. She said something about Father, didn't she? Is he dead? He is, isn't he? Is that what they've come to say?'

I knew, past comforting. I flew across the chilly floor and buried my face in her skirt, clinging wildly, even though she stroked and comforted me.

'No, my pretty. It's not that. They say your father's alive. He's here. He's come to your mother.'

I felt her shudder.

I was out in the passageway in a moment. Two giant shadows stood either side of a shaft of misty moonlight that slanted so as to leave their faces in darkness. A smaller figure stood in the pale light at my mother's door. Her woman Ruan.

I flew at them. Ruan gave a smothered laugh. Gwennol tried to catch me and clutch me back to her side.

'Hush, my lover. Your father doesn't want you now.'

She could not have held me. But as I fought for the door strong hands, that should have belonged to Britael, my father's boyhood friend, gripped my wrists like a vice. I wrestled with him, scratched and bit. He tried to fling me from him. My little head rang as it hit the wall and my brain rang louder with the voice that should have been Britael's, but never could be.

'Take your claws out of me, you little screech-owl, or by the Hounds of Annwn, I'll put that on you that will bind you stiller than stone from now till morning.'

Oh no, not Britael. The words of power. A man whose

22

strength lay not in swords, though he would bestow swords on others. I had met Merlyn.

I sank my teeth into his hand.

In that instant of agony I heard my mother's cry. That sound is screaming in my ears still.

Then Merlyn laughed in my face, a great shout of triumph. And from inside Ygerne's chamber Uther echoed his shout.

So my brother Arthur was made.

In the morning Bryvyth told me that Uther had killed my father.

Chapter Eight

This lusty legend proves too much for the Victorian sensibilities of Alfred Lord Tennyson. In 1859 he completes The Idylls of the King, *twelve books of poetry chronicling the ideal rule of Arthur. There are sins and failings by many at the court of Camelot, but Arthur is always noble. Tennyson cannot allow his stainless king to be fathered by adulterous trickery. He would rather deny the consistent record of the earliest chronicles. So others will always doctor the evidence they find uncomfortable.*

True, before Arthur can wed Gwenhyvar the poet makes the knight Bedivere repeat to her father a sanitised version of the traditional story. He is careful to have Gorlois slain and Ygerne hastily remarried before Uther beds her. King Uther himself dies childless before Arthur is born. The only part that Merlyn plays is to receive the newborn baby at a secret postern-gate and whisk him away for fear of Uther's rivals.

But Tennyson himself has invented a different coming for his sovereign.

This second tale is told by the Queen of Orkney and Lot's wife, named here as Bellicent. I, Morgan, do not exist for Tennyson. Bellicent is a daughter of Ygerne by Gorlois, and Arthur's loyal sister.

This is her story:

The place, Tintagel, still. The time, a night of storm. The witnesses, Merlyn and his master Bleys. They spy a dragon-winged ship, poised upon a wave so high it seems to sail in heaven. From stem to stern its sides are bright with shining people. This vision is gone as soon as seen. The two mages drop to the cove and watch the breakers fall, each mightier than the last. The ninth great wave draws half the deep into itself, and full of voices, all aflame it roars upon them. And in the flame is borne a naked babe to drop at Merlyn's feet, who seizes him and cries, 'The King! Here is an heir for Uther!'

24

HERSELF

Thus Tennyson's Arthur comes to earth even more immaculately than the Christ child. A boy born of no human parent, on either side, heaven-sent for our salvation.

Yet even Tennyson makes Merlyn riddle:

> 'Rain, rain, and sun! a rainbow on the lea!
> And truth is this to me, and that to thee;
> Sun, rain, and sun! and where is he who knows?
> From the great deep to the great deep he goes.'

Chapter Nine

I know the truth. I was there.

Certainly there was a baby, born of a woman in the usual way. And very certainly it was a boy.

How could I forget that? The exultant cry that cut through the howling of the south-west gale. A man-child! Victory to Merlyn.

Elaine, Margawse, Morgan, all Gorlois's daughters. And now the Mother's curse had broken and Ygerne was delivered of her first son. Look at Uther Pendragon, dancing a jig with Merlyn. Drunk as lords, that Midwinter night, king and sage. The torches flaming and the wine running. Everybody celebrating. No one as drunk as the High Lord of Britain, as drunk as the High Lord of magic. They had got what they wanted.

That cry screamed in my ears like a hare when the weasel is at her throat. I had heard another cry, uttered in triumph but sounding in my childish heart my father's death-knell.

Those long, hard fingers on my arm. Those steely eyes. A more than physical power that transfixed me and would not let me through my mother's chamber door to where they said my father was.

And then that shout, unbearable. A woman's ecstasy.

Nine months before this cry of triumph.

I was skilled at mathematics, even before I went to the nuns' school. Gwennol, who had nursed Ygerne and then her daughters, had taught me to track the stars and seasons. For a wise woman, that counting has one particular end: the regeneration of life.

On the women's side we knew well who the shape-shifters were who had penetrated Tintagel, even before the Pendragon boasted openly of it. But we could count too how short the days between my mother's husbands. We knew how unpredictable are women's wombs.

Uther boasted of victory. How could this male baby be anything but his? Nine months since the Duke was killed. Now Cornwall had suffered its final defeat. He had got the son that Gorlois could never give Ygerne.

Was Merlyn so confident of his own prowess? Did he never wonder?

Arthur came as their Midwinter baby, the turning of the sun at the darkest time of the year, to light the heart of Britain.

He lit my heart.

Full of resentment, I crept, soaked by the storm outside, into the chamber where my mother lay sleeping. The midwife was drunk on the floor. The baby drowsed in his cradle. And Gwennol was stooping over him, murmuring charms.

I raged at the foolish fondness in her face.

I blamed him then for all our wounds, for my father's loss, for Gwennol's rape, for Keby's throat cut by the well, my old home burned. For Uther's coming. I lashed her in my anger.

'Poor Gwennol! Did you think he would be your baby? Did you think they would give him to you when the wet nurse had finished with him? Were you dreaming of dressing him, and playing with him, and singing him to sleep, as you did with Gorlois's daughters? He's the eldest son of the King of all the Britons. Did you think they would leave him here in Bossiney with you?'

I darted to the cradle.

The baby stirred and opened milk-blue eyes.

I had never held an infant in my arms. I was the youngest daughter. I must have seen other babies but I did not notice them. Nothing prepared me for that soft peach-bloom face that looked up at me so innocently and opened almost in a smile. I had no warning of this fire that leaped in that core of my body discovered only once before. I did not expect to fall in love with my brother.

As Ygerne woke, and reached fearfully for her baby, I snatched him up from his cradle, heedless of her cries and his. I bit my lip till the blood ran and then . . . I nipped his neck, with a tiny precise incision.

He gave one cry, no more. I had wounded myself more deeply than him. I left my kiss upon his neck, meaning our blood to mingle. I marked him for mine. I think it did not sink deep enough to reach his heart.

The child was not left with us long enough for his christening. Uther had planned it for Epiphany, the feast of the wise men's gifts. Merlyn had other schemes.

But the magician disappeared himself the night before Christmas. Merlyn served the high magic to win temporal power. Not for him the feast of the poor child in the manger who would be a crucified king. That is the way of the white-robed Christian saints, who are loved by the poor. It is also the wisdom of women like Gwennol who sanctify the ordinary.

Midwinter too is a time for giving gifts. Merlyn should have remembered that.

The flames leaped on logs to keep back the wild winter day. We three sisters stood around our mother's knee while Uther looked on fondly. Elaine was still fair and virginal, with the soft flesh of childhood not quite melted to maidenly slenderness, though she was promised in marriage to Nentres of Garlot already. Margawse flaunted her unbound hair as fiery as the blood that beat between her thighs and would not let her hungry body rest. And I, Morgan, ugly as a moulting crow, born painfully after long waiting, the third girl, a bitter disappointment to my parents.

What should we give him, this tiny golden brother in Ygerne's lap? I stood and stared at my mother's bright green skirt with its ribbons of daffodil-yellow brocade. They had wrapped him in lambswool and swansdown, so that only his wide blue eyes peeped out at us. But his tiny flesh was born of woman, like mine. Strip away the warm cloth on which he rested, and he had known Ygerne's body beneath. He had travelled down the same red road as myself. Why did one entry into the world bring such anguish, and the other so much joy?

Elaine was pink with self-consciousness. This was a solemn moment. She would cuddle him afterwards. She, who had mothered me when our own mother would not even look at me, loved babies, but she shrank from the messy way by which they are got. She was hesitating on the threshold of womanliness. The ceremonies of adulthood still confused her, yet she was not displeased that everyone was looking at her now, admiring her. Everyone? Were all our household ranged around the hall alike to her, Uther's warriors, Ygerne's waiting-ladies, old councillors, children, serving-maids, male slaves? Did she not, unconfessed even to herself, prize more highly the regard of men? She did not seem to. She was vain enough to boast of rivalry in dress with other young women, as though their opinion was the most important thing to her. But I had seen one man stir her. Uther Pendragon had ways that could set any maid blushing. He made no exception for his step-daughters, even in front of Ygerne.

He had tried his charms on me once. But only once.

What was Elaine holding out to the baby? A stone I had never seen before. A crystal pure as herself. Clear, flawless, cool. His little fist closed round it and at once the jewel became a lively pink, warmed by his hand. She kissed his brow.

'Hold it tight, little brother. Keep it safe. In this small stone there are riches, treasure, corn for your horses, and whatever your heart desires to eat and drink. It can draw precious gems and gold to itself, and perhaps a crown. Prize it above all other friends. It is plenty.'

The baby stared solemnly.

Margawse pushed past her, laughing. She could never be serious. Quick as a leaping flame to take Elaine's place and the centre of the stage. Tossing her hair, that was brighter than all the jewels threaded through it. Knowing the firelight from the great hearth warmed her creamy skin. Eyes rolling round all the men, taking her time, creating an audience, flashing that special spark that seemed to kindle anew for each one of them.

Her hands were nursing a cup, warm copper. She was hugging it to her newly swelling breasts. The metal was doubly inflamed. You could imagine it pliant, melting, cradled there. She held it out now, provocatively, above the baby's face. His large blue eyes swam up to it. His hands were bound in the soft wrappings. He was too young to snatch for it.

Mocking, she waved it. A little liquid splashed him red.

'You will drink deep from this, little man. You will intoxicate all the women of Britain. Queens shall fall to you, and maidens pay you their ruby tribute.'

Then she raised the cup to her lips and sipped from it

herself, watching him over the rim with her laughing green eyes. I was curious to know what stained her mouth so crimson.

She kissed the baby full on his yielding lips.

'Wealth and women,' my mother laughed, and rose with the baby guarded in her arms. 'A fortunate child!'

She would not look at me. She never looked at me if she could help it. But every other eye in the room was on me as she turned away. I sensed their shrinking back. They saw the truth about us. Ygerne the Wise. Afraid to take the gift of her third daughter.

I seemed to freeze, a waterfall silenced into icicle. My mother at any rate I was certain of. I was her daughter as well as Elaine and Margawse. This boy was my brother as much as theirs. I could play the fairy queen too.

Ygerne must know, as everyone did, that I had loved Gorlois more passionately than either of my sisters. Did she guess that I had cursed him too? She could not have paled and started from his shade more fearfully than she did now from me.

I dropped my gaze from her averted eyes. I willed my mind upon my little kinsman. How near indeed was this my brother? They do well who say a man's closest bond is to his sister's son rather than to his own child. Only our shared maternity is certain.

Did Uther in his man's pride never doubt? Whose daughter was I? Whose son was this in front of me? Frightened, I clutched the gift I had brought. Suppose I had guessed wrong?

Gwennol's hand pushed me in the back. I stumbled forward, angry at this loss of my rehearsed dignity. My small hand gripped my mother's bright green skirt, detaining her. Ygerne turned, looked down, cold, repelling.

'Let go my dress.'

'I have a gift for the baby.'

'He does not want your present.'

She was too frightened to clothe her rebuke with smiles and pass it off to the court as a mother's pretty scolding. For the first time in my life I discovered a great truth that until now I had used without understanding: that I had power over people. I would not need to wait for my apprenticeship of spoken spells and brewed charms. The Goddess was already present in me. The realisation made me strong and joyful.

I loosed my hand and reached up to the baby in my mother's arms. A moment's pause. I concentrated, and then she lowered him unwillingly. My fingers parted the swansdown. With my left hand I laid my present across his heart. The first little hunting spear that Gorlois had given me. The fine blade stabbed my nine-year-old heart with the recollection of autumn forests, galloping ponies, a laughing man. Farewell to childhood innocence.

'I shall never use this again. I must be a woman now. Take it, and see what you can do with it.'

I kissed the spear, but not the child. I was still not sure of him.

I had armed him with his lance. Would he understand how to use it?

But Ygerne shrieked as the weapon touched the baby.

'Unlucky gift of a killing blade! Take that in payment! He owes you no blood!'

She tore a pearl from her hair and threw it at me. The skein was snapped, and all the precious drops slipped from their net and tumbled at my feet, glistening like fallen tears among the rushes. I raised my steady eyes to meet her terrified look.

Uther burst into laughter and even hugged me. He was more than satisfied. His son a gold-giver, a womaniser, a mighty warrior. What could the boy be but another Pendragon? I watched and wondered. One half of this infant was Cornish, that much I knew for certain. Half of myself. But more than that? Was this the last secret child of Gorlois? Was he the foal of Cornwall's Horse, or the spawn of the Head Dragon? And which would draw him more surely into my arms again? I could find no clear sign.

He had the spear now. I must wait till he could use it.

Ygerne was wise. Ygerne must know. But Ygerne would always tell the tale that suited her purpose best.

I pestered Gwennol afterwards. But she scolded and pinched my lips with her calloused fingers.

'Hush, my lover. Do you think my little old bit of magic could have been stronger than great Merlyn's?'

The baby was three weeks old. Epiphany was to be his naming-day, when the Church claimed him for her own and my mother's clan received him. Nectan, the saint, would christen him in our chapel. Druid or not, Merlyn would surely be back for that. This child had been his making, more than Uther's. In this sun-gold baby lay the sorcerer's great hope for power once Uther died. I could imagine how he would take him from their Christian hands, how he would hold the infant in his arms, say over him the words we must. He would look on him keenly, feel the beat of his heart, smell his small sweet breath. Not drunk with joy and wine this time, Merlyn would know if Ygerne had cheated him.

And if she had? Would he ever tell Uther?

'Lucky for him the lad's as fair as a corn-dolly,' I overheard one soldier gibe to another. 'Gorlois was raven-black. Else we might have thought the duke had moulted a feather or two before Dimiliock!' And he stuck his fellow in the ribs so they both doubled up with coarse laughter.

'Ah,' said the other, wiping his eye. 'But her Elaine's as fair as a lily, and the queen says she was Gorlois's daughter.'

'Aye, true enough. But she and Uther are two of a kind. Still, she's a wise woman. If it had been another like that black cat Morgan, she could have changed him with her arts to the right sort.'

'Best not to crack that joke in his lordship's earshot. It would break his dam's heart if she lost her precious pup now.'

I stole, like the black cat they thought I was, softly past.

I was old enough to calculate the moons, young enough not to know that wise women do not lie with their husbands on the eve of battle.

On Epiphany Eve all the court was revelling in the hall, even Ygerne, while in the queen's bower the solitary wet nurse was snoring over a jug of ale. I crept, this time unseen, into the dimly lit chamber and leaned over the cradle of my baby brother. He was a beautiful boy.

Tonight, after Camlann, this beauty is marred with blood and sorrow. On that night too, I looked upon him with the same dread and love.

I feared and hoped what might come to me from my brother. And I feared for him.

I took the baby. Loving and hating him as I had done Gorlois. Cherishing and condemning him as I did my own self. It was January, a night of tempest more terrible by far than that summer storm that had once lured me out on to the cliffs alone. But I felt the same powerful call, to the sea, and above all, to Tintagel.

I longed frantically to carry him westward beyond the sunset to my island that very night, clasped in my arms. I struggled against the gale to Tintagel Cove and fought my way through the waves to stand buffeted by the wind on a high rock. Drenched, I turned to the ocean from which I had come. I lifted one hand. My spirit summoned the ship that would carry us both to the Fortunate Isle of Joy. Beyond all reach of hurt we two would play glad games for ever.

It did not come. The breakers showed no pity. And as I shivered and sneezed, even the vision was snatched away. Behind me, shouts rang louder than the gale. Armed men clattered in haste and anger on to the beach. The Pendragon yelled curses and threats across the angry water. Old Gwennol sang pleas to me, harder to resist. High in the chapel of Tintagel convent, candles pricked. Then Merlyn stretched out his hand and acted.

I felt my being stiffen, body and spirit.

My power could not withstand him. I was only nine years old. I let the baby fall. I watched my brother's small pale face sink beneath the swell, helpless. The ninth wave crashed round my shoulders, stunning me, and carried him to Merlyn's feet. I heard one fierce exultant shout.

'By the power of the old earth and the older moon and the three dark Mothers.

'By the power of the bright face of Ludd and Gwydion and Llew.

'By the power of the Father and his Christ and the Spirit of Wisdom!'

'I name you . . . Arthur!'

And they were both gone.

A baby was taken from me. A fifteen-year-old youth, on the first step of manhood, appeared from Merlyn's tutelage with his sword in his hand. After an irretrievable interval of silence, which changed the course of Britain, I made Ygerne affirm this was her son and Uther's.

It is probably true.

Chapter Ten

I am the fairy godmother.

In the mid-twelfth century, Geoffrey of Monmouth tells the world of Arthur in his History of the Kings of Britain. *It is a tale of battles, thrones and statecraft. His good fairy surfaces later in the* Life of Merlin. *Within twenty years the Jerseyman Wace has turned the chronicle of Arthur into Norman French with his own robust embellishments. Before the century is out the Anglo-Saxon Layamon has seized upon the tale. In his hand the anti-Saxon hero is changed into, ironically, the quintessential Englishman. You might say the conquest of Celtic Britain is complete. Two chapters in Geoffrey have grown into a swashbuckling saga. Wars, jousts, quests, voyages. Good colourful stuff, a boy's own story.*

Wace does not mention Morgan. But Layamon knows of Argante.

He tells how, as soon as Arthur was born, elves took him. They enchanted the child with magic most strong, they gave him might, to be the best of all knights; they gave him another thing, that he should be a rich king; they gave him a third, that he should live long; they gave the prince virtues most good, so that he was most generous of all men alive. And thus the child thrived.

At the end, the wounded Arthur believes that

'I will fare to Avalon, to the fairest of all maidens, to Argante the queen, an elf most fair, and she shall make my wounds all sound; make me all whole with healing draughts.'

Two women come, and take him in their ship.

In Brittany they have guarded an ancient tradition well. We are the Margot-la-fées. Not long since, no woman would bear a child without invoking our help. It is not safe for the baby to start upon the road of life without our fairy blessing.

34

HERSELF

While the mother struggles in labour on bed or birthing-stool, there is work of a different sort being done in the room next-door. Lay the table with the best you have of linen, silver, crockery. Serve up a meal that will not dishonour Otherworld queens. Now, is all ready and fair? If you have not displeased us, we Margots will enter your house.

In that other room there is blood and pain. Here is peace and seemliness. The child will be born whole and healthy.

And we have brought our gifts.

We offer this baby a name, a character, and a destiny.

It is more than five hundred years since we first gave our blessings to another hero of the French romances, Ogier the Dane.

Six fays come to watch over his birthing and weep when his mother dies. They lean over his cradle and caress the baby. They shower on him their gifts of strength, courage, success, beauty, tender susceptibility, so that he shall surpass all knights.

Then Morgan comes last.

Oh, yes. Are you remembering The Sleeping Beauty? *Are you waiting for the story to turn on my wicked fairy's curse?*

I hate to disappoint you.

My gift exceeds all the rest. It is myself I bestow on the baby Ogier. His destiny is that he will never die by the hand of man. After a long, hard-fighting life of glory, he shall come home to me, to my island of Avalon. There, in my welcoming arms, his blessing will be fulfilled. I offer him a never-ending youth and unwearied joys as my lord and love.

I keep that promise.

Chapter Eleven

For that theft of Arthur, I became Uther's prisoner. He feared the darkness in me, calling it devilry. Darkness is for plotting, grief and love. Men go to war by daylight.

Arthur was gone, and Merlyn with him. Uther had served his purpose. The Pendragon was right to be afraid.

The prison he sent me to was Tintagel convent. That high, hard, windswept roost, almost an island, but for one lofty neck of rock that linked it to the land. Leviathan, with all the ocean before it, caught by its tail. The nuns' lime-washed cells speckled the cliffs like a sea-gulls' colony, but their songs were sweeter. Within their chapel and their library they enclosed pearls of great price. They clung like limpets to the rock, those white-gowned women. No gales could shake them, nor druid curse dislodge them. When they were swept away and armed men took it for a fort in the end, it was because their own faith faltered.

I was an unwilling heiress of their treasure. Furious, rebellious, appalled to be confined within a space whose circumference barely measured a mile. I know; I walked that tiny plateau time after time, counting each stride, hearing the waves battering the rocks beneath, thinking how short a step I would need to end it.

I could not believe it. I, who had galloped with the hunt through the Forest of Trigg, who had urged my exhausted pony after my father to the uplands of Bodmin Moor, whom Gwennol had allowed to run and climb and dream freely on the sandy shore.

I raced for the farthest outcrop of the headland. I might have dashed myself from that height the very first day.

Someone came after me. The nun they had given me for my foster-mother, Luned. A scared and sallow young woman, more fitted to theology and mathematics than the care of a child. Her hands were rough, her muscles sturdy on her thin bones. She was no aristocrat. My royal status cowed her. The High King's step-daughter sharing her cell! And it was whispered that I was the devil's child.

I balanced, leaning on the wind, and taunted her from the outermost shelf of rock. Beneath me the breakers swung, almost too far away to be heard.

I reached out a wicked hand.

'You are afraid?'

'Of course!' Her flash of anger pleased me. 'Get down.'

'Climb up here. Stand beside me,' I ordered her.

'I cannot. Get down at once.'

'Climb.'

I fixed her with my gaze. Slowly, against all the instincts of her fearful flesh, against all the reasoning of her clever mind, I watched her obey. She could have prayed. She could have yelled for Bryvyth. But she did not. I savoured the taste of sovereignty.

I had no power over my own life. I had lost my freedom. But I had gained my first subject.

I used my power cruelly. I dragged her to the very edge and forced her to look over. She retched her stomach up.

I laughed at her. 'Bryvyth said you were to look after me. That you were to guard me from harm. You couldn't keep a crow from the corn.'

But in that moment of peril, leaning out over the windswept ledge, I had seen a sight that shocked and fascinated me. An older nun, gaunt as a scarecrow, perched on the narrowest foothold of rock on the side of the cliff with her hands raised to heaven in prayer and the ocean before her.

That night, in a cell so close that we could scarcely move without touching each other, Luned undressed me. She had no need to do it. I was nine years old. I had been parted from my nurse Gwennol for the first time. But I was a neat and capable child. I could shift for myself.

Her arms went round me as she lifted my gown. Her cool hands brushed my flesh. Her breath quickened. I knew that I had power over her of another sort.

The Abbess Bryvyth was another matter. I loved her for her strength. I envied her rumbustious faith. When I transgressed, which was often in that first year, she beat me with birch-twigs. Afterwards, she would crush me to her in a hug, scolding and laughing. I believe that in secret she flogged herself for my sins too.

The food was plain, my bed was of bracken in the cell I shared with Luned, my unadorned clothes a cause of mockery to my fellow-pupils for a High Queen's daughter. The hours of prayer and study were long, the work delight.

I learned to write in Latin and Greek, scratched on slabs of slate. In time I came to handle heavy volumes lovingly transcribed from Egypt, Carthage, Rome, Jerusalem. I watched my tutor Rathtyen unroll fragile scrolls and saw how her hands caressed pages even of Hebrew. My fingers traced the compass marks of geometric interlace and spiral. My eyes feasted on the colours and gilt of illuminations.

Geometry, philosophy, theology, the science of calendar and stars. Literature, poetry, rhetoric, disputation. Weaving, embroidery, calligraphy, design and painting. All these the sisters taught me.

In time, I sang the liturgy with them.

There was knowledge at Tintagel that the scholar Rathtyen could not teach me, nor Bryvyth either. But there were those who could and did. In her hunger for wisdom, the far-reaching pilgrimage of the soul, Bryvyth had gathered round her all the keen minds of the west. Among them were the daughters of druids, newly baptised. They found the holy life of the Christian nuns not too dissimilar to their mothers' training. They were noted for herbal lore and astronomy and the breeding of animals. Such knowledge is power. Knowledge is dangerous. It should not be left lying where children can find it.

These women had entered the Church. They had not left the older faith. Christ was their Druid. The Mother was holy.

Gwennol committed me to their care. She came to see me, secretly, rowed in a little coracle round the headland in the mists of dawn.

Luned knew. I wanted her to know. I had stood on the threshold in the pale moonshine of May Eve until she woke, wide-eyed and fearful. I waited, seeking her eyes, not knowing what I hoped. If it had been Bryvyth watching over me, she would have yelled and scolded me back to my bed. If I had tried to run, she would have thrown back the blanket, come after me with huge strides, wrapped me in those powerful arms, marched me back to the cell and barred the door. She would have whipped me. She would have fought with every weapon that her strong love could show her to save my soul.

Luned's voice was high with anxiety. 'Where are you going? Come back to bed.'

I scorned to answer. Where was there for me to go but Tintagel Head? I was a prisoner. If I were found beyond that causeway Uther would have me killed.

And still I waited. She was a clever woman. Could she really not guess?

She came and stood beside me. I took her hand and pulled her round to face the mainland. The lights of Beltaine fires blazed all along the coast and on the hills beyond. Out of the darkness, new life was being made.

'Come, Luned! Come now!'

I started to run towards the fires. I could hear the drums quickening the rhythm of my blood. The pipes were calling to me. Gwennol had kindled those flames as a sign for me.

'No! Come back to bed!' she cried. 'May Eve is not for us. We leave all that behind us when we take our vows as virgins.'

I did not heed her. I do not know what I meant to do. You cannot run far on Tintagel. The cliffs are below you on every side.

Then I stopped, startled. There were muffled voices beneath me on the zigzag path that led down to the cove. Hope streaked across my mind with lightning brilliance. Gwennol had come to me!

'Who is it? Who's there?' I shouted.

'Hush.'

There was a shocked silence from below, and then came a wavering banshee wailing that should have chilled the blood. I saw the flicker of white hurrying down to the beach from the nuns' huts. I guessed the truth and burst out laughing.

Very early next day, I was abroad again. I watched a coracle slipping out of the cove into the misty dawn of May Morning. A close-cloaked figure sat crouched in the stern. I did not need to see beneath the hood to know who she would be. Solon rowed it, my father's old slave whom I had known since babyhood, a man weathered and silent as a storm-struck oak-tree. He was wise too.

I was standing forlorn on Tintagel's high meadow. In all the island I had found no may-blossom to greet the summer. As I watched the boat, even at that distance I read the hunger in Gwennol's look as she turned her hooded head up to search for me. I was her baby, the last Ygerne would ever give her. Little Arthur was gone. He would never be hers to hold. She would not let the nuns have me entirely.

I raised my hand to her. I doubted her eyes could see that far.

Luned came searching for me. I expected a scolding, but to my surprise she crowned me with summer flowers. Her hands were shy and awkward arranging them in my tangled hair.

I smiled for her. 'Thank you, Luned. You have crowned me your queen.'

She tried to fight a little when she saw where I was leading her. 'In the name of the Father and the Son and the Holy Wisdom, do not go there!'

Yet she came after me, down the steep and stony track that wound between huts where nuns still slept. She hated heights. She feared the sea. For all her sharp mind she was physically inept. My chest was aching, like a waterskin overfilled with tears. Luned could not stop me. I might do anything I wanted. She was my foster-mother. My sins were her failure. To protect her own pride, she would not report them to Bryvyth.

I lured her, unwilling, over the rocks to the great shelf of stone alongside deep water where ships could moor. A small fire was burning, its flames beginning to pale in the growing light. Gwennol had left a basket beside it. Under the dock leaves my eager fingers discovered two fish and a handful of herbs. Hidden beneath the last leaves was a sprig of may-blossom. A harmless-seeming gift. But for me, as I snatched the scented flowers to my face, that May Day was the first of many years of lessons in the way of wisdom.

I forced Luned to feed the fire. In vain she protested that the mist was lifting, that day was near, that the chapel bell would soon be calling us to prayer. I made her help me cook the fish and eat it. All it needed was a coaxing smile. The handbell rang out above our heads. The smell of frying fish betrayed us. We were both thrashed. Luned's penance was heavier than mine.

I trod the left-hand path. Nuns smiled at me and gave the sign. I sat on their thresholds, followed them observantly through the shippens, chanted a hundred times a day the charms they sang me. Bryvyth never saw. Her vision, and Rathtyen's, was too high, too wide, too full of sunlight. She was not curious enough about the darkness.

Luned did not dare to betray me. She told no one of Gwennol's visits. I was her charge, a heavy responsibility. Luned was ambitious. Rathtyen, who should have been Bryvyth's heir, was beginning to waste with a sickness that turned her face grey and racked her with pain. The librarian Cigfa was known for her skill with the pen and her scholarship, but Luned, for all her youth, was growing in importance to rival her. She had a head for mathematics above any other nun. She taught me sometimes, but for the most part she was busy ordering the provisions and trade of the convent and overseeing the outlying farms. We had a reputation. Ships came to our little quay in the cove from as far as Phoenicia and Cyprus. Wealth of tin and corn and fine textiles passed through Luned's hands. She paid for manuscripts and wine and metalwork. Bryvyth trusted her.

Yet I began to find a comfort in the convent's order. The dark-eyed saints painted in splendour on the chapel walls looked down at me with compassion. I felt Christ's wounds more sharply than my own. I loved the chanting.

My childish wild rebellion slowly froze. I had almost lost hope of change. As long as Uther lived I should not win my freedom. I saw my classmates leave, blushing and self-important, to be married to husbands their fathers had chosen for them. I passed the threshold of womanhood, recognising with pride and awe the signs in my body Gwennol had taught me to watch for. Luned had never spoken of such things.

Then Bryvyth sent to Uther, far away in Winchester. She told him I was a woman grown, and no schoolgirl now. Three horsemen came with his answer. I saw the manes of their mounts stream in the wind and their hooves send divots flying from the turf. They spoke of freedom. I ran to meet it.

Luned panted after me. For once she physically restrained me.

41

'No, Morgan. Wait! Don't you see?'

I tugged and struggled, careless if I was hurting her. I thought she was trying to hold me back because she wanted me with a love more selfish than Bryvyth's. I had tried her sorely. I was endangering her ambition and her soul. Yet still she would not have me leave Tintagel.

We saw the men come out of the guesthouse and Bryvyth with them. She was folding her staff close to her chest, as if to hold herself from striking them with it. They sprang to their horses and rode away. They had brought no spare mount.

With despair I watched them go, from the guesthouse where Uther had come to seize my mother. I saw I should never be free of the sight of it now. Bryvyth summoned me with the news. I screamed then, and beat my head on the stones of that prison. I made for the high headland where I had run that very first day. I flung myself weeping on to the flat, bare rock.

A cold hard hand descended on my head. Piala had found me. The hermit who fasted and prayed on the outermost gale-swept ledge. She uttered one word: 'Sister!' The touch was chastely removed. Piala spoke but seldom to anyone.

That day she sat beside me, silent for hours except when the chapel bell chimed thinly and she rasped the words of our communal prayer. She made no attempt to offer other comfort. I learned from her endurance. Later, I witnessed, though I could not share, her ecstasy.

Soon after that day, Bryvyth called me to her, sitting in the sunshine outside her cell.

'You are sixteen now, girl. Womanhood was late coming to you. You will not be free or married while Uther lives. You must make a life for yourself. You are a clever girl. If you took the veil with us you would soon become a great scholar.'

I met her gaze steadily.

'That is not why you want me to take my vows. The only true reason for becoming a nun is the love of Christ.'

She laughed with delight and hugged me. 'I knew I couldn't fool you! You go straight to the heart of the matter every time. Think about it, Morgan. You've had a bitter coming. But if you were to surrender yourself to Christ in

42

Tintagel willingly, it could turn to joy you've never dreamed of.'

I almost did it. I humbled myself for weeks of preparation. At the Feast of All Saints I would take the white veil. I walked to my solitary vigil in the convent chapel on Samain Eve.

Samain. Did some deeper layer of Bryvyth's mind suspect? Why else should she choose that most dangerous, spirit-filled night of the year to try me, when even Christian souls stay safe indoors and jest uneasily around the fire? All pagan fires are out. This is the night of darkness, when the barrier between the Otherworld is down. Why must she make me kneel alone through those hours of terror for my final test? Did she need so much to be sure of me?

For a while she prostrated herself on the floor beside me. Then she kissed me, and said a blessing over me, and left the chapel. She did not leave me without light. Candles glowed all around me, making shadows softly furred as moleskin, out of which the faces of Saint Anne and the Holy Marys watched me tenderly. An oil lamp burned on the altar below the Christ Pantocrator with his fingers raised to bless me.

I should have been safe.

Do not think I am the Devil's child. In our theology there is no Devil but the fiend in each one of us. When with my nails splitting I scored the faces of the painted saints, when with stung fingers I pinched out the candle flames, when with a breaking heart I overturned the cross, I was not striking out in blind defiance. I did not attack the Christ to desecrate his name. I loved that bleeding Lord. He bore my wounds.

But I was embracing darkness. I was crying out to the children of light: 'Why do you deny the other half of creation? The un-male, the un-virgin, the Great Mother. Can you not see what you are doing to us? God did not tear the universe in two, to set the right at war against the left. The kingdom of heaven is here, in the sanctified earth as well as the starry heavens, in the blood and the seed and the springing growth. She conceived us in wholeness. She did not give birth to a false dichotomy of Either/Or. Her ancient wisdom embraces Both/And. Let us weep together over our wounds. Let us be joined.'

I fled to the kitchen, and put out the fire there too. We

must not be afraid of the dark. We must make it holy also.

No, I deceive myself. All this I understood much later. Just then I raged against my loss of freedom. I had been hurt, I wanted to hurt back. I would wound even those I loved.

There, by the fireless hearth of the kitchen, Luned found me. She must have seen the sudden darkness in the chapel. That night, at least, she showed a kind of courage, to venture out of doors on Samain Night searching for me through her terror.

I had made my decision, on the cold chapel floor in those long night hours. All this time, unknown to Bryvyth, I had been undergoing another preparation. Samain is holy to the Wise.

There is a hole under the heart of Tintagel, as though a sea-serpent had bored its way from the cove to the open sea. It is not quite straight. At its beginning you cannot look forward and see the sky clear at the other end. You must enter in, and trust yourself to the shadows, under the island's enormity of stone. You must stumble on, past the rose and the green and the black dripping rock, to where the passage turns and the pure light flashes and the sea-pools greet you on another shore. You must choose your time carefully. High tide covers both entrances.

The nuns were forbidden it. They never spoke its name.

No human act can make such places sacred. Their fascination is already present in their creation, calling to us in the shape of living stone. If we are wise, we respond to their leading.

Gwennol came there, and others with her, like insects creeping along the burrow of the snake. Nuns from high Tintagel convent, wise women from Bossiney, some men. That Samain Night for the first time I went to meet them in that cave, leaving my gown and shift upon the rocks.

Luned struggled to hold me back, shocked and terrified. She called me defiant, angry, evil. And so, in part, I was. Yet I went loving too. I ached for wholeness. She never knew my heart. My virgin body feared what must be done. My scholar's soul wept for the life it was losing. But most of all, I dreaded that the old faith I was fleeing to might prove only a different side in the same war.

That first time of my offering myself, in the Mothers' Hole, there was darkness and cold, and then a sudden flaming warmth. Flesh surrounded me from which I shrank in revulsion, for all my resolution, and then came pain. The waters rose and met. All fire was quenched. We struggled to regain the shore and our separate selves. There was no ecstasy, only a hard commitment of the will.

I have done better since.

I have tried to keep the balance. I have sought to heal our wound. It has not been easy.

Luned had followed me, unprepared, too scared to turn back alone. She got a baby from that night. They cast her out of Tintagel.

The full truth of what we had done was not revealed till later. Still, I was punished cruelly for my desecration that night. I bore it gladly. I knew by the strength of her anger how much Bryvyth cared. I had hurt her as deeply now as Uther had wounded me.

She banished me to the farthest pinnacle of the headland for a month. I was not left alone, of course. There was the hermit, Piala, roosting in her seaward-facing cleft of the cliff. A gaunt, grave woman. She spoke so little that the words grated strangely in her gravelled throat. Yet she could sing with a wild haunting cry like a buzzard's scream. I listened to psalms and litanies flung across the wind to the endless ocean as she stood with arms upraised, gown tugging like a banner, face lit with the western light.

And she was wise, wise in her silence, wise in her rarely falling word, wise in the even rarer touch of her dry, cold hand. She understood my yearning for a spirit greater than the body's frailty. She could not have known the wound I had submitted to. It would have horrified her. Yet, in the month I spent with her, she healed it.

There are those who say that Tintagel means the 'Stronghold of the Constriction'. Others hold that it is the 'Place Where Two Waters Meet'.

I have known both truths.

Chapter Twelve

I am the maiden from the sea.

Geoffrey of Monmouth called me Morgen, 'Sea-Born'. Waves beat around my traditional dwelling-places: the Isle of Avalon, Tintagel, Sicily.

Where did I surface from?

The Irish know a mermaid, Muirgen. In The Destruction of Eochaid *she is a prisoner. Her tale is tragedy and loss.*

Once upon a time, in the days of King Eochaid of Ulster, an enchanted well overflows its banks. The flood pours out unstoppably. The terrible inundation sweeps away palace and people, all the sweet harps and the running horses, the courtiers and slaves. It drowns the familiar farms and forests of Ulster beneath a huge sea. Only two creatures escape in the whole country, Eochaid's shape-shifting daughter Liban and her pet dog.

For a year they survive in a chamber underwater. When they emerge, there is nothing for those two to see anywhere but a vast loneliness of empty water.

Well, she is wise. Since this is the only world left to them, Liban turns herself into a salmon below the waist and makes her dog an otter.

Three hundred years the pair of them swim the watery waste, without parents, without companions, without clan.

At last the waters drop and form Lough Neagh. The hills rise green again around it and life returns to its shores.

Ireland has changed. The Christians have come.

Now here's Bevan mac Imle, a monk, sent to Rome by Saint Comgall of Bangor on a mission to Pope Gregory. The pilgrim sailor comes winging over Lough Neagh and hears rising out of the depths a chant like angels.

When Perceval, on the Quest of the Holy Grail, reaches the destined Castle and sees the sacred vessel, he fails, out of politeness, to ask the correct question. Because of that, the Maimed King is not healed.

Bevan is no Perceval. With the proper curiosity of the scholar, he enquires: 'What can be making such music?'

Is this the question that can heal her sorrow?

After three hundred years, the fishy princess falls in love at first sight with the holy man. Liban parts the waves to reveal herself and tells her story. Then she bids him keep tryst with her in a year and a day at the lake isle of Ollorba.

We shall never know what joys she has prepared for him in her own sphere.

On the appointed day men sail across the lake to the island with nets. They catch her. Fergus is the fisherman who hauls the mermaid into his boat.

Her faithful dog-otter is left whining behind.

Crowds stand on the beach to gape when they bring her ashore. She is a marvel to look at: the face and body of the loveliest of maidens from the waist up, the powerful scaled tail of a salmon below.

To be even half a fish disqualifies her from humanity. She is clearly out of her element. They confine her in a vessel of water. The curious flock to stare at her.

A freak is a valuable commodity. Three men argue over the ownership of Liban: the monk Bevan who found her, Fergus the fisherman who caught her and Saint Comgall of Bangor himself on behalf of the abbey.

They decide that Heaven must settle the matter. At Bangor, the rule is already a perpetual fast, but they make it stricter yet. Strong prayers are made. A revelation is granted.

This is their answer: the mermaid to be laid in a chariot yoked to two stags, and then the beasts to be let free to carry her where they will. The wild deer leap away and carry her over hill, through glen, across forest and meadow, until they come to a halt at last in the town of Tec-da-Beoc. The people come running out to see the wonder. The clergy take charge.

In Liban, two worlds are caught in a single person. It must not be allowed to continue. She cannot be both magic salmon and mortal woman. She must declare herself either one or the other.

They offer her the choice: to be baptised and shortly depart to heaven as a proper Christian, or to live on for another three hundred years in the way of magic.

Christian monks wrote down this story. They say — well, wouldn't you expect them to? — that she chooses to end it there and then and do the decent thing. And after all, it can hardly be said that any of them have given her cause to want to stay among them. Saint Comgall himself baptises her. He names her Muirgen, 'Sea-Born'. She dies a holy death soon after.

From then on, the people of Tec-da-Beoc worship Liban Muirgen as their own particular saint.

Muirgen's true story will have been older still, before it was edited by the Church to render it suitable for a Christian audience. Who can say now who was the human sailor whom Liban charmed in the first telling of it? Or what taboo his fairy lover put on him, which he broke, to make the wild stags gallop her away from him? Or whether in those watery depths Muirgen is singing still?

In this story Muirgen is a victim, not the wise ruler of her own island. A man carries her away in a boat, and not she him. You need not waste your pity. This is not how it was.

Chapter Thirteen

I was glad when they told me Uther Pendragon was dead. Do not mistake me. By then I cared nothing for the man himself, one way or the other. It was ten years since I had taken his baby son to the sea, only to watch helpless as Merlyn snatched Arthur away from all of us. No, I danced for joy on the sea-pinks of the cliff because soon I would be free at last.

Mark was my kinsman, Gorlois's cousin. The same pride, the same interest of clan-blood united us. He must avenge my shame.

He summoned me to Bossiney.

You cannot know how much I lived in that short chariot-ride that took me from Tintagel convent to the Duke's hall. I would rather have ridden horseback and astride, but instead I had the Abbess Bryvyth sitting beside me as chaperone. Left to herself, she would have stridden the way barefoot with her crooked staff in her hand, proclaiming her poverty with pride. But, big brawny woman though she was, she knew when to play the part of the high lady. Bryvyth had been Gorlois's friend, and I was Gorlois's daughter, riding to reclaim her right, a princess too, by my mother the High Queen Ygerne. Bryvyth was stateswoman a well as abbess. She understood secular symbols as well as the sacred. She knew what belonged to the wounded dignity of my family. And so, this chariot.

So short a road, and half a lifetime of living to catch up. I had forgotten nine-tenths of what I had been denied on the sea-washed rock of Tintagel. Dogs, eager, warm-coated, noisy, casually fouling the street. The small children of peasants, dirty, playful, self-centredly absorbed in their tiny worlds, startled into wide-eyed shock and excitement as our wheels were almost upon them. Woods bright above with the yellow-green scalloped leaves of oak-trees, secret with moss beneath. A freshwater stream. The curious stares of ordinary men and women.

I had lived ten years in that holy fortress. A dizzying neck of rock, a bank and ditch, a stout gate and a porter's lodge, had separated me from the common world. I felt exposed, with all my nerves laid raw. Yet underneath the trepidation I burned with excitement. I was coming back to my world, my inheritance.

Bossiney now. A shock. Uther's Bossiney. Curious how I always remembered it the way it was in my father's time, before it burned.

I made myself cross that hall I had left defiantly at nine years old. As then, I bore myself high-headed, queenly. My heart was thrilling at the sight of my dark-browed cousin. He was so like my father. I held out my hands to him in a cool greeting. My face I kept still. Inside was triumph, festival. I seemed to hear all the sweet birds of Rhiannon singing for me, glad horses neighing, the bells of Cornwall's saints sounding. This was my feast-day!

I did not lower myself to plead for my release. It was unnecessary. Mark was my kinsman. My equal in pride, in blood-tie with the land of Cornwall, in ambition. He pierced beneath the ice I had armoured myself with. He saw through my steady gaze into my leaping heart. He was shrewd enough to calculate the meaning of my eagerness even before I did.

The Pendragon was dead, and Britain was washing apart in fragments. Dumnonia was splitting into east and west. It was not enough for Mark to be war-leader, Duke of Cornwall, as my father had been proud to style himself. Soon he would proclaim himself King west of the Tamar.

And I was Gorlois's last daughter, unmarried, and still in Cornwall. Bossiney had been my father's dun. Tintagel was Gorlois's own gift to the nuns. My sisters had realms of their own now. Elaine ruled with King Nentres in Garlot, the distant deep heartland of Britain, and Margawse was further off still with King Lot in storm-wracked Lothian. Only I was left in the west, a full woman now, with all my father's authority in my eyes, and something more that Mark had not – the royal blood of my mother Ygerne in my veins.

I thought I had found an ally. He saw a rival. Mark was

no fool. Those who whisper he wore ass's ears slander him. He was suspicious of claimants to his land and his wife. He was right. All this my mind allows him.

But not my heart. I cannot forgive the avidity of his stretched smile, nor the dark peat-fire of satisfaction that burned in his eyes, nor the power over my life he so clearly felt and enjoyed when he spoke my sentence.

'Pendragon was no fool to keep you close. Take her back to Tintagel and set a watch on the island. See my cousin gets no visitors. Have her shown to you every seventh day.'

Darkness smothered my soul like an eclipse of the rising sun, a day that never dawned. All creation should have been appalled at it. I opened my mouth and thought I screamed. Yet the silence of centuries of solitude seemed to dull the air as though his words had deafened me. I thought a multitude of gulls rose clamouring from the rocks and beat about my head. But no blood flowed, no feathers fell, I heard no sound. They must have taken me away. I remember nothing of the journey back. I was blind to the new-found world he had robbed me of.

Since then I have pitied Mark. We have both been unjustly maligned, I for revealing Gwenhyvar's faithlessness to my brother Arthur, he for accusing his wife Essyllt and his nephew Trystan. We have worked together to uncover their treachery. But that night I cursed him, weeping.

It was Gwennol saved me. She bought my liberty at a terrible price. That little, earthy, ageing woman who had nursed Ygerne and me. A witch clever enough to interest Merlyn once. Did she do it for love of her last baby? Or was she the Wise Crone moving her pieces on the sacred board-game? Did she sacrifice the castle of Tintagel to win the freedom of the queen?

As soon as he saw it, Mark coveted Tintagel for a stronghold. What man has not? That impregnable fortress, cliff-girt, with only a single causeway to the land. Gorlois knew more than he did of its old reputation. He feared it so much he gave it to the keeping of the holy women.

Gwennol surrendered Tintagel to Mark as the price of my release. She betrayed the nuns. There were many who had both trodden the chaste discipline of Christ above, striving for glory beyond the stars, and also danced to the hot life-giving rhythm of the Mothers beneath, in the dark where the waters meet. Some followed the drums for fear, some went to find their freedom. Others made a mockery of one and used it for a cloak to cover the other. That is not how I acted. I would have sought the hard joining of our hands across the battle-line; the meeting of truthful eyes, even in anger; the dialogue. The same hands created us. The same heart calls us to her. We need both Father and Mother. In many bodily acts and many languages, souls turn to worship the one light. Some also bless the dark.

I never deceived Bryvyth, though certain of my actions I found it prudent to keep secret from her. If she had discovered this, I would not have denied it. She knew what I held true, and why I would not take her veil. I believe she loved me more for that but never ceased to pray my heart would change. But others she trusted counterfeited.

Gwennol revealed it all to Mark. Like a clear moon pitilessly rising, she let the light fall fully on Tintagel Cove. She savoured her revenge on Bryvyth for setting the cross on the top of the holy island. She made the abbess witness the betrayal of the sanctuary they both loved. I was not there to grieve for them.

First, Mark demanded that Bryvyth surrender the island to him. Bryvyth refused him roundly.

Then Gwennol beckoned her witness, who was hiding her face from Bryvyth at the back of the crowd.

It was Luned she forced to stumble forward and confess the truth publicly. Poor learned, timorous, ambitious Luned, robbed of both veil and baby. She was Gwennol's pupil now. I had sent her to Bossiney. I found her useful later.

Now she was pushed out, shaking, to stand before Mark and his court. There were a number of the wise among both high and low at Bossiney. She must have been very afraid. With Mark's relentless eye fixed on her, she revealed everything. The cave, the masks, the fire, the blood. Her baby.

When the abbess learned of the doubled truth of her beloved Tintagel, her heart broke. She rounded on Luned, with dry-eyed fury.

'Curse you! Curse you, that did not tell me this at the very first. Curse you, that you have spoken of it at all.'

But what better witness could Gwennol have chosen to uncover the dragon-pool under Tintagel's foundations? The convent collapsed. The firm faith of its nuns in Christ had rotted from the core and now the faith of the people in those holy women crumbled.

The nuns that had stayed true to the high ideals of Bryvyth left, singing a bitter litany of exile. Bryvyth went last, stooping under the weight of the cross. The wise jeered at her, as they had mocked when she came.

Difficult, that leavetaking. Bryvyth had reason to rue my coming.

I was left there, by my wish, alone. I stood on the highest point, beside the old standing stone carved now with the signs of Christ. I watched Mark ride in across the causeway with his young warriors. As their hooves touched the island, the horses broke into a gallop. The men were yelling in triumph. Tintagel was theirs. Mark drew rein in front of me, while they circled us. He saluted me mockingly.

'Cousin, I keep my word. What are you waiting for? You are free to go.'

As I rode across the causeway with my escort, I stared with aching heart after the bowed back of Bryvyth going south. Then I turned to find Gwennol.

She never saw my freedom. The Mothers took their revenge. The instant Mark's men touched the island, the old woman was struck senseless to the earth. I leaped from my mare and ran to cradle her in my arms, as long ago she had held me. When she opened her eyes again, she was blind.

Mark has had no joy of Tintagel. He should have feared the power of the Mothers, as Gorlois did. Essyllt betrayed his marriage-bed there, with her lover Trystan.

Still, his ambition had triumphed. I could not remain in Cornwall now Mark wished to be king. We were too alike. Our thoughts matched too well. And the Cornish people loved me. I was Gorlois's daughter returned. I was the romantic prisoner freed. I had come back to them transformed, beautiful and wise as Ygerne.

He got me a husband rapidly. A kinglet, of course, because we were of the same blood and I must not demean him. A Northerner, to send me far away from Cornwall. A Christian, to keep my ancient powers in check.

Urien of Rheged, fourteen years old, just coming to manhood that May. I had already been a full-grown woman for five years.

I rode north with one thought in my head: '*Somewhere in Britain my brother Arthur is alive, and Merlyn is holding him.*'

Chapter Fourteen

I am the Washer at the Ford of Barking.

In an old Welsh legend, all the hounds for miles around used to gather at night beside that mysterious ford and bark to wake the dead. There was no one brave enough to go down and find the reason, until Urien Rheged came. What he found at the river's edge was a woman washing.

At the dead of night I had set the dogs howling and raging to chill the heart. If you are a Christian you would call them the Hounds of Hell. Brave, warlike men glanced in the dark towards the shuttered windows and feigned deafness, sleep, nightmare. I was that nightmare.

In the darkness a young man was awake and dressed. A boy on the threshold of the warrior's way. He girded on a weapon of steel, new-made for this night and all his fights to follow by the last of a long line of master smiths to his family. Teilo was a Smith of the old magic who knew how to temper sword and spirit. The lad bore a weapon of flesh too. His mothers had formed it in the womb, both sheath and shaft. He was Urien of Rheged, the boy-king, fatherless now. He came twice armed and doubly virgin to the eve of manhood.

Come, Urien, by the howling of my dogs I summon you. Come, Rheged, your father's war-band watches you knowingly. Come, boy, down the dark wet path that leads from the curled womb of childhood into the world that awaits us all. Your mother's pain expels you. You are slipping from her, terrified, alone.

He had no comfort on this road, of horse or escort. Not all the spells of druids or prayers of saints were made to keep him from this meeting. This was our purpose. Tonight he must cross the threshold. Even his Christian mother prayed for his courage, not his safety.

His steps rang on the road, crunched on the shingle, came to the water's edge, as though unwillingly. I murmured a word. My hounds whimpered and were still.

The water divided us. I knelt on a stone, insistently washing the nameless weave of obscurity in the cold shock of the stream. I lifted and wrenched. Starlight, death, fame dripped from my hands.

He stood at the brink. Only a little tremble in his voice as he called across.

'Who are you . . . Lady?'

'It is for you to name me, Urien son of Cynvarch.'

'What must I do?'

'What your father did before you, Urien Rheged.'

He splashed across the shallows, the longest passage of his life in those short steps. His shadow fell across me where I lifted my head.

'Show me your face, then.' His breath indrawn fought the reluctant words.

'It is for you to uncover me.'

I stood taller than him now, this lad of fourteen years. Nine unbound tresses clad me from crown to waist. His hands were dry, warm even now. The hair brushed back across my shoulders.

The moon was young, and I was old. Just enough light to show him wrinkles, blackened hairy chin, jutting eyebrows, warts on nose. I brought him the foretaste of reality. I offered no promise for myself or for him. He must take me as I am.

They had bred him well. His hand found mine. Only a second and his hold was firm. The hounds were nudging round our legs. They were herding us towards an opening in the hollow hill. His grip was tighter now on mine as he left the last familiarity of the sky.

Darkness and silence now, beyond the moon's gaze, the way found only by the reaching foot. A passage down into the earth. He had lost one mother, he must enter another. I slipped his hand and moved ahead. He could not feel me now.

They had prepared the entry well. Invisible horrors assaulted him on every side. Shrieks echoed round. Lights leaped on fiery eyes and were instantly smothered. The

56

blackness was more awful now that he had glimpsed something of what it covered.

He could have turned back. How much of this had he been taught, how much did he guess, what did he believe, this Christian child of holy Brychan's daughter? I heard his stifled cry, the swift slap of his boot-soles on the rock. He was following me still. Well, the lad was determined.

Halt here. A huge and hollow hall, in total darkness. We were all hushed, to know what he would do.

Nothing had prepared him for this. I sensed a child's uncertainty. A hand groping and falling back. I was out of reach. Was he meant to act or wait? I must not help him. Leave him awhile to the stillness of his senses. Nothing to see, nothing to hear, nothing to feel, nothing to know.

Presently I heard prayers whispering from his lips. The name of Christ. Young Urien wanted to be a man and a king. He would undergo the rites they set him. He would meet our challenge. But he would never be truly ours. Still, let it be.

We were coming to the unveiling of the mysteries.

The lights began to sparkle, dazzling his astonished eyes. Illumination spread on ranks of men and women, robed, some masked. It flared on rock walls painted with mythical truths. It reached towards the soaring cavern roof too vast to catch the light. Some secrets must always remain covered in darkness. Urien blinked and staggered, as he adjusted his senses. He had not expected to find himself the centre of such a magnificent company. Teeth grinned at him from familiar mouths but the eyes were masked and watchful. Do not distract him. Let him not miss what follows in the haze of scented smoke from pinewood torches. He was already dazed with wonder and faint with fasting.

Behind his back I was preparing myself.

And now at the far end of the cavern, the curtains parted. Once, only once for him tonight, the youth carried the bleeding spear across that floor. Once, now, the maiden's hands were bearing the brimming grail of life past Urien's eyes. Would he understand?

'Boy! Speak now what is in your heart.'

Was it a hound or a man that barked at him? Urien son of Cynvarch was boy-king of Rheged, with all his life stretched out before him. He would not leave here without the manhood he had come to get. He asked his question.

'What do this spear and the vessel signify?'

A sigh of satisfaction from the ring of watchers.

'She is waiting for the wound that will make her whole.'

Following their pointing hands the boy turned. I was enthroned on a golden bed, set about its edge with letters of precious stone and hung with rich tapestries. My head was veiled now in white. Apart from that, I did not seem in this moment to be any other than I was when he met me washing at the ford.

And so he came slowly to my bed. His breath quickened and caught as I drew him down. Before them all, he mated with the moon-scarred Crone. The cavern thundered with their shouts of triumph. And when he put back my veil, still shaken, he found neither the Crone nor a blushing Maiden. I had become for him full-breasted Woman, beautiful beyond all expectation, holding out arms of love to welcome him. For Urien the Man I lay revealed as Queen, Wife, Land, Sovereignty, Joy.

I had wetted his weapon. The earth was made whole.

Then Urien seized hold of the woman and had his will of her. She said, 'The blessing of God on the feet that brought you here.'

'Why?' he asked.

'Because it was my fate to wash here until I should conceive a son by a Christian. And I am the daughter of the King of the Otherworld, the land of Annwn. Come you here at the end of the year and you will get the child.'

And so, on a May morning, young King Urien of Rheged came to his wedding-day in Carlisle. Scarcely a week new-made as warrior and man, he waited on the steps of the church in his feast-day clothes. Around him stood the bishop, his powerful cousin King Gwendoleu, chieftains, nobles, men of the north. His kin had picked him a stranger for a bride from faraway Cornwall, once Uther Pendragon's step-daughter, but now a grown woman with few friends. They had chosen me as a princess who would have no power to lend him if he should grow ambitious.

Well, we would see.

As I rode under the Roman gateway, he would have seen

a bride in virginal white, with a chaplet of flowers on her head, sitting a white mare astride. I, Morgan of Cornwall, scorned the stiff tissue of royalty, and the gold and the bright colours of an earthly queen. Today I wore May-Maiden white, an older authority. I had braided two ribbons in my hair, of green and red, for vegetation and blood.

There was a ripple of anger through the reception-party, as when the wind shakes the embroidered curtains across a door. They thought I mocked the Church and the northern aristocracy with such a simple gown. Indeed, I challenged both.

Startled but courteously-bred, Urien took a step forward to help his bride from her horse. A serious boy, who did not disgrace his own gorgeous wedding-garment. He raised his youth's eyes to see my unveiled face. The cry that broke from him then shocked the crowded street.

It was not what they thought, when I parted my unbound hair and smiled winningly down at him through nine black tresses. True, May-Maiden though I seemed, I was years older than he was, and proudly pagan. Yet he had known me older far, ancient beyond any imagining. He had taken hold of my hand in the night. He had followed me under the earth. He had entered my womb. I had taught him manhood. I became Woman for him.

I was his Goddess.

And so Urien Rheged returned at the year's end and the woman of Otherworld Annwn gave him a boy and a girl, Owain his son and Morfudd his daughter.

We have done well together, Urien and I.

Chapter Fifteen

Farewell then, Urien. This is a battle you had no heart for. Arthur, the gold-bearded, laughing-eyed, high-hearted, conquering friend of your youth. Modred, your clever, comely, valiant, vulnerable nephew and foster-son. Morgan the Wise, your beloved wife. We have strained the strings of your heart between us.

You cannot watch and wait on the high ridge while Modred's desperate remnant flings itself on Arthur's too-chivalrously equal force and, fighting for their lives, begins to win. Too many names, great rallying cries, are missing: Gawain, Gareth, Cei, gone before this. Those that survive this day will think they have lived too long.

Spur your horse, then, with a grim pitilessness of grief and anger, down the short slope into the thick of the fray. You did not wait for the long horns to summon you. You have disobeyed Arthur. In your heart you know already he will not live to reproach you. How can you have it sung that the King of all the Britons fell at Camlann, and Urien Rheged did not lift his hand to stop it?

Modred is not yours. Modred was never yours. Did you sometimes fear that he might be mine? By Arthur?

I have deceived you. I intended you no harm. I respected you. Forgive me that I could not love you as you deserved.

I have loved only one.

Does that drive the stern fury in your arms, wielding the sword two-handed, forcing the horse to twist between your knees, almost without thinking? Do you rage against the cruelty of the world that sets your sword against your family, my family, against the family of Britain, for our family? Do you blame me?

You will never blame Arthur.

Are you fighting for me? Do you believe somewhere in your

loyal, just, loving Christian heart that if dark Modred dies and golden Arthur wins, heaven will triumph over hell, Britain will be restored, I shall be saved?

No, Urien. I am what I am. Not good or evil. My ancient faith takes no account of morality. My metaphor is not the battlefield, right against wrong. I till the harvest-field. Birth, fullness, and death. All are necessary. Accept them. I am both darkness and light. Accept me.

Watching, unseen, I flinch from the shock of steel and the crack of wooden shields, from the almost human scream of wounded horses and the dreadful animal howl of mutilated men. My tears water the pastures of Camlann. Death is required, but not this disharmony. I have no power to stop this stupidity, this pride, this ambition, this self-sacrifice, this patriotism, this heroism. Did I precipitate this?

I stood for truth. Modred was Arthur's son. Gwenhyvar was Modred's lover. Nimue was protecting them. I said so. Others would have winked and kept silent.

You bore the burden of a lifetime's silence, Urien. One fierce and furious argument we had. Do you remember Tristvard? That handsome bard, before young Taliesin came to bring glory to your court and immortalise you.

Poor Tristvard. Not so winningly boyish as Taliesin. Brown, waving hair, a little crooked in one leg but otherwise exceedingly well-made. Deep hazel eyes, laughing and sympathetic. A taste for fine wine and an expert eye at assessing the jeweller's art. Not one half Taliesin's skill in harping, nor a divine poet. But a good conversationalist, pleasant company to while the time away for a wife who had been cheated of her years of girlhood. He was a little older than me. You were too often away at wars and cattle-rustling.

Do not mistake me. This was no seduction. I chose him, not for the pleasures of the flesh, though I will not deny them. Bodies were meant to be enjoyed, not thwarted. But mating is holy, not a careless sport. I was a queen. I was the Goddess. I must be served. There are seasons. There are rites. The joy of the earth must be recreated in me. I did what I must, well, and gladly.

Owain observed it. A child of eight. He chattered of it openly to others. They told you.

You came disguised as Teilo, my Woman who hides his

61

manhood behind a wimple and a female skirt. Not like you to counterfeit. You never saw that Teilo was once the Smith who had forged your manhood's sword. It was a more bitter irony than you intended. So jealousy humiliates us all. So disguised, you received from Tristvard's own lips the message that he would meet me at the sacred ford.

You, of all men, should have understood the meaning of that place. Terrible your wrath. You could not, would not comprehend. You, the son of sainted Brychan's daughter. You, the upright Christian king. You saw only adultery, violation, treason. In your own kingly form you struck off Tristvard's head, there at the water's edge. Then you rode back and threw the bloody sword at my feet.

I was outraged. I did not feel the guilt you heaped upon me. I had no fear that you might kill me too. I snatched up the stained weapon, the sword of justice fouling the patterned Roman tiles. I was the Mothers' priestess. You had attacked her son. I could have slain you for it.

No time for guards to unsheathe weapons or leap across the floor to stop me. Barely space enough for my women to scream. Owain was watching, staring, strangely smiling. Always a dangerous child, though on the surface so like you.

No. A momentary faltering. I had seen the tears of pain in your eyes. Pain for Tristvard our friend, wastefully, needlessly dying this ugly death. Pain for me, for the lost wife of your dreams whom you would never now have. Pain for a young man's hopes dashed against the walls of reality. I saw your innocence lost in your own deed, by your own hand, for your own honour.

In that heartbeat's hesitation my arm slowed. And someone sprang. Another eight-year-old. Light, and lithe, and passionate. Our daughter Morfudd.

She snatched my wrist and clung to it. The blood of Tristvard, clotting on the blade, smeared her cheeks, her hands, her dress, as she wrestled with me.

'No! No! Mother, you mustn't! Father is crying.'

The guards were round us. Not one of them dared to touch me yet. My husband was staring at me. Your eyes seemed hollow, empty, dark blue tunnels into which I could go down and find great rivers of grief, caverns of disappointment, and springing green, even in this shadow, the obstinate living fern of love.

In silence, we embraced. We kissed, in the reek of Tristvard's blood that stained us both. I would not dishonour you again. I would be discreet. You would accept me for what I am. We were the king and queen. I was united with you.

The battle of Camlann has touched you less than most. The Raven's wings have been dark over your life. I have also sheltered you. You will grieve for Arthur. You will search for his body. You will not find him.

You will never see me again. In the morning you will turn your horse's head to the north. You will leave the land of legends and ride for the cold clear winds of reality. Take Taliesin with you.

Go well, Urien.

Chapter Sixteen

I cannot be Urien's wife, if I am Arthur's sister.

The Welsh Annals give 537 for the date of Arthur's death at Camlann. It was probably earlier. Urien of Rheged fell about 590.

> *'A head I bear in my shirt,*
> *The head of Urien who governed a court in mildness —*
> *And on his white breast the black raven gluts.*
>
> *'A head I bear on my sword:*
> *Better his being alive than that he should go to the grave;*
> *He was a castle for old age.*
>
> *'A head I bear that supported me,*
> *Is there anyone known but he welcomed them?*
> *Woe my hand, gone is he that sustained me.'*

How did we ever come to marry? I was never more than a legend, the fairy love, and later the sister, of Arthur. You certainly lived, the king of Rheged in North-West Britain in the last quarter of the sixth century. Urien Wledig, Chief among the Men of the North.

We know you, because of Taliesin. Fortunate indeed that friendship between the prince of battle and the prince of poets. Twelve precious poems have survived to us from Taliesin's own lips. They praise you richly.

> *'He has a warlike demon,*
> *The king of the baptised world.*
> *As you plunder, you scatter,*
> *You make glad the poets of Christendom.*
> *Arise around your triumphant rustler-lord!*

64

HERSELF

An unassailable fortress, bounteous, famous,
The anchor of his kingdom.
Like a fiery sphere, like a familiar song,
Like a magnanimous sea is my shining lord.
He slays, he hangs, he nurtures, he dispenses,
He kills in the front line.
Gentility is around him, and a heap of riches.
Great and unflagging his fury against the enemy,
Great is his bounty to poets and women,
There is esteem and welcome in the hall of the men of Rheged,
Offerings of wine and jubilation.
And gold, gold, gold and gift.
I shall not cease yearning,
Unless I praise Urien.'

Truly, you are a mighty king, and popular. Your admirers intend to exalt you still higher by uniting you with me. Any hero worth his salt is drawn into the list of Arthur's war-band. My dowry for you, a higher honour: to be not Arthur's comrade only, but his brother-in-law. Only a sister's son ranks closer than this.

Owain, your son, is also historical fact. Taliesin sings his elegy. Early, Owain becomes a legend of his own, my son and yours.

Early too, our wedding must have been, before the corruption of my character could harm you both.

Taliesin honours you, and so do I. You are a creature of your age, as bloody and barbaric in your defence of Christianity as I in my celebration of paganism. A thief of cattle and horses, loving war for itself. You are as gentle in your court as you are grim on the battlefield, as generous with your gifts as you are rapacious in plunder. I do not blame you. Both of us are true to what we know.

Unfitting your end for so renowned a warrior.

You are white-haired already. Your sons in their northern lands have begun to mock you, throwing the hazel twigs of derision in your face. But the strife of Camlann between brother Britons was long ago. Now the Angles who have lived with us quietly in the North East are massing. Fflamddwyn, the Firebrand of Bernicia marches on Rheged, demands hostages from you and Owain.

On a Saturday morning, the Battle of Leven Forest.

' "*Have my hostages come?*
Are they ready?"
Then answered Owain,
The scourge of the east,
"*They have not come,*
They do not exist,
They are not ready.
And the whelp of Coel
Would be a pathetic warrior
Before he would pay anybody a hostage." '

Slaughter then. Fflamddwyn is beaten. The crows get red in the wake of the ageing king.

East now, and war against King Theodoric takes you and your victorious allies to the shores of the North Sea. Rhydderch Hen, Gwallawg, Morcant, Urien, kings of the North; Aedan of the Dal Riada Scots and Fiachna of Ulster. Proud chieftains all. This is Morcant's country. And Fiachna seizes Bamborough back from the Bernicians and installs an Irish garrison. In Morcant's citadel.

Honour has been wounded.

You quarrelling kings all stand at last in the whistling grass of the long low strand that fronts the island of Metcaud, which others have called Lindisfarne. Three days and three nights you besiege Theodoric. Then tragedy strikes.

'*Eurdyl will be joyless tonight,*
And multitudes will be so besides.
At Aber Lleu has Urien been slain.

Decapitated is my lord, his opponents are powerful.
There is commotion in every region
In pursuit of Llovan Llawdivro.'

The greatest of warriors is struck down. But how could spear and shield protect against the sliding blade of treachery? No final battle for you. No glorious fall under the rush of blood-spattered horses. No English spear to run you through and let the daylight in.

Yet just as finally, in secrecy and darkness, your white-haired head is severed from your body.

HERSELF

'This frail white corpse will be covered today
Under earth and nettles:
Woe my hand, that such a step could have happened to me!

This hearth, will it not be covered over by the ants?
More accustomed it was to bright torches,
And harmless festivities.

This hearth, will it not be scratched up by the fowl?
Want would not approach it
In the lifetime of Owain and Urien.'

Howl, you winds. Great Urien Rheged is dead. Carry his desecrated body west on a gore-soaked bier. Who has ordered this? Who hated Urien so much that they would see the greatest British king dead sooner than the English one? Who has fed the ravens with this generous mead-giver?

The traitor King Morcant, Urien's closest ally.

Would it surprise you to learn that his name is frequently given as Morgan?

Chapter Seventeen

Three years after Owain and Morfudd were born, I held another baby in my arms. Difficult to say this, difficult to think it, even.

Arthur's son, Margawse's child.

There! Four words, and it is done.

My brother and my sister were his parents. His father's father, Uther, had killed his mother's father Gorlois. His only grandmother was Ygerne.

Perhaps you will think it was the incest that shocked me, and so it did. I was convent-bred. I had lived with women who had chosen the cool, hard discipline of chastity, though I had seen that shot through with the fire of religious ecstasy. My soul still ached for that high commitment.

By an act of conscious will I had chosen an older, more physical way. I was the Lady. Many a night I danced barefoot and naked. I had held common flesh, made holy by my touch. I had given myself in a sacred union as the Goddess, even if afterwards I had walked away into a vast cold loneliness.

Did Margawse mock the sacred marriage? Or did I rage against her because we were both Gorlois's daughters?

I had seen my father's corpse brought home from Dimiliock. For love of Ygerne, Uther butchered her husband. They brought him home to us. The laughter silenced. The war-like muscles stilled. The blood of his great heart blackened a hundred jagged cuts, as though in a frenzy Uther's men had danced round their fallen enemy, stabbing and slashing in triumph. The poets still sing this romance.

And where was Uther? Merlyn the enchanter used his magic to change the Pendragon's face to Gorlois's, charm him through the shut gate of Tintagel by night, smuggle him into Ygerne's bed. Solely to get this boy, this Arthur. A political act.

How could my red sister hug the flesh of her half-brother,

the fruit of our mother's unholy union? How could she open her legs for him?

Merlyn had orphaned the three of us for Arthur.

Margawse knew all this when she took him. Her blood flows redder than mine. She was bred in a rustic court that called itself Christian but still knew earthy, violent ways. No white nuns had schooled her in their gospel of forgiveness or chastity. She would have scorned either. Margawse is female, animal. She did not care how close a kin he was to her. She enjoyed the bodies of men. She wanted vengeance. She chose the most appropriate way.

Merlyn had kept Arthur close hidden till the time of his manhood. The lad did not even know he was the Pendragon's son, still less that he had sisters.

He came marching into Caerleon with his standards shining and the tall war-horns braying triumph. He was a boy of fifteen, and already he was victorious over the Saxons in Lindsey. All Britain seemed likely to throw itself at his feet. He was strong, he was golden-haired and ruddy-cheeked. His limbs were whole and hard-muscled, his flesh unmarked. He carried a merry charisma about him that had older men jostling each other to swear him their swords and devotion, and he had laughing blue eyes that could turn women confused and rash.

Yet he had enemies, our kings of the north who had never met him and were jealous of his sudden fame. Lot of Lothian, Margawse's husband, Nentres of Garlot, Elaine's, Gwendoleu of Solway. Even young Urien was wary at first, before he saw Arthur.

We three queens made a guarded magic for our own chiefs and this our refound brother. Too soon to say which of them would serve our purpose best. Then we rode with our menfolk to a camp outside Caerleon. We came all of us prepared to make war against Arthur if he proved too proud. Wise women that we were, we obeyed the necessary laws. In all our journey south we sisters did not once lie with our husbands to sap their battle-magic.

Lot and Nentres were haughty: they would not go into Caerleon to do honour to this lucky boy like the soft southern chiefs. Urien was younger. He longed to see Arthur himself. And so did I.

I was not chosen.

It was Margawse we sent, ravishingly dressed, to spy out his camp and assess the man.

Yet, in his youthful arrogance, Arthur never thought it strange that the flame-haired Queen of Lothian, twice his age, magnificent in beauty, consort to hostile Lot, should come to his camp and consent so easily, merrily to share his bed after supper. He would have considered it, if he had stopped to think, merely his right. None of us told him his parentage then. He never asked.

She came back laughing. I dashed to tear her face when she rolled wantonly on the grass boasting about it. Luned and Teilo had to drag me off her.

I fled home to Rheged. I fasted and dressed in black and sat at the gate of Lyvennet giving myself to the healing of any who passed.

Six months later, it fell to me to tell Arthur the truth.

He came as guest to my fortress in Rheged. How can I recall, unshaken, that moment when he walked in through my gate? My brother, my king, my little child. Not sixteen years, but war had already set her brand on him. He was no longer the golden-downed boy of Margawse's sport. This was a man. The Red Ravager. The Bear of Battle. I had my tribute for him ready. I had brought his mother Ygerne, widow of Uther, once High Queen of Britain. A quiet woman in white, hiding her face in her hood. He learned from my lips and hers that he was the Pendragon's son. There in my high courtyard, above the apple orchards.

I met the full force of his joy. His hands reached out for mine. His face was alight with all the new vision of his future. This was all my doing.

I held a cup in my hands. The wine beat on the sides like the surge of my blood. Our eyes engaged.

'Stop!'

Merlyn sprang like a wildman out of the forest of men and dashed my cup aside. Consternation. Fury among my people. Suspicion had been sown. Pride was endangered. It all ended in laughter. Arthur drank my welcome. But the moment of meeting was spoiled.

Round and round the spiral turns, and we are always parted.

Ygerne was my mother too. I could not hide what followed logically from that.

I showed him we had two other sisters. Elaine and Margawse. Even Margawse hung her head and blushed as she met his horrified recognition. But the smile was more wicked as she took her hands from her swelling body to let him see.

He read in our faces that this could not be Lot's.

And so this child. This little dark-eyed baby. Why did I want to scream every time I looked at him?

Because he was Arthur's son, and I was not his mother.

It is out. Many times I have had to remove a buried javelin point from a man's flesh and seen the bright heart-blood come spurting after it. In that swift moment of danger I must stem the tide. That is my work. I am the healer. It was not so easy to staunch my own wound.

I am more a traitor to our family than Margawse was, in my heart. I would have willingly ignored Uther's lust, Merlyn's deception, the Abbess Bryvyth's holy condemnation. And not for revenge. Do you think it strange? When Margawse told me she had lain with Arthur, I had not seen him since that night when I leaned over his cradle and carried him out into the storm. A girl of nine with her infant brother. Why did I shriek like a woman robbed?

Arthur and Morgan. The Lord and the Lady. I think I always knew we were essential to each other. In us the fractured worlds of gender, politics, tribe and faith should have been made whole. He is the warrior. I am the healer. Our conjoined power should have made this baby.

Modred. His small red fist gripped round my finger. His dark eyes on mine, it seemed, so knowingly.

The spiral twisted, and we were back in the same dangerous region, a generation later. Lust, treachery, a vulnerable baby boy.

I could not stop this castle spinning, even though I knew clearly what was coming.

Merlyn could not allow this. He was as arrogant with his magic staff as Arthur with his weapon. This baby would not be permitted to live.

First, there was a more immediate danger. Modred was born in Lothian, on May Day. At the height of the festival

71

King Lot was drunk. I met him striding to his wife's bedchamber. Margawse was generous to him, as well as to others. Four sons he had, Gawain, Agravain, Gaheris, Gareth, and they were truly his. But Lot was a pagan who feared the old taboos. He had ridden to Arthur's camp at Caerleon under a warrior's ban. He had not touched his wife for a month. This son could not be his.

I feared his human anger. Margawse must guard her own life, I took the child.

We rode south in our chariot through a landscape that did not seem like summer, all three of us nursing our loss. Luned, who might have succeeded Bryvyth as abbess at Tintagel. She was now my servant whom I had schooled in another wisdom. Teilo, who had once forged Urien's sword and hammered runes of protection into its blade. He had tried to play the Master Smith over my Ladyship. I had taught him thoroughly to know the left-hand way of power. So he served me now in the dress of Woman. And I myself, feeling the pain of Arthur's baby sucking my half-dried breasts.

I nursed a greater dread of another man's vengeance than Lot's. When I heard that Merlyn was approaching our fortress at Lyvennet, I did not run. I knew what he had done in Lothian. I knew the story of Arthur's dream. His feasting-hall set on fire. How Arthur must tear out the blazing beam before the whole palace was destroyed. Merlyn's interpretation: a child of treachery was born on May Day. Arthur's warriors must seek it out and exterminate it. No baby from that festival time must escape alive.

It was not for the enchanter's face that I searched when Arthur came storming up to the gate at the head of his war-band. This was the father. My paps had fed his son. He could not do this to us.

Yet I was frightened. I knew that, even so young, war had hardened him. I set a woman's trap for him, a woman's lesson. In the great hall of Lyvennet I laid out the holy evidence of my wisdom. A hundred May-time babies, born of female bodies from male seed. A hundred tiny, noisy chicks lifted from their nests, all washed and dressed identically.

'Arthur,' I smiled. 'You are not yet our king, but you have won much for Britain. Your sword has saved the future of these children.'

One boy alone mattered to him. Arthur of Christian Britain could not have, must not have, a son by his sister.

I saw him stop. I saw the fury in his eyes. Those wide, blue, winning eyes that can turn a woman's loins to water, flashing now. I saw how Saxons see him in his battle-madness. I was denying him what he wanted.

'Get these women out.'

I hardly heard him for the noise of crying.

'The women are my witnesses.'

There were men behind him, unwilling to put their hands on weapons. Cei, Bedwyr, Gawain. Younger, less famous faces. Surely they could not, in cold blood, take them all.

Merlyn was sweeping round the hall, picking his hasty way over tiny bodies, peering into wrinkled, squalling, placid, sleeping features. Ygerne would have known at once. Blood would have spoken to blood. Merlyn's magic was too high for this.

Arthur sprang on to the dais. He seized my arm. I knew, we knew, that even Modred's death could be no more than a shadow between us. I felt myself sway to meet his warmth. He sensed his victory. Eyes softened, melting mine. Hands became tender. Arms surrounded, supported, drew me close to him. My head went down upon his shoulder. I had no strength.

His voice caressed my ear. 'Give me my son.'

Oh, Arthur, I would have given you all I had.

With a last resolve I murmured, 'Last year you could not recognise your sister. Now it seems you do not know your own child.'

He struck me, in my own high hall, in front of my people.

I thwarted his pride. He took them all, because I would not give him Modred.

That nightmare claws me still. Warriors gathering those babies up and heaving them into a cart. My women screaming. Spears pinning them to the wall. My own guard bleeding. Urien's face. His hero and his wise wife gazing across the hall at each other's eyes, appalled. But Merlyn's plan for Britain could not be endangered by a single child, or by a hundred. His Arthur must serve the male imperative.

And I, in women's way, would not betray one solitary, treacherously-got baby to save all the rest.

One last wracked plea, 'Do not do this, Arthur, for your soul's sake!'

But Merlyn signalled. Arthur's eyes hardened and he stared back at me as though I was a stranger. They tried to amputate the past. I too believed in Arthur's dream. I understood that Modred would one day betray Arthur. And yet . . . That cart was full of little Modreds, none of them wholly perfect, not one conceived in a union of unspoiled trust. None would be all their parents had hoped for if they grew to adults. Flawed, vulnerable, harmful, particular in their failings, human. As he was.

We all of us need our dream of the ideal King Arthur. Arthur himself could not live with the evidence of his own reality.

I gave one piercing shriek and tore my face, not for Arthur's son, but for all the rest. I sent my Woman, Teilo, after them to bear witness.

They went through Rheged till the cart was full. They came to the banks of the Solway Firth at evening. There was no need to stain their swords with innocent blood. They piled the babies in a boat. They pushed it out into the tideway. Merlyn signed to his chief. Arthur's own hand was the last to leave the stern.

The cold sea took them. The boat scraped rock and foundered. The raucous gulls feasted.

Merlyn should have known better. The truth was inescapable. Just one baby was saved. Modred was fostered in a fisherman's cottage. I sought him out and found him.

Chapter Eighteen

I am Modron, the Mother.

The Welsh never called me Morgan. That is a masculine name, and usually an ill-omened one. In Wales there is a sinister man called Morgan, who like me is water-born. He lives at the bottom of Lake Glasfryn in the parish of Llangybi. His is the name that mothers use to frighten their children. He knows the naughty ones and he will rise from his gloomy lair and carry them off. They disappear, of course, under the water and are never seen again.

Geoffrey's Morgen, you remember, took men away to bliss in Avalon.

Oddly enough, though this Morgan is male, the family who own the land around Glasfryn bear on their crest a mermaid.

I stole no child. My child was taken from me.

There is a tantalising collection of threefold sayings, the Welsh *Triads. Each group alludes to three ancient tales. You might call them a catalogue of the fabulous history of Britain. Some of the stories they point to are known to us; others are irretrievably lost.*

One Triad lists:

'One of the Three Fair Womb-Burdens of the Island of Britain: Owain son of Urien and Morfudd his sister who were carried together in the womb of Modron daughter of Avallach.'

Avallach is King of Annwn, the Otherworld.

It is a daughter of the King of Annwn who meets Urien Rheged at the Ford of Barking and gives him a son Owain and a daughter Morfudd. In the medieval romances Morgan is queen to Urien and the mother of Owain. So I must be Modron, must I not?

All Europe knows me. In Latin I am Matrona. I have dropped my name like a benediction over towns and waters. The River Marne is holy to me. As Modron, I settled in Britain with the

75

legions. My image is often sculptured threefold. I appear as a triad of myself, the Triple Woman, the Mothers.

Mother to whom?

Where Modron is the Mother, Mabon is her Son. You can find our sacred stones still scattered around Hadrian's Wall. We have no personal name. Modron means Mother. *Mabon is* Son. *That is the essence of our being.*

'One of the Three Exalted Prisoners of the Island of Britain: Mabon son of Modron.

My child. Son of the Mother.

We have a fine collection of old Welsh tales, the Mabinogion. *Listen to the oldest one of all, Culhwch and Olwen:*

Arthur's young nephew Culhwch is mad with love for Olwen White-Track the Giant's daughter. And the whole crazy, mythical court is horsed to win her for him. This is the hunt to end all hunts. A preposterous inventory of impossible tasks to prepare the roaring Ysbaddaden for the marriage he does not intend to grant and furnish his daughter's wedding-feast.

There are no instruments in the world can dress the Giant's hair, so exceedingly stiff it is, but the razor and comb and shears that are caught between the ears of the enchanted boar Twrch Trwyth, and they may hunt that beast through the length of Britain and Ireland but he will never give them up willingly.

There is only one hound in Britain that is fleet enough to chase this boar, and that is Drudwyn, the whelp of Greid.

Only one leash in the world is strong enough to hold Drudwyn, and that is the leash of Cors Hundred-Claws.

Only one collar in the world can stand the strain of that leash, and that is the collar of Canhastyr Hundred-Hands.

And the collar may only be held to the leash by the chain of Cilydd Hundred-Holds.

There is not one huntsman in the world may manage that hound save Mabon son of Modron. But where is he to be found?

An immemorial grief. I bore a baby son. He was snatched from between me and the wall when he was three nights old. And in all the ages since the dreadful shriek that revealed my loss, I have never known where he was taken or whether he is alive or dead.

Of all the many wonders the giant demands, it is Mabon my son that Arthur says must be found first. And the four he sends on that task are Eidoel my nephew, Gwrhyr Interpreter of Tongues, with Cei and Bedwyr.

They seek the oldest animal to tell them where Mabon might have been heard of.

The first they approach is the Ouzel of Cilgwri, and this is what she says:

'I came here as a young bird and found a smith's anvil. No work has been done upon it save by my beak of an evening, and now there is not so much as a nut of metal not worn away. In all that time I have heard nothing of the man you are asking for. But for Arthur's sake I will guide you to one who may know more.'

She takes them to the Stag of Rhedynfre. But:

'It is not I you need. When I came here I was scarcely more than a fawn, with a single tine on either side of my head. This ground was bare in those days except for a solitary oak-sapling. I have watched it grow into a mighty tree with a hundred branches. I saw it fall. I have lived on while it decayed to a red stump. From that day to this I have heard nothing of Mabon, son of Modron. But I will lead Arthur's men to one older than I.'

On then to the Owl of Cwm Cawlwyd. Her eyes are solemn.

'I have seen this valley before us filled with forest and laid waste by men. A second wood grew up in place of the first. That too was felled, and this that you see is the third. And as for me, I have flown so many nights that the roots of my wings are no more than stumps. Nevertheless, I have heard nothing of the one you seek. Yet for Arthur's quest I will bring you to one who has lived longer still and flown farther than any of us.'

So to the Eagle of Gwernabwy and the same question.

'When I came here I perched on a pinnacle of stone and pecked the stars each evening. Now the mountain I stood on is only a hand's-breadth in height. And no word has ever come to me of Mabon son of Modron. But I may yet be able to help you. Flying far in search of food I came once to the lake of Llyn Llyw and sank my talons into the back of a mighty salmon. That should have been a feast for many a day. But he proved stronger than I was, and drew me deep down under the water so that I barely escaped with my life. I summoned all the eagles of my clan to return and destroy him. He met us with messages of peace. The Salmon himself came swimming to the surface and begged me to take from his back fifty tridents that were torturing him. For gratitude to me he may be willing to tell you something.'

And so at last to the Salmon of Llyn Llyw, a vast shadow underwater, in the tidal waters of the River Severn. He is ancient beyond believing, the wisest of all the animals. Here they have dipped so deep into the well of time that at last they dredge up the age-long memory of a mystery.

'It is little indeed I know, but what I have heard I will share with you. With every tide that has ever been, I have swum up the Severn. And each day and each night I hear a cry of distress at the bend in the river, under the wall of Caer Loyw at Gloucester. It has wailed and lamented from a damp deep cell at the water's edge almost since the beginning of time, and I have heard no cry to equal it for sadness in all my life. Let two of you ride on my shoulders and you may judge for yourselves who that prisoner may be.'

So Cei and Gwrhyr Interpreter of Tongues ride the Salmon. And when they come beside the wall they hear a lamentation on the far side that would destroy your heart.

Gwrhyr calls, 'What man is that who grieves so sorely in this house of stone?'

'Alas, and never had man a bitterer cause to lament. I am Mabon son of Modron in the cruellest imprisonment that ever was.'

'Can you be ransomed, or must you be freed by fighting?'

'I shall never be got out except by a battle.'

When he receives this news, Arthur summons his war-band. With all but two warriors he assaults the gate of the stronghold. But Cei and Bedwyr go leaping up the current on the back of the Salmon. While the fight is fiercest, Cei breaks through the wall and carries the prisoner out on his back. So Arthur comes home in triumph, bringing Mabon, a free man, amongst his pack.

Mabon rewards them all by hunting the monstrous boar Twrch Trwyth and his seven vicious piglets across Ireland and Wales and into Cornwall. Many of Arthur's best men are slain in that hunt. Spurring his horse into the midst of the Severn, Mabon snatches the razor from the boar's head while another gets the shears. But worse mischief still is done in Cornwall before they take the comb and even then Twrch Trwyth escapes into the sea.

So they shave the Giant for Olwen's wedding, and he must give up his daughter to Culhwch. And then, they cut off his head.

I, note well, am this Mabon's mother. The story says nothing *more of me since that night, unimaginable ages ago, when I lost my baby.*

To the Welsh, as to the Romans, my principal function is motherhood.

Even the bards have no words to tell you how, for longer than it takes a mountain to wear away to dust, I grieved for that theft of my son.

Chapter Nineteen

So there you are, Modred, your wrecked humanity crushing the sunless buttercups where you fell. My fosterling. These arms shielded you under my shawl in your babyhood when Arthur was hunting your life to destroy it. They have not enough strength now to lift you from the earth. I must let you lie. Bedwyr and Lucan have carried Arthur from the battlefield in grief and honour. Your corpse everyone has left to the crows.

Your destiny is fulfilled; treachery is triumphant. Who will remember now your valour, your courtesy, your good counsel?

You were called one of Three Royal Knights of Arthur's Court. The bards said:

> *'No king could refuse them on account of their beauty and wisdom in peace. In war no warrior could withstand them, despite the excellence of his arms.'*

Arthur trusted you.

Gwenhyvar could not withstand you.

Nor could I.

The battle-cap on hair black as a Cornish chough's wing is encircled with silver, and silver loops your broken breastplate. Too soft a metal to withstand the thrust of Arthur's lance. You and I always chose silver rather than gold. We were more at home in the moonlight than in the sun. Did we in our deepest being accept the secondary place that others allowed us? Or did we cherish the truths revealed to those who alone have the courage to listen in darkness? That wisdom endures only as long as we shun the lust for gold. Silver blackens, neglected. Who notices the moon when the sun is in the sky?

Arthur's gold could not protect him, either.

So the shadow falls on Morgan and Modred. We are the figures of disloyalty. Our original fame is tarnished. Villainy is all they have left us of our birthright.

'Three Dishonoured Men who were in the Island of Britain: The third and the worst was Modred, when Arthur left with him the government of the Island of Britain when he himself went across the sea.'

Death has not long since passed this way. The blood is still bright where the gash severed your throat and silenced the song that was almost as pure as Taliesin's. Life has gushed out over your breastplate. This flood will darken by nightfall. A dreadful deed by a weapon never made for this. Caliburn has flashed in the sun for the last time. That Lady who lifted it up for us from beneath the lake is weeping now a salt ocean of tears for what her gift has done. With the most famous sword in the world, King Arthur has killed his own son.

Your wounds are terrible. I kneel beside you, lowering my head to the armoured body I may not lift, and I glimpse the last pale light of the sky clear through the lance-hole in your chest. Was ever daylight cursed as this? You never let us see into you so plainly while you lived.

Robbers are creeping on to the battlefield as the shadows lengthen. You need not fear them. You were robbed before you fell. At your conception your mother Margawse robbed you of honour when she twined with the scarce-bearded Arthur in his bed, and never told him that she was his sister. You were the apt reversal of Merlyn's plans. You were her sweet revenge for the death of our father, the honour-price for the seduction of our mother. Her hostage for Arthur's fame, triumph, his place in the heart of every Briton. How could you feel for him? You were not made to be a human child, the fruit of love. You were formed as our tool.

Your father would have robbed you of life, when he knew. When at Merlyn's bidding he cast you out to sea, he feared you would steal from him a golden crown and a golden reputation.

Morgan and Modred. We are the Sea-Born. I named you.

81

I saved and reared you. My wisdom hid you from Arthur's wrath. I have made you what you are.

You were the child of stories. I held Arthur's son on my lap by the fireside, my arm encircling you, your sleepy head against my breast. I crooned songs for you. In dappled sunshine we walked through the forest and made its ancient trees and new-sprung flowers our college. In gales we struggled to the tops of mountains and, laughing, claimed the far-spread lands and oceans for our own. I taught you the speech of beasts.

I thought you listened wisely. Your little, knowing face turned up to mine. Your small warm hand gripped tight around my fingers. Those dark eyes seemed to drink my knowledge deep.

I told how wisdom might still bind up the wounds of warfare. How Gorlois's and Uther's blood had been united. How all the hurt and loss of Ygerne's daughters could be made good through Ygerne's son. How, though despised, I wielded a power of my own to equal Arthur's. I was the Healer.

You saw how deeply I was hurt.

On the eve of manhood you learned that you were the Pendragon's child. Margawse's vindication. Arthur's shame. Merlyn's nightmare. Morgan's hope.

But secrecy had darkened your childhood. Too long for a child to be without a father. Too bitter to learn that yours had willed your death. What breastplate could I have buckled on you to shield you from that? You saw yourself his living doom, who should have been our reconciliation. Arthur had claimed the sunshine; we were left the night. Today at Camlann, Merlyn's worst premonitions have been realised. Twenty-one years late, Arthur has slain his son.

Let me slip that circlet of gold from your head. The colour does not become you.

The victory is elsewhere. Arthur's shame died when you fell. The bards will rob you of your bright renown. Modred the traitor, who destroyed King Arthur's Britain.

There, I have bloodied the wings of my cloak in the thickening tide. Too late to hold your young life in. Our time is over. We, the women of the Arthur story, will bear the blame for this day's work. Vengeful seductresses, false queens, untrustworthy enchantresses. We are the evil to Arthur's virtue. Forgive us, Modred. You deserved better of history than this.

I cannot heal you yet. The blood begins to clot. The chill is claiming your flesh as the sun goes down. The final battle is still to come. I drowned the power of Caliburn's scabbard long ago, that could close all wounds. Now only the naked slaying blade remains. Wait for me, Modred. Arthur is still alive, and armed. And I must steel myself to play the warrior-woman. Can your father bear to cast away his sword to join the scabbard, and in that surrender make us one at last?

Let me close your eyes to a world that held too much pain. See in this sleep the laughing of fair women, the rush of racing horses, the break of spray on ships that will carry you to my Summer Isle. Believe that this, at least, can be true. Do not yearn for this world. It has wronged you too much.

Men mourn for vanished Arthur. His praise-songs will echo down the centuries. Hero-tales will multiply. Women will measure manhood by him.

Where are the laments for Modred?

Hear me, you stars.
I sing him resolute and honourable on the battlefield,
Comely and courteous among women,
Just in judgment, a gifted artist.
Generous to poets.
Swift horses pricked their ears
To the whisper of his voice,
Hounds' hearts took courage
From the touch of his hand,
The salmon lay still
Under the stroking of his fingers,
And blackbirds alighted
In the clearing where he sat.
He was a fatherly prince in caring
For the slave and the servant in his court,
He, too young to nurse his own firstborn
Before he died.
He was a peacemaker, gathering round the table
Painted Picts and pale-haired Angles,
He for whom the Britons
Tore themselves apart.

This was Arthur's son. The king's maternal nephew. Blood of father, blood of mother, doubly royal. The courtly prince, gifted beyond his brothers. The ideal Celtic hero. One thing alone this wise, brave warrior-scholar lacked. The blessing of his father and his mother.

I have loved him from the depths of my being. It was not enough. I was not his parent.

Chapter Twenty

I have had happier fosterings.

One is the hero of the thirteenth-century romance Floriant and Florete.

The king of Sicily is murdered by Maragoz, his steward, who then violently lays claim to the queen's hand. She flees the palace, trying to reach shelter in the castle of a faithful retainer. On the way, the pangs of labour overtake her and a boy is born.

I am Morgan Sea-Born. I and two other fays have been disporting ourselves at night out in the salt water. We are returning at midnight from our moonlit swim when we discover the fatherless child beside his sleeping mother.

I am the fay of destiny. I foretell that he shall become a great knight one day. But now, this baby is in danger. Take him up quickly, then. Bear him away to my own sanctuary on Mongibel, Mount Etna. Here I baptise him Floriant.

The boy is well brought up. I have a tutor who teaches him all the arts and the skills of chivalry that a noblewoman's son should know.

I cannot keep him. At fifteen years of age he comes to me and begs to know who his father was. I withhold the saddest part of his history from him for a while. I tell him his father was a king, his mother, a king's daughter. Now his heart is set on rejoining that world. I knight him myself.

Next day a magic ebony ship sets sail for my brother Arthur's court at Cardigan. I wave farewell. I have hung the boat with wonderful silken tapestries, embroidered with tales of Troy, from where the British ancestors came long ago. He has many marvellous adventures on the way and to crown them all, the lad arrives at court just in time to win a brilliant victory in a tournament. He does me credit. He bears my message commending him to Arthur's service. He is welcomed and honoured.

My foster-son has proved himself to be a valiant young man.

It is time for the truth. One of my maidens has been following his adventures secretly. Now she delivers a letter to him from me. Here is the whole sad story of his father's murder, the queen's persecution, Floriant's wayside birth. His mother is still not safe. Even as he reads this, the castle of her retainer, which has been her refuge, is being besieged by the treacherous steward Maragoz.

Arthur and Floriant set out to rescue her.

It is more than Maragoz they have to fight when they reach Sicily. The Emperor of Constantinople is laying claim to the land. Arthur fights bravely but Floriant excels himself. The Emperor is repulsed. The steward is beaten. The queen is freed.

But Floriant has taken a very serious wound: he has fallen in love with the Emperor's daughter.

Difficult to win her father's consent, of course, but Floriant is a bold young man and the lovers succeed. Floriant marries Florete. He is made King of Palermo.

The story takes a familiar turn. The valiant young warrior becomes a staid, inactive husband. People start to criticise him behind their hands. The loyal Florete recalls him to his knightly reputation. Together they leave the court in search of adventure. They head for Britain again, the land of magic and marvels. There the court welcomes the 'Handsome Savages' from a far island.

Floriant beats a dragon.

But another sultan is besieging Rome. Concern for his kingdom takes Floriant back. He retires to Palermo.

Age is beginning to attack him. I see it is time to call him home.

Now Floriant sights a white stag on a hunt. It is, of course, an animal from the Otherworld. What hero of romance ever refused to follow that magical beast into the depths of the forest? Or ever failed to lose contact with his followers? The creature leads him up the slopes of Mongibel to a beautiful castle and dashes in through the door. Floriant charges after it.

A threshold is crossed.

The stag has disappeared. I am there, on my couch, waiting for him to return after all these years. I have not changed. But he has. Gently, I tell him the truth he does not want to hear. He will die if he stays longer on earth. I have sent the stag to fetch him. If he will live with me now, he will never grow old. There are maidens to welcome him, monsters to fight with, like the Sathenas with gigantic ears and the Pellican who devours a girl *every day. Plenty of occupation for a hero. Arthur himself will soon be here.*

Time passes easily in Mongibel, with feasting and singing and hunting and fighting, all a man could desire. The women I offer him are incomparably fair, but still he grieves for an earthly one. I hold council now with the same two fays who found him long ago after our midnight bathe. Shall we let him go? No. We will bring Florete here instead to share his bliss.

Floriant is my foster-son, not my lover.

I have other expectations.

No need to tell you why I feel no jealousy of Florete.

Chapter Twenty-one

Modred had disappeared. The sea had taken him. I paid the woman Fencha and her husband well. They were discreet.

Slowly the wheel turned, the Goddess smiled. I dared not own him yet, but in a fisherman's cottage at Mabon's Stone beside the Solway Firth a little baby crooned and suckled. The Son was born. The Mother would watch over him.

Still, I had power.

The Church, as so often in his turbulent youth, laid a heavy penance on Arthur for those babies. This time, he walked barefoot from Bath to Glastonbury. Then Bishop Dubric laid hands on him and forgave him. Merlyn they did not absolve.

So the stage was cleared for Arthur to be acclaimed High King. For that they needed Cornish Gwenhyvar.

Merlyn arranged the marriage. We were Arthur's sisters. We were summoned.

I could not sleep that night. It would break my heart to see my brother married. I could not bear to stay away.

Caerleon, where all of us but I had first met with Arthur. Where Margawse had lain with Arthur. Where Gwenhyvar would marry Arthur soon. A place of bitter memories for me, and the knowledge of worse to come.

And now Merlyn, coming to *us* to ask for help? Uther Pendragon's sorcerer to Gorlois's daughters? There was strangeness here. Something was wrong.

Merlyn. A creature out of our past, haunting our present, shadowing our future. What could he need from us a week before Arthur's wedding?

I watched him coming into the room where we sat, Elaine, Margawse and I, our faces avid with curiosity. An old man bowed down with the weight of the magic he had used. Bent as a shepherd's crook, and almost as thin. His skin hanging loose on almost fleshless limbs. Hair so fine and light and white it floated in the lightest breeze like unhooked spider's webs. He looked at us sideways, as wary as we were.

An old man with young eyes.

I felt the lurch of my heart that told of treachery. And then he smiled.

Merlyn was not so dried by age and not so stiff with enmity to us that his blood could not run faster when he looked at me. I sensed his double desire. I kindle that lightning in the air when men are close to me. He wanted my body for his own. Merlyn was a sorcerer. He needed me also for a higher use.

I felt my power grow.

'Emrys Merlyn does us honour.' Elaine spoke for us.

'The honour is mine, to come into the presence of three great queens who rule large realms of the Island of Britain through their husbands, but hold a greater majesty in their fair persons.'

'You sentenced my son to die,' Margawse accused him.

He shrugged and spread his hands. 'Blood has to be shed for the good of the land. You know that, Margawse.'

Yes, she knew. We all of us knew the laws. Merlyn himself had taught my sisters for nine months, after Uther married Ygerne. A dangerous education. Gwennol our nurse used the caring, nurturing magic of birth and fruition and death. Merlyn had wider visions, ambitions, strategies. The high magic of kingdoms demands a higher price.

He never taught me this. He feared me, even as a child. I got my education in the Christian convent where Uther confined me. There I learned that blood has been shed once only, for the whole world and for all time. I wove the wisdom of Gwennol and the nuns together. It should have been healing enough.

All this time Merlyn's eyes were on me. I felt his urgency.

'You robbed Margawse of her son, and me of my freedom, and all of us of our father. What do you want from us now?' I asked.

'Arthur is your brother.'

'So you tell us.'

'Ygerne confirmed it.'

I bowed my head.

'Yet, in your wisdom, you have gone straight to the nub

of the matter. Tongues will wag. They were dangerous times. Uther's son was fostered in secret. Nimue, Lady of the Lake, was a discreet guardian. He survived. That much is victory. He has gained much from Nimue's teaching. That may be gain, if he uses it wisely. But there is always a price. For a king-in-waiting, something was lost.'

'Legitimacy.'

His turn to bow.

'I see we understand each other.'

And now the blood was starting to hammer in my veins. He could not be asking what I thought he meant, surely?

'The nobles may question Arthur's right to royalty. Needlessly, of course. He has generations of purple through Uther Pendragon, and a crimson brighter than that in the blood of Ygerne. But still, the visibility of the thread was broken. He emerged from the mists.'

'The war-lords will hail Arthur as their battle-leader, the Imperator? But they may yet dispute his claim to be our High King?' Margawse was laughing softly. 'Yes, you are right. Even now Lot would trim Arthur's beard before he gets too great, if he could persuade the others to back him.'

Elaine leaned forward, with that slow deliberation that hushed talk and drew all eyes to her.

'But you are marrying him to Gwenhyvar.'

Gwenhyvar the Giant's Daughter. Gwenhyvar, King Leodegran's child. Young Gwenhyvar of Cornwall, whose mother was cousin to Ygerne and who could bring Arthur as her dowry the most ancient, most sacred bloodline of all. The Kings of the West, who claimed descent through their maternal line from the still more revered Queens of old.

A slight pause, long enough for us to hear the buzzing of a fly upon the window-ledge. Knowledge crackled between the three of us as though we had touched hands before a thunderstorm.

'What is wrong with Gwenhyvar?' asked Margawse innocently.

'Wrong? Wrong with Gwenhyvar!'

'Gwenhyvar is flawed.' Elaine's voice came deep as a man's, startling from her fair, plump face.

'What do you see?' Too quick now, Merlyn, to challenge her.

'What do I see?' Her eyes were dazed now, her voice thick and heavy. 'I see a woman with a sword.'

She shuddered, as if a goose had walked over her grave, and shook herself awake. She looked around at us questioningly. She did not know what she had said.

'A woman with a sword?' Was that my own voice or Merlyn's shriller than Elaine's, trying out the words, testing the possibilities. I shivered too.

I sensed a sexual excitement in Margawse beside me. We were all looking at Merlyn. Had we helped him? Had we frightened him? Had he got what he came for?

He was like a miser with a bag of gold, who hears the thieves approaching and knows that he must trust his hoard to others' keeping. He cannot bear to let it leave his hands, and yet he dare not wait.

What was this flaw in little, royal Gwenhyvar? What was driving Merlyn to us a week before the wedding?

Legitimacy.

The word came back to me with the force of trumpets blowing. Merlyn had come from Celliwig in Cornwall. Bedwyr was following from Cornwall bringing Gwenhyvar. Gwenhyvar would not bring Arthur what she promised. Gwenhyvar was flawed.

My power was reaching its height.

'I see you understand.'

'And you ask *us* to help you?'

'Not me. Oh no, my bright and midnight Morgan! Arthur.'

He knew. He had stood in his wildman's garb in the high fort of Lyvennet and seen Arthur open his arms to greet me after fifteen years. He had seen the meeting of our eyes. He had read my heart.

'The woman with the sword. And the sword is in the stone. The High King must draw the weapon from her rock.' Elaine made facts sound like a dream.

'You want us to legitimise Arthur!' Margawse cried out in amazement.

Merlyn bowed very low.

The eyes of the three of us met and locked. So Ygerne had affirmed Uther, though never Gorlois. So we had each authenticated our own chief. His men would hail him as their battle-leader when he raised his sword. But we holy women took the sword into ourselves in the sacred rite. We would release it only for him we had destined to be King.

'You would trust us that far?' Elaine spoke for all our bewilderment.

Merlyn smiled, that dancing childish smile that had enchanted even old Gwennol to think herself a young girl.

'You are Arthur's sisters.'

He lived for schemes of power. He thought we saw the same world he did. With Arthur High King, his sisters the Queens Elaine, Margawse and Morgan would be powerful ladies. Our ritual assent must make Arthur's right unchallengeable. It would also proclaim our own authority. The secret power of our royal blood would be acknowledged publicly, in the world of men and war-hosts. With the lure of temporal power Merlyn baited the trap of magic for us. He partly succeeded.

'Are you not afraid that a second son might come from that rite?' Margawse taunted him.

We saw the flash of anger in his eyes.

'That nightmare is past and over. Even the Church is ready to anoint King Arthur now. Whatever further sons and daughters he gets need not trouble his sleep.'

'No. What Arthur once did, stays done,' Elaine murmured.

A long silence filled the room, as if in a tent enemy battle-commanders pondered the terms of a truce that might or might not secure their boundaries. We mused on wounded honour, larger empires, old bitterness. I struggled to call down wisdom, to hold the balance, to satisfy the Goddess. We saw between us a young man's face, blue, laughing eyes, a joy of muscled body raised on northern hills to race a horse and fling the spear, a baby born in Cornwall, cradled always in the arms of the women of the West.

'Well?' smiled Merlyn.

His eyes were on me. He knew my heart. He was coming to the moment of his greatest victory. Once, he believed, I had tried to destroy the baby Arthur. Now, I must authenticate him king. Uther Pendragon's son. By offering me political power of a sort, he hoped to curb my more dangerous powers for ever. If I am the land, and Arthur mates with me, then I shall be his love and his Goddess for the rest of our lives, never his rival.

We both knew we had come to the moment of decision. I would not hesitate. The ninth great wave that had torn Arthur from my arms in the sea at Tintagel would bring him back to me in the thunderous foam of our meeting.

I opened my mouth to assent.

'We must draw lots,' Elaine's voice came quietly.

A start broke Merlyn's fixed attention. An instant of fear as his eyes left mine. He shrugged it off. 'As the Goddess chooses.'

His gaze was back on my face, intent now, as if he could will the outcome of the lottery. And mine on his, as if I wished he could.

So slow and fumbling, Elaine's plump fingers. She cut three straws. Two short, one long. So childish a game to settle the future of Britain.

Merlyn must hold the straws. I could feel the enchanter summoning power into his sere hand to guide our choices. We closed our eyes and drew in turn. Elaine was the eldest. I was the last. Margawse took the long straw.

Margawse took the long straw.

Margawse took . . . My soul screams to this day. Margawse took what I never had. Twice over! In laughter and fornication after his victory feast. In solemnity and terror before his king-making.

I was there, in the cavern. I was the Grail Maiden. I carried the vessel of abundance past his eyes.

But Margawse was the Stone. The rock of the Island of Britain. Arthur's weapon was in her. She let him draw it out. And the cavern roared with a mighty shout that must have shaken the fortress of Caerleon.

'Arthur the King!'

One voice had cried out in protest before that ceremony. Nimue arguing furiously at our threshold in Caerleon.

'Merlyn! Emrys Merlyn, what are you doing in there with those witches? You do not need them. Gwenhyvar is coming.'

She never guessed. No rumour from Cornwall reached her to make her doubt the truth of Gwenhyvar. She never met Gwenhyvar's sister Gwenhyvach until it was far too late. She feared when she saw Merlyn restoring our authority to us. She never forgave him. I shudder now when I think how she imprisoned him, solitary, powerless, under the spell of his own giving. Merlyn, my adversary, who understood, as I do, how darkness must balance light.

Nimue was never as wise as Merlyn.

And nor was I.

When we made Arthur king, we affirmed Gwenhyvar's right to be queen.

Chapter Twenty-two

I become Arthur's sister.

I was originally less, and more, than that.

In Geoffrey of Monmouth's Life of Merlin, *I am one of nine sisters on the Island of Avalon, and Arthur is not my brother. I am the most beautiful of all, the senior. I teach my sisters mathematics and astronomy. I am unmarried. I lay Arthur in my own bed.*

In his other book, the History of the Kings of Britain, *Geoffrey gives Arthur a single sister.*

Uther's brother, King Aurelius, lies dying in Winchester. A huge and brilliant star is seen in the sky. A beam of light from it ends in a ball of fire which spreads into the semblance of a dragon. From its mouth shoot two more rays. One lights the Continent; the other crosses the Irish Sea and sparkles into seven smaller shafts. Three times the vision appears and terrifies the country. Merlyn interprets this portent. The dragon is Uther. The ray of light over Gaul and beyond signifies the conquests of his son. The second ray denotes his daughter, whose sons and grandsons shall hold the kingship of Britain.

Merlyn is the Pendragon's court magician, and he is sound enough on the subject of men. But he seems to have been distressingly inaccurate in his assessment of women.

Uther takes the crown. Arthur is born. He is followed a year later by a sister, Anna. She is the daughter of both Ygerne and Uther Pendragon.

Ana is the Irish goddess of war, but that is probably a coincidence.

Arthur fulfils his destiny.

Anna marries Lot, Duke of Lothian, brother to Urien. She becomes the mother of Gawain and Modred. But Modred seizes the crown only to lose it ignobly. Both sons fall in the civil war. Gawain seems to die childless. Modred's two sons survive him, but are killed by Custennin, the new High King.

The sister's bright future turns to tragedy. It would be wise to avoid any relationship with this family.

Anna disappears from the later stories.

It is Chrétien de Troyes, late twelfth century, who first brings me into this turbulent dynasty. He calls me Arthur's sister. There are two of us: the mother of Gawain, whom he never names, and Morgain.

I bestow on my friends and relations great gifts of healing ointment. I am the lover of Guingomar, Lord of Avalon. I have brought the powers of my fairy island with me into the human scene.

When the memory is strong of the matrilineal clan, the emphasis is on Gawain's generation. A man, even Arthur, derives reflected glory from the daring exploits of his sister's sons. There are more stories about Gawain's sisters than about me.

As we move to patriarchy and absolute monarchy Arthur and I become more important.

When Robert de Boron writes his Merlin in the early thirteenth century, Ygerne has acquired three daughters. The eldest, unnamed, marries Lot, the second, Urien, and there is a third, whose name is Morgain. I am put to school, where I achieve outstanding success. I am known as Morgue the Fay.

The Huth Merlin follows. Morgain becomes the second daughter, wife of Urien, mother of the hero Yvain. Morgue the Fay survives as a separate, husbandless third daughter.

By the Vulgate version of the Arthurian romance Ygerne has had two husbands before Uther and produces five daughters, wives of Lot, Nentres, Urien and Karadan. Morgain alone seems to remain unmarried.

I am sometimes Gorlois's bastard, sometimes Ygerne's.

So, for a time, the Otherworld side of me struggles to hold on to my independent existence against the human female role of wife and mother. Then I capitulate. Morgain and Morgue are one. I am married off, sometimes to Lot but most frequently to Urien. Well, I have ceased to be the fairy mistress of Avalon and an earthly lady requires a husband. Since Arthur has become my brother he cannot share my bed, can he? Still, the shadow of my past falls sometimes on my husband Urien, making his kingdom of Gorre a delectable paradise or a dangerous

Otherworld reached only by a perilous bridge, hard to escape from.

The older tradition still surfaces. Arthur does indeed lie with his sister. Because of the new relationship, that union is shameful now, not joyful. In it is sown the seed of Arthur's downfall. Modred, who in earlier stories is called Lot's son, is now the child of Arthur's incest.

It is Margawse's bed Arthur is lured to now, not mine. I have lost him.

Chapter Twenty-three

Gwenhyvar, the Giant's Daughter. Gwenhyvar, the 'White Phantom'.

Another pain. I must stand in the church at Caerleon and watch her walk demurely past me to marry Arthur. A child scarcely fourteen, as pale as milk, with hair like the bleached fronds of oats. And yet, I admit it, beautiful in a pure sweet way. Such innocent virginity can quicken men's pulses as much as Red Margawse's eager heat.

Yet as she walked past us to the altar I heard the indrawn breath of the wise women ranked around me, Elaine, Margawse, Luned, Teilo, my Man-become-Woman in his new blue gown. Merlyn had chosen Gwenhyvar for Arthur, and Gwenhyvar was not a child of the Wise. We sensed an opportunity.

We underrated her. Gwenhyvar's power was not in spells or ritual. All the enchantment she needed lay in her own shy, sweetly-smiling self. Without high magic, she worked more harm than all the rest of us.

It seemed power fell into her little hands without her willing it. I witnessed the nuptial mass that joined her to my brother. Then we prepared her for a second ceremony at a different altar. Two churches, two processions, two coronations. One for Arthur, in the Church of the martyr Aaron, for Archbishop Dubric to anoint him in front of all the men. The other, in the sister Church of Saint Julian, to crown Gwenhyvar in the presence of all the women.

There were those who thought this was merely a matter of convenience. Neither church was large. Half Britain had come together for this king-making. Arthur needed all the friends he could win. There were many like Lot who had opposed this crowning. The boy could have remained Duke of Battles, War-Leader of Britain, nothing more. He could not afford to offend the dignity of any chieftain by denying him standing-room at his coronation. He needed their total affirmation. There was no space for women.

We saw it differently. Though that was true, there was an older truth. Merlyn had not chosen Gwenhyvar for his Arthur lightly. It was more than the hero's whim for a pretty West-Country face. Merlyn had calculated that the blood of Gwenhyvar ran royal with the inheritance of the old kings of the West. Our blood, through Ygerne, taps that same source. True, Arthur was also Ygerne's son. But our lineage and, it seemed then, Gwenhyvar's, was certain, our upbringing a matter of public knowledge. Arthur's was clouded. He was spirited away from his parents as a baby. Fifteen years later a youth appeared. We had only Merlyn's testimony they were the same, and Ygerne's wise instinct.

But now, this doubt. Might Gwenhyvar also be false?

We royal women felt our hearts quicken as we escorted the bride to this second altar. We knew what was happening here, though she, as yet, might not.

The silver trumpets sounded for her. White doves were carried in front of her and released. She wore a pale blue gown trimmed with snowy ermine and pearls. She seemed the moon-queen to Arthur's sun, his consort, helpmeet, the sweet reflection of his glory. But she meant more than that.

Bishop Bytwini, in white and gold, waited to greet her with her crown in his hands. She knelt, colouring faintly with proper modesty. He marked her forehead with holy oil. A bell sounded distantly from Arthur's church. And in the hush that followed, the golden circle descended on her silver hair. At that same instant, the nave rocked with the shouts of acclaim from all her noblewomen, and across the town came the deeper roar that told us the Church had made her husband king.

'Receive the Staff of Britain. Wield it well.'

Into her hand, that seemed too small to grasp its weight, Bytwini placed an ancient rod of stone. It gleamed grey-green in the candlelight. A network of shadows traced the carving of strange heads, bird-beaked above, human reversed below. An ancient symbol for a Christian queen. We helped her rise. The stiff cloth of her mantle weighed down her shoulders. It was an effort for her to straighten them and turn to face the congregation. She summoned a radiant smile for all the ranks of ladies massed below her.

'Thank you,' she said. 'I will care for the land, as Arthur will care for me.'

So young, and Maiden still. She did not realise her Arthur was High King because he had wedded Gwenhyvar the High Queen.

Now I and my sisters must prepare her marriage-bed.

Chapter Twenty-four

I am the wise healer.

I do indeed arrive early at Arthur's court, and for a wedding.

By 1160, only ten years or so after Geoffrey of Monmouth introduces me in his Life of Merlin, *I have crossed the Channel and begun a new career in the French romances. The courtly Chrétien de Troyes is one of the first to welcome me. He calls me Arthur's sister. He makes only three mentions of me, but they are significant.*

In the story of Erec and Enide *the lovers celebrate their splendid wedding. Among the long list of guests, which includes Maheloas, Lord of the Isle of Glass, an island where thunder is not heard, where lightning never strikes nor tempest blows, where neither toad nor snake live, and it is never too hot or too cold, comes Guingomar, Lord of the Isle of Avalon, of whom it is said:*

'We have heard of the latter that he was Morgan the Fay's lover.'

Years later, after unhappy wanderings, Erec and Enide return to Arthur's court. When Erec is discovered to be sorely wounded, the joy of everyone at this reunion is turned to grief. Arthur sends for a precious ointment made for him by Morgan his sister. It is a sure cure. Any wound, or nerve, or joint anointed with it is certain to be healed within a week if the salve is applied once a day. Though Erec declines to wait that long, my ointment gives him immediate relief.

The third time Chrétien refers to me is in the tale of Yvain, *the Knight with the Lion.*

Yvain is the French equivalent, though the connection is not made here, of my own son Owain.

The hero comes to a magic stone. When water is poured on it a violent storm arises and a fearsome knight gallops up to defend it. Yvain fights with him and gives him a mortal wound. He pursues the fleeing knight back to his castle so furiously that he himself is trapped when the portcullis falls and his horse is sliced in two.

He is rescued by the damsel Lunette, who gives him a ring of invisibility. She hides him in the castle till the knight dies. Then she persuades her mistress Laudine that the famous Yvain is just the husband she needs to defend her. After a suitable time she produces him.

Yvain in turn defends the stone, till Gawain comes and pours the water that invokes the storm. Yvain comes rushing up. After the fight, there is joyful reunion. Yvain is persuaded to return to Arthur's court. The lady Laudine gives her permission, but charges him solemnly to return in a year's time.

Of course, he forgets. Too late he recalls his pledge. Already the damsel Lunette is storming into Arthur's camp. She calls him disloyal traitor, liar, deceiver, and tears Laudine's ring from his finger.

Yvain, overcome with remorse, runs mad and naked in the forest. A lady and her two damsels pass that way and spy him deep in slumber. One of the girls is despatched for a closer look. She rides up and recognises Yvain with much amazement by the scar on his face. She returns weeping with the news. A plan is formed. They leave him asleep and hasten to their castle to fetch an ointment.

This is a priceless gift from Morgan the Wise. It is kept with the respect it deserves, in a box locked inside a case. The lady entrusts it to her damsel with a warning. It is extremely precious. She is not to be lavish with it. Since Yvain's disorder is only in the brain it will be sufficient to rub just a little of the salve on his temples. The girl is ordered to take great care of the remainder.

She returns to the forest, leading an excellent palfrey and bearing fine men's clothes. She goes boldly up to the naked madman. But in her eagerness to cure the lost hero she rubs his entire body till the box of ointment is completely empty. Then she hides behind an oak-tree, leaving the clothes in view.

Yvain sleeps in the sunshine, and the black despair seeps from his pores and leaves him whole and sane. He wakes to find himself in his right mind, and as naked as ivory. He is ashamed and bewildered at the evidence of his wildman self. He sees the clothes in front of him and blushes that whoever left them may have recognised him in his bestial state. He dresses his unkempt body and tries to rise. He, who once hunted stags barefoot and ate them raw, finds himself suddenly so weak he can hardly stand. The damsel watches.

After a tactful interval she rides up, as though she had only just now come that way. Yvain hails her. She makes a pretence of searching through the trees towards the cries until she finds him. He begs a loan of the spare palfrey she is conveniently leading, and she invites him to her lady's castle till he has recovered. The request is not wholly disinterested. They are expecting shortly to be attacked.

By now, standing so long under the trees, the girl has had time to think. Her first rash eagerness has cooled. She realises that the lady's box she clutches in her hands is empty. Morgan's ointment is all gone.

She is an intelligent girl. The pair of them have to guide their horses across a bridge over a swiftly roaring torrent. It takes only a moment to fling the box away and see it lost among the cataracts. That bridge is known to be perilous. She will say her palfrey stumbled and the box slipped from her grasp and fell as she almost plunged into the gorge herself.

The lady is delighted to see Yvain restored. He need not know how he was cured, or that they observed him in his nakedness, witless. Men's dignity is fragile. But she has not forgotten the ointment. She summons the girl aside. In private she requests the return of the box and the rest of the precious cure it should still contain. Now it is time for the damsel to tremble as she tells her falsehood. She is right to be afraid.

The lady is seized with grief and fury. She has lost the best and dearest possession she ever owned. Morgan's gift is irreplaceable. She has won a knight to defend her, but he has proved more costly than she bargained.

Chrétien is always courteous about women. Note, I am Morgan the Wise. I am the Healer. The gift I give is the most precious thing anyone could possess. I can heal any hurt, of body or spirit. I am still the magic woman who offers love to a lord on the Island of Avalon. But it cannot be Arthur now. I am his sister.

So who is this Guingomar, my new lover?

103

Chapter Twenty-five

I have had many men. I am not promiscuous. I serve the Goddess.

I committed a kind of blasphemy when I prepared Gwenhyvar's marriage-bed. This was not how it should have been. We crumbled the herbs of bitterness to a fine green powder in the folds of her sheets. She would never notice the ergot blighting the rye in the corn dollies we had woven so elaborately and hung over her bed. Even the too-sweet oil of the lamps we left softly burning was tainted.

'She is not one of us,' Elaine said. 'She will bring trouble.'

'Her son shall not inherit over mine.'

I had not told even Margawse where her baby was hidden. Men rarely saw the bitterness with which she mourned both the murder of Gorlois and the loss of Modred. She laughed when she took her revenge. Only I knew the pain.

My loss was different. I must watch Arthur come storming down the corridor towards us, laughing and flushed with wine and lust as a man had a right to be on his wedding-night. His mates ran hard on his heels, cheering him on. And I must join the mock-battle, struggle in the arms of excited young men, pretend that I was trying to keep Arthur from his bride's bedroom door. Pretend!

It was over. We were hot and dishevelled. The door slammed and we were all left on the outside. The men panted and grinned and trooped sheepishly off to down more drink. I leaned, breathless and yet scarcely able to breathe through the tightness that was banding my breast, against Arthur's door, against Gwenhyvar's door. Not long to wait. I heard her small glad cry before the door burst open again and Arthur was brandishing the bloodstained sheet of his triumph on the point of his sword.

Bedwyr seized it from him and raced off. I heard the roar of acclaim from the hall.

The door closed behind Arthur again. He never saw me.

Now they slept. And there was nothing left for me but to join the feast.

I too got drunk. How else could I have borne that night? And I was ashamed and afraid of what I had done. I had been bitter at others before. Gorlois, Luned, Uther, Teilo. I wounded them sorely. Today I had desecrated the Mothers' own bed. Had I hurt Arthur as well as Gwenhyvar?

I felt a strong imperative to purge my sin. I had angered the Mothers. What would come of any union I made that night I dreaded to think. Still I must offer myself. I must make restitution. I must mend the weft.

I chose him calculatingly, even in my fuddled despair. Not kingly Urien. I would not foul my own marriage-bed that night. I honoured Urien, though it has been hard for him to understand. We made a better couple than you might think.

Who, then? Accolon. Yes, that was appropriate. A callow youth, a masculine version of Gwenhyvar. The same slim small bones, the straight pale hair, the blue-grey eyes that showed light without depth. He had payed me pretty compliments, excited to find himself at Arthur's court. I could see him sitting at the corner of the table now, looking over his goblet at this famous company, wondering how a young man with no great pretensions as a warrior could rise to greatness here.

Well, stand up then, Morgan. Carefully now. The floor's as unsteady as a ship.

Light up your face with your best smile for him. Advance towards him. Hold out your hand. He pales and backs away, then blushes and edges uncertainly forward to meet you. You have shattered his young blade's poise. He does not know what to do. Arrest him with your eyes. Soften your lips. You have him now. It does not matter what you say. He cannot resist.

'The hall is warm and the noise too loud. It will be sweeter by the river. Will you escort me, sir?'

Breath was indrawn. Heads turned our way. No one challenged me.

I had no need of this man's safeguard. I had another bitter, surly watchdog. Even tonight, even though he knew plainly what I meant to do, Teilo was following me. I had ended his manhood. Yet he would watch over me while I did with another man what I had denied him with all women. My people are more loyal than I deserve.

'Madam, you honour me.'

Accolon was both eager and overawed. In his eyes I read more of ambition than lust. This was Arthur's sister.

One face I must not look at as I left the hall. It might have broken my heart, if that were possible, as I was breaking his. Forgive me, Urien. I did not choose this marriage. I would not willingly shame you on any other night. It is well that you are more drunk than I am, from the cup I held to your lips. In the morning you will not remember this. Tonight the banshees howl. The Mothers must have their dues.

Forgive me too, Accolon. Your sin this evening was only that you resembled Gwenhyvar. It cost you dearly.

Chapter Twenty-six

I am the jealous woman.

Accolon was not my first.

Chrétien de Troyes names Guingomar, Lord of the Isle of Avalon, as the earliest of my lovers to appear in the pages of medieval romance. We get no more than a passing mention.

'We have heard that he was Morgan the Fay's lover.'

My name weaves through the lays and literature, shifting and changing. Morgen, Morgain, Morgue, Morgan. So does Guingomar's.

In the twelfth century, while Geoffrey was writing chronicles and political prophecies and Chrétien romances, the Breton minstrels were singing their lays of love and heroism.

In one of these lays we meet Guingamor, a valiant young knight of Brittany. He has never cared anything for the love of women until a fay captures his heart.

He meets her, in the traditional way, on a perilous boar-hunt. He finds her irresistible. She leads him away to her beautiful castle where he forgets the mortal world. Three hundred years seem like three days, but at last a longing to return stirs in him. She lets him go, but warns him that the world is dangerous to him now. She tells him the rules of faerie. He must eat nothing while he is away. He disobeys, of course, and this lively, lusty knight, still apparently in the prime of manhood, sees all his strength shrivel until he becomes a feeble old man of incredible age. The fay takes pity on him and sends her messengers to bring him back to the Land of the Ever-Young over the water.

This is a common tale.

A more skilful of those Breton poets is Marie de France. Naturally, with a name like that to distinguish her from all the other Maries, she lives in England. She writes between 1160 and

1190, a contemporary of Chrétien's. She may be Abbess of Shaftesbury, half sister to King Henry II, but she can tell a good love-story.

Her hero is Guigemar, also beloved by women, also scornful of their love. His downfall this time is a stag-hunt. He falls behind the rest and spies a doe with her fawn half-hidden in a thicket. He draws his bow and shoots. The arrow wounds her, but then flies back and pierces him too. The bleeding doe cries out that she is killed. She pronounces her curse on Guigemar, that no medicine, no herb or root will cure his wound until he is healed by her who will suffer greater pain for his love than any other woman.

Guigemar sets out to seek the land across the water where he can find relief. He rides through the forest till he comes at last in sight of the sea. He has been anticipated. A fair ship is waiting anchored. He goes on board. There is no crew, no pilot, no other passengers. All the same, the ship takes off at speed across the high seas.

It takes him to a port with a high tower defended by a wall on every side except the seaward one. Here an old man, the lord of the city, has imprisoned his beautiful young wife out of jealousy. She takes Guigemar into her tower and heals his bleeding wound. Love blossoms rapidly for the hitherto unsusceptible hero. He lives with her secretly until, after a year and a half, her husband discovers the pair together. Guigemar gets off more lightly than the lady, and is ordered to flee in his ship. Eventually she too escapes and the magic ship is waiting to bring her to Brittany. After much difficulty the lovers are reunited.

The fairy mistress and the human woman have separated. The fairy is beginning to sound vindictive. Never mind that the man has mortally hurt her; this is the hero's story, not the fay's. The human woman suffers too.

So on to the next century and the romance of Lancelot. *He is called:*

'The best knight in the world.'

He is a late arrival in our story, as is his foster-mother, the Lady of the Lake. In Geoffrey of Monmouth's history, Modred is Gwenhyvar's lover.

But the French are jealous of the daring literary exploits of the

British, especially Gawain. *They need a hero from their own side of the Channel to outshine him. Enter Lancelot, from Brittany.*

We are passing on from the chronicles of kings and battles to a different kind of story. What was treachery to his sovereign in Modred becomes in Lancelot the new ideal of Courtly Love.

This doctrine assumes that no self-respecting medieval woman can be in love with her own husband. Granted, love is of slight consideration in these aristocratic betrothals. They are about power and possession. My daughter's hand and half the kingdom in return for killing the dragon. The lady needs some compensation. A romantic 'ami' whose heart and body are totally hers. Courtly Love allows her complete autocracy over his actions. She may command him to do anything, however unreasonable. He is inspired to superhuman deeds to satisfy her, and rewarded by, at least, her smile.

It is the love of Lancelot for Gwenhyvar that destroys Arthur, and the whole Round Table with him. But this courtly couple are portrayed as the hero and heroine of high romance. We must not blame them. Somewhere there has to be another villain and a villainess. Modred and Morgan. So the author requires a reason for me to hate Gwenhyvar.

Meet . . . Guiomar.

He is portrayed as a handsome, valiant knight, nephew to the king and queen. Morgan is Arthur's half-sister, lady in waiting to Gwenhyvar. In the first version I am ugly, but in later tellings, though I am dark I am silky-skinned, my body perfectly modelled, my hands elegant and I am merry and clever. I am also the hottest woman in the Island of Britain and the most lustful.

After a brilliant feast at court the guests troop off to bed, but in a small chamber deep in the palace I am still embroidering a headdress for my sister, Lot's wife. And Guiomar lingers after the rest have retired. We salute each other debonairly and soon he is winding the golden thread for me. We please each other. The needle slips from my hand and we fall to hugging and kissing. When he sees that I am as eager as he is, we move to the bed.

We love in secret. There is more passion on my side than on his. One day Gwenhyvar is attracted by the sound of our quarrelling and finds us in a compromising position. To avert shame from the court she warns Guiomar that his life will be in danger if Arthur hears of our liaison. For love of her, he deserts me all too readily.

109

In my distress I flee the court and seek refuge with Merlyn, who adores me. He teaches me great enchantments. I bear Guiomar's son.

The author says that Arthur searches for me unceasingly.

Later, in the Livre d'Artus, *I have my revenge on Guiomar. With the art I learned from Merlyn I create the Vale of False Lovers, my Valley of No Return. Deep in the forest, through a wall of air, come men who have proved untrue to their lovers. They do not get out.*

In a more sadistic version, I punish the woman too. I fasten two lovers in sight of each other, but out of reach. I make my rival believe she is encased in ice from her feet to her girdle, and wrapped in flame from her girdle to her hair.

I rage and grieve for Guiomar, my lost love. But he is not the original one. When I cry out in my restless sleep for the man whom Gwenhyvar stole from me, it is a far more famous name.

Yes, I am jealous of Gwenhyvar.

Chapter Twenty-seven

Gwenhyvar. Well now. You strayed like a slender-legged filly tossing your mane in the sunshine, too near the lair of wolves. No matter that we squabble among ourselves, Arthur, Margawse, Modred, Elaine, Morgan. We are family.

Still, I have found you a place of safety. Abbess Bryvyth is a warrior-woman of God. She lost Tintagel. She did not retreat from Cornwall. She planted her cross by the River Fowey. It is a nice irony. The white nuns, who kept me Uther's prisoner in my girlhood, and freed my mind to possess the circular earth and starry universe, they will guard you. I cannot save your sons. Nothing of Modred will remain. I think he knew it.

You must have been the only one of us who slept soundly last night, the eve of Camlann. The nuns will have seen to that.

Gwenhyvar. I almost called you 'the queen'. But you are not queen now, are you? You never should have been. You were not the right woman. Britain will not see Arthur again in your lifetime. Modred is already dead. Two tiny strips of flesh, twin boys, mewl in their baskets. You never gave Arthur so much, and the one son you bore him died straining for his manhood. And these? My tears flow faster now, for these are Modred's sons. I think the nuns in their quiet convent cannot shield them long.

Cornwall. The blood flows back to the heart. The far southwest. We were all born here. Arthur, you and I. We come home for our final leave-taking. Custennin of Dumnonia will take up Arthur's fallen crown. Modred's sons, Arthur's grandsons, he will not allow to live. Oh, Gwenhyvar, what have you robbed him of?

You have drunk the nuns' soothing draught, and you lie in darkness, your face serene. Younger than I, and fairer in your sleep. You have known more happiness than I did. I have ended that.

111

You will wake in a narrow hard bed in an anchorite's cell underground, with only a wind-eye for God to see you. Too late you have vowed yourself to chastity and prayer. Too late for everyone but yourself. Tomorrow they will tell you Modred is dead, and you will weep. They will tell you Arthur was carried away and has been seen no more, and you will shudder and fear the future. When Custennin's men come, the Abbess Bryvyth will belabour their ears. They will search the holy place for you, in spite of her. I think they will not find you. But they will find your babies. The convent cannot hide them.

Gwenhyvar, the Giant's Daughter. Gwenhyvar, the White Phantom.

I remember you, pale and slight as thistledown, walking up the church aisle to your wedding with Arthur. And we, all the ranked powers of warriors and wise women, turning our heads to stare and get the measure of you.

I heard the triumphant hiss of breath behind me. Teilo, my servant, that had once been Smith. He was a great master of magic before he met me. He should have known. You fooled him. You almost fooled me too.

He thought you had no magic in you.

In part, he was right.

You did not weave and work at enchantment, like Nimue, Lady of the Lake, coaxing the keys to wisdom out of Merlyn, casting her eyes over my store of herbals from the open door, running her fingers seductively even up Teilo's arm. She wanted power. You accepted it as your right.

You were the still, hollow centre of Camelot's world. And into that well flowed all the life and love that made it brilliant: Arthur, Gawain, all Margawse's and my sons, our daughters too, grey warriors from the British Isles that had known your father, young fighting men from beyond the Channel, even from Africa, the bards and pages, and Modred.

I almost said 'my son'. No, Arthur's son. You learned the truth too late. Too late for you; your bed was fouled already. I saw the horror in your eyes when I declared his provenance before the court. I heard you scream. Yet not too late to save Arthur, if you had wished.

That difficult, painful reconciliation with his son. Were his hands softer now in middle age than the hard-riding, fighting youth's that reached out, oh, so reluctantly, no doubt, to lift the baby Modred from the cart? His son, his firstborn prince. A vast litter of screaming May-born infants bagged up in a boat like kittens to be drowned. And Arthur's mistake. The brat that should not have been got upon his sister.

He did not know. I scream that at you, Gwenhyvar; he did not know when he got Modred. But you knew, when you got Modred's sons. You knew by then who Modred was. Arthur was ignorant of that second treachery as he reached out those sinning hands to touch and hold his adult son.

You did not warn him, and you did not let Modred go. And still the honour and the love rained down on you to fill your hollow like a limpid pool. So clear, so pure, so transparent is Gwenhyvar. You seemed to will nothing. You merely let it happen.

You were like Olwen White-Track in the old tale, who was also the Giant's Daughter. She sat and smiled, and for her wedding feast impossible quests were undertaken, treasures stolen, countries ravaged, warriors torn to death by savage boars, Arthur's band devastated. She got her husband.

So you walked up the aisle, the meekly blushing bride with lowered lids. So you were crowned. You stole from Arthur the sceptre that we had entrusted you with. You tore the kingdom from him and reigned yourself. You coupled with his son. Your royal blood legitimised Modred's coronation.

And I consented to it.

There was one woman who did not. Gwenhyvach, your half-sister. Little Gwen, a thing to be hidden, a daughter to be ashamed of. Our story is full of the unacknowledged parts of ourselves crying out to be loved.

I will not ask again who was the false Gwenhyvar, and who the true. I can still see the mark of Modred's hand flaming on your cheek, the tears of outrage in your eyes, Gwenhyvach's smile. Only this I knew: if you were not our true queen, sickness would haunt the land, the crops would wither and the cows and ewes bar up their wombs.

The plague is here.

I leave you now, your children born, emptied of queenship, marriage, motherhood. Pale, exhausted, fearful of the spiritual warfare I have sent you to.

You brought us to Camlann, and you find refuge in a nunnery. Where will the rest of Britain shelter from the storm?

Chapter Twenty-eight

I am the Wild Huntsman's lover.

I am tempted by lesser men, who might have loved me better, as in the thirteenth-century tale, Li Jus Adan.

In the French city of Arras it is their custom to entertain Morgan, with her attendant fays, Maglore and Arsile. One evening, the table is richly laid in preparation for our arrival with fair linen, gold and silver. These citizens know what is due to us.

We have come prepared to bless the town. Always we fays offer both promise and danger. Arsile and I are laughing, well-pleased with what we find. We deal out riches, love, beauty, success to the two hosts who have provided this for us. Townsfolk raise their goblets to us. We are welcome here.

But there has been a small oversight. No knife has been laid for Maglore. Insult! Anger! Fear! For this omission she will deal them pain, famine, poverty, sorrow. We are not to be trifled with or crossed. If you accept our favours you are committing yourselves to our service. You neglect us at your peril.

The feast resumes.

Who is this at my elbow, breaking in on the merriment? Crokesot, messenger of the fairy king, Hellekin. He brings an entreaty to me from his master, but I am too busy holding court. These humans please me. I, at least, am honoured here.

Well now, here is this excellent young man, Robert Soumeillons, offering me his hand and heart. I like him well. I could stay here with him, in this safe, sunny, ordered city among men who adore me. The idea is tempting. I am on the point of saying yes.

But someone is insistently interrupting. Crokesot again. What is this message from his fairy lord, that will not wait?

Hellekin the Huntsman, they call him, leader of the Furious Chase. A winter king, grey as the storm-clouds that sweep over Europe when the bitter nights outlast the trembling days. You hear the howling of his hounds and hide your faces to the wall as the

Wild Hunt goes past. Do not walk out by night, do not let them catch you; you will not come home.

Hellekin the Huntsman wants my love.

I laugh and say he sighs in vain. I am giving my hand to the human.

Crokesot plays on my imagination. How could the fierce fairy soul of Morgan the Fay be satisfied here in the summery city of Arras?

Oh, the pull of the wild dangerous Otherworld against the solid comfort of an earthly marriage. Have I still the courage to fly the night sky with my fairy lover? Or the strength to turn my back on Hellekin, the sense to stay with a human husband? Which will I risk: heartbreak with the Huntsman or disappointment with the predictable Robert?

Young Robert Soumeillons pleads for my constancy. Crokesot and Arsile argue more passionately for Hellekin.

Passion wins. I choose the Storm-King.

The feast is breaking up. A lady comes to beg my help to disgrace a man. I take flight, singing.

Do not trust me. I am dangerous. I will break your heart.

Arthur, the Bretons say, leads the Wild Hunt.

At Cadbury too, there is an old track called King Arthur's Lane. On a rough night the spectral king and his hounds can be heard bearing down on the unwary.

I will embrace the tempest that is coming. I will ride the storm.

Chapter Twenty-nine

On Arthur's wedding-night I lay, still haunted by my painful imaginings, in a crowded guest-room of his Roman castle. A tiny hand gripped mine warmly. I came back unwillingly to my body. My little daughter Morfudd was leaning over me.

'Ssh!' A childish scolding.

I followed the nod of her head. We were not the only ones awake. A vast grey shadow was sliding across the painted wall into the darkness of the doorway. I did not need Morfudd's hand dragging me across the room to know what she would show me. The bed of my eldest sister, Elaine, was empty.

And I, who had done so much hurt already to Arthur, Urien, Accolon, was filled with fear. Elaine meant our brother harm. I was the Healer. I had vowed these hands to making men and women whole. I had given way to meanness.

With stealthy haste I followed. And Teilo, once again, followed me. Too late we saw her coming from Gwenhyvar's bridal chamber. She was carrying something swathed, enfolded against her breasts. She still moved smoothly, but I thought her feet dragged heavier than before.

Elaine was all the mother of my own blood I had ever known. Ygerne had rejected me, a third daughter, the seal on her failure in a warrior's world. I had sat cradled in my sister's lap, a fierce, wild, ugly child, leaning sleepily on those same fragrant breasts that passed me now.

Lullabies hummed through my head. I found it hard to move. I watched her slipping away into the dusky garden. I have always struggled to understand Elaine. Little spoken of, quieter than any of us, as wise in magic as Ygerne, our mother's favourite. More innocent than I was as a maiden. More gentle a mother than passionate Margawse. Growing more mysterious as she aged. What was she taking away tonight?

A cold draught eddied along the colonnade, stirring the hair round my face. I shook myself awake and forced my feet into urgent movement. I do not have the Sight, as Elaine does. I dreaded what I would find.

Outside the couple's door, sleep lay unnaturally heavily on Gwenhyvar's women, on Cei, stretched with his hand on his dirk across the threshold, even on Arthur's dog. Our shadows passed over them like uneasy dreams. The door yielded lightly.

Some lamps still glowed, too sweetly.

Arthur and Gwenhyvar slept in each other's arms.

No blood, no devastation. That is not Elaine's way. I cannot say which would have been the greater grief.

A sword lay naked on the bed beside Arthur's hand. Caliburn.

Even on his wedding-night he would not be parted from his true love. The weapon lay, half lapped in the folds of the bearskin coverlet. The scabbard had dropped, unregarded, into the rushes on the floor.

A naked sword, in a bridal bed? Had Arthur been boasting of his bare blade to tease Gwenhyvar?

It lay only a hand's-breadth from Arthur's grasp. But now those victorious hands held softer skin than the golden dragon-scales wrought by the elves of Avalon for Britain's champion. Gwenhyvar was snuggled in his embrace. Gwenhyvar I could not touch. But this I could rob him of.

I picked the weapon up. I almost dropped it with a sense of shock. It was like lifting a corpse. Even as my hands closed round it I felt its falseness. The dragons were there, with tongues of flame. The letters hammered along the blade. This looked like Caliburn. This was not Caliburn. Elaine had taken the sword forged in Avalon for the greatest King of Britain, trusted by those before us to Nimue, the Lady of the Lake, as guardian, given ritually to Arthur at his coming to manhood. With that, he had driven the Saxons to take the first steps back to the long shores. It was his talisman of victory and meant to win our peace. Elaine had left this one in its place.

A poisonous, jealous thought crept through my mind, like a viper, jaggedly patterned. Could my sisters feel about

Arthur as I did too? Were they my rivals as well as Gwenhyvar?

Or had Elaine melted into the night serving a deeper purpose?

Arthur stirred in his sleep, and murmured against Gwenhyvar's cheek.

I was a wronged woman; I was a Wise Woman. I held that treacherous counterfeit in my hands and looked down at pretty sleeping Gwenhyvar, that false substitute for Arthur of Britain's true mate. Heart and duty warred, like wild dogs against a disciplined hound.

I lifted that false Caliburn. I cannot say where it might have fallen.

A small voice shocked us both: 'No, Mammy, don't do it!'

Owain, my son, in the room, and Luned, terrified, chasing after him. Those wide accusing childish eyes. The high, clear voice.

Arthur's castle erupted into rage and horror. The door was flung wide back. Cei's knife was in his hand. A babble of women's voices broke like a floodtide above a swirl of shifts.

With all my art I held them, powerless, back from the door. I heard Arthur roar behind me.

'*Morgan!*'

I must not turn and see his blue eyes blazing at me without love. I must not see him shielding pale, shocked Gwenhyvar. I must keep my strength. I threw down that gilded, useless toy that had replaced the Lady's gift, as Gwenhyvar had replaced the true wife of the High King of Britain. Let him snatch it up and keep it if he loved the look of it. It would betray him. I seized the only thing of worth left in the room, Caliburn's scabbard. The Lady's talisman of healing. Gwenhyvar would not know how to use that. Only the true blade and the true sheath must know each other. I would guard this better.

With that protection, I sped through the doors, like a sudden wind on the lake that agitates the surface and is gone. Teilo yelled for horses. He flung Owain aside. This was no time for children. My people were armed and rushing to meet us. Our mounts were ready in moments. We sprang astride and charged the gates. Beyond was night and freedom and a vast cold loneliness outside the walls. I would not be welcome again in Arthur's court.

Arthur pursued me.

My brother and his men ran us down in a wood. Urien was with them. I led my people down into a cold hiding-place. I whispered runes of concealment over us.

We lurked like stones in chilly bog-water. Over our heads the skeleton of a sacrificed horse swayed creaking from a branch, hung with the dark tatters of its hide. It was an awful place. What had happened here, that the Great Queen of Horses had demanded this offering from her people? What had I sacrificed?

The men quartered the muddy shore of the hollow, but their mounts shied back from the creeping ooze and the swinging bones that creaked against the darkness. They passed us by, unrecognised, and the sound of their horses' hooves was lost in the wilderness.

I turned myself to stone. I had stolen Arthur's healing. I have not felt warm since.

Chapter Thirty

I am the traitor.

In less than a hundred years my character has changed from Geoffrey's healing fay to what it has since become. Before the mid-thirteenth century I am already the vindictive seductress, enemy of Arthur.

I harm Arthur, Urien, Accolon.

The Huth Merlin *tells how Morgan lures all three of them: Arthur my brother, Urien my husband, Accolon my lover.*

They are out hunting. A great hart appears, as always. The three of them pursue it and are soon separated ten miles from the rest of the pack. They chase him so hard their horses are ridden to death under them. The stag leads them to — where else? — the bank of a river. They come upon the beast in his death throes in the water, with a brachet biting his neck. Arthur the king claims the prize.

But the real adventure is only just beginning. A ship comes speeding down the stream and comes to rest lightly on the sandy shore. She is hung with silk, right down to the water's edge. Night is falling, and they step on board. Out of the darkness a hundred torches flame, and here are twelve damsels to greet them on their knees, lead them to a stateroom richly hung, serve them with choice food and wine. Then, a luxurious cabin for each of them, and sound sleep.

When the three of them wake, Arthur is in prison, Accolon is sitting beside a strange fountain, and Urien is in bed in Camelot in my arms.

Yet I mean him harm too.

First, Arthur learns that there is only one way he may win his deliverance from the tower. He must fight in the place of the cowardly lord of this castle to resolve a quarrel. His adversary is the lord's younger brother, but he is badly wounded before the appointed day. I arrange that his role will be played by Accolon.

120

For a year, Arthur has left Caliburn and its scabbard in my safe-keeping. Note how completely my brother trusts me. When he sends me a message requesting his sword for this fight, I supply a counterfeit, which arrives just before he takes the field. I have already despatched my dwarf to Accolon, carrying the true Caliburn.

The contest begins. Naturally, neither combatant knows his opponent's real identity. Arthur cannot win. His opponent has the sword that ensures victory. The king has also lost the scabbard that protects him from hurt. He loses much blood. But still he fights so bravely that Accolon is sorely wounded too.

It is the Lady of the Lake who rescues Arthur, as she thwarts all my evil plans. When Arthur is at his last gasp, she realises what is happening. She strikes Caliburn from Accolon's hand by magic. Arthur seizes it back.

Now the battle turns. Arthur has Accolon at his mercy. At the point of the stolen sword, the young man confesses everything: his name, my guilty love that has schemed to set us both on the throne, and all my plots against Arthur's life and Urien's.

Accolon is forgiven. The blame is all mine.

His pardon comes too late. Accolon dies of his wounds. Arthur himself now lies in a convent, gravely ill. Yet he is not so weak that he cannot despatch my lover's bloody body to me, for me to see what I have done.

Ignorant yet of Accolon's fate, I believe there is still one more thing I need to do to complete my triumph. In Camelot, I send my maiden for Urien's sword, and carry it to his bedside. As I raise my arms to strike the final blow, Owain our son, warned by this maiden, comes rushing in and grabs my hand. He threatens that if I were not his mother, he would smite me dead. I beg for mercy and secrecy. He grants me forgiveness, on my solemn promise that I will never harm Urien again.

I make no promise for Arthur's safety.

My brother's gruesome present for me arrives at court, with the taunt that he has Caliburn again in spite of all my evil. I stare at the corpse of my young lover. I must not show my heart is breaking. I plead with Gwenhyvar to let me leave. In Arthur's absence, she is unwilling to allow me to go, but I prevail.

I will seek out Arthur in his convent now. I will be revenged. The frightened nuns are reluctant to let me see him, but they do not dare to forbid his sister to enter his chamber.

The sword has been separated from its sheath. He sleeps with Caliburn naked in his hand, his boyhood love. All I am able to steal from him is the scabbard. When he wakes, weak as he is, and finds it gone, he calls for men to pursue me. He shall not have it back this time. As I flee, I fling the scabbard deep into a lake past all recovery. Arthur is vulnerable now. His end is marked from here. I have, in effect, slain him.

I turn myself, my horses and my followers into blocks of stone, and so escape the hunt. I barricade my castles. It is my turn to taunt him that he cannot touch me. I am a shape-shifter and, but for the Lady of the Lake, I would have done him worse harm.

Arthur threatens me in his turn.

I send a damsel to him with a richly jewelled mantle as an offer of reconciliation. Again the Lady of the Lake interferes. She orders my damsel to put on the mantle herself. The unhappy girl falls dead in front of the king. My mantle burns her to cinders.

I am accursed. Urien, my husband, is exonerated. His loyalty to Arthur is beyond question. I nearly killed him too.

But Owain carries with him a hint of suspicion. He may be too much my son. He is expelled from the court. His cousin Gawain indignantly insists on leaving with him.

Owain is reinstated later. I never am.

Chapter Thirty-one

Yes, I ritually killed the scabbard. Almost a suicide.

Do you think it strange that I, of all women, should cast away the power of healing?

You do not understand how dangerous that power may be, how close the scabbard marries with the sword. There is only a fine line between new-won life and sudden death. It needs a great exertion to drag the sufferer back from the brink. In one rash movement we may find that we have overplayed our force and stepped too far.

The killing sword may also win us life. Nothing is simple.

I feared the power in our hands.

A sacred cave above Din Eidyn, Lot's stronghold. A spring ran from the entrance, staining the rock red. Inside, a raised slab of stone, as though the gods had made this chapel for us knowingly.

We laid our tributes on it. Elaine the Fair, our lily-maid, now heavy in the body with the change brought by the bearing of a single child, put down the sword as though it were a thing of massive weight.

Even in the shadow, the gold danced. Flesh-hungry dragons strained from the hilt, opening mouths from which red tongues shot out to lick at cold blue steel. The blade was awesome. Few smiths would know the magic of that hammering, the metal softened and bent and hardened, over and over again, growing stronger with each tripling. The ancient tracery scored in its final setting, spelling a simple truth for those who have the wisdom to read it:

TAKE ME UP.

And on the reverse:

CAST ME AWAY.

One question had hammered in my head since I saw Elaine

coming from his chamber, smothering it in the folds of her bosom.

'Why?'

Dull her voice. I could not tell if she knew what she said, or if the spirit spoke through her.

'Let him discover he is vulnerable.'

A threat? A fairy wisdom?

I thought Elaine's eyes read the future more clearly than the present. She saw the handsome, blue-eyed youth riding a high-stepping horse through cheering crowds, claiming his right to the heart and body of every woman, sliding that sword so easily into the entrails of Angles, Saxons, Picts.

I saw a boy, shadowed by doubts and plots and rivalry. A casque of fragile bone shielding the source of immense dreams. A little life-span weighed down with the vast pains and hopes of this mighty Island.

I matched the scabbard along the weapon's length.

A simple case of black leather and wood, much used, but serviceable still. Banded with silver, once patterned with magic, that had worn so smooth its mystery was almost lost to sight. The fingertips might feel, faintly, the uncertain evidence of wisdom. A lining of old red silk so frail the blade had parted its threads. A plain and quiet thing to lie alongside that flamboyant hilt and blade. Unless you knew.

'Where one has gone, the other must follow. They belong to each other.'

I was not sure what we had done. We had not taken kingship from him. That was a different sword. This was his battle-weapon.

Red Margawse shrugged and laughed lightly, 'A High King's wedding is not so common a feast that I would have left it readily. But you two had created such a pother with your plots that it was impossible for me to stay. It will be a long time before we are invited to that court again. That being so, I brought away a keepsake of my own.'

Her creamy fingers twined between the sword and scabbard, knotting them firmly together. A belt. As simple as the sheath. Black leather, soft, supple and scuffed with use. Old silver clasps.

She lifted it carelessly. It raised the scabbard easily. The tension spread across the table to the separated weapon. The knot grew tight around the pommel of the sword. The leather stretched and strained against the weight of gold. The soft edges of the belt began to split and part.

'No!' I shot out a hand involuntarily. 'It is too frail!'

Elaine's larger hand descended over ours and took the belt from both of us. She unhooked it from the sword and from the scabbard, folded it lovingly and tucked it in her breast.

'Leave it with me. I will make it stronger.'

We made strong spells to keep them.

A time of trouble followed. Ravens came swooping from the east and the north croaking their news of disaster: young, spirited men, wearing gold torques, left as bloodless corpses on the field of battle, strong walls breached and sanctuaries desecrated. Books burned and virgins bloodied. Celtic Britain was shrinking.

Arthur was gravely wounded.

I could not shriek or weep when they told me. The skin of my face felt cold. I thought I had died, still standing.

Had I done this?

Screech-owls sounded in the night, bringing back old scenes, as Luned and Teilo watched over me anxiously. In the faces of these two I read the power I had used.

I remembered a little boy, Howel, in the school at Tintagel. I was older than him; he was in love with me. Always he was at my elbow, bringing me gifts, coaxing a smile from me. I was a serious scholar. One day I toiled over a page of Euclid, meticulously copying a triangle and the bisection of angles. The diagram was exact, the theorem clearly written. The scroll would not disgrace our schoolroom library. Howel came, nudging my elbow to show me a tabby kitten. The ruler swivelled. The nib tore the page. My work was wasted.

I jumped up in a towering anger and cursed the child.

Next day I had forgotten it. Released to freedom, I led a wild game of hide-and-seek across the cliffs. I loved both speed and danger. I fled to the southern side, out of sight of the nuns' cells. On the steep grassy slope I darted behind a boulder and crouched, waiting. The children's cries sang overhead, distant as skylarks. Then a breathless, chuckling laughter followed me down. Howel had spied me. I did not see him slip. One sudden cry, short, high and final. He somersaulted past me. The rocks devoured him. The sea washed him away.

I have tried to hold the balance. I have striven with passion and might and obedience to be wise. It has come hardly to me.

Teilo still bears the scars.

He came to me in Rheged, Lord of high magic to my Lady. He was the Smith. I showed him the herbs of healing. He scorned them. I placed beside them the seeds of death. He took away both.

I had another maiden then, younger than Luned. Erith, golden and merry, and respectful of no one, except the Mothers. She was much less of a scholar than Luned, but far more wise. When I sent them to the forest to gather fungus she had teased me laughingly that great Merlyn could make and unmake kings without such simples. It flicked me on the raw. Arthur had vanished. I could not find out where Merlyn was keeping him and we had all lost sight of Merlyn himself. The years were stealing life from me. I was Urien's wife. I was carrying Urien's child. Once more, I lashed her with my tongue.

Teilo took her. By force, in the forest, with those strong Smith's arms. He made her drink the potion he had brewed with the darker herbs. He scorned to use the ones I had given him to bring life back. They carried her home to me, purple, twisted, terrible. Had I caused this?

My curse drove him mad. It wracked me too. Owain and Morfudd were born that night in grief and pain. I never forgot Teilo. That awful tilting of the balance out of true. He fled to a Christian hermit, to Nimue, even to Merlyn. They could not mend him. Three years later I drew him back to me. And only then he told me that the day I cursed him, his wife fell dead of poison and he was blamed for it. Should I have taken a knife and cut these healer's hands from my wrists, that wreak such havoc in the lives of others?

He came back to me disguised as a woman, and Woman he has remained. He chose the way of death to prove his power over me. I have taught him the path of life.

I did not know how great my power to heal and harm. I did not know how much Arthur depended on Caliburn for victory and how far on himself. Bright clouds of magic and prayer swirled round us both, dazzling our sense of what we were and did. We could not see ourselves, or each other, clearly.

Arthur lay at Celliwig, near to death. We sisters held his sword and scabbard.

We were the land. We were the stone. We were Britain's healing.

I went to Elaine in Garlot, Black Annis Hill, and begged the weapon and its sheath from her on my knees.

'For a Daughter of the Ocean you are strangely impatient. How long does it take for a cliff to be eaten away or a new island to be formed?'

'But it is Arthur who is being eaten away. The King. The Lady's champion.'

'Kings come, kings go. The Island remains.'

'It is not the same. It will never be the same if the Saxons advance.'

'The Romans came, even as far as Cornwall. The Island you love is partly their making. Before us, it was different still.'

'Then why Arthur?'

A heavy pause. 'Or one day Modred?'

'Is it only Merlyn's ambition? Against our rivalry?'

'We gave him his sword of kingship. We have not taken that away.'

'You have stolen what alone defends that right.'

'He loves his first sword more than the other. Does he understand yet that Caliburn is the King's servant, not his god?'

'He is young. He may die before he learns that lesson, and Britain will be overrun.'

'And if we give it back?'

'Let us at least take the risk. He is our mother's son.'

And so, with her unwilling authority, I went to Margawse. She was more ready.

'It would be a shame to see the maggots crawling out of the darling flesh of him. Give him his toy.'

She gave me the sword and scabbard from the secret hiding-place in Lothian. The belt was missing.

It was a far, hard journey to Celliwig in Cornwall. And when I arrived, I was not welcome.

Cei turned me away from the gate of the fort rudely. 'He has wise women enough to look after him. The nuns and, if magic were needed, Nimue.'

'They have returned? She and Merlyn!'

'The Lady came alone.'

A quarrel? Some shift of power? Merlyn deserted Uther when

Arthur was born. I did not believe it. Arthur had not achieved his destiny yet.

Lean low. Smile. Keep my voice sweet and reasonable. He must understand.

'Friend, you have a traitor in your camp. I must speak with my brother.'

Words stung my face, like hazel twigs thrown for scorn. I struggled to hold the sense of them.

'Be off with you, woman. It would shame the king as well as yourself if we have to remove you by force. But I will do it if you are still here one hour from now, Arthur's sister or not.'

Never a courteous man, Cei, or a wise one.

What wounded dignity kept me from handing the sword and scabbard over, there at the gate?

I summoned Accolon out of the fort secretly. We met in a clearing in the woods that freezing winter morning. I entrusted Caliburn, sheathed, into his hands solemnly, and with it the message Cei would never have delivered.

'Tell Arthur, we found these separated, even on his wedding night. Always, we offer him the weapon in the stone. Always he sees his glory in the naked blade. What we have allowed him to take, he must return. Tell him that truth and joy wait for our meeting.'

He had no time to carry my message. Nimue came galloping through the wood with her red cloak streaming from her shoulders. She saw the weapon in his hands, but whirled on me.

'So it is you! You stole Caliburn from Arthur, and the scabbard with it.'

But Nimue, Lady of the Lake, had stolen from Arthur a truer friend even than that.

'Where is Merlyn? Why is he not with Arthur? What have you done with him?' I challenged her.

The radiance of her smile showed how much she relished the power she had now taken for herself.

'I, responsible for the great enchanter Merlyn? You sisters could never overcome him yourselves, and yet you believe I have?'

'Where is Merlyn now?'

I sensed her falter, and fear sprang across the gap from her to me.

'*Where?*'

'U . . . under a great rock . . . of his own free will! . . . He wearied me with his lascivious attentions.'

'You coveted Merlyn's power.'

'You sisters are too bitter. I offered him love and I got what I asked. The power that Merlyn had belongs in a woman's hands, doesn't it?'

And in that one word 'had' I heard the truth.

'How long will you keep him prisoner? He is your prisoner, isn't he?'

Silence, as long as the silence of the grave. It will never be broken. I felt the world slip from its pivot and tumble into the void. The balance of our enchantments was overturned. I must have screamed.

'You cannot do it! You made the great spell of binding, and you did not learn how to unloose it! Merlyn is trapped for ever, isn't he? There is no one, no one, who could break that now except Merlyn himself, and he is sleeping. He will not come back to Arthur ever again!'

The rest was chaos. Nimue stretching out the finger of power to forestall me. Accolon drawing the sword in a flash of dragon's breath. His horse bolting. Both sword and scabbard lying in the snow where they had fallen, one black, one golden, crystals of ice melting around their silhouettes. So near each other. So small a space of snow between them.

Nimue and I dived for them, I darting forward from the sycamore tree where I stood, she swooping low from the saddle of her roan. I swear I meant to give them back to Arthur. But not from Nimue's hands, with Nimue's words.

She snatched up Caliburn exultantly. Brandishing the sword aloft she galloped off, taunting me. I was left clutching the scabbard to my chilled heart. Nimue, of all wise women, knew its ancient power. She was the present Lady of the Lake. She knew how the weapon and sheath both came from Avalon. She understood that the scabbard of healing was worth ten times the sword. In the moment of decision she had let me keep it because she saw it was the sword that Arthur loved.

Arthur had not been able to undo what he had done, and nor could I. I still held the scabbard in my shaking hands.

We found Accolon hanged, caught in the branch of a tree.

Chapter Thirty-two

Am I myself the ambivalent Lady of the Lake?

Both of us live in magical realms across, or beneath the water.

We are both the foster-mother of heroes.

We both rescue orphaned princes and whisk them off to safety. We train them in warfare and nobility. We tell them their parentage. We send them back into the world.

We heal their madness and their wounds.

We are skilled in enchantments.

Both of us are pupils of Merlyn. He loves us lustfully and unwisely. I also am accused of imprisoning him in his tomb.

We are both benevolent and dangerous.

The world cannot live with this ambivalence in one person. It requires that characters identify themselves as evil or good. Especially if they are supernatural. A polarisation, then: the protective Lady of the Lake versus the malignant Morgan.

It is the Prophecies of Merlin *written by a French-speaking Italian in the thirteenth century, which speaks the worst of me.*

Merlyn, my tutor in magic, is attracted to me, but he has another sweetheart, Nimue. Because of her boasting, I have called her a whore. To win her favour back, he praises her and reviles me:

Nimue has a more natural gift for enchantment and more subtle art than any woman in the world.

I am the child of heat and lust; she, of paradise.

I purpose and work evil; she acts well.

I kill good knights; she helps them.

I am the enemy of orphans; she fosters them.

It is true that I work against Lancelot and Gwenhyvar, whom Nimue encourages. Did I destroy Arthur? Might he have survived if he had stayed innocent of their falsity and the good fellowship of the Round Table not torn itself apart over those two?

Nimue and I are enemies because of this. Her good against my evil. And yet . . .

130

In the Prophecies of Merlin *all women are dangerous.*

I wish to get rid of Nimue. When she sets out on a journey, I order fifteen knights across the sea to capture her and I send a message to King Claudas to lay an ambush. She hears of this in time and guards herself, but she is fearful that I will harm Lancelot. Merlyn she does not trust. He is too fond of me, and on friendly terms with Claudas.

Merlyn leads her into a cave in the forest, which contains a tomb. Only she can find the way there. For fifteen months they stay together. Then I enter the forest.

I am searching for Merlyn. When the Lady of the Lake hears my hunters' horns, she is afraid. If Merlyn helps me, I will kill her fosterlings, Lancelot and his two cousins.

Merlyn assures her he will never again leave this cave. She begs to stay with him. He makes this lover's plea: that after his death she will be buried here with him, in the same tomb. Nimue suggests he lie down in it, so that she can test if there is room for two. The moment he is in, she slams down the lid, and fastens it with the magic he himself has taught her. No one may open it now.

Now she reveals another motivation. I have taunted her. I told her Merlyn had boasted to me that he took her maidenhood. Too late for him to swear before God that the charge is false. Merlyn is lost to the world.

It is all my fault.

Chapter Thirty-three

Arthur recovered, even without his scabbard. The hands of the nuns from the River Fowey must have been skilful, and their prayers were strong.

I nursed the scabbard to my heart and an image in my mind. That small cold space of snow between Caliburn and this sheath. The flakes of ice melting around their separated shapes, flowing together, almost meeting. Soft yellowed moss beneath, waiting for the sunlight to turn it springing green.

So narrow a distance. I would make a great leap of love across it. I would show Arthur he need not fear my ambition or my jealousy. I would heap on him a gift of such generosity he must believe I meant him well.

What should it be? Some precious, healing ointment in an alabaster box? A harp so rare and sweet you would think Rhiannon's birds nested among its strings? But Arthur was whole and warlike again, and music did not seem to move him as it did me. What was appropriate from Morgan the Wise to her Arthur the King?

We had given him royalty. In our blood, in Margawse's flesh, in the ritual sword. Let me be overwhelmingly generous then in affirming it. I had offered my womb, and lost. Let me give him my hands, my eyes, my heart. Arthur should have from my fingers a mantle fit for the Emperor of Constantinople himself. A gorgeous thing. A magic thing. An imperial gift. Let me show how I both loved and honoured my brother.

I set to work. I sent for costly velvet, woven on Venetian looms, dyed richest purple. I beggared Urien's treasury for jewels. I laid in coils of gold and silver wire and heaped up basketfuls of bright embroidery silks. I smiled on Teilo. I let him remember he was once a Smith. He was never a silverworker, but his hands were clever. He had the adept's feeling for the soul of metal. He knew the spells of smiths. Under my coaxing he drew out gold and silver almost to the fineness of sewing thread.

I sketched designs on scrolls of parchment. The nuns, Rathtyen, Cigfa and Eira, had taught me well. I knew the mathematical secrets of interlacing, the dimensions of spirals and circles and Arianrhod's Wheel. I let imagination flow in cats and griffins, serpents of resurrection, vines of plenty. And for the Pendragon, one immense, spectacular dragon danced glittering scales around the border and opened its flaming, laughing mouth upon the collar. The lining should be of shimmering gold silk.

I told my sisters of my plan. Margawse was wild with jealousy as she watched me cut the rare, rich cloth. Elaine said little.

All through the fast of Advent I and my women stitched that miraculous cloak. Drops of my own blood darkened the purple from my too eager fingers.

With every twist of the pattern, with every loop of the needle through the cloth, I whispered a spell of turning, binding, meeting.

At last, just before Christmas, the lavish embroidery was finished. Arthur would celebrate the Christian feast in Carlisle, ten miles from Lyvennet. All that remained to sew was the plain gold lining. And then, we would both rejoice.

When I had set the last stitch of silver, I had Luned and Teilo spread the great mantle across the floor under the lightest window. All the women crowded to look and gasp and admire. I had woven my soul into this embroidery. I could only offer it now. I put my needle away. I had my women sweep up the clippings of silk. An immense weariness came over me. For Urien's sake we all fasted through Advent. But Christmas was almost here.

I lay on my bed, hugging the dream of my love-gift which warmed my heart like the healing scabbard. I closed my eyes in deep exhausted sleep.

Elaine woke me, kissing my feverish forehead, almost a maternal touch. She smiled down kindly.

'It is finished, little sister. Luned and Teilo and I have sewn in the lining.'

I felt a sudden, childish pang of disappointment. This

133

should have been entirely my gift, not Margawse's, not Elaine's. All the plans, all the expense, all the months of skilful painstaking labour had been my doing, or that of the people of my court. I did not want to share my heart with either of my sisters.

Still, it was done. That last plain, simple stitching. The mantle lay, spread out as I had left it, but the jewels and precious thread of the dragon winked more secretively now in the winter lamplight.

I stroked the encrusted hem, took a handful of the soft purple cloth. I would have gathered it up, wrapped myself in it, as soon it would wrap Arthur. But Elaine stopped me.

'We must fold it carefully now. It would be a pity to crush it or loosen the jewels.'

She signalled to Luned and Teilo. With a care I had hardly expected, even in such loyal servants, they folded the widespread mantle. Luned's trembling hands seemed unwilling even to touch the embroidery. Teilo tucked the golden lining out of sight more tenderly than a mother with a baby's crib. I called for the softest of deerskin bags, large enough for it to lie easily within. Blushing, a grown woman and Urien's queen, I kissed the last smooth fold before it was wrapped from sight.

Should I have suspected? We are three and we are nine and we are one. Each of us sisters holds within herself a triune being, Maiden, Mother, Crone. We cannot be separated. What is done, even by a part of one of us, belongs to the pattern. Did Elaine bring death? Or was it the malevolent hag within myself that could not forgive Arthur, even yet?

I was the Maiden again that morning, feeling my eyes dance and my cheeks glow as I stood in the frosty yard waving to the chariot that was taking Luned and Teilo to Carlisle with my gift for Arthur. Soon, soon those wheels would come rumbling home, like the drums before a festival. Luned and Teilo's faces, that looked so tense and fearful now, would be satisfied and smiling. Arthur would reward my messengers generously. The doors of Gwendoleu's Roman castle where my brother kept court would be flung open to welcome me for the Christmas feast. Arthur's arms would open. The glory and softness of that purple cloak would enfold us both. I was as eager as a village maid daring herself to send a love-token to her first sweetheart.

I did not have the Sight.

The chariot brought all three back to me in the grey, cold afternoon. Teilo, Luned, the mantle. Teilo was trembling so that he could hardly speak. I could not see Luned, till he showed me. Once my people had carried Erith home from the forest like this, after Teilo had killed her with poison. Poor, pale, plain Luned, who had once been one of Bryvyth's white nuns, was wrapped in death in the purple winding-sheet of my extravagant love-gift. Teilo, who certainly blamed me, would yet not allow me to touch even the hem. He turned it back with cautious hands and showed me her face, accusingly. Black, twisted in agony, tongue bitten, bulging eyes. I covered my own face in horror. I could not deny what I had done.

Luned, my tormented foster-mother at Tintagel. Luned, whom I had led against all her pleading to the Mothers' cave. Luned, whom I had robbed of her scholarly ambition and schooled in a more dangerous, earthy wisdom to serve me. The earth would have her body now. But what of her soul?

They called me Morgan the Healer! And yet, let me be honest, it was not Luned I truly shrieked for. It was for my own lost love. This was Nimue's doing. She stopped Arthur as he reached out his hands to take my gift. She made Luned try the mantle on herself. What would have happened if Arthur had trusted me? Would I have killed him? Could all my spells of love have triumphed over Elaine's? The Crone is not the last you see of us. The circle turns, unbroken. Summer, winter, spring.

Winter was here.

On Christmas Day I shunned the feast Urien was celebrating already in Lyvennet. The magnificent mass of the Nativity, the seething cauldrons of meat, the pipes and drums, the clowns, the horseback games.

I took Caliburn's scabbard, with only Teilo for escort. We drove in a chariot, jolting over the frozen ruts. The ancient leather and soft smooth silver were warm against my heart. In a chapel between Lyvennet and the Long Lake the saint's handbell was chiming the Christians thereabouts to the Great Offering. The door was shut. Behind us voices were rising in a sweet litany of praise, hearts were giving voice to prayers of thanksgiving. Beside the lake it was bitterly cold.

Too late to yearn for Bryvyth's strong enfolding arms. I left the candles and the hymns for the wind whining in the bare twigs of birches and the chill blue light on icy scree.

Above the far, overshadowed end of the Long Lake, where the mountains rear around it, there is a smaller tarn, treeless, black, unguessably deep. It was a fitting place. The Lady is One. All the waters are hers. I gave her back her own.

Caliburn can never now find its true mate this side of Faerie. The scabbard has gone before us.

Tonight we must follow.

That Christmas Day I flung it out over the lake. I felt its warmth ripped from my hands as though the skin was tearing from my palms. One swoop like a wounded blackbird's flight. Brief, awkward. The dark surface opened to swallow it. It sank so swiftly. No chance to call our dreams back. The healing power of the sheath, that should have married the killing power of the blade, was mine no more. We could have made that union, Arthur and I. Man and Woman. The earth balanced. Her people free and whole.

I have used only the healing of any wise village woman since then.

The blade remained to Arthur.

There is an enchanted island, set amidst springtime waters. The sword must come to meet the scabbard there.

Chapter Thirty-four

I am the loser.

I figure in many contests. Since I have now become the wicked enchantress, I cannot be allowed to win.

In the Prophecies of Merlin *I am derided, a buffoon.*

In one story, my friend, the great enchantress Sebille, has a lover, Berengar. I steal his son. Sebille pleads with me to return the child. I pretend to agree, but I mutter between my teeth that I will not unless Berengar leaves Sebille for me. The child's nurse, Flor de Lis, overhears our quarrel. She warns Berengar. In the night the two of them take the boy and flee.

In the morning, Sebille finds that she has been abandoned. Both lover and child are gone. She accuses me furiously of deceiving her. She calls me names, seizes my hair. I am showing my age. I cannot withstand her onslaught. She drags me across the floor by the hair, then kicks me repeatedly on the mouth and nose. I bellow like a wounded bull, but I am too decrepit to resist her strength. I am left lying half-dead, unconscious. I only revive after three days.

I appeal to Bréhus the Pitiless to avenge me. I get no sympathy from that quarter either. He tells me mockingly Sebille will always outwit me. I am abandoned by all my friends and lovers. Humiliated. I can only weep and nurse my bruised and swollen face.

It is the third of our trio, the Queen of Northgales, who makes a patched peace. You may tell by her very name how far from the writer's sympathy she stands. Northgales: the land of the North, the land of the Gaels, the sinister unknown. The wars of Arthur the Briton against the invading Saxons have long, long passed. The Saxons themselves have been defeated since. It is the conquering Norman the minstrels sing and the poets write for now, in French. We Gaels of the west and north are natives, savages, impossible to understand, dangerous.

The Queen of Northgales will not accept my complaint against Sebille. She forces me to forswear my hope of revenge.

There are many stories that link the three of us: Queen Morgan the Fay, Sebille, and the Queen of Northgales. We are, as we were always in our more distinguished beginnings, wise in magic. We are also, as we have lately become, quarrelsome, vindictive, sowers of disunity. The three of us form

'a company unequalled in felony.'

We receive a challenge from the Lady of Avalon, who is not the same as the Lady of the Lake. Yes, you may well look surprised. Avallach, you remember, was my father. Avalon is the island I ruled in wisdom.

I am indeed a loser.

The Lady of Avalon is revelling in delight at some magic rings which the maiden Ayglantine has brought her from India. These she is determined to put to their greatest test, against our powers. One ring confers invisibility. With the other, the wearer can persuade anyone to give her whatever she asks.

These secrets are not revealed to us, of course.

When we hear her challenge, we put our heads together, we witching three. We shall be shamed if we refuse this contest. One of us must bring the overconfident Lady down. Which will it be?

I let the others ride on ahead of me.

The Queen of Northgales pits her skill in magic against the Indian rings and loses.

Sebille goes next. There is more respect shown here, in her name. The clerks who study the classics know the Sibyl's name. She is the figure of prophecy, the wise foreteller. But she comes from our pagan past.

She is also cast down.

I am not there to see them lose. I ride, reading in my book of enchantment; I arrive for the final round at the last moment and laugh when I find my friends have failed. The Lady of Avalon is smiling. She is tasting triumph. Our eyes and wills engage.

Our battle is in an open court before a tall stone tower. The first move is mine.

Once, I could fly through the air from the Isle of Avalon to Brest. Now I summon a legion of fiends from hell. I command half of them to take the form of hideous birds and the rest to merge into a devouring dragon. My birds shall lift the Lady out of her own yard and transport her helpless to the top of that tower. She shall feel the earth reject her. She shall feel the beaks of my ravens pluck at her hair. She shall look down into the waiting dragon's mouth. Exultant, I can see her fear.

The demons fly to do my bidding. In her extremity one of her hands flies to its twin and twists the first little circle of gold. Rings are always potent. I should have ordered their beaks to pluck her hands away from each other, and ignore her hair. Why are my servants rushing about now here, now there? Why is the ground covered with flaming dragons pursuing mine? Where has the Lady gone?

My attempt has failed. The Lady of Avalon returns to visibility.

Now I await her turn. The second ring. I should have feared this more. I should have come sooner to see my friends' downfall. I might have been wiser.

It is not blood she draws from me. I should have preferred that. I, Morgan the Wise. I, who surpassed the world in mathematics and astronomy. I, whose healing salves King Arthur called upon when the men he loved were bleeding in their last hour. Other stories. Other authors. Here, I am humiliated.

Her request rings about my ears. I open my mouth. No sound comes out. Not a donkey's bray, or a sow's snuffle. I gape and flap my lips like a stranded fish. I am out of my element. I, Morgan the Fay, in a house of magic, and nothing to say.

The crowd in the Lady's court watch and grin and begin to whoop as I obey her command.

My hands unfasten brooches, buckles, laces. No hedge of mist to shield me. No castle revolving to spin me from their eyes. The clothes are falling from me. Why should I mind? I, the Maiden? I, who dance skyclad for the Goddess? I, who have drawn so many men to my nakedness?

But the mantle drops to the stones, and the gown, the shift. I am down to skin, like an unclad baby, powerless and bare.

No, not a baby. A cry of shame bursts from me. The magic veneer of beauty with which I deceived men's eyes has been stripped from me. The truth is revealed.

I am old and ugly. My flesh is wrinkled. My dugs droop low. My stomach scrapes the ground. A devil has taken my clothes up to the high tower. The Lady of Avalon sends fire to burn them.

139

And all around me people are laughing at me so hard they cannot speak.

Time was when an older people knew and reverenced the clothing of true worth, when a naked woman was a symbol of most potent might, a sight to stop the irreverent dead and make the believer incline the knee in respect. A woman past menstruation achieved her greatest power when the well of mysterious life no longer leaked from her.

Not here. I am among Normans who proclaim their majesty in stone-built towers and not in oak groves. I am under the Roman church that decks its priests in gold and lace and builds cathedrals shutting out God's sky, and scorns the unworldly Celtic hermit close to bliss in the clearing by a waterfall. I am surrounded by knights who buckle themselves in cases of armour and have no notion of the glory of fighting naked, on foot, with only the patterned protection of pinpricks that etch the symbols of the gods on living skin. They have never known that utter simplicity, that openness to the elements. It speaks no power for them.

I am bare. I am an object of derision.

No man is so reviled in the romances.

Chapter Thirty-five

I had not seen Arthur's face for thirteen years. Urien's cousin Gwendoleu fell, and we moved our court to Carlisle. There we held many feasts and horse-races and contests for warriors. Arthur never came. Urien was welcome at Caerleon and Camelot, and our son Owain had sworn his sword to Arthur's command, but I was banned.

I nursed one hope still, Modred.

Modred, my foster-child, but not my son. Red Margawse's cub. And yet he was growing as like to me in looks as an adolescent boy can be to a grown woman. I saw in him my childhood self. He might have been the boy that Gorlois always wanted. Only, he was Arthur's son and Arthur did not want him. He did not even know the boy was alive.

Now I must set Modred on the most dangerous passage he might ever make, to offer his new manhood's service to Arthur. He would ride without weapons, because I wished Arthur to arm him himself. He went bearing no name of father, because his father was not yet ready to bear the truth.

I dressed my gift with pride. White became his night-black hair. I had prepared fine bleached linen and a tunic and breeches of soft, limed-white leather. My hands caressed his swansdown collar in farewell.

Cornwall. A little baby boy wrapped in swansdown. My childish gift of a lance. Arthur would not remember that.

I had persuaded Urien to give our young man a pure white mount. Modred handled the stallion well. He spoke to horses. They understood his voice.

'Well, are you pleased with him?' Urien teased me. 'I do not remember you took so much trouble over Owain's weapon-taking.'

'Modred came to us with nothing,' I said. 'Let him leave us richer.'

What am I saying in this mumming? Am I making a mockery of his impure origin, denying the past: Arthur's lust, Margawse's adultery, Merlyn's revenge, my concealment?

Modred knew it all now. Last night I had taken him up the fellside to where a standing stone looked out over the sea and the inner lakes. I sat crosslegged upon a boulder, the storyteller, and made him listen at my knee to the tale that would end his childhood.

I had been his mother. I had told him many stories. In the dusk his pale face turned up to mine. His dark eyes were pools filling with knowledge. He made no sound.

I told him everything, from the day when Uther set eyes on his grandmother Ygerne at his crown-wearing feast and wanted her.

When it was finished, he took my hand. He was only fourteen. It was the strange thing about Modred that he always behaved to his elders as if he were twice their years. My schooling at Tintagel was hard, but I was never so completely the mistress of my feelings. Would it have been different if I had not let him see me give way to passion? If Modred had followed his own heart?

His touch caressed my fingers. The stars were pricking through the dusk. When darkness fell, the trial of his manhood would begin. But as the light faded from that limitless seaward sky, he was the one who seemed to reassure me.

'An acorn falls into the ground, and from its rottenness springs a miraculous new oak-shoot. I am that shoot. The winter is over. We shall make the spring ours. I promise you.'

He had a winning smile.

Did I believe that: that through Modred we could make a new beginning, turn back the pages of all our lives and find the first leaf clean, no word of black-inked tragedy left to mar it?

Now, on this crisp morning, the men were impatient to go. Modred's hand took mine again, strangely warm out of his snowy sleeve.

'Mother.'

That word that somersaulted my heart. I had cast the spells of opening for his birth. I had rescued him. I had brought him up. I was his guardian, and I must let him go. I was not his mother.

I am not his mother. I am not his mother.

But his hand held me more firmly. 'I will not forget you. The lays of the bards at Camelot can never sing on the strings of my heart as truly as the tale you have told me. Your story and mine. Our wrong will be righted. I shall make him love us both. I will pierce him with the weapon of love he hands me himself. It will break through his shield of suspicion and his breastplate of pride. I shall knot you together with hairs plucked from my own head and seal it with blood from my own veins.'

And so he has.

I smiled. I was sick at heart, with the emptiness of the days without Arthur's son. I longed to believe that he spoke the truth, that he meant the truth. He was going to his father's court. This was the purpose of all my fostering. But I searched his dark, intelligent eyes and I was not sure how to interpret his speech. I saw myself suddenly in my nephew's face. I saw how others must see me. I could not read his mind. I mistrusted him.

Over and over again I have tried to cross this water. There is a chasm between me and Arthur. If I have seen a sword-bridge I have walked its slicing edge. If the way has been threatened by lions, I have grappled with them. If the only passage has been sunk fathoms deep in monster-haunted waters, I have plunged down. And always I have been repulsed. I bear the scars.

Arthur would never trust me. Not though I had once stood like this, his large hand holding mine with greater warmth than Modred's smaller one did now, his blue eyes burning for me like the flames from coal, his breath loud and unsteady in the sudden silence. I knew he felt the magic thrill between us.

Is that what he feared? My enchantment. The wisdom I never could or dared to use in this my deepest interest. It meant too much. I cared too deeply. I was the Lady. I have bound myself under a stern discipline.

I have asked nothing for myself from the Goddess. I have worked much good for others. I have not bewitched Arthur. Even now the barge of death is nearing, he must come to me as a free man to a free woman.

What if he will not come?

143

I looked into the impenetrable tunnels of Modred's eyes and I could not tell how shallow his pretty words were. I understood why Arthur did not trust me.

I was too wise, too powerful for my brother. Caliburn's scabbard was worth ten times the sword. He thought I kept it still. Would I dare to tell him I had cast it away?

Urien leaned from his horse and kissed me, laughing.

'Have you two done? The day grows stale with standing. Let the lad go. You did not hold on to the hand of my first-born Owain as long as you do to this fatherless foster-son of ours.'

He was a generous man, but I dropped Modred's hand as if a snake had struck me. Owain was Urien's son, and Modred was Arthur's. Urien had been witness when Arthur took those babies, a young man torn cruelly between wife and hero. He must have guessed who this child's father was, though it was never spoken between us. Did he know truly who was the mother?

Modred smiled at both of us, unnervingly at ease on his first day of manhood. He was a handsome boy, in a sober way. Tall and slender-hipped, though a little large in the chest, as if his swelling heart needed more room than most. Yet I could see more of myself than Arthur in him, except for that winning smile.

He wheeled and waved and cantered off bravely beside his foster-father, and a piece of my heart was torn away, like a shoot from a parent tree that may or may not take root in a different garden.

They told me afterwards he carried himself with dignity when Arthur knighted him. But they said my cautious Modred blushed like a girl and dropped to his knees when he met Gwenhyvar. She gave him his man's sword. Her small pale hands held the blade of his weapon as he swore to serve her with it.

Chapter Thirty-six

I am the enemy of lovers.

In the royal chronicles of Geoffrey, Wace and Layamon, Modred is named as Gwenhyvar's paramour. In the romances, this lover becomes Lancelot. She spurns Modred who brutally tries to force her into a bigamous marriage.

Lancelot and Gwenhyvar. He is a French invention. Chrétien de Troyes is responsible for his popularity.

One must make allowances for national jealousy and the tenor of the times. Arthurian stories, the Matter of Britain, *are all the rage in France. Jongleurs recite dramatically the 'chansons de geste', their heroic epics, to crowded courts, but romances are beginning to bloom for more private reading. Ladies sit in window-seats in the scent of roses and dream of chivalry.*

King Arthur is British, and his most famous knight, the golden Gawain, is British too. It would be nice for the French to imagine one of their own in that glamorous circle of the Round Table.

No sooner thought than done. The well of creativity is a bottomless cauldron to satisfy any desire. In Chrétien's story, The Knight of the Cart, *Gwenhyvar is abducted. It is an old theme. But this time British Gawain fails to rescue her. It is the Breton Lancelot who succeeds.*

His story develops rapidly in other hands.

The baby Lancelot is born in Brittany. He is a prince, fleeing with his royal parents from a city betrayed. On the journey, his father dies of heartbreak. A magical lady seizes the boy and before the eyes of his grief-stricken mother she leaps with him into a lake. The poor queen retires to the conventional nunnery.

Safe in this Otherworld, the child grows up, handsome, skilled, brave, proud, taught by fays, but ignorant of his origins. At last, reluctantly, the Lady of the Lake gives in to his insistence and admits his approaching manhood. He shall be knighted by none other than King Arthur. They cross the Channel, that barrier of water between reality and magic, and she conducts him to the court. The lad is dressed in white and armed in silver, riding a white horse, and all his train are similarly white-clad. They make a dazzling sight.

Lancelot has had a sheltered boyhood. He falls in love at first sight with Arthur's sovereign lady, Gwenhyvar. In a few words of queenly courtesy to this blushing youth she expresses the hope that he will be her 'ami'. Does she mean her friend, or her sweetheart? He makes his momentous interpretation, and all the unwritten pages of romance spring into joyful life like birdsong at dawn. Arthur dubs him knight, but Lancelot contrives that it is from Gwenhyvar that he receives his sword.

The centre has shifted. Arthur is no longer the pivot of the story. This is not the tale of how Britain came into being and found the greatest of her kings. This King Arthur does not fight the Saxons, to hold the dream of a lost Roman Britain against the grim reality of pagan invasion. His wars are now in distant Europe, against the Romans. At home we are being shown a greyer, unromantic overlord. No wonder Gwenhyvar looks for interest elsewhere.

The glamour is with Lancelot. He is the perfect flowering of the medieval ideal of Courtly Love. For Gwenhyvar, he will do anything without question, whether it is to satisfy her smallest, ignoble caprice, or a quest of the uttermost honour. For her smile, he will suffer any humiliation, rise to any height. She sets the goals of knighthood. She is knighthood's reward.

And so elaborating on Chrétien's Knight of the Cart, *the thirteenth century romances weave ever longer tapestries.* Lancelot of the Lake, *the* Prose Lancelot, *three massive books out of the six that form the* Vulgate Cycle *all bear his name. Arthur is dwindling in importance. Gawain is fading. Lancelot is*

'the best knight in the world.'

And Morgan the Fay acquires a new role.

I am now the jealous enchantress who loves, not the heroic Arthur, but Lancelot.

Remember Guiomar, who jilted me at Gwenhyvar's command? I have been given a reason to hate her. Hurt and humiliated, and according to one version pregnant, I flee to Merlyn. Besotted with me, he teaches me all his magic. I am an able student.

Note how my status has diminished. Once I was the fairy queen of the Otherworld Island of Avalon, who taught astronomy to her sisters and offered her wise protection to Arthur. Now I am reduced to Merlyn's pupil.

Guiomar is not the only man to reject me for another woman, even before Lancelot arrives.

I will have my revenge. I create my Valley of No Return, the Vale of False Lovers. Its walls are air. Knights ride through the forest and do not realise they have come too far until it is too late. Good women, sometimes, and all baseborn people may pass through the mist as they please, but false knights never.

It is a pretty enough place. Streams flow and flowers bloom. There is a chapel at the entrance for spiritual comfort. Young men and damsels dance and sing. I have provided good food and courteous servants. But these knights are condemned to perpetual dalliance. Their punishment is to be confined where there is no warfare, no quest to be pursued, no giants to slay, where the requirements of courtly love cannot be met. Only a knight who has been stainlessly true to his lady-love can break the spell. So none have escaped me.

Into my hidden web blunders Lancelot. The entry, that has been all too easy for some, I make hard for him. To enter my domain he must grapple with fierce and clawing dragons, cross the inevitable chasm by a narrow plank bridge, topple fearsome knights. He struggles manfully until a ring given to him by his foster-mother, the Lady of the Lake, reveals them all to be nothing but my enchantment.

On he presses to my castle, through flaming doorways, up staircases, slaying knights with axes. In hot pursuit he chases one of my guards through every room of the palace until he bursts out at last into a beautiful garden. Oblivious to impending disaster, I lie asleep on a luxurious couch in a curtained pavilion. My cowardly defender rushes in and takes refuge under my bed. Too late he disappears from view. Lancelot storms in after him and overturns my couch, tipping me unceremoniously on to the ground. I wake, screaming, to see both men bolting out of my tent again. A little later, Lancelot reappears carrying the knight's head. He proffers it to me, kneeling, with profound apologies for my rude awakening.

The freed prisoners now come crowding in to congratulate

Lancelot. My defences are down. The spell is breaking all around me. I curse the woman that he must love so faithfully.

This is Gwenhyvar's doing again. Guiomar is forgotten. I have been awakened to a new desire. Jealousy and revenge are focused on another man now. I set my will on becoming Lancelot's mistress.

I feast him and all the men he has freed. I too have a magic ring. When I place it on Lancelot's finger as he sleeps that night, I cast him into a deeper slumber still and carry him to a prison deep in the forest.

We are not done with rings yet, by a long way. On his left hand he wears the gift from the Lady of the Lake which uncovers enchantments, on his right, another, Gwenhyvar's love-token. I have demanded this one from him, as the price of his freedom, but he swears he will never let it go while he still has the finger it encircles. I could slip it from him easily now he is asleep but I am terrified of his wrath when he finds it gone. Yet I must separate him from that ring. I need it to disclose Gwenhyvar's adultery to Arthur.

Gwenhyvar is the woman I hate most in the world. She has robbed me of too much.

I feast and fête Lancelot. I offer myself to him with all my arts. He does not want me.

Yet we both play by certain rules of honour. I agree to release Lancelot to fight at the Dolorous Tower. Afterwards he duly surrenders himself again to be my prisoner. Still I cannot get the ring from him.

Well, sleep then, Lancelot. This time I have drugged you with wine. Daring, I ease Gwenhyvar's ring from his finger and carefully slide another in its place. This was Gwenhyvar's gift to me, the twin of his own. But, like human twins, there is a small and subtle difference. Each bears the image of two lovers embracing. On his, they hold a heart between their hands. On mine, their hands are joined. When Lancelot wakes, I wait with palpitating heart to see if he will detect this substitution. Nothing yet. We play at courtesies. Many times in our conversation I draw his attention to his hand. He regards the ring fondly. He has noticed nothing sinister.

Now is my opportunity. I despatch a wise damsel, armed with Gwenhyvar's love-token, to Arthur's court. She tells them they will never set eyes on Lancelot again. The queen, overcome with distress, makes for her chamber. My damsel holds her back. She will not tell her story except in Gwenhyvar's hearing.

Lancelot, she says, has suffered a great wound at the Dolorous Tower. Repentance has barely saved his life. Henceforward he will go barefoot and in sackcloth, never sleeping more than one night in the same place, renouncing arms of war. Nevermore will he be called 'the best knight in the world'. And for what sin? In my nest of lies I have laid this living egg of truth. Through all these years Lancelot has been betraying his king and his friend, lying with his queen.

Here is the proof. The damsel returns Lancelot's ring to Gwenhyvar. It is all over. The queen falls fainting. Then she recovers — both health and good fortune.

Arthur will not accept my story. Gwenhyvar's wide-eyed simplicity pleads for them both. Yes, she gave Lancelot her ring. Yes, he has sworn to serve her. But in chastity and honour, as Arthur's loyal friend. So open and innocent her face, Gwenhyvar, who never uses magic, never studied the arts. My face betrays a lifetime of application. Her magic is in her person, not in her deeds. She beguiles everyone. Arthur believes her.

In jealous rage I keep Lancelot prisoner, not for hate, but out of passionate love. I make him dream that Gwenhyvar has been unfaithful to him with a younger knight. In this dream, Lancelot draws his sword to kill his rival, but Gwenhyvar stops him. When he wakes he will find the proof this was no dream. I have laid his unsheathed sword beside his hand.

So strong my own resolve, I underestimate the depth of a man's despair. He will not eat, and lest he die, I, in my bitterness, am eventually forced, against my will, to let him go. Only this he must promise me: not to go near the queen until the year is ended. Without this hope, he declines into madness in the forest, where the Lady of the Lake finds and heals him.

A century earlier, you will recall, it was my ointment that cured Yvain's madness for a lost lady, in a forest.

Once more, a maiden of mine lures Lancelot to my castle. I entertain him lavishly, dress him in scarlet, pledge him from silver goblets, bed him in a chamber fit for King Arthur. Only, the windows are iron-barred, overlooking a garden. He is not my prisoner, you understand, merely my honoured, if reluctant, guest.

So Lancelot remains confined till Christmas. When the cold eases, he opens the window to look out. A man is painting an ancient history, and over each picture he writes the meaning of the scene. It tells the tale of our Trojan ancestors, and how Aeneas left Troy, and Brutus founded Britain. And it comes into Lancelot's mind that his own exploits ought to be so recorded.

He begs the painter for brushes and pigments. Then, on the spacious walls of his chamber, which is no cramped cell, he begins to paint the romance of Lancelot and Gwenhyvar, all his own brave deeds, all her rewards.

Unseen by him, I come each night to gaze on him with love. I see from these pictures with pain where his true love lies. Each morning he wakes, and when the sun falls on his paintings he kisses his image of Gwenhyvar.

Two fruitless winters pass and it is Easter again. The roses are opening in my garden. I have created this beauty for him. But May undoes us all. One Sunday morning he watches a bloom unfold that seems rosier than all the rest. It speaks to him unbearably of Gwenhyvar. He has to have it, but it is beyond his reach. With superhuman strength he breaks the bars apart to kiss it, press it to his eyes, pluck it, hide it in his bosom. The barriers are overthrown. So Courtly Love makes heroes out of frail, flawed men. Lancelot, fired by Gwenhyvar, is free, in the hush of sunrise.

He hurries across the garden, finds an open door, seizes weapons, armour, saddles a horse. Only the porter is awake yet. My man is surprised to see a strange knight hurrying out of my castle at this hour, but whatever he suspects, it is not the truth. Dreadful my grief when I find Lancelot fled.

He has left a message at the gate for me. 'Tell your lady Lancelot of the Lake greets her as

"the most disloyal woman in the world".'

This, from the man who is committing adultery with his king's wife.

Chapter Thirty-seven

I sensed the truth, even before that ominous May Day when Gwenhyvar was abducted in the Summer Country.

When Modred came of age I had persuaded Urien to give him Caerwenloe. This is the old haunted fortress north of Carlisle where Gwendoleu's bodyguard made their last stand after their king had fallen to the sword of Rhydderch Hael. Many men became ravens' meat and their bones are there still. They lie uneasy.

Modred was not Urien's blood, and the fact that he was my nephew was a thing never spoken between us. Urien had sons of his own to inherit the vast lands of Rheged. This one place for Modred, then.

Did I ill-wish him?

I had shadowed his boyhood enough with dark tales of our family. One secret alone I had kept till that last evening: that he was the child of Arthur's, unluckily got, who had been launched in the ship of death into the Solway.

What dark thoughts kept the vigil with Modred afterwards through the night that brought him to manhood? What painful resolve had he come to by morning? He rode with Urien to take service at Arthur's court with a smile on his lips and all my teaching in his heart. We none of us understood what Modred thought.

Should I not have told him the truth? Did I believe that the hurt which Arthur's coming had brought me might be made whole by Modred's restoration? Or did I even then seek satisfaction, twisting the spiral back to our beginning?

Did hate weigh heavier than love?

Well, pagan Gwendoleu fell fighting Christian Rhydderch, and now Urien ruled a wider kingdom. At Caerwenloe one mad survivor babbled of old battles under the apple trees and

151

striped pigs rooted where the bodies of warriors were too hastily buried. The ravens are never still over Caerwenloe.

Gwendoleu left another legacy, an ominous chessboard of gold, whose silver pieces move by themselves. This is a dangerous game that sometimes ends with death. Urien would not touch the board. Owain took it. He played it once with Arthur. Bloody, the outcome.

Modred, who should have inherited Britain, had nothing of his own. Give him the deserted halls of Caerwenloe, the fallen beams, the thistles in the courtyard.

Modred was a scholar before Arthur enrolled him as a warrior. He was intelligent. He had artistry. When he came back to us as a young knight from his first border skirmish I took him to Caerwenloe. His eyes flamed. He walked around the walls, his hands caressing the broken breastwork, fingering the splintered timbers, touching the bloodstained earth as if in recognition.

He turned and hugged me, laughing.

'I will make it a place of song and feasting, a ballad to beauty. Its cauldrons shall be filled with bait for the finest harpers, artists and embroideresses. Arthur himself shall envy it. I will build a hall that would not dishonour even Gwenhyvar.'

Two years he took repairing it. He planned it all on parchment before he built. He asked my advice. Many hours we spent together, with our designs spread over the mosaic floor of Carlisle's palace, like children with their toys, like generals before a battle. Did Urien, descendent of King Coel, lord of the old frontier of the Wall, frown just a little to see his rival's stronghold newly fortified? It was a single homestead he had allowed his foster-son, but it carried a dark inheritance. Urien was Christian. Gwendoleu's Ravens had attacked the Cross. He saw our heads bent together over the shaping of a new fortress. Some things we would not alter. Old blackened pillars carved with signs and faces too holy to be destroyed, hollows in the earth, time-honoured hearths. Modred had been taught by monks from the White House, but he was pagan at heart. How would he use what Urien had given him?

It seemed, for gaiety and sport! Who would have thought our solemn black-browed boy could flower into such a hospitable courtier? My sons told me he had become Arthur's favourite, already wise in counsel for one so young, but an entertaining wit and a marvellous horseman. In the sunshine of Arthur's approval he had blossomed.

So would I have done.

How many nights my bed was ready for him, my body perfumed and waiting. I have made something less than the Sacred Marriage with other men. Arthur never came for me.

But now he came to visit us in Rheged for Modred's sake. I had been up in Caerwenloe. It is a potent place. Arthur arrived at my palace in Carlisle before I returned. My home was invaded by fighting men, horses, servants. By my High King.

When I rode through the gates and found my world changed, Owain came limping across the courtyard to meet me.

'Arthur is here.'

And all the trumpets of Britain sounded on the hills.

I wanted to rush to welcome him. Yet I was afraid to meet him.

Eighteen years now since we had met face to face, since our hands had touched. Those years would have changed much.

I hurried to my rooms and prepared myself with trembling care.

That evening I stood in my hall with all the beauty that art and nature could bestow. A rich purple gown, precious stones and gold in my hair. Perfumes of Arabia and creams of springtime flowers. Radiance flooded me from within. I felt I must be outshining my jewels.

He was there in the doorway, golden and laughing, as though the years of our separation had crumbled into dust. We walked towards each other. Skin touched. Our hands entwined. I knew that leap like lightning in my body was matched by the conflagration of his. It was a wonder we did not enfold each other there on the floor of the hall in front of all our people, so great our longing.

'Welcome, Arthur.' I meant a thousand times that. 'I am grieved beyond measure that my brother the king should honour my hall with his presence after all these years and another woman than I should offer him her cup.'

153

I waited for the first words I would hear from those lips since he had called for his guards to kill me on his wedding-night. That was all past. It was over. Gwenhyvar could not remain between us.

'A welcome as rich as this was worth waiting for, lady.'

His eyes slipped from mine, lingered over my face, seemed to caress my hair, my body. His hand hardened on mine.

'Purple becomes you. Did you fashion the embroidery on it with your own hands?'

My eyes followed his. I had chosen a marvellous purple gown, patterned in gold and silver, stitched with all my artistry, like the mantle I had sent him as a love-gift long ago that did Luned to death. He had forgiven nothing.

I snatched my hand from his.

Had he only come for Modred, then? I saw how fire warmed his eyes when he looked at the young man, even before he knew this was his son. Blood called out to blood, Arthur's to Modred, mine to my brother, against all reason.

Yet he had wanted me.

No, I was wrong. Arthur wanted something from me. Power.

When supper was over, and he stood disturbingly near me above my stool, I watched the firelight playing on his grizzled hair. I was a woman almost past childbearing. He was a king who spent more time in the judgment-seat now than on a warhorse. The wine was beginning to blur old enmities.

We had added a jewel to our treasure that year. Young Taliesin, prince of poets, whose hands were as skilful on a woman's flesh as over his harpstrings. He was enchanting his audience. Under cover of his song, Arthur leaned closer. I heard the urgency in his voice.

'The bishops speak to me too often nowadays of heaven. That is not what I want to hear. The world is slipping away from me too fast.'

I gasped. I feared for the moment the whole hall must have heard it. But I twisted my head and the face that I met told me cruelly that he did not mean what I had hoped. Turn back the years and start afresh? Arthur and Morgan. Young and free. Before Urien, before Gwenhyvar. No, never free to love each other. Merlyn had seen to that.

My royal brother was asking me for renewal of his man's

strength. Did he truly believe his sister had such power? That I was what the common people called me, when they found I spent long days alone in the forest, beside the sacred wells? Morgan the Goddess, mistress of the Land of the Ever-Young? I saw hope and ambition in his eyes. This was a man past the prime of manhood. From his marriage he had only one sickly son, Anir. Did he understand the enormity of what he was asking? Was he prepared to pay the cost?

I never cheated him. I worked all night, with Teilo and Taliesin to help me. Teilo went crippled in a woman's gown, because he had tried to deny the truth of half our existence. Taliesin was young, but wiser, a pretty boy, his face unmarked, though he had a fearsome magical birth from the great Mother Ceridwen. Poetry is truth. A bard who sings from the heart, as Taliesin does, carries the light of youth in his eyes, even to old age. He sang while I worked. He may not have known how he helped me.

Next morning when the horsemen gathered in the foggy courtyard for the start of the hunt, I dressed in my priestess's robes, black, gold-banded across my breasts. With all solemnity, I handed the cup I had brewed for Arthur. I would not explain. He must make the hard pilgrimage to understanding alone. I did not give him then the elixir of eternal youth he wanted. I offered my cup of truth.

He nearly failed to take it. Those hard blue eyes, that had learned what it is to take and hold kingship by the sword, met mine and held them. He partly grasped the truth, that this was not what he desired. Was it fear that made him hand the cup to Taliesin, standing by his elbow with a boy's dream in his eyes as he looked up at his hero? Poor Taliesin. That cup was fear to him! Even though he had watched me while I brewed it, how could he know it would not have hurt him?

But Arthur of Britain was never a coward king. At the last moment he snatched my goblet from Taliesin's unsteady hands. The sharp-scented wine splattered his clothes, his horse, the frosty ground as he swung it to his lips and downed the rest.

'If that is your price! See how well I will trust my beloved sister!'

He had got half of what I intended. The rest will come hard to him.

Two days later there was another hunt. Word came to me in Carlisle that Arthur had been taken suddenly ill out on the fells with a fever-chill. They had helped him to Caerwenloe.

I sensed a sudden darkness before me, as though I had ridden to the very brink of a chasm. Arthur had humbled himself to plead with me, and I had refused him. Now he was ill, and not as young as he wished to be, and I was afraid for both of us. I do not have Elaine's Sight of the future, but I sensed the darkness massing over us. Modred must be the bond that would draw us together, though I could not see how.

I must go to him.

I had fast horses saddled. I called for the most skilled of my people, Taliesin the bard, and Teilo the Man turned Woman, and Tegau my Christian maid. Would they think my cup had harmed him? Today I meant only good. We packed healing ointments. We flew to him over the rough wet ground with the rain lancing coldly through our cloaks. Had they welcomed him fittingly?

I rode through the battlements with a lift of satisfaction and pride. Caerwenloe was a fair haven for Modred now, after such early shipwreck. He had furbished it well. The gable-ends were carved with dolphins, the doorposts with vines. For the principal rooms my skilled needlewomen had embroidered hangings that told ancient tales. There were our ancestors: Brutus, who gave his name to Britain, Corineus who founded Cornwall. The battle with the giants Gog and Magog. The ship of Solomon bringing the Grail. There were wonders on every wall, and mysteries. My sisters Elaine and Margawse had exclaimed with rapture when they saw them.

I should make Arthur well. There would be music in these halls again to astound and delight the ear. Taliesin to sing of Arthur's exploits. Old man Llywarch himself should come to lament his lost youth in poems by the fire. Morgan the Wise would be the brilliant hostess at his table. Modred had not been persuaded to take a wife yet.

The servants had done well. There were roaring fires in Caerwenloe, already there was the smell of baking bread and simmering meat. They had laid Arthur in the guest-chamber.

Modred had proved courteous and hospitable. But young

men would not stay indoors for the gale or the rain or an infirm king. The hunt was not finished yet. They had their manhood still to prove.

I opened the chamber door and stole to Arthur's bedside. His face was fevered. He lay in a bed deep with heather and goose-down. The curtains were thickly woven. But this hill was high and exposed. The wind sneaked under the door.

Why had Modred let our High King, our Arthur, lie in any room less than the best? Summon the servants.

'Get your master's room ready. Warm linen sheets, heat stones for his feet, bring lamps and braziers. My brother should lie nowhere but in the chamber where the master of Caerwenloe has his broad bed, in the Raven's own nest.'

I expected no question from any of Modred's servants to my commands. These were all my people. I had trained them. I had given them to him for his household. After the first startled glances, the work was swiftly and well done.

Arthur was stirring.

'It is I, Morgan. I am here. Do not be afraid.'

Give him a strengthening draught, hold the cup to his shaking lips. It was not often anyone would see Arthur so unmanned. His hand was hot where mine rested cool against it.

'How do you feel, Arthur? Can you rise? We have better entertainment for you than this.'

In the weakness of illness he was obedient, though not so swift as my slaves. He trusted me blindly. I was Morgan the Healer.

They seated him in a chair, wrapped him closely in wolfskins, held a canopy over him.

'I can walk, damn you! I'm not an old dotard like Llywarch Hen.'

'Hush, brother. Let me decide what is best. I am Morgan the Wise.'

Carry his chair carefully. Shield him from the rain. It is only a few steps across the court.

I walked ahead of him through that old hilltop fort and felt its dark magic stir beneath my feet.

This chamber I had not entered for a year and a half. Modred always slept alone at Caerwenloe, master of his own soul in his own house. I had sewed tapestries for his walls

157

with loving hands. A sound ship sailing. A father fondly holding his son. A brother and sister with hands entwined. I meant it to be a room for blessed dreams.

I eased the door open on my foster-son's sanctuary, blinked back the fondness that blurred my sight. I had helped prepare this room like the nursery of a much-wanted child. The bed was wide and softly sheeted. Its hangings were an enchantment of colour. My feet sank deep in furs. You would not have guessed so chaste and hardy a warrior as Modred would have chosen to furnish a bedchamber so unsoldierly. There were longings in Modred none of us suspected.

Every wall was painted . . . *Painted?* A sudden shock. Where were the embroideries I had stitched so carefully through all those sunlit summer afternoons, those winters of eye-straining lamplight?

Gone. He had illuminated these lime-washed walls with his own hands, with his own dreams, not mine. Look, read his story. Urien's scholar-priests had schooled him to write a fair hand. The captions were written overhead. Here is the baby boy. Here is the broken ship, the drowned bodies of infants. Here is Modred nursed by the fisherman's wife. Here is Urien bringing his foster-son to court. Here is Gwenhyvar presenting Modred with a sword. Here is the River Camel, and the Michaelmas feast at Celliwig in Cornwall. Here is Arthur's war-band hunting, dancing, wrestling, jousting with spears. Here is Queen Gwenhyvar giving the prize to Modred.

Turn the corner to the wall opposite his bed, where the light would fall upon these pictures before he slept and greet him when he woke. There is the white stag with a golden collar in the forest. There is Modred separated from the rest and giving chase. There is his plunge into the river, and on the other side . . . three maidens in white who lead him inside a flowering hedge. So soft the grass, so skilled this painter, so sweet the waiting, rosy flesh that he portrays.

Had this happened? Would it ever? Was it only the same hunger that kept my own unfulfilled body awake? Would they always torment us out of their fullness, Arthur and Gwenhyvar, secure in the receipt of love upon their thrones? Would they always enjoy what we had not?

Too late to turn back. We had crossed the fatal space.

No arguments from Arthur now as he sank into the warm,

soft, pillowed bed. What could I do but sprinkle sweet-scented herbs on the brazier, set Teilo and Tegau to watch? Let Taliesin's harp strum soft airs to soothe him. Leave him to sleep and dream.

Why had I brought him here to this most private chamber? Why had I laid bare Modred's soul? The truth must break us, before we know that we need healing. Do not be afraid, brother. Mine are the arms that will hold your fall.

The rain was over, and drops fell slowly from the thatch. The hunters had not yet returned. I glided into the chamber and found Arthur waking. His eyes came round to meet mine, wide, intelligent, yet a mite bewildered.

I sat on the bedside then, and took his hand. Laughed gaily.

'Poor Taliesin's throat is dry. When ballads fail, we have prepared other tales to entertain you in this room. See around you. Whoever Modred of Good Counsel's mother was, she has bequeathed him an artist's hand.'

'You yourself are famed throughout the land as an embroideress.'

'Modred is my foster-son only, though I would that he had been more.'

'Amen.'

Only because that meant his nephew?

I shivered. When and how would I tell him who Modred's father and mother were?

We sat, like man and wife, examining those pictures. Would you believe we smiled and exclaimed with fondness over the cleverness of the lad we both loved? Arthur could read well enough for a soldier. Could he not understand the captions that spelt out his fate? 'Here is Arthur.' 'Here is Gwenhyvar.' 'Here is Modred.' 'Here Modred is making love to Gwenhyvar.'

Did he wonder afterwards if this was all a fevered dream of his, or Modred's? Did these scenes ever happen?

Shut up our lips, shut up our eyes, shut up our hearts. Was his soul crying, as mine did? We would not drain this cup of truth. It would have destroyed us.

And so it has.

Did Modred truly love her?

Chapter Thirty-eight

I am the betrayer.

The bearer of unwelcome news is rarely rewarded with gratitude.

Already by the mid-twelfth century, when my legend first appears, the Lay of the Horn *is being sung. I am not yet named as the supplier of this horn of fidelity.*

It is Pentecost, and a brilliant feast is being held at Arthur's court. A comely youth enters the hall bearing a magic horn. It is richly fashioned from ivory, chased with silver and gold, and hung with bells which ring with the marvellously sweet sound of fairyland. When it is blown, the hearers lose all control of their actions, servers are struck motionless, plates in hand, stewards totter and stumble with unsteady jugs, knives cut the finger and not the loaf. Around the horn the gold and silver inscription runs: 'This message Mangons of Moraine, the Fair, sends you.'

The horn has been enchanted by a fay. If a man whose wife has been untrue to him even in thought drinks of it, the wine will splash his breast. The King of Moraine has sent it to Arthur as a friendly gift.

Of course, Arthur has to take the challenge. He shouts for wine, but when he drinks, the liquor spills. In fury he seizes a knife and is about to stab the unfortunate Gwenhyvar. Gawain, Cadain and Owain hold him back. The queen, defiant in her distress, offers to prove her innocence by the ordeal of fire. But Arthur has other ideas. Every man of the court must face the same humiliation. They drink, and each one splashes his clothes, while the ladies' faces burn with amazement. Only one husband escapes: Caradoc, whose wife Tegau becomes a legend for constancy.

Arthur recovers his good humour and enjoys the joke. He gives Caradoc the meddlesome horn and Cirencester.

160

By the fifteenth century, in the Fastnachtspiel, *I am the sender. Arthur and Gwenhyvar are planning a feast again, to which all the crowned heads of Europe will be invited. Suddenly Gwenhyvar remembers. They have failed to include Arthur's sister, the queen of Cyprus. Arthur refuses adamantly to have me.*

I am furious at the insult. I send a maiden to his feast bearing the magic horn which betrays the unfaithful wife to her husband. He is not to know which queen has sent it.

Arthur drinks and splashes his breast. He makes to strike Gwenhyvar but Gawain prevents him. Other men are similarly humiliated. Strife breaks out. Only the King of Spain stays clean and smiling. My maiden returns, and I am in high glee at the disunity I have caused.

A knight accuses Gawain of disloyalty with the queen. They fight, till Arthur separates them and denounces the evil the horn has brought. Merrymaking resumes.

In the romance of Tristan *and Malory's* Le Morte d'Arthur, *I am again the one who sends this horn to betray Gwenhyvar. Now the woman herself must drink. But my plans, as usual, are foiled.*

Two knights, Lamorat and Driant, meet the man I have sent to Arthur's court bearing the horn. At first he will not reveal its secret or the name of the sender, but Lamorat unhorses him and makes him confess.

This Lamorat spies an opportunity. He has a quarrel with King Mark of Cornwall, who once forced him to continue fighting in a tournament after he was already weary from beating thirty knights. His thirty-first opponent was Trystan, Queen Essylt's lover. It is true, Trystan did not wish to fight him and only did so on Mark's orders, against his code of honour. The fact remains that Lamorat was beaten. The defeat still rankles. Now he sees his chance to be even with both Mark and Trystan. He orders my knight on pain of death to carry the dangerous horn to Mark's court, instead of Arthur's.

The queen Essylt is made to drink, in Gwenhyvar's place, and a hundred ladies after her. Only four drink cleanly. Terrified, Essylt protests her innocence and asks for a knight to defend her honour. Mark swears a great oath that his queen shall be burned.

The danger is averted. Once more, it ends in laughter and goodwill. It is the barons who rescue her. They say Essylt shall not be burned

*'for a horn made by sorcery that came from Morgan the Fay,
as false a sorceress and witch as then was living. For that
horn did never good but caused strife and debate, and always
in her days she had been an enemy to all true lovers.'*

I shall have to try again.

Luck comes my way. This time Trystan himself rides, unaware,
to my castle and asks for lodging. We do not at first recognise
each other. I entertain him warmly, but in the morning when he
wishes to leave he finds he is my prisoner. I treat him well, but
I will not release him until I learn who he is. He is reluctant
to tell. Our proper names are our true and vulnerable selves. They
should not be readily uncovered.

At supper my paramour, Huneson, seeing me laughing with
Trystan on the other side of me, burns with jealousy.

Trystan decides his freedom is worth any risk. He pays my price.
When I learn his name, I wish too late I had not promised to
release him. But I keep my word, on one condition. I entrust him
with a shield. Its field is gules, and on this blush-red ground stands
a knight, with one foot on the head of the king and the other on
the queen's. Trystan is to carry this shield to the Castle of the
Hard Rock, where Arthur has cried a great tournament. There
he must acquit himself as valiantly as he can.

He asks me the meaning of the strange device. I tell him it is
a knight who holds both King Arthur and Queen Gwenhyvar in
bondage and servage. His name I will not disclose for the present.

I am motivated by my passion for Lancelot. He has scorned
me, and so I will betray his adultery to Arthur.

Jealous Huneson chases after Trystan to kill him, but gets a
mortal wound himself instead.

It is dangerous to spurn me. It is dangerous to love me.

Trystan enters the lists and brings down many knights. As he
watches, Arthur wonders at the shield. But Gwenhyvar guesses
the meaning, and her heart is heavy with dread.

I have sent a damsel anonymously to the tournament. She
secretes herself in a chamber close to Arthur. Hearing him
marvelling aloud what this device can mean, she seizes her chance.

*'Sir King, wit you well this shield was ordained for you,
to warn you of your shame and dishonour, and that belongeth
to you and your queen.'*

162

Then she is gone.

Arthur is angry, and demands to be told who she was. No one can enlighten him.

But Gwenhyvar knows for certain this must be my doing.

No one has yet beaten Trystan and so been able to demand his name. When it seems that he may escape unknown, Arthur himself takes the field, with my son Owain. They bring Trystan to a halt and insist on knowing at least where he got the shield.

'Sir,' he said. 'I had it of Queen Morgan the Fay, sister unto King Arthur.'

But he cannot tell them the meaning of the blazon. Nor will he disclose his name. When Arthur fights him for it, he knocks the king down and after him, Owain. It is Lancelot who pursues him from the field, finally overcomes him, and brings him back to Camelot to be welcomed as Sir Trystan, knight of the fellowship of the Round Table.

A doubt has been sown, but Arthur's suspicion does not yet rest on Lancelot. When at last I spell out the truth for him, Arthur will not believe me. He thinks I am lying out of spite to all of them.

Mark's marriage-bed is betrayed by Trystan and Essylt, Arthur's by Lancelot and Gwenhyvar. It is assumed the reader will take the lovers' side. You may sympathise somewhat with noble Arthur, but certainly not with King Fox of Cornwall.

Mark also tries to tell the truth. He sends letters revealing it to both Arthur and Gwenhyvar. He too is rejected.

Later, I send Mark a poisoned lance with which he stabs Trystan.

We Cornish are dark and untrustworthy. We spell danger to Camelot.

Chapter Thirty-nine

Anir, Gwenhyvar's only child, was dead, a broken body on a hurdle of spears. A hunting accident, some said. The lad had tumbled, wrong-footed, over a cliff. Caliburn is a dangerous blade to carry without its protecting sheath.

Arthur knew that I had destroyed the scabbard now. He cursed me for it. My hands ached empty without that power. Could it have saved Anir? Was I to blame for that loss?

Others blamed Arthur.

And I? I nursed a terrible fear that, after all these years, Arthur did not truly want an heir. Great Arthur, victor of Mount Badon, High King of Britain. Surely this Arthur could not die? I saw the furious energy in his actions. I watched the rivalry in his eyes when young men boasted of their exploits.

I had spent a lifetime making ready this better son for him, his first-born, my little foundling, Modred. He might yet fling the gift back in my face.

Now Owain came galloping north with worse news still. Gwenhyvar had been abducted from Camelot. Horsemen were scouring the countryside for her in vain. Arthur was summoning all the wisest women of Britain to help him find her.

'The bishops will not like that.'

'Arthur has always walked uneasily with those gentlemen, since he tried to steal Saint Padarn's tunic and got the worst of it. They need his sword, but they do not trust him,' my son laughed.

'All the same, do not mock the Church. The land needs wholeness. Male and female, light and dark, the east and west. The join will not be easily made.'

I seemed to see a shadow flooding over the land, sweeping

away little silver-haired Gwenhyvar, the white monks and nuns, leaving our darker power unchecked.

'Merlyn!' I wanted to cry. For even the wiles of that great pagan sorcerer, who had done me so much wrong, had served the demands written in creation. He had let the Church use Arthur, for Britain's good.

But Merlyn was gone. Who guided Arthur now? If Nimue fought the Church because she wanted power, then I must challenge her, and strive to hold the balance.

Who had struck this blow at Arthur's pride, at Camelot's peace, at Britain's unity? Who had taken Gwenhyvar, and why?

I obeyed the summons.

The hill to Camelot was steep, the gate dark and strong. My brother was waiting, angry, on the other side. My treacherous heart skipped like a week-old lamb. But disillusionment followed and despair hung cold and heavy on my shoulders as a sodden cloak. Though I was hundreds of miles away blessing the fields in Rheged that May Day, he blamed me for the abduction of his wife. I saw his grizzled hair, the pent-up energy in his stiffening limbs, the baffled fury in his eyes. Beneath my smile, the muscles of my own face ached.

We must embrace. We were the High King of Britain, the Queen of Rheged, royal brother and sister. The court was watching. The stiffness of our faces repelled each other. But in that closeness our bodies pressed and pulsed. When we parted he was rough and I was cold.

'Where is she?'

'You did not seek my blessing or my sisters' to wed Gwenhyvar. Why should you need our help now she has left you?'

'Left me! Damn you, didn't Owain tell you she was snatched from here by fiends of hell? A troop of masked huntsmen who vanished into the mists of dawn, leaving not so much as a drop of their cursed elf-blood behind them. Only her cry for help upon the air and my nephews wounded fighting for her.'

'Poor Gareth. Owain tells me he took a dangerous gash. May I see him? I have some little skill to heal him.'

'You? You stole Caliburn's scabbard! We are all hurt now.'

165

'I did not speak of enchantment. There are other ways to heal.'

'Gareth. One of Margawse's brood. You knew he would be Gwenhyvar's bodyguard. Will you sisters even wound your own children to damage me?'

'Damage *you*? So that is why you have summoned us out of Lothian, Rheged and Garlot? For yourself. Because Arthur's pride is hurt. Is that all Gwenhyvar's captivity means to you? Is her danger nothing to you for her own sake?'

I saw by the crimson in his face the shot had struck home. And a treacherous tide of delight surged in my own body. Arthur no longer loved Gwenhyvar. Long, long ago that wedding of the golden laughing prince, his sweet and silvery-blonde princess. Creatures of fairytale when I was already old with grief. Gwenhyvar had scarcely changed, as light and shallow now as then. Even the loss of her son had scarcely touched her. With the young men of Arthur's court she seemed still more girl than mother, though always prettily circumspect.

My brother had grown beyond her. Arthur lived a king's life. He had made hard decisions. He had forced his enemies to surrender and then ordered slaughter. He had seen old friends fall defending him. He had leaned on counsellors, only to find them gone. Merlyn the magician, sleeping under a rock. Now even his foster-mother, the Lady of the Lake, had left him. She had swept off indignantly when she quarrelled with the Church. Only Bishop Bytwini, his chaplain since childhood, remained. He stood behind Arthur now, wary of me as always, reproof in his face. He must have berated Arthur strongly for summoning the wise women to this council.

None of them could give Arthur back his son. He believed we could. I bowed courteously to the bishop.

'Peace to you, Father,' since he did not bless me first.

With pain I saw him turn his face aside.

Margawse was there, dangerous with excitement as always. She was angry at Gareth's wound.

Elaine arrived last, slow, ponderous, the fat wrinkles of her face inscrutable. Elaine has the Sight. Elaine could tell us nothing.

A cold summer then, Camelot almost bare of men, the

country scoured in vain, the air empty of news, like a day
without birdsong.

The men came, and reported failure, and rode off again.
Modred had been missing a long time, and Taliesin with him.
I feared more than one thing from their absence.

Arthur met me walking along the ramparts, looking over
the wilderness of meres towards Glastonbury. For once his
eyes begged, rather than challenged, me.

'Morgan . . .' I let my look encourage him. 'If someone
has taken her off to spite me, why does he not send a taunt
to say so? What does this silence mean?'

I did not want to hurt him, but he must know the truth.

'That Gwenhyvar may be dead. Or that she went with him
willingly, and not as a spoil of war.'

I saw his fist ball and grind against the white stone
breastwork. Guilt? Rage? Grief? I would not judge him now.

'Can you do nothing? Morgan the Wise, they call you.
Some of them whisper, Morgan the Goddess.'

I shook my head in part denial.

'I have told you how I let go the scabbard. I have used no
great enchantments since then. Only the ordinary magic of
birth and death. Well, let me try. Tomorrow is Samain Eve.
You have forbidden any woman to leave the fortress until
Gwenhyvar is found. You will have to let me go.'

His eyes darkened. 'Where?' He suspected that I would
not tell him.

'Where else but the most powerful spiritual centre in the
country?'

Our gaze travelled to that hill rising like a faery fortress
across the marsh from Camelot. Old Ynys Witrin,
Glastonbury. An ancient, still spirit-haunted Tor, and at its
foot, the earliest Christian church in Britain, if you believed
the legends.

'The place is doubly holy. This is the threshold of the year.
Samain is the night that brings two times together. The
barriers are down. From the unseen world spirits come back
to feast with the living again.'

'Samain is dangerous. Good Christian folk stay safe
indoors.'

'Arthur the soldier has risked a night attack before.'

'I will escort you.'

167

'No!' Too quick my protest. 'You are not initiated. What I must do is not for you to see.'

I knew how that must sound. Why should my brother trust me, knowing our histories?

But I was right. He was a general used to taking risks. He saw no other opening.

'Go then, if you must. I do not doubt you have protection better than Gareth's sword gave Gwenhyvar.'

Like a bitter, sulky boy. But would he grieve if I too disappeared?

There is a causeway to the island, among willow trees. I crossed, with a few attendants, and paid my respects at the abbey. A simple collection of huts, a church for choir and pilgrims, a guesthouse and farm. The monks dressed simply in white. This place knew more of Jerusalem than Rome. It understood the potency of mysteries better than the power of law. Holiness shone in the monks' faces. Beneath their courtesy I sensed a fear of women. Yet we shared a common language, these mystics and I. They knew very well the Tor was a battleground of spiritual warfare. That was why they were here. Could I persuade them it was a truce I sought? I must speak carefully. There was no gain in offending their Christian sensibilities.

Abbot Congar's face registered alarm. 'You would keep vigil on the Tor itself? On Samain Night! Lady, beware of pride. Are you so armoured for spiritual battle you would risk your soul where even the priests of Christ fear to watch?'

I smiled, meekly. 'I am a woman. I come in great need. For my sister Gwenhyvar I have vowed this penance. The powers of darkness will beat about your door tonight, Father. Me, they may overlook. The Lord will shelter those who trust him on a mission of love.'

This was not subterfuge, though it was circumspection. That night I felt the power stirring in me again. That night I believed the join might yet be made. That night I had indeed come in love.

With some amazement, Congar let me pass. He offered, hesitantly, to send monks to pray with me. I felt his relief when I refused with a smiling shake of my head.

Did he watch us climb the Tor, treading the sacred serpent path that winds around the breast of the hill? He cannot have lived so close under that omphalos, Beltaine and Samain, keeping vigil in his candlelit church, and not have known that others kept their old feast on the highest point.

I was the king's sister. He let me go.

I had been careful to bring both men's and women's magic. This was a great drawing together I must do tonight. For once, I must give power back to Teilo, who, until he crossed me, had been a master Smith. After twenty years in a woman's dress he had come to understand, unwillingly, through great bitterness, more of the balance than he did when he dared to challenge me.

That night, I put hammer and sword in Teilo's hand again, the mirror and comb in mine. Build the fire high, let the iron ring. Let the images dance in the sparks. Sharpen the edge, hammer the drum, scare this evil away. Part the hair, kneel, let the polished bronze reveal the truth.

I was not Elaine. I could not see yet what I had done.

Dawn, exhaustion, the fires paled, and the light of All Saints' Day dawned purely on the watery waste below us. The chants of Christian monks came sweetly on the air. A cart rolled in across the causeway. I had no sense of victory, only foreboding.

A long path down into the safety of the meadow. The monks had been praying for me. Let them think what they would. I must not show indignation or shame. I must hold the balance. Abbot Congar was hurrying to greet me. The dew of morning was wetting the hem of his gown. How must I look to him, after such a night? Relief, concern, a wary courage, courtesy, all these struggled in his face. I murmured meaningless pleasantries to reassure him.

But there was a stir of excitement among the younger monks. I turned my head, and the smile froze on my face. The cart had stopped; the occupants climbed down. Gwenhyvar was standing there, pale-faced under a great dark hooded cloak. Her eyes looked red with weeping. Modred was beside her, with Taliesin.

Six months, our High Queen had been missing. Beltaine to Samain, while the year turned round from summer to winter. The two young men had been gone almost as long, seeking her. Modred was modest, as always, while Gwenhyvar poured out her gratitude to him for rescuing her.

169

Who was responsible? Gwenhyvar was incoherent. I could not get sense out of her. She was terrified of Arthur's wrath. I did not blame her. One name kept surfacing, like a branch to cling to in a flood. 'Modred freed me.'

Taliesin looked thin and nervous, and pocked with sores. When I questioned him, he babbled of a watery captivity, of foul serpents and the Little People, of unholy fires and dancing, of Modred saving him.

Take Modred then, march him into the abbey orchard. Let the dew-heavy grass wash my penitent's bare feet and the last yellow leaves drift down to crown my hair. In the name of the Goddess I demanded the truth of my foster-son, Arthur's child, who was not my own.

'Why were you gone so long? How did you find her? Why must it be you who brings her back now? Can you not see how it must look? How can this help us?'

Modred listened and smiled at me, gently, courteously, ever-evasive.

'The departed return at Samain. Arthur lost Gwenhyvar. I am bringing her back to him.'

'Who abducted her? Where has he hidden her all this time?'

'The king lost his wife for six months only. His son has been missing for twenty years.'

'He will think we took her. He will accuse me too.'

Still that smile.

How could I shape the words for what I must not believe? I had spied on a young man's dreams painted on his bedroom walls.

'Do you think you can wound Arthur and not damage me?'

'You tell me my mother was Margawse. Had she not more reason than you to harm him?'

Oh, cruel Modred. I spun away from him. He should not see the tears that flooded my eyes, though he must know the cause too well.

Gwenhyvar was Arthur's prized possession. Let it be only that. A jewel stolen from one man's storehouse to another's court and now put back again.

Do not look at Gwenhyvar and see that she is a woman, still young and desirable, though she has had a full-grown son. Do not remember that Ygerne seemed young and desirable to Uther, when she had full-grown daughters.

Weep for yourself; do not weep for Arthur yet.

Arthur came swiftly enough when he heard the news, and I, like a fond sister, must lead the shaking Gwenhyvar into the abbot's private chamber and stand by her while Arthur shouted his questions.

We each nursed our fears. The abbot was troubled. A simple wattle hut with the sign of the cross was no place for a High King's judgment-chamber.

'I cannot tell you who he was. He came always at night and masked. He kept me on straw, and fed me bread and water.'

'It seems to have suited you as well as swan's meat and honey and a bed of goose-down. Taliesin is weak and full of sores, but your flesh is soft and blooming.'

'I was the High Queen! He would have known that Arthur must one day call him to account for how he treated me.'

'Why should that stay him? It was death already for him to have laid hands on you. But I must find him before I can kill him. It is curious how you cannot say one word to help me.'

There was a name which none of us spoke. I knew the fear that made Arthur shout at her. He had seen those pictures too. Modred was waiting with Taliesin in front of the fire in the guest-hall.

Oddly enough, it was Abbot Congar who rescued Gwenhyvar from Arthur. For once I was glad of his war between good and evil, devils and angels.

'Sire, your adversary may be more dark and difficult to find than you know. There is a legend here of shadowy Melwas, Lord of the Summer Country, who lures the unwary traveller across his bridge into a grim fortress from which none returns. The prison your lady speaks of, with its fiendish jailers, has all the horrors of his den. That must be why even your warrior Modred could not come at her until Samain Night, when all such barriers are down.'

Congar himself was a mighty warrior in prayer. He believed in, and respected, the power of those spirits he called his enemy. At Glastonbury, their two worlds stand very close.

'Devils have lain with women, even nuns. My queen must be above suspicion! Lady, you had better retreat to a convent and take yourself to prayer till this is settled.'

'Sire!' the abbot protested. 'The Church will not allow you to put away your wife for no good cause.'

'Good cause? Have I not cause enough to doubt her?'

But as we entered the guest-hall, Modred turned slowly from the fire, with his face warm. He seemed not to have heard their furious argument. One hand reached out to Gwenhyvar, no more than the courtier's gesture to salute his queen. His smile was reassuring.

'Your majesty, I am more glad than I can say that I came in time. Before I slew him, the gatekeeper confessed that on Samain Night their dread king would come and at last enjoy his prize in the sight of all his foul court at this most unholy feast. Forgive me, lady, these words must pain you,' as Gwenhyvar gasped and paled.

But Arthur looked from one to the other. Then he gave a great shout.

'Then it was true? No man or demon has touched her since me!'

'I am still yours,' Gwenhyvar whispered.

Possession. The Queen of Britain. The soul of the land. Still Arthur's.

After that, it was all celebration. Modred our hero had broken the curse. Gwenhyvar was saved. Taliesin of the Radiant Brow had been rescued. Honour was salvaged. Banish all fears of flesh-and-blood enemies. There are good people and there are evil. They are not the same. If Modred had brought her back, apparently undamaged, he could not have been the villain who spirited her away, could he?

They searched the marshes. Of course, they did not find Melwas's castle. In a land of mist and magic, what would you expect? The witching night had passed. We were in winter now.

But Arthur still could not let it rest. He was home in Camelot, within man-made walls. He was a human, Christian warrior. Melwas was now too shadowy an opponent. He needed revenge, a culprit here.

He should not have turned back to Nimue, Lady of the Lake, as subtle, shifting, unpredictable as the marsh itself.

She had returned, from whatever ways she had been searching for Gwenhyvar. She and her warrior-women had scorned Camelot's protection. She looked at us sisters, and

172

in her changing face I saw the current of contempt ruffled by a cold wind of apprehension.

Incautiously, Nimue accused us.

'In your extremity you run back to the women who have always betrayed you. What could I do for you now, that these cannot? It was for those who stole Gwenhyvar away to restore her to you. As I see they have.'

Her blue-green eyes flickered over the three of us, Elaine, Margawse, and me. But they came back to steady into stillness on Elaine, the eldest. I am the healer. My hands are potent but blind. Margawse's heat is all for the present moment, generously giving herself. It is Elaine who has the Sight. She should have known the guilty face.

'She can tell me nothing,' Arthur defended his sister.

'Cannot, or dare not.'

When at last Elaine rose in all her massive power from her seat to answer Nimue's taunts, the Lady of the Lake had reason to regret her rashness and quail.

'A contest, then? You and I, to see whose net can catch the bird of truth?'

'You are trying to trick me. I never claimed to have the Seeing!'

But they were both Arthur's wise women. He ordered the trial. Nimue would have run from the challenge but Elaine was on her feet, facing her, an overwhelming presence.

Arthur compelled them to make the test. The hall was prepared. The fires were lit, the sprigs of druid-wood laid to hand, the rune-stones set.

Bishop Bytwini stalked from the room at Elaine's first words. A stillness gripped the court. The scented smoke seemed to carry me far away as though I saw them all from the height of a circling crow. I could watch dispassionately Arthur's frown, Gwenhyvar's pale face, the unnatural calm with which Modred waited. I saw Nimue and Elaine sinking deeper and deeper into trance. Their hands moved alternately the sacred ivory rune-stones that would shape the truth.

The tension was shattered by a harsh gasp.

'Modred defiled her!'

Possessed by her spirits, Elaine would not have known what she had said. But in that same terrible moment of revelation, Nimue gave a ragged scream.

'It was Morgan's doing!'

You must believe I would have given anything for that to be true. Let Nimue accuse me. Let posterity blacken my name for thousands of years. Let them trumpet across the centuries that I was Arthur's enemy. Anything but acknowledge the truth in my sister's words. I would not believe it. Modred was my lifetime's work. I had saved this young man from death. For twenty years I had shielded him, nursed him in my heart, fostered him in my home, reared him only for Arthur.

Only? No. This was Arthur's royally got son, my gift to him. And with that gift, I would pledge our blood to him, and be rewarded with his gratitude and love. In Modred, Ygerne's daughters, Uther's son, should be made one at last. The terrible chasm that Merlyn drove between us, I would bridge. I saw the future ripped from us, hope scattered to the tempest.

'No! No!'

Swords were already out against Modred. The court was in an uproar. Arthur was on his feet, face blackening with rage. The little baby whom the fisherman saved from shipwreck was face to face with death again. Only I could rescue him, as I had shielded him twenty years ago from the wrath of his father.

Tell Arthur only the truth. Elaine was old. Her powers were fading. Her wandering sight was unreliable. Offer him the greatest truth of all, that must triumph over any accusation.

I took my foster-son's hand and led him up to Arthur. The younger man looked steadily at the older's frown. I joined their warriors' hardened palms together.

'Arthur! Modred it never could have been who fouled your queen. Modred, of all men, you have no need to fear. Brother, I give you your own son.'

I felt a great wave rear. A long, hushed moment. I waited for the pain when it would smash and overwhelm us all. Then it exploded harmlessly in spray and sunlight. Arthur was laughing at my news incredulously. Margawse was kneeling before him, blushingly, as she confirmed the truth of my story. His arms were open to receive his son, while the whole court cheered. Modred was smiling.

On the floor behind me, Elaine began to stir out of her trance.

My nerves are tuned to truth, even though my touch is blind. I felt our doom in the moment before Modred slipped my hand to embrace his father. Even before I heard Gwenhyvar scream.

I had handed Arthur a poisoned apple.

Chapter Forty

We weep for what we may not have.

*We are the Morgans of Brittany. Not the gift-bearing Margots.
You would call us mermaids. There, you can see us already, can't
you? Fabulous females in a magical seascape of coasts and islands.
The jade and purple water over silver sand and kelp-strewn rocks.
And I who sit, coiled half in and out of the tide that laps so
lovingly around my iridescent tail. Golden hair, green eyes. The
white hand that endlessly combs the curling locks. Sweet face bent
to admire itself in the silver mirror, that looks up through its lashes
to smile so winningly. Predatory.*

*And singing to call down the stars and raise up the dead. Such
songs, such voices would stir a monks' cemetery. Or so it seems
to you who live on land and feel such longing in your bowels when
you hear us.*

*We call the fishermen in their sturdy leather craft. We lure the
Phoenician galley wine-laden from the East. We entice the warlike
pirate ships from human takings.*

Come, mariner, I am all yours. Take me.

*The planking splinters on the rocks. The hide is holed. The mast
cracks and falls in a ruination of sails. The seaman plunges, not
reluctantly, into the sea's embrace, into my arms.*

*Soft limbs twine around the stiff canvas of his smock. My eager
lips seek through his beard for his still-gasping mouth. My heart
knocks with a violent joy on the ribbed cage of his sinking body.*

*Hold him now. Love him. Enjoy him. He is mine at last. All
that I ever wanted. He shall have his heart's desire. Draw him
down to palaces of coral beyond mortal dreams. Feed him on rarest
crustaceans, from dishes of pearl and gold. Unstop amphoras of
red Rhodian wine and let us be merry. Bed him on softest couches
of pale green dulse. Let seahorses dance for him and porpoises
tumble. I am a virgin. He is my first. Let the ocean rejoice.*

Rest here our first entwined fall on the floor of sand that the tide lightly strokes. The eyes of the sea-anemones are curious. Sharks smile. Can you still hear me sing through this green wall of water?

Open your lidded eyes. Look on me. You have me entirely. our dreams are manifest. Lift that limp hand. Stroke my blue and silver side, let your fingers stray over delicate scales, fondle the fragile fronds of fins, cradle my breasts. See, I am hanging my hair over your heart. Feel, I am brushing your cheek with my long lashes. Awake for me. I am opening and thirsting for you.

Nothing. He does not move. He will not move. They will never move. Ten thousand times I have called my first love down to me. And I am still a virgin. Still untouched. Unloved.

They are all cold.

Storm now, and an intolerable wailing. Lightning flashes curses. I beat the fists of my rage upon the rocks. It will not rouse him. They lie, white faces, swelling corpses, bleached, picked bones. The sea is salt with torrents of my limitless grief. Why was I made so? Only to chill what I would most inflame?

Still I must sing. I must rise to the rocks, take up the mirror and comb. Calm the sea, bring out the moon. I have so much to give. An ocean of unspent love. Why will he never take it?

The Morgans weep for men they never meant to destroy.

Chapter Forty-one

I bound their hands together with Caliburn's old belt.

Long ago, when Arthur lay wounded at Celliwig, I took the sword and scabbard from their sacred cave in Lothian. I intended a restoration. It led to a fatal separation.

One thing Elaine kept back, not telling me why: the belt that should have held both sheath and weapon together. It was nothing magnificent. Worn black leather with silver clasps, fragile from the hard use of ancient battles, a slender strap on which to hang both Arthur's life and his victory.

Now the sword and scabbard had passed out of our hands, one snatched away forcibly, one surrendered willingly. We still held this link. We had lodged it safely, in the high hill above Margawse's capital at Din Eidyn.

As Modred grew to manhood, Elaine began to weave. Her feet hardly moved from the hearth, her eyes seldom lifted, her hands were always busy. She plaited a new and brilliant band to twine around the old. Three magical colours: white, scarlet, black.

White for the Virgin, purity of spirit, the high ideal, the untouchable huntress.

Red for the Mother, blood and life, generously given, hungrily taken.

Black for the Crone, our inescapable death, and no less bitterly feared though we know the white will be born afresh.

The colours twisted and spiralled; the belt was new-made and strong. It was finished at Camelot, while Gwenhyvar was still missing. Elaine laid it in my hands with that hooded smile.

'Our season is approaching. Arthur has got the sword back, and you have lost us the scabbard. Bind him with this.'

So, in that fateful, irrevocable moment when I joined Modred's hand to Arthur's, I tied that belt to both. The new wrapped round the old. The strong supporting the frail. Modred and Arthur in each other's arms.

Then Gwenhyvar screamed and flew to Nimue. My old enemy was writhing on the floor, still drugged with trance. And the rafters of Arthur's hall seemed to shiver still with the echo of her accusation: '*It was Morgan's doing!*'

Forgive me, Nimue. You saw more truly than you knew.

Forgive me, Merlyn's shade. You warned of the truth when you interpreted Arthur's dream. His hall ablaze on May Day. A burning beam that must be dragged out and destroyed before it ruined the rest.

Not Moses, this, rescued from the Nile to lead his people to their Promised Land.

I had given him Modred.

I did not remain the Virgin. I could not be the Mother. I had become the Crone.

That night I was shown for a few moments all I had lost. After a splendid supper Arthur took my hand. Never had fire warmed my skin with a more welcoming glow. My brother embraced me joyfully. He had discovered his son. In gratitude he was ready to forgive me anything that night. I never felt myself more joyful in powerlessness, more yieldingly woman, more strongly cherished than leaning on my brother's chest in the circle of those mighty arms. Before the whole court Arthur kissed me, as all my life I had dreamed our lips would meet. What did we care whether those who saw it sighed with romance or stiffened in disapproval? For us this flawed world had vanished. Gwenhyvar, Urien, and all the rest were on another shore. Tonight Arthur the King and Morgan the Queen were joining at last in an Isle of Bliss across the ocean. Tonight . . .

Illusion. A land of dreams that could not be.

Arthur took Caliburn from its false sheath and offered it to Modred.

'Symbol for symbol, emblem of oath. I have the belt. I lay my sword before you two. Morgan, let you and I give up our warring powers. Shall we make Modred our heir and give him Caliburn, and go down into a happy old age?'

At last he was giving up his pride, as I had surrendered mine. The scabbard had passed from sight. He was offering the sword of victory to his son.

179

The terrible reality forced its way through the charmed circle of the arms still enfolding me. Truth shackled me like a woman torn from her man by slavers. Arthur was married to Gwenhyvar. I had reared Modred. Modred had stolen his father's queen.

I was the Healer. There can be no cure that leaves the poison in the wound. I must lance it out. I must cut this foulness away from him, though the knife slipped in my trembling hand and killed me too.

See how I loved you, Arthur. I feared that what I must say now might destroy you. How could these who witnessed it think my bitter flood of tears betokened rage and hate? I howled for both of us.

'No! No! Do not trust Modred!'

Tear from his chest the ancient sword-belt I had just restored to him. See my own grey hair caught in the buckle that should have bound us all together. What's left now? Caliburn, the unsheathed blue blade glinting wickedly in the firelight. Modred was my gift to Arthur, Caliburn his to Modred. But I had spoiled the feast with my accusation. The moment was marred.

He hurled me away from him. The fragile, ancient leather snapped as I clutched the sword-belt in my hands to tear it off him. The new, bright weaving slipped its moorings. Modred smiled.

Arthur snatched Caliburn back, cutting my palms. He must not believe me. It was a matter of man's pride. His queen deceive him? His son, his new-found heir, betray him? I insulted Arthur the King. Morgan the Wise was always false.

But he would keep his sword.

I lay sleepless all night with that broken sword-belt under my cheek. I was marked next morning. Grey dawn showed me the desolation of reality. I had given Arthur his son and then blackened his name. I had accused Gwenhyvar of adultery, Modred of treason, and both of them of trespass against the taboo of consanguinity. I bore my punishment. I myself had longed for what was doubly forbidden me. I was Arthur's half-sister; I was Urien's wife. It was never possible.

I destroyed that sword-belt, the magic binding made to bring weapon and sheath together. I had cast the scabbard away willingly, offering the sacrifice of my power. That giving away was never matched by Arthur.

I killed the belt in bitterness. I hacked it in pieces, with fingers bruised and reddened by the marks of the scissors. I washed the bloodstains on it with the rain of my tears. I flung the rags on the fire and heard the wet leather hiss, smelt the foul smoke of ruin. Modred was all I had had to give. I had spent my life's work shaping that blood-bond. Now I had destroyed him.

Even in the darkest night we cling to shreds of impossible hope. One thing of Arthur's remained to me. That spring I had asked Taliesin to steal a keepsake for me from Arthur. Perhaps I had more of the Sight than I knew. I should not be close to him ever again after this. I wanted no jewels, traded from one court to another. No goblet looted in war. Something of himself, unregarded, precious only to me.

Taliesin was a sympathetic young lad. He understood. He brought back a shirt of Arthur's, taken from his bedchamber. His eyes sparkled with pride in his own audacity as he handed it over, softened in pity as he saw how I struggled to receive it with dignity.

I wore Arthur's shirt at night next to my skin. It was muddied from hunting, stale with his sweat. I hugged it to me in the secrecy of the night. It was all I should ever have of him around me now. The linen grew warm as a lover's skin and the stiff stains moved against me like calloused fingers. The smell of him stirred my blood. I could not let this go. In my dreams, one day I would yet wash all these stains clean for a wedding garment.

Dreams. By day I watched, with incredulity and fascination, their power grow. Gwenhyvar and Modred. I had done nothing to stop it.

Arthur flung himself off to hunt in Cornwall, leaving Gwenhyvar with Modred for protection. They say he lodged at the hall of Gwenhyvar's bastard half-sister, Gwenhyvach. He came back furious to prove his manhood and his own might.

There is a hill in London, looking out across the River Thames. It is a holy place, and made holier still by what was buried there. The head of Bendigeit Brân, the Blessed One.

Like a child asleep on its mother's lap, like a wounded

warrior that lets his horse carry him safely homeward, like swallows that follow their heart to their nesting-grounds, so are we to Bendigeit Brân. He is our peace, he is our safety, he is the heart of Britain. While his miraculous head lived in the earth on the White Hill, hope would always triumph, no enemy would finally overrun us, we would be the Island of the Mighty for all time.

Arthur said, 'It does not seem right to me that the Island should be defended by the strength of anyone but my own.'

He dug up the Blessed Head. The white bleached vessel of great Brân's skull. He set it on a stake in another place for the crows to mock at. He overturned our cauldron of regeneration.

Chapter Forty-two

I am the fay who bestows fabulous gifts on the men I love.

I give Hector his wonderful horse, Galatée. Alas, this is a love that turns to hate when the Trojan hero flouts me.

In Jaufré *I give the hero an amazing tent.*

Jaufré hears me crying for help and runs to my aid. I am standing on the brink of an enchanted spring. My handmaid appears to be struggling for her life in the water. Jaufré leans over to rescue her. I steal up behind him and push him in. Then I leap in after him. I clasp my arms around him and together we sink deep down into a beautiful land beneath the surface.

Jaufré survives the experience. He and his friends see coming towards them a baggage train. I announce myself. I am the Fay of Mongibel. He has pleased me well. I am heaping gifts on him as his reward. Greatest of all of these is my tent. It can be folded so small it may be carried in a single cart. When it is opened out for a banquet it spreads for half a league.

What is Arthur's Round Table compared with this?

I give Julius Caesar a magical horn and a son.

Yes, truly, I am his wife. In Auberon *Morgan is stolen in infancy by a fairy king. He keeps me for ten years and teaches me all his enchantments. On his deathbed he leaves me his precious ivory horn. If it is blown by one of truthful honour it can summon twenty thousand armed warriors in an instant. Clearly I offer a valuable dowry for the right man. The doting parents of Julius Caesar covet this for him. They persuade him it makes me a highly desirable bride. The marriage is arranged. His own mother, Brunehaut, is a queen in faeryland. She also brings a legacy, an enchanted golden goblet. If an honourable man circles thrice around it and makes the sign of the cross over it, it will be filled with a limitless quantity of wine.*

Our son, who receives both these gifts, is Auberon, a little fairy king, dwarfish, but otherwise of great beauty. He lives in a dangerous enchanted wood. The ignorant warn Huon of Bordeaux that any traveller who speaks to the dwarf will never come out of the wood again. The truth is the opposite. Anyone who responds when Auberon addresses him will receive a rich reward. The punishment for not returning his courteous greeting is death.

Huon discovers this just in time. Auberon gives him Julius Caesar's goblet and my horn.

We offer limitless joys. It is not wise to spurn us.

Chapter Forty-three

I had threatened Arthur's manhood with my accusation. I compelled him to prove that he was still the unchallenged king. The fragile truce between Britons and Saxons could not bear so great a war as his pride needed now.

Unluckily, he found a cause in Brittany big enough to engage a hero-sized army. King Hoel, his uncle, had lost a niece, poor Helen. The girl had been seized and ravished by a barbaric giant who hurled rocks on his attackers from Mont-Saint-Michel. She died in the monster's arms, but Arthur avenged her, smiting the blood-smeared giant through the brain and ending the terror.

Yet over the mountains was a weakened Rome that still demanded tribute, though it could no longer keep its subjects safe. The men of Greater and Lesser Britain would show them who was master now. They would raise their own standards for all to kneel to: old Rome, still older barbarians, upstart Saxons and encroaching Angles. *We are the British, the Cymry, Arthur's people. Fear his sword.*

He did not leave Britain unprotected. Gwenhyvar was already High Queen. He appointed as her war-leader and his regent, Modred.

When they brought the report to me, they told me that Modred had pleaded modestly he was unworthy to rule. 'Let the honour fall to someone more mature, better loved by the people.'

Did he turn his eyes to Gwenhyvar when he said this? Did he mean the sword of government was rightly hers? What need did Britain have of a regent, while she reigned?

Arthur would listen to no argument. 'You are my son. I am putting this sword into your hands, damn you.'

Not Caliburn, you understand, but the Sword from the Stone.

185

He must have done this to defy me.

I heard the news and in my mind I saw that sword. This weapon of our peace Arthur the Soldier had hardly wanted and had too little regarded. Caliburn had been Nimue's gift to him. This one was ours.

I must not let myself remember how he got it.

And he is leaving this sword of sovereignty with Modred?

Far away in Rheged I felt, as if in my own bones, the great burden Arthur put off when he handed over the royal sword. It had been a weight too heavy for other men to lift, though he had once parted it from Margawse as lightly as a squire grabbing up a weapon for a friend on his way to some war-game. I sensed his youth returning. This is how Arthur of Britain would always choose to live his life, brandishing Caliburn on the battlefield, not sitting as law-giver with this solemn, civil blade before him. My spirit was grieving. Arthur, I had the strength, the wisdom that you scorned for this great task. I could have borne that sword for Britain. Instead, you left me carrying an empty sheath like an unclosed wound.

So Modred was entrusted with the sword of government, and Arthur kept his battle-magic.

But the known pedigree of frail, pale Gwenhyvar was inked with old royal blood. Did it take the wise counsel of Modred to make her understand the power and destiny in her lineage? She was High Queen of Britain. Arthur, whose descent from Uther Pendragon was always uncertain, had taken his sovereignty from her. I witnessed it.

I was there when, in a church filled with women, in token of that Cornish blood, Ygerne's blood, our blood, she was independently crowned. Gwenhyvar was High Queen in her own right.

Even through my heartbreak I had felt that thrill of affirmation, when Bishop Bytwini raised the circle of gold above the altar and turned to us. Gwenhyvar sat enthroned before him, gorgeous in cloth of silver. Fourteen years old, her violet eyes huge in her solemn face. The choirboys hushed. The white nuns lifted their faces. We listened. And on the waiting air Archbishop Dubric's bell chimed from the sister church where Arthur sat.

'Vivat! Vivat Regina!'

And all of us were crowned in womanhood as the circle

descended on Gwenhyvar's head. The heavy greenstone sceptre swayed in her little hand.

Now, twenty-one years later, Arthur left Britain in Modred's hands. He was gone a long time. The country prospered. We had a feeling of peace, as when the sun shines warmly on a day in early spring and all the flowers open.

Angles from the Humber came to trade in our markets. The border farms reported less trouble than usual from Pictish raids. Laden donkeys passed us, driven by half-scared people setting out to reunite with kinsfolk left behind in the Saxon east. The long truce of Badon was crumbling to reveal a larger peace.

Then the news stunned us. Gwenhyvar declared herself Queen Regnant. She was repudiating her consort Arthur.

Once more, I was torn in two. I was Arthur's sister. How could I support this? I was a royal woman of the West. How could I argue against it?

Gwenhyvar summoned all the nobles of the Cymry to a high council in York. The women were especially bidden. Such lords as Arthur had left behind to keep the land came too, Urien from Rheged, Cador her foster-father from Cornwall, Taliesin Chief Bard, the bishops. But most of all the women, secular nobility and abbesses.

All round me the great hall in York was loud with commotion, anger, hope, calculated ambition, shock. Our female world was suddenly full of remembered possibilities.

But *Gwenhyvar?*

Nimue came. She who had been Arthur's foster-mother, now turned with the wind to lap a different shore. I stiffened to see her enter, carrying the jewelled symbol of government laid ceremoniously across her palms. She placed it in Modred's hands, as regent. Then Modred, kneeling, delivered the sword of sovereignty up to his High Queen.

Now Gwenhyvar had them both. The greenstone sceptre and the jewelled sword. I saw they were too heavy a burden for her to hold. Soon she must offer the sword back to Modred, as her new consort.

I am the Mothers' daughter. I am all my sisters. But in Her name I had loved men, and a man. My woman's pride lies partly in my power to heal and enable men, ennoble them. My woman's strength should enrich both of us.

187

Could I help Gwenhyvar depose Arthur? Should I help her tear this sword from him forcibly? My own pride and power I had surrendered long ago, when I sank the scabbard. Blood and love were all that remained to give. I, Arthur's still-loving sister, stood silent while the great 'Aye!' to Gwenhyvar thundered around the walls.

Yet Nimue was there behind them, eternally young, eternally changeable, guardian of Gwenhyvar and Modred now. Her fair face sought out mine, calculating, as she read my soul. She knew they must win me over. They mistrusted me, even in my powerlessness. Merlyn they had disposed of long ago. Me, they still feared.

I should have known that Gwenhyvar would have a second, less noble weapon. This one was forged to hurt. That treacherous blade slid between my ribs, aimed at my heart.

The High Queen burned with an almost maidenly indignation when Bishop Bytwini challenged her.

'You have no right to put away your lawful husband and your king.'

'No right?' Her violet eyes swept round the women of her court, gathering up loyalty, resentment, self-satisfaction, shame.

'I have been left barren for many years. Your king has wasted the seed, that should have fertilised me, on lesser wombs. I will show you the proof. Speak now, my women, which of you has Arthur persuaded or forced to lie with him?'

Was that all his sin? Arthur had been hot-blooded from a boy. But Gwenhyvar was no ordinary wife. To be untrue to the sovereign High Queen is to be an unfaithful husband to Britain. Did she accuse Arthur of that?

I watched the slowly climbing hands. How few stood modestly still. Chaste Christian Tegau, Caradawc's bride, was one. I could not bear this.

'You hypocrite! Answer for yourself. Adulteress!' I screamed at her.

Gwenhyvar was enjoying her power. She almost smiled at me.

'Yes, Morgan the Faithless, one woman defied him, despite his threats to bind her silent. In her anger and distress she unfolded the tale to me, showed me her bruises, washed my feet with the tears of her wrath.'

Gwenhyvar's hand reached down from the dais and took another. She led a tall and softly blushing noblewoman out before me. Young, raven black of hair, slenderly made, her eyes as green as mine.

Arthur had been unfaithful once too often. He had offended against more than his Queen. While his own son was committing adultery with Gwenhyvar, Arthur had assaulted the virtue of . . .

Morfudd, my daughter.

No, do not try to comfort me. Do not tell me he saw in her the mirror of her mother's youth. Those words would seal the tomb on what I knew already. I was old. My womb was dry. Hope had fled. My furrowed face spoke charms of wisdom not of beauty. The enchantment of youth had passed to my daughter, my beautiful, winsome, winning Morfudd. The magic of youth is what Arthur could not bear to let go. With his offering of himself, she had inherited everything. He would never have eyes, or arms, or heart, or bed for Morgan the Wise now. I had lived too long. My time was over. He had forced on my daughter what he had never offered me.

His time was over too! Modred my foster-son would avenge this hurt. I could have forgiven Arthur easily for marrying Gwenhyvar, pretty irrelevance that she seemed at first. But never this cruel severing of present from future hope. This was the final wound that would slay us both.

The cheering had died. The thronged council chamber was hushed. I sensed the heart-rending pain in Urien at my side. In spite of everything, he remained Arthur's man. Nimue was watching me. Her voice whispered like the first trickle of water through a breaking dam.

'Now, Morfudd! Your mother must give her verdict now.'

My daughter was coming towards me. Cheeks warm with remembered injury, her head held proudly high. Green eyes intent on mine. Her hand reached out.

'Mother?'

My eyes on Morfudd's serious face, this all-too-flattering mirror of my own, my wrinkled hand in her smooth young one. My spirit in her flesh. I heard a stranger's voice cracked with unbearable grief affirm the death sentence on all of us:

'Aye! Vivat Gwenhyvar!'

189

Chapter Forty-four

I am the jealous mother of a lovely maiden.
The stories twine like water-snakes.
  My daughter's name is Pulzella Gaia, *the Merry Maiden, in a fourteenth-century Italian poem of that title. My spell has cast her into serpent shape. Brave Gawain comes riding by from Arthur's court. The beguiling snake begs him to tell her his name. A knight-errant does not readily reveal that, but, ever-susceptible to female charms, Gawain complies. My spell is broken. He has won himself a fairy lover.*
  Pulzella Gaia rewards him generously. She will grant his every wish. There is just one condition – there always is, with a fairy mistress. Gawain must disclose their love to no one, ever.
  Of course, he does. Gawain is a boaster. He attends a tourney at the court. When all the other knights start proclaiming the beauty and virtue of their ladies, it proves too great a challenge for his pride. He describes the unmatchable charms of his Pulzella Gaia.
  Once more, I have my daughter in my power. Pulzella Gaia must surrender herself to the spell of her vindictive mother, Morgana the Wise. This time, I imprison her in a tower of my own castle, Pela Orso. Here she is condemned to stand, waist-deep in water, her lovely legs transformed into a fish's tail.
  To be a mermaid is not an enviable condition. It is a punishment.
  Gallant Gawain is not the man to accept such a defeat easily. He sets out on a quest. He will find and free his love again. He forces his way into my castle. He lifts my daughter out of the enchanted water.
  Now it is my turn to suffer the same punishment. He leaves me floundering in her place. Then he and Pulzella Gaia ride merrily off to Camelot.

There is a version that makes me more cruel still. There is less of shape-shifting, more of sadism, in this story.

A century earlier, in the Prose Lancelot, *I play no part in it. Gawain arrives at a castle and hears the piercing screams of a woman. He rushes in to find a damsel, naked as a needle, standing in a marble tank up to her waist in boiling water. She pleads with him to lift her out, but for all his efforts he cannot do it. So she must wait in agony till the best knight in the world comes to deliver her. Through her tears she tells him she has not yet suffered enough for a sin she once committed.*

You will have guessed that Lancelot is now the one destined to be her long-awaited rescuer.

By the fifteenth century, Malory — more of him later — has no doubt whose wickedness is at the bottom of this. It is certainly not the maiden's fault.

For five years the poor girl has stood boiling in scalding water in the tower of Castle Corbin. In this story too, Gawain fails to release her. Then Lancelot comes. The searing iron doors of my prison unbolt themselves for him. He bravely enters the chamber, hot as any stew, takes the damsel by the hand and pulls her out.

She reveals that I, Queen Morgan the Fay, with my crony the Queen of Northgales, are the ones who devised this torture. Our motive, jealousy, because the damsel was called the fairest lady in the land.

Unlike Pulzella Gaia, this lady is not my daughter. But that tradition survives, like so many others, in Brittany. A maiden changed into a serpent. A fairy daughter in a prison.

The Bretons still tell of the unhappy offspring of a Margot-la-Fée. Her misfortune is to be the most beautiful maiden in the world. On a certain day of the year she is transformed into a snake.

Her mother, the Margot-la-Fée, implores a peasant to go to a point in the road which she describes to him. There he will see a snake, which he is to cover with a basin.

The peasant obliges. To be doubly sure, he sits on the basin and stays there till evening. At sunset he lifts the cover, and is astonished to find a radiantly beautiful maiden. In a rush of gratitude, not wholly explicable, she offers him a rich reward for her freedom.

Am I responsible? Am I the vindictive, ageing queen, envious of the beauty of the next generation? Or am I, as Modron, the grief-stricken mother, seeking help to unspell my child? No doubt you have formed your own opinion.

Chapter Forty-five

I was a wise woman, and I had acted in anger. Well, perhaps I am what they call me, Morgan the Fay. It is dangerous for a man to be false to his fairy mistress. Mistress? I was never Arthur's lover though once I believed that was our destiny. I did not consult the Goddess, she who is always tender to wronged women. I had been hurt, and I hit back.

Gwenhyvar and Modred were married, and Modred was crowned High King, though Bishop Bytwini refused to perform the ceremony. He fled to Glastonbury. I also could not bear to witness that. Bitter enough that I had affirmed my rival Gwenhyvar's right. But to see Modred, Arthur's son, wearing the crown of Britain, Arthur's crown? If I acknowledged that, our field was stripped of harvest. My brother's time, and mine, was over.

Pretend it has not happened. Imagine that slender circle on Modred's black hair is false gold and not the true Welsh metal. Which of us can distinguish truth from falsehood?

'Three Futile Battles of the Island of Britain: And the third was the worst: that was Camlann, which was brought about because of a quarrel between Gwenhyvar and Gwenhyvach.'

Little Gwen. Gwenhyvach. She came limping into the court at York, the Loathly Damsel. We Celts are a race proud of our bodies. Tall, white-skinned, hard-muscled and slender from joyful exercise, our hands nimble with harp and needle, our tongues ready with wit and story, our hearts brave for the danger of horseback or swordplay. We are scornful of slowness, ignorance, cowardice, deformity. The Good God Dagda is not a moral giant; he is the god who is good at everything. That is our ideal.

This lady was hunchbacked, and crookedly so. The left

shoulder rose to nestle against her ear. She was short and stout, with legs, to judge by her ankles, as thick as logs. Her face was blotched with purple and her mouth hung awry. Her dun hair was straight and lank.

We were most of us there to witness her arrival. Gwenhyvar herself, silver-blonde, Red Margawse, still merry and passionate, I, Morgan, in all my pied beauty of glossy black hair and fair white face, no longer young but handsome still, and our lovely women.

We were not kind. We were a proud, aristocratic court who tittered behind our hands and moved away from ugliness. I had lived closer than most to misfortune. Charitable white nuns were my teachers, and wise women like Gwennol my nurse. I had healed many. I had held the hands of the dying. I had provided gifts of another sort for those whom nature had wronged.

This deformed woman had an uncommon dignity. It held us stilled now and curious, watching her come through our ranks to where Gwenhyvar had half-risen from her seat by the fire, with Modred at her side. Gwenhyvar was gripping the dragon-carved armrests and Modred had turned his face to her in surprise and alarm.

I knew this lady, Gwenhyvach, Little Gwen. So did Gwenhyvar, Big Gwen. All Gwenhyvar's filial love was centred on her foster-father, Cador, Duke of Cornwall, battle-leader of Dumnonia as once my father Gorlois had been, before Uther killed him. But Cador was not the father who gave her royal blood. That was Leodegran, of the old kings of the West. And she claimed her mother's line was older still. By that lineage she had the right to be what she was now, our sovereign Queen, and Modred her royal husband.

And Gwenhyvach, poor twisted Little Gwen? She was known as the daughter of Leodegran's high steward's wife. I say the wife advisedly, because the girl had been richly endowed, in wealth if not in looks. She was indeed a high lady, we allowed her that, the unspoken admission of a strong vein of royalty mingling with a respectable but lesser blood. Leodegran's bastard daughter, half-sister to Gwenhyvar.

Gwenhyvar bristled like a kitchen cat that sees an unwelcome sibling come to share her bowl.

'We bid you welcome to our court, sister, though you come

to pay us your homage a little late. All the nobility of Britain was at our marriage and Modred's coronation.'

'So, you are queen in more than name now?'

'I was always queen, from the day I married Arthur. I was crowned as he was.'

'And no doubt you think you should have been High Queen before that?'

'My royal blood was right, from both my parents, but I needed a champion to uphold my rule. I am no Boudicca screaming her wrath in a war-chariot.' She turned very sweetly to Modred, and he smiled with manly warmth and took her hand.

The Lady Gwenhyvach flushed. 'You throw that in my face? You are right. I have no husband to fight for me, while you have two.'

Anger flashed in Gwenhyvar's face, like a flame leaping between two peat-turves and as quickly smothered.

She seemed to soften a little to this travel-stained sister. 'Is this the reason you have given yourself the pain of your long journey to York from Cornwall? Someone has wronged you? You come to my court to ask for a champion?'

Gwenhyvach spat. A shocking act. It told us she knew that we despised her coarse appearance, and she did not care. Only I, who have looked deeper than most into pools of pain, knew how this bitter behaviour was the dam that held back grief.

'Your court! As if old kings of Britain were not as plentiful as dock-seeds, and as rank in their growth. King Leodegran? What was he? My father as well as yours. Does that make me High Queen?'

'You are his bastard.' Gwenhyvar was whispering hollowly now. She must have been gripping Modred's hand. The smile had left his face and he was watching her curiously.

Little Gwen smiled, a horrid transformation of her marred face, as when the sun peers out from beneath a massive storm-cloud and paints the sky with threatening colour.

'So it is said. And you imply she could not be the Sovereign of Britain who had Leodegran's steward's wife for mother and not Leodegran's queen.'

Modred spoke now. 'Her mother's blood was thought more potent than Leodegran's. I pity you, lady. Fathers are treacherous. I should know. You speak aloud now what was

195

only whispered before. You were raised as the steward's daughter, though one Leodegran favoured strangely. The truth of fatherhood is not easily told. Our faith lies in our mothers. Gwenhyvar's dam, Leodegran's queen, was still more royal than he was. She comes of that ancient line that flows in the veins of kings and queens like the mighty Severn that is an artery from the heart of Britain. So Arthur claimed his royalty from the same line through his mother Ygerne, if one could be sure he was her stolen baby. And I, by my mother Margawse, carry the same blood that fits me to wear the crown beside Gwenhyvar.'

'You understand well, young man. You have done half my work for me.'

'Do not listen to her,' Gwenhyvar urged him. 'She was always a mischief-maker. We have offered to give her whatever boon she came to ask, and she has spurned it. Harper! Some music to lighten the gloom. Why could we not have Taliesin with us to make our spirits dance?'

But I had sent Taliesin away to Brittany, to break the news of her betrayal to Arthur.

'Music, is it?' grinned Gwenhyvach, as the first notes graced the air. 'Would you have me sing my lay to the hall? The ballad of Gwenhyvar the Steward's Daughter?'

'Louder!' Gwenhyvar called. 'Are there no pipers handy?'

But Modred moved his hand. Only a gentle gesture, yet the harp stilled. Gwenhyvar was High Queen, but Modred had a deeper authority.

'Come, sister.' How strange that word from this young man to her whom bodily misfortune had aged to the appearance of twice Gwenhyvar's years. 'Sit by us upon this stool. You have ridden far. Some wine, there! Let me take your cloak. Drink with us, and then tell your tale.'

'I have no patience to hear her. Come, love. Escort me to my chamber.' How hard it was for Gwenhyvar to force that smile. How thin and white her lips appeared, stretched over those bared teeth.

'No tale, unless she listens to it.' Gwenhyvach was enjoying herself now. She was seated warm on a stool by the fire. She was the centre of attention. She knew we all love a story, and the stranger the better. As the firelight leaped on the crooked crags of her face we sensed that this might be more unusual than most.

196

Modred put out a hand and caught his wife's arm. Her difficult smile was wasted on him. He did not turn his face to hers. Gwenhyvach had hooked him.

And now I thought Big Gwen was near to fainting. I moved her chair for her and she sank into it with a fluttering gesture of her hand as though to force aside unwillingly a curtain of spiders' webs. I signed for wine and she drank it unsteadily. Modred looked at her, briefly, and then back to Gwenhyvach.

Gwenhyvach's smile was wide and bitter. 'I am myself one half of my tale. Look at me. No, don't turn your eyes away in embarrassment. Stare all you want. Now look at my other theme, who calls herself the High Queen Gwenhyvar. Very fair, is she not, for one whose husband has left her many times for other women or needless wars, whose only son is dead on the threshold of manhood, whose womb is barren?'

That made Gwenhyvar colour.

'The world has blessed her with a royal upbringing, a mighty king for a husband, and now a bigger throne. Why then has the Goddess cursed her?'

'Cursed Arthur, not . . .' Modred's quick movement silenced his wife.

'Because her fairness masks an ugly truth, while my loathsome exterior is the prickly husk which covers the sweet kernel of virtue wronged. Pluck up white Gwenhyvar, like a mushroom left till evening, and you will find a foulness of slugs and maggots in your hand.'

'It is you who are cursed for a liar! Look at her, and judge where goodness lies.'

'She knows the truth, even while she calls me liar. She knew, from the night the steward I called father summoned two girls of fourteen to his deathbed. Yes, we are both the same age, though you would not think it to look at me. Our lives have been very different. Would I have graced his court as King Leodegran's daughter? Would the High King Arthur have married me?'

She spat again.

'No. Such men are proud. Women are their possessions. Daughters and wives are jewels to be boasted of and displayed. Beauties to outshine other men's treasures. What use was I to an ambitious man? A crooked girl-child. An ugly daughter. A terrible failure for King Leodegran's queen.'

'*You?* The queen's daughter!' It was Margawse who asked, relishing the salacious scandal.

'So Donaut, the king's high steward, confessed to us, dying. Fortuitously, his wife had borne a daughter a few hours earlier than the queen. Fair as a tear-drop on the cheek, his little Gwen. Will it be heartache then for him to exchange this perfect one for the other? Not difficult. His daughter will be raised as a princess and Leodegran's shame will be saved. Who cares what our mothers felt? My royal dam bowed to necessity to retrieve her failure. Her lowlier one was allowed two sweet years as Gwenhyvar's wet nurse, feeding her own child at her breast like a royal guest, while I was passed off to a commoner woman. Well, I do not complain of that. Deformed as I am, it is enough that they kept me alive. Those who knew the truth feared to lay hands on royal blood and snuff out my warped little life. They let me grow, though others have whispered I must be the devil's daughter.'

'And so you are to say what you have said!'

'Why then did Leodegran reward my foster-parents so richly? What was the steward's Little Gwen to him?'

'His natural daughter! All the world guessed that.'

'Or his legitimate and too-unnatural child.'

'Unnatural indeed to spread such lies about our parent who recompensed your mother generously.'

'Do you deny it, who stood with me, one either side of that deathbed, and heard the truth?'

'How could that be? You say Leodegran bought Donaut's silence. Was the price not high enough? Your story falls.'

Gwenhyvach shrugged. Whosever child she was, I sensed a power in this woman I had looked for in Gwenhyvar and never found. It has nothing to do with fathers. It runs in the mother's blood.

There was consternation all around. Nobody knew what to think, or how far it was wise to reveal which they believed. Gwenhyvar was glaring. Little Gwen grinned at the havoc she had made. And Modred stood unsteadily, his eyes on Gwenhyvar his wife.

'You knew that story? Even before you married Arthur? That you were no queen's daughter, and maybe not even a king's. You claimed the throne of Britain. You married me. Now all that founders, like a tower built on a mire!'

He drew his hand back, he, my courteous, gentle Modred, ever chivalrous to women, ever careful in judgment. His movement sliced the air. The blow slapped against Gwenhyvar's cheek with such bitter force we all winced from the sting of it.

'Modred.' I took his arm. 'The truth is clouded.'

He looked from Gwenhyvar to Gwenhyvach with more brilliant tears than hers in his eyes.

'I know what it is to be rejected, unacknowledged, unlovable.'

My voice was as dry as the rustle of an oatfield in a summer drought.

'Will you still fight Arthur for her now?'

'Gwenhyvar was always the means, and not the cause. I fight falsehood. Arthur denied the truth of who I am. But if she is the false queen, my weapons are rotten. I cannot win.'

So young his face. So old the depth of despair in his eyes. My hand on his.

'You think you see the truth, that Gwenhyvar is false. Then give her up. Give Britain up till Arthur dies. Let her not ruin you both. Make peace with your father.'

'I had no father. And when I lose, Arthur will have no son. Which of us will you aid now, Morgan the Wise?'

I looked to Gwenhyvach for help. She grinned more savagely. 'A plague on both their sides! I'll play no High Queen for you. I am too marred.'

Over her head my troubled eyes met Modred's.

'You may be right. I have betrayed the Lady. Arthur was Ygerne's blood before you were Margawse's. Our old king is not dead yet. The battle between you has still to be fought.'

He bowed and walked away from me, a young man without hope. It was over between us.

My daughter Morfudd was comforting the queen.

Who among us could tell which was the false Gwenhyvar and which the true? Elaine would have known, but Elaine was far away in Garlot. Margawse and I left Gwenhyvar's court together and rode south for her fortress on Black Annis Hill.

Too late to withdraw my challenge to Arthur now. The fatal blow had been struck.

Rumour met us on the road that Arthur's fleet was approaching Britain.

Chapter Forty-six

I am both beautiful temptress and Loathly Lady.

In a fourteenth-century gem of English alliterative poetry, Sir Gawain and the Green Knight, *I issue my enigmatic challenge to Arthur's Camelot.*

The king and queen and their court are young, they are merry, it is the Christmas season.

Into their New Year banquet erupts my champion, a giant of a man. But it is not his size alone that startles them. He rides right into their hall very handsomely dressed for the occasion, without armour, and he is fairly formed, with flowing hair and beard. Yet the man is entirely green, from the curls of his head to his stockinged feet. His clothes are all the same hue, rich with green gems and gold. Even the horse he bestrides is grass-green, its mane braided with gold. In one hand he grasps a holly-bough, in the other, a mighty axe.

Green is the colour of the supernatural. Always it offers two possibilities: both promise and danger. You do well to be wary of us. But those who prove faithful can win incomparable riches and joy.

So the Green Man rides a circle round the hall, staring into all their faces, holding his branch of evergreen and that monstrous helmet-smasher.

This is a wonder then, to satisfy even the king, whose custom it is not to sit down to eat until some new adventure is shown him. The court is hushed till Arthur finds his voice and offers his hospitality.

The stranger will not stay to eat with them. Nor will he say yet who he is, or where he has come from.

When he issues his taunt to the court it causes consternation. He asks for a champion among these beardless boys brave enough to play a game with him. The challenge is this: to seize the Green Man's axe from his hand and then smite off his head with it.

He promises to stand quite still. Then that knight is to present himself in a year and day to suffer the return blow.

So why does brave Arthur blanch as he meets the stranger's gaze? It is not customary for the king to accept single combat when he has a retinue of knights to fight for him. Why should Gwenhyvar scream and stagger near to fainting? She knows the falsity that stands to be exposed. They both understand the meaning of the challenge. This game is indeed aimed at the sacred head. Arthur's reputation is in question. Only a man whose honour is unstained could survive this test unscathed. Is this why the court is shocked and silent?

The Green Knight roars with laughter. Arthur must take the bait. Red-faced with shame and rage he springs to take the axe, come what may. As he hefts it, the giant stands before him, stroking his beard and arranging the neck of his tunic.

Gawain saves Arthur. Gawain his nephew is loyal to both Arthur and Gwenhyvar. He knows the shameful truth, but he has counselled his brothers to silence. Now he steps into this perilous breach and separates Arthur from that moment of reckoning. Gawain says he will not be missed, he is weak and unwise. The court judges differently. In whispered council they speak of foolhardiness. Good men argue of waste and women weep, but he gets his way. Arthur grants permission. Gawain shall take the adventure of the Otherworld. It will be a great loss to Arthur's court if he does not come back.

The Green Man bows his head, laying his long hair over his crown to bare his neck. There is a moment of horror when Gawain, unwillingly, lifts that mighty axe. Will it strike clean for him? The bright blade falls and the hall shrieks as the unlucky head rolls severed across the floor. Now is the time, now is the urgent danger. Here is hope of rescue. Kick the bleeding head from one to another, lose it under the table. Separate it at all costs from the gory green torso still standing upright, spurting blood, before the appalled Gawain. Everybody knows that a sorcerer cannot live again unless his head is reunited with his body.

But the green arms grope and the huge body arches itself over the floor and the hands snatch among the bloodied ankles. He has it by the thick and verdant hair. The head grins.

More macabre still, he does not set it on its wounded neck but tucks it under his arm as he mounts his emerald horse. It speaks to Gawain now, who must carry the burden of Arthur's honour.

'*I am the Knight of the Green Chapel. Meet me there on New Year's Day to take your turn.*'

They hang the bloodstained axe over the royal dais.

Little merriment now at Arthur's board, though they try to laugh it off. What are they thinking, each of them, as they lower their eyes to plates of untasted food? What is their friend to die for? Why should they fear that Gawain will fail?

The year rolls by to All Saints' Day, old Samain. Gawain leaves court amid lamentations, riding his good horse Gringolet and bearing the holy Pentangle, the Endless Knot, on his red shield. He does not know the way to the Green Chapel. The weather is bitter. He quests through North Wales, on across the wintry Wirral, into the unknown, alone.

With just one week left in which to offer his life and save his honour, he comes on Christmas Eve out of this icy wilderness to a borderline. Deep in an oakwood he finds a moat of deep water, the sort of boundary you always have to cross between reality and faerie. Beyond, a shimmering white castle rears its turrets and pinnacles above impregnable walls.

The welcome is warm indeed. Ready servants, fine clothes, leaping fires. The genial lord, a man of stupendous size and fiery-red face, offers him hospitality, wine, and a sumptuous bedroom. He is the host, but not the real master of this castle.

Midnight approaches. The company wend their way to chapel. Two ladies enter. Gawain is captivated.

The wife of his host is a radiant beauty, and young. As she leaves the chapel, he strides to squire her. Her snowy breast and throat are bare and tempting. Her brow is hung with pearls. Her walk is alluring. In this story she has no name. Let mine suffice for both of us.

The castle's true mistress walks beside her. She is old. She is short, she is squat, and her buttocks bulge. Within her close-swathed wimple she is ugly of nose, and swarthy of chin, and her black bushy eyebrows meet across her rutted forehead. I am the figure of sovereignty. I take the highest seat in the hall. I rule here.

Gawain does not recognise his aunt. And it was not my golden nephew I had hoped to be entertaining by my side this Christmas night. This is not who I intended to face my challenge, not what I designed it for. Still, the message of doubt has been implanted in Camelot. So let us play the game out to its conclusion.

Give the lad good cheer, then, and light him to a soft dreamless bed.

Three days of feasting, till St John's Day. Gawain makes ready to leave with the other guests.

The host detains him. When Gawain protests that only three days remain for him to achieve his quest, the lord is loud with laughter. Gawain's search is over. The Green Chapel lies only two miles from here.

There is no need to be on your way in the morning, Gawain. Stay with us. Three more days, then, to live and laugh and forget your fears. But you are weary with your wandering and our merrymaking. You need to renew your strength. Let the men go hunting while you sleep late and rest and enjoy the ladies' company. Only one game we propose to you, since it is festival-time. Each evening, your host will hand over to you what he has taken in the day's chase, and you must pay back to him what you win indoors.

So you lie in soft, warm, heedless sleep while outside the lord and his pack go bounding away to hunt the hinds. And you are prey of another sort as the door slips open to admit a lady who bolts it firmly behind her. The curtains lift and the host's wife is sitting on your bed. You feign sleep, but her closeness cannot be ignored. You pretend to wake, and find her smiling over you. The wrapper slips, and rosy flesh shivers deliciously in the morning air. Her arms imprison you. She offers more. How can courtesy refuse the shelter of covers warmed by your body? But nothing else. You fight gallantly with words where no armour stands between your skins. At long last she releases you. You have taken from her no more than one entwined kiss.

For the rest of the day, the old lady is as merry with you as the young one.

When the host displays his pile of butchered venison, you pay that kiss back to him exactly, to his amusement.

The second hunt, and the wild boar springs across the savage mountains, a giant, ghastly, solitary beast. Desperate for life, he backs against a cliff and hurts many hounds before he is driven into the river and falls to the castellan's sword.

So desperately you defend your honour before you yield to temptation. This time, when you are offered the boar's head, you give back two warm embraces to her husband, and nothing more.

How would Arthur have conducted himself in such a trial?

203

Whose bed is Gwenhyvar in now?

Amid the evening revels, the younger lady flirts with you disturbingly.

So we come to the last day of the old year, and the final hunt. Tomorrow the test. Gawain must offer himself at the Green Chapel to be beheaded.

Now the twisting fox is not more subtle than the host's wife to dodge past your defences. But the fox falls to the gallant hounds and loses its skin. And in my castle, Gawain is proof against the urges of the flesh but falls to a more insidious temptation. His hostess offers him a ring. He will not take it. The lady unfastens a girdle from her waist, green silk with a golden hem embroidered simply along its edges. He refuses that too, but she warns him not to despise its plainness. We have woven art of another sort into this embroidery. No hero who wears this girdle can lose his life. Gawain accepts the talisman and puts it away secretly.

Will he give this up?

Do not condemn him. He is the sun in all our skies, Gawain the Golden. Our lust for life.

His host comes striding in, red from cold hunting, striving to make this last dismal eve bright with his laughter. Gawain is quick to meet him and restores to him . . . three kisses only. A rich exchange for a red fox-skin. But is it enough?

The last evening passes as merrily as it can under the circumstances.

Gawain's prayers are said. New Year's Day dawns, bitterly cold with driving snow. Gawain is armed and ready. At the very last, in this treacherous temptation to dishonour, he does not totally hide the truth. Over all the rest he has strapped the lady's girdle. The green silk stands out bravely against his red surcoat. Nothing is said.

Men will hold on to what they have. They must make themselves invincible, at all costs. How could they be expected to submit, naked, to the wounds that others would give them?

Gringolet is led out. Gawain takes his shield. Farewells are spoken. A servant of mine is chosen to show him the cheerless path.

One last temptation. They have scaled the snowy fells. The horrid place is near. My man warns him to turn aside. This Green Knight is unmerciful. No one rides by his chapel and lives to tell of it, be he knight or clerk. Gawain should take his way homeward. His shame will not be revealed.

Brave Gawain will not be persuaded.

With no hope now except in lasting honour, he descends a wild ravine. He finds no church there between the towering cliffs, only a grass-grown mound above a foaming river. This barrow has two dark entrances and is hollow within. The Green Chapel is holy to an older deity.

The air is hideous with noise. The giant waits on the crags out of sight, grinding his axe. Now he comes whirling round the rocks, vaulting across the torrent, striding through the snow with his four-foot blade.

Gawain must stand his turn. His neck is bared. His head is bowed. He glances up as the axe comes whistling from the sky. In spite of all his courage he flinches. The blow stops short. He suffers the Green Knight's reprimand.

Now he must be firm as rock. His hands hold frozen earth. His open eyes are fixed on the winter grass through the snow beneath him, small spears of hope. Around his loins the fragile cord of our woman's giving burns with its accusation of weakness and its promise of life.

The Green Knight heaves his axe. Once more its fall is stayed. Still Gawain waits, till in a rage he bids the giant have done and strike.

The axe descends, and its hurtling fall blots out hope. Sharp pain strikes through Gawain's stretched skin and screams, 'She was faithless!'

The wheeling earth steadies. Only the stream is rushing in his ears. Gawain leaps away to defend himself. The Green Knight laughs. It is the host.

There is blood in the snow. Blood from Gawain's neck. Blood burns in his cheeks too as the host merrily tells him our plot.

His name is Bertilak. He has followed my bidding. I am the mistress here. I am Morgan the Fay, Morgan the Goddess. It was I who ordained this challenge to Arthur's court, the Beheading Test, the quest for the Green Chapel, the hunts, the kisses. Gawain has won his life by his good faith and honour. That was the secret of the taunt. Three blows averted for three temptations resisted. Yet he failed to submit to the rules of my game completely. He would not trust his life to my sense of

205

honour. He clung to the magic girdle. His neck will go scarred for ever by this one nick.

Well, he understands now what Arthur never has.

Still smarting from that one wound, Gawain will not return and meet me face to face. He takes my green girdle back to Camelot and shows it as the badge of his shame. The court adopts it as a decoration of honour.

My plot was aimed at Gwenhyvar. It usually is.

How does Arthur feel when this tale is sung of Gawain?

Chapter Forty-seven

Gawain is dead.

I heard Margawse shriek for the eldest of her four tall sons by King Lot. He was the last of them to die, fighting in Arthur's quarrel with their half-brother Modred. Her cuckoo child, Margawse's youngest son, and Arthur's firstborn, was all she had left now. Must we cut the tangle of our family to shreds before the knot was slipped?

Arthur had landed from Gaul with his hardened war-host. Gawain was slain, staining the beach like a bloody sunset. Winchester fell to its returning king. Gwenhyvar fled.

We met her on the road and gave her our protection. She could not tell me when and how Morfudd was lost.

Now Cornwall had drawn us back for the final battle.

Yesterday Modred stood at bay with the survivors of his allied army, Angles and Saxons, Irish and Picts, on a bluff of cliffs above the River Camel where it goes hurrying through a narrow valley to seek for the western sea under the watch of the happier hall of Celliwig.

And so we sisters came there, riding through the dusk from the convent where we had left Gwenhyvar hidden. We stopped beside the water's edge.

Modred still had Nimue. Oh, yes. The Lady of the Lake, guardian of warriors, friend of lovers. Ambiguous. As fickle as a pool in times of plenty or drought.

We were both opposites and too alike, the Lady of the Lake and Morgan Sea-Born. Both of us served a more ancient Lady. Both of us loved our fosterlings fiercely. Both of us used these men as instruments for our own designs.

Nimue. Look at her now, flying from the battlefield like a swift white water-fowl from the hunter's bow. The moonlight catches the sparkle of golden breastplate and silver helmet. Her spear shafts the stars. She is still beautiful. She will spirit other protegés away. She will teach other young men war.

We Cornish sisters delivered to Arthur the Sword in the Stone, the blessing of the Island of Britain, sovereignty. She gave him Caliburn. He loved that more.

Do not despise her. She has shielded Arthur well. I might have destroyed him before this.

She should not have protected Modred and Gwenhyvar. She set her shield between me and Arthur. No spear could reach him. But she blessed the blade that would take him from the back.

Yet she went in fear of me. So did they all. They knew I had thrown away the scabbard, that came from Avalon. Myself I could not so easily drown. I was born with power in my hands, to heal or cripple.

Am I to blame for Camlann?

Last night . . . Last night! It seems dark ages before this . . . Nimue found our camp. Margawse, Elaine, I, Teilo, Taliesin, our women and guards, kept our various vigils beside the River Camel.

It was the dark before moonrise. I sought a silence by the water. No one followed me.

Over the hills there was the convent, where Bryvyth had set up her cross after Tintagel, where Gwenhyvar lay like an unlucky gambler, stripped of royalty, husband, lover, and now the twins in her womb. All night in their chapel the nuns would be praying for us. I felt that warmth and power like a fire banked under turves. Tears trickled cold on my cheeks. I should like to be there. I should like to leave the rich dress of a queen for a simple white gown. I should like to surrender authority to my High Lord. I should like to feel my face bright with their joy and certainty and not creased by the care of my more ambiguous faith.

I was Morgan the Wise! Some had called me Morgan the Goddess. I must hold the balance of the world.

Arthur, my brother, lay very close. Modred, my foster-son, nearer still. Between them, Camlann would be a battlefield tomorrow. I had brought them together.

I heard a plash more regular than a moorhen's launching. Oars were approaching. Men's voices challenged from our camp, women's replied. Who would come at night, risking the readied spear? War was men's business now, since the Romans trampled their way to victory over Boudicca. This could only be Nimue, the young-old, the ever-returning, abroad with her spear-maidens, in the dark.

I was as suspicious of her as she was of me. We encompass too much. We love too widely. It is always unwise to assume too readily how we will act. Our worlds are not limited by one side or the other. We may be now here, now there. We may abandon you both. You may tear us in two.

Walk softly up the path, then. Listen to their parley.

'Did you know there was plague in the land? Arthur is growing old. The earth cries out to be renewed. You would surely not desert Modred on the eve of his battle, would you?'

'Desert him? We are here, as you see. We lie scarcely a bowshot from his camp, even for an arm like mine.' Margawse's voice teased her lazily.

'Your nearness has endangered many men before now!'

'Gwenhyvar is almost as old as Arthur. Her womb will be dry soon.'

'Gwenhyvar is carrying Modred's child.'

Light, mocking laughter. She did not know it was a double burden.

'Is she not still?' Nimue's voice rose sharply. 'The child is born? Where? Are they both alive?'

Silence. Twin boys. They may live till tomorrow. But after Camlann . . .

'Where is the Queen?'

Gwenhyvar had laid down queenship. The nuns would hide her well. She would take their veil. We sisters knew that. Nimue could not.

'I would speak with Morgan. You have done too much harm already. And we all know what Elaine is waiting for. But Morgan . . .'

'Morgan is here.'

I stepped out from the thickets of gorse, far from the campfire. Let the starlight catch my face, no more. Let her doubt me, as I am doubting myself. Let her grieve for both Arthur and Modred. Let her fear for her wisdom. Let her lay down her magic.

I sensed an awe in her tonight I had not often felt.

209

'Will you fight for us?'

'I am Morgan the Healer.' Could she hear the bitterness in those words.

'You armed Modred.'

No. I sent him to Arthur's court. Arthur made him a warrior. Gwenhyvar armed him.

'You three kept the Sword in the Stone of Sovereignty. You bestowed it on Arthur. You gave your voice when it passed to Gwenhyvar.'

'You gave him Caliburn.'

'It was you destroyed the scabbard.'

'I cast my power away, but Arthur keeps the naked sword.'

'So fight against him! Modred is your weapon. You would not reject the child you made?'

Visions of making, in Avalon, of a child at Tintagel, of the Lady lifting a sword for us from a lake, of the scabbard sinking, a baby boy in my arms once more.

'*Tomorrow, Arthur Pendragon will surrender his sword to me.*'

How could she understand?

The flash of victory in her face. Elaine had the Sight, Margawse the will, Morgan the power. Nimue believed she had won us.

The starlight tricked the surface of the water.

No one could win this battle.

'There!' she gasped out. 'I told Modred you would never forgive Arthur.'

Oh, Nimue! How could I answer that?

Her warrior-women rowed her away. I could not suffer the thoughtful gaze of Elaine, Margawse's bitter smile. I stooped inside my tent and searched the dark interior of my travelling-bag.

Taliesin lowered his harp, Teilo half-rose. I gestured them to remain still. It was not darkness or solitude I feared, though I was very afraid.

I took the only thing of Arthur's I still possessed, the shirt he had worn for hunting, which Taliesin stole for me.

Even now, more than a year afterwards, it held the warmth, the smell of Arthur. Old mud crumbled to dust among its creviced fibres. Sweat stained its sleeves. A thread of dark blood showed where a bramble had caught his careless arm. It smelt of life and strength and laughter.

I left the campfire far behind. I walked along the river's bank until it widened into a vast mere. There, where the brook flowed out at a stony ford, I knelt with the last living remembrance of my love in my hands. I dipped it in the cold flowing stream. I watched through dazzled tears all its stains and sweat and impurities swill out into the current that would carry them seawards, on into the ocean, and the ultimate west. The linen between my fingers was pure as a wedding-smock now. Nothing of Arthur left but a chill, clean, bloodless garment.

Once long ago, I knelt at a ford and washed. And Urien Rheged came and got me children. Last night I knelt again, washing a man's shirt in the River Camel, and no one came.

Forty-eight

I am Urien's lady.

Urien, Urbgen, the City-Born.

Early in the thirteenth century the Didot-Perceval *tells how the princely knight Urbain becomes the defender of a ford.*

Urbain is the son of the Queen of Blackthorn. He sets out through the forest in search of adventure. On a tempestuous night he spies a lovely woman riding a mule at high speed. He pursues, and she leads him to her secret castle. There she welcomes him in warmly and pledges him her heart and body in return for his promise to remain with her and her maidens. To him, the castle is surpassingly beautiful, but to all other eyes it is invisible. It stands beside a ford.

Urbain must defend the crossing and challenge all comers.

He fights loyally for his lady for almost a year.

Then Perceval comes. The gallant Urbain calls on a damsel to provide this callow intruder with shield and lance. Alas, he falls to the younger knight's borrowed weapon. His year of delight is ended. It is for Perceval now to defend the lady's ford for a twelvemonth.

But young Perceval has another quest in mind. He refuses.

A terrible crash, a tumult of smoke and shrieks, thick darkness, follow, denoting the destruction of the lady's magic castle. Her voice calls curses down on Perceval. She cries out to Urbain, warning him to flee or lose her love.

A flock of black birds swoops down on Perceval, pitilessly striking at his eyes. Urbain, renewed in courage, joins them in the fray.

Fighting for his life, Perceval pierces one of the birds through, and as it tumbles to the earth it turns into a beautiful woman, dead at his feet.

Before his horrified eyes, her feathered sisters flock to snatch her up and carry her skywards.

Urbain, twice a loser, smiles wryly. Young Perceval need not lament his blow. All is well. These black birds are the fay of the ford and her maidens. They are flying the lady's sister to Avalon. There, their mistress will restore her dead to life.

Following his lady's command, he then departs, leaving Perceval his horse. Soon afterwards, he himself is taken up with great rejoicing to follow the black birds.

The horse disappears too.

Morgan the Fay, they say, allows Arthur to return from Avalon in the form of a raven.

Chapter Forty-nine

Slaughterbridge. Such an insignificant valley, the upper reaches of the Camel. So small a stream to carry this deep-laden barge of grief. The meadows lie soft and quiet. But walk a little way upstream and the valley darkens, a stern cliff rises on one side, the river runs swift over rocks, old hills close in.

Tragedy lay all around us. To the south stood Caer Dimiliock, where my father Gorlois fell trying to defend Ygerne's honour from the hands of Uther Pendragon. Over that western hill, Tintagel, where in the night of her widowhood my mother waited for her husband's executioner to become Arthur's father. Let us finish it here in Cornwall, where we began, Arthur Pendragon and I.

No, this was not my contest yet. First came the men's fight.

The war-band of Arthur the king came over the Cornish skyline, and found his son.

Modred was camped on the bluff above the Camel, facing him, with his back to the sea. Not far left for him to flee. Beyond this coast ships have carried the heroic dead out to the blessed islands in the farthest west.

Pitch here, then, the ragged remnants of your host, my foster-son, with the door of your tent to the east and your weapons sharpened. No peace is possible. You have stolen Gwenhyvar. You have enjoyed the High Queen of Britain. You have known sovereignty.

The old king was cuckolded and widowed by your bigamous wedding. He has lost his crown, he has lost his son, his dreams are dead. The spring tide of Britain has turned. It will never reach to the same high-water mark again, but he'll bear us all down in the terrible grip of his undertow.

Or will he?

Come. Listen, behind the lamp-lit walls of the grey king's tent. Is not this the Arthur of old, Arthur the soldier, Arthur the Red Ravager?

'Well, what's the news from the scouts? Are that pack the beaten curs we thought?'

Bedwyr was exultant. 'We've got them squeezed in our fist like a bundle of old rags. One twist, and they'll fall to threads! Angles, Saxons, Picts, Irish! They can't even talk the same language, or agree on the same type of warfare.'

You could almost hear the grin on his face in Arthur's words. 'You'd back Rome's discipline, eh? The way of Ambrosius and Constantine, the tradition of the British Emperors, against a stew of pagan tribes.'

'Tribes! Since they ran from Winchester there's barely enough of the rabble to put together a clan. We'll overwhelm them at daybreak.'

Arthur's voice was loud with indignation or wine. 'Does that match with my honour? Would you set wolfhounds on to run down a hare? Shall I have it sung that Arthur the Briton got his kingdom back from a boy in unfair battle?'

A hesitation round the cross-legged chieftains. You sensed their eyes questioning each other.

'Modred's no boy.'

'We've borne some heavy losses, too.'

'Great Gawain is dead.'

'Gaheris. Gareth.'

Beloved names dropped like leaves from trees. Too many more lay unnamed. They were numbered in death only as spears, save to the distant wives and mothers who still named them daily in their prayers, pleading for life long after the crows had feasted. Unnamed, save to their vengeful comrades.

'You are not suggesting you'd meet him in single combat?'

Well, why not? Surely Arthur's cause was just? Modred had taken his queen and country. Arthur was the anointed king. The Church was with him, in the person of his chaplain Bishop Bytwini here in the tent, as well as in their prayers. Arthur's invincible Caliburn still lived in his hand.

Was it a father's fatal fondness that made him draw back from a duel at the ford? Or did this king gone past his summer need the cloak of cohorts to keep off the whistling blast of

215

his New Year son? Did he weaken himself with the frailty of pity or fear? Cover it with pride.

'How many divisions does he have left?'

'He could make up six, at the most.'

'And ours?'

'Say, nine.'

Arthur struck his fist so his armour jingled angrily.

'By God, I will not have the bards sing I crushed my own son like an ant under my boot. He'd be the one they'd keen the laments over, while I bore the calumny. The victory shall be mine on the field, and in the feasting hall! Six divisions against six! I'll bring back sovereignty from this day and my warrior's honour.'

Again that pause. The shadows shifted across the tent wall. Did Bedwyr shrug before he said, 'Well, so be it. There's no harm done. We hold the high ground on the east, where the land slopes smoothly. If Modred leaves his perch on the cliffs to cross the river, our reserve of horse can be down the hillside to stop him in a moment.'

'I forbid it. Let Urien of Rheged hold his Northmen off. He has no stomach to fight against his foster-son. Let Owain keep back too.'

Owain? A treacherous weakness of relief flowed through me. So the son the Mothers allowed me was not to fight against the son who was denied me. Owain's spear would not be the one to kill Modred. Did Arthur mistrust that Rheged's dread Raven-Band might yet turn against him in this final battle? Owain was, after all, son of Morgan the Fay.

There were younger but wiser chiefs, Modred's generation.

'Do not despise your adversary, sir. Modred of Good Counsel is a canny strategist. He'll fight you with his head as well as his heart.'

'He has no heart, that would so betray his father.'

His friends could offer no salve for this pain. Bishop Bytwini was present, a warrior in prayer, to recall him to his duty.

'We must first prevent this battle, if it is possible. The man must repent his sacrilege. This war is a scandal. Briton against Briton.'

'Britain against a mongrel pack of scavengers!'

'The king against his sister's son, sire!'

Ah! That was the wine-jug overturned. The bishop had courage. Fathers have killed their sons in many dynasties, but the tie of sister's son is far more sacred. You worked more than blind revenge when you lay with our brother, Margawse my sister. You made a union at once sinful and sacrosanct. He cannot escape that bond.

'Do you deny my right to take back what that skulking whelp has stolen?'

'The Church anointed you. For all your sins, you have ruled us as a Christian king. You have protected our bodies and our buildings, and we in our turn have armoured you with our prayers. If this battle must come tomorrow, you can count on our loyalty. We will do our duty, assault Heaven with prayers for your victory and curse the enemy who opposes you. But I charge you solemnly to seek peace first. Win your son's soul, if you can, as you value your own.'

'All right! I'll offer to spare the puppy's life. Will that content you? Modred to surrender his arms, hand back the crown, take ship to exile?'

The bitterness of a man who knew no terms would be accepted. This battle could not have been avoided, could it?

'And Gwenhyvar?'

Eyes hidden behind his hands. Fists clenched and tearing.

'Gwenhyvar is not my wife or queen. Gwenhyvar is not my . . . Gwenhyvar is not . . .'

No. If Arthur survives this battle, Gwenhyvar . . . is not.

Poor pale frightened Gwenhyvar in her secret cell above the Fowey. She may lie paler yet.

If Arthur should come whole from Camlann . . .

Hush, my love! In darkness, I hugged my arms around myself for pity.

'A parley, then?'

'Tomorrow morning.'

'Who will carry the message to his camp?'

'Is Idawc out there? He knows the traitor. They were initiated into my war-band on the same May Day.'

Chapter Fifty

'Three Fortunate Concealments of the Island of Britain:

'The Head of Brân the Blessed, son of Llyr, which was concealed in the White Hill in London, with its face towards France. And as long as it was in the position in which it was put there, no Saxon oppression would ever come to this Island.

'And Arthur disclosed the Head of Brân the Blessed from the White Hill, because it did not seem right to him that this Island should be defended by the strength of anyone, but by his own.'

'The third of the Three Unfortunate Counsels of the Island of Britain: the three-fold dividing by Arthur of his men with Modred at Camlann.'

'Three Futile Battles of the Island of Britain: and the worst was Camlann, which was brought about because of a quarrel between Gwenhyvar and Gwenhyvach.'

'There was a sad battle, provoked by wanton passion, Camlann, through slaughter and pursuit; and fair Gwenhyvar, lively nurtured, yellow-haired, brought it about.'

The tradition is deeply-rooted, that Camlann was caused by strife among Arthur's women.
Whose word should you believe?

Chapter Fifty-one

Ask Idawc, the Agitator of Britain, how it came about.

Look at him. The curling moustaches, the yellow hair bound back in a high pony-tail, the clan marks blue on cheeks and arms. Fire in his grey-green eyes and his colour high. No disciplined Roman this.

He was eager to take the message. Arthur was offering to come to the water's edge. The old king would talk to Modred face to face. He would steel himself to look into the dark eyes of his son, who had stolen his queen and people from him. More than the Camel between them now, since they last met. Could Arthur really bring himself to offer peace?

His hand fell heavy on Idawc's wrist. The young man flinched and laughed.

'Your touch strikes cold for a summer night, my lord.'

Arthur's voice croaked a little, like a Cornish chough.

'My heart may be warmer than you think. You know my son. He has been brother-in-arms to you since I shaved the pair of you in Caerleon and you took weapons in my service. I thought no more of him that day than that he was Urien's foundling. I came to love him, before I knew he was my own. But you enjoyed the years I wasted, fighting beside him, drinking wine with him, wenching . . .'

'Wenching? Modred? Never. He's as chaste as a nun!'

That chilled them all. Custennin of Dumnonia coughed to cover the chiefs' embarrassment. Arthur whipped his hand away as if a snake had struck him.

Urien's voice came steady, reasonable as always. A true friend. 'Forgive me, Arthur. When Morgan brought the boy home, I thought no more than that she wanted to save some noblewoman's shame. Yes, I suspected it might be Margawse. But only much later that you . . . Well, I have already cast my die against him, after he handed the sword you trusted

219

him with to Gwenhyvar. I couldn't turn him from his path. A young man will always argue with his foster-father. Better a friend of his own age.

'Idawc, you've been his battle-mate before this treachery. Make him see sense. Smooth down his prickly pride so he comes to this parley in a mood to listen. We'll find a way out for him, with honour. The lad has his life before him. He is Arthur's only son. He can afford to wait.'

'You'd still acknowledge him as heir to the throne after this?' Bedwyr was on his feet. From the time they were boys together in Nimue's house he had run with Arthur. Blind loyalty to his hero was all he knew.

But Urien had reared Modred. 'When Arthur has gone, it will be another world. It seems Modred has made the people of Britain love him, in a short space. It was always so in Rheged. In God's time, if they want him, he may make a good king.'

'The people of Britain love him? Witchcraft! Your wife was behind him.'

I heard the pain in Urien's answer. 'They tell me she stayed away from his coronation.'

Lucan's voice pierced the hubbub, like a second barbed spear entering the boar's throat from the opposite side.

'It is true the young man appears unnaturally favoured at winning love. Have you forgotten Gwenhyvar?'

That growl of anger. Custennin turned it to advantage.

'They are saying that Arthur's queen may not be the true Gwenhyvar.'

Ah, so that tale had reached Arthur's camp, had it? Or had he always suspected, since that month he lodged with Gwenhyvach in Cornwall? Was that why he came back flinging himself into war in Gaul and Gwenhyvar into Modred's hands? Did his man's faith in himself falter, like Modred's, when he doubted his woman?

'If she has proved false to her king and husband now, might she not indeed have been false when she married him? Let her go, Arthur. She was never worth you. Let Modred keep her. If she is not the daughter of Leodegran and his queen, she brought no sovereignty in the blood you shed on your marriage-bed.'

Uneasy stillness. They were only half Roman, these men.

Was Uther Pendragon's inheritance alone reason enough to affirm Arthur High King? Would they begin to mistrust the sword we sisters had given him?

'Are you proposing to wed Arthur to Gwenhyvach instead?' Bedwyr was contemptuous; his laugh barked like a buzzard. 'Do you imagine he could go to bed with that crone and wake up in the morning to find a beauty beside him?'

'Men have found joy in stranger marriages than that.' My husband's voice was barely audible. Oh, Urien Rheged, I have wounded you. It has been hard for you to hold Arthur as your king and friend, and Morgan as your wife. You loved us both too well for your own peace.

'Get to their camp,' Bedwyr ordered Idawc, 'before the sun comes up and takes us unprepared.'

Moonlight was clear as day now. The stars barely showed around it. Even this late, scattered camp-fires blazed like dragon's eyes. Sleep would be slow in coming for some, and some would never sleep again. Idawc carried the herald's wand, and the skinned wood gleamed, a pale shoot of life. But brighter sparkled the gold on Idawc's breastplate, the battle-torque with the boar's head at his throat, the studded guard on his forearm. Two spearmen followed him.

He passed out of the old king's camp, into the unlit no-man's-land. This was the most dangerous walk, down into the valley and the rushing ford, that seemed colder and deeper at this hour. Do not blame him if he strutted and jingled his weapons more than was necessary. Better the sentries on Modred's side knew that he was not coming stealthily, as a spy. They heard his horn, and the notes for parley came small and forlorn to ears that were tuned already for the battle-call. They would sleep lightly tonight, these warriors, if they slept at all, with their weapons within reach.

Heraldic staff or not, Modred's sentries in the shadow of the cliff challenged him sharply. Whatever their kings debated, let it be seen that the men on both sides were ready and strung for war. Idawc laughed, a white-toothed grin that bared gums redder than the sap that wept from his alder-rod.

'By Brân! Don't you recognise me? Idawc, son of Mynio, that played hurley with you and Modred, and once gave him a knock on the head that laid him out cold!'

'Idawc the traitor,' the sentry growled.

221

Swift movement of the two spearmen behind their herald. He stayed them with a quick lift of his hand. They were all tense. It would take only a little spark to start a conflagration. But the rules of parley are strict as the rules for single combat. Honour is everything. He was led up the steep path to Modred's tent.

Can you bear to follow?

The flap lifted and a young man stepped outside. He stood with his back to the moon. The peat-dark eyes did not catch the light of the stars.

I do not want to hear this. I do not want to hear Arthur plead with his son. I do not want to hear the old king beg for the last of his life from the young one. How could great Arthur parley for the return of Britain and his queen?

What price would Modred set?

Modred was beaten.

How could I wish my brother not to plead, but to march on and grind this smouldering ember into ashes?

I had fed Modred at my breast.

'Idawc ap Mynio! Have you come back to taunt me? Or would you change sides again?'

Oh, yes. When they picked Idawc, his spear-brother, for this mission, did those grey-bearded veterans remember the jealous pride of the young?

Idawc, left behind to guard Britain, when his brothers were off winning glory in Gaul. Idawc, fired by the young man's hope in a younger king. Pledging his sword with the dream of becoming Modred's war-leader. Idawc, chafing as the news was of peace, of diplomacy, of Modred swearing treaties with Saxons and Angles and Picts. Idawc, riding the lonely frontier, restless to see the dust of an enemy war-host, for his horn to vibrate with the battle-alarm. What honour for a warrior in the pride of youth, with his fame still to make, in a settled confederation of the Islands of Britain? What praise for the Red Ravager in peace?

Fire in his heart then, when he heard that Arthur's fleet was swooping towards the coast. The fighting king, hero of Mount Badon, was alive still, he was returning in vengeance, he and his glorious war-band were not entombed somewhere in Gaul. Modred? His new crown was a mockery, a girl's chaplet of daisies. Modred's word of government, entrusted him by Arthur, a small boy's wooden toy. Arthur was the man, Arthur was the soldier. Arthur had the fighting sword, Caliburn. Gallop then. Leave Modred's service. Be there on the beach. Pledge Arthur your spear again as you did in that first, proud, face-warming, unforgettable day, when the king declared you and Modred his warriors and his men.

Now Idawc must turn his spear on his companions. Modred, so long his friend and newly his prince, swept in from the north. Arthur's band was trapped on the beach. They must fight for their lives. In the first bloody onslaught, as his foot touched once again his native soil, Gawain fell. Blood spurted from his mouth into the tide-washed sand and his shadow covered it with his collapse. He was gone, in that dangerous no-man's-land between high-water mark and low. You would believe the sun had fallen out of heaven. Arthur threw back his head, careless of shield. Before the charging enemy, he howled to the sky like a mad dog.

Idawc was rushing in front of him. His armour took a javelin aimed at Arthur. His leather-stiffened wrist hurled it back and found his mark. A friend was dead.

Old men were dying around Arthur. The young were here.

'Remember me, sire? I am Idawc! Bless my weapon.'

Had the tide turned again?

Why did Arthur choose this young man to persuade Modred to a truce? Idawc's voice was scornful. 'You assured us Arthur would not return, but you see he has. Your legitimacy fails. He holds the sword.'

'I keep the sword of government. He has only Caliburn.'

'Only! The weapon that won him twelve great battles, that took Mount Badon? Caliburn is all the legitimacy Arthur needs. You're beaten, like a fox trapped in a hole that has no back door. You can lay down your puny sword in disgrace or leap over the cliff at Tintagel. There is no other escape.'

'My father sent you with this message?'

Idawc's tone assumed a mockery of formality. 'King Arthur of Britain greets Modred the traitor. He will meet you tomorrow morning on the banks of the Camel, to set out the terms for your surrender.'

'Just that?'

'Did you expect more? Did you think he would bargain

223

with you for your life? Man, you stole his wife and crown and sold our country to her enemies.'

'I sought to govern in wisdom. My . . . father . . . handed over the sword of regency to me with all solemnity. Gwenhyvar was High Queen. I laid the sword where it always belonged, in her good hands. She chose to end her marriage to her consort. I, of all men, could most believe his infidelity. I married her. I rule beside her now. She is my legitimacy, more than the fighting-sword she gave me.'

'Gwenhyvar! Haven't you heard? They say she's Leodegran's bastard and Gwenhyvach should have been High Queen.'

That bitter wound Modred could not admit, though blood was blinding the eyes that had once discerned so wisely.

'Gwenhyvar is true! She is, and always has been, Britain's royal lady. I defend her right and honour against all who slander her!'

'You defend your own tin-pot crown. Or you would, if your Germanic friends hadn't scurried back east behind their hills at the first glimpse of a real British war-host.'

'Is this herald's talk? Why has he sent you to me? I have heard bards' satires that would raise smaller blisters on a man's face. Does he think Britain's woes can be healed with scorn and bitterness and taunts?'

'Healed? Did you think we had come to Cornwall for healing? Arthur conquered you at Winchester. You have no hope left. Arthur has come to seize back what is his.'

'He cannot do that. He can enjoy the whole of Britain, as I would have done, by the marriage of east and west. If he tries to rape her, the spirit of one or both of them will die. Britain will lose her wholeness. Even the Church of the West would not send saints across the eastern frontier to save a Saxon. Someone must end the bitterness and close the circle. That was my mother Morgan's teaching.'

'Morgan . . . !' His cruel, mocking laughter spoke for all Arthur's men. 'That mischief-maker? You'd fight us to the death for that old bitch? Is that your answer?'

Modred was known the length of Britain for his wise counsel. Yet it cost my foster-son dearly to answer this levelly and with self-control.

'Tell my father I respected his deeds once. But if that is

how he speaks, I am determined never to surrender my sword of good government to his sword of war. Let him rip it from my dying hand first. I can see that his army is stronger than ours. But I will not surrender and witness all I have worked for undone. I would rather he killed me.'

'Arthur gave you life, as he gave you that sword you boast of. He will take both back.'

'Does he forget he tried to take my life once before, when I was born? Tonight, I am alive, and I hold the Sword from the Stone my mother gave him. Tell him to remember his grey hairs. His time is over.'

'That is your answer? Meet him at the river then, mid-morning. Your anger should put a good edge on his own weapon.'

'My fighting-weapon will go sheathed to that parley. Be sure that yours are. One naked blade, and I will warn my warriors to storm to my defence and overwhelm Arthur's traitors till the Camel runs with shameful blood.'

'We know the rules of honour as well as you do, boy.'

Idawc turned with a swirl of his green cloak. He was well pleased. Swift the steps that brought him back to the river. The ford was crossed in three leaps and he was in Arthur's tent.

'Well? Will the lad see sense? Is he grateful for the mercy I'm offering him?'

'The traitor will meet you tomorrow morning. But he will yield you nothing. He taunts you that you have outrun your day. He says he has not fled here but drawn you down into the trap of Cornwall. The Mothers will not allow you to slay their Son. He trusts your sister Morgan.'

The shadow of a cup was hurled across the lamplight. Wine splashed the tent-wall.

'Always that accursed name!'

'Parley all you like. She will not let him surrender. You cannot be free of Black Morgan till you have killed Modred.'

225

Chapter Fifty-two

I am the mother of Owain.

Among the collection of tales in the Mabinogion *is the curiously technicoloured thirteenth-century* Dream of Rhonabwy.

Our hero sets out on a quest with two companions. On a filthy night they seek shelter in an even filthier homestead. The floor is treacherous. Where there is not a bump there is a hole, and it is so slippery with cow-muck and urine a man can hardly stand. They wade through dung and holly branches that the cows have chewed to seek a refuge on the floor of the main hall. A dusty dais at each end, and a sulky fire on one wall. No hostess to greet them save a snaggle-toothed crone, throwing a lapful of husks on the fire to keep off the cold and filling the place with choking smoke.

Not a civil word can they get out of her. The master of the house comes home, a bald, wizened, red-haired man and a skinny purple-faced little woman with him, carrying sticks. No supper but bread and cheese and a cup of watery milk. No bed but such foul straw, with branches sticking through it, as the oxen have left unchewed, and it is barely covered by a threadbare blanket alive with fleas, a half-empty pillow and a dirty pillowcase.

No bed, that is, save one. Tormented by bites and scratches, Rhonabwy claims for himself the couch he was not offered. At the far end of the hall a yellow ox-hide has been spread alone on the boards of the other dais. Here he betakes himself to sleep, and dreams.

He enters a land which is, and is not, Britain. A familiar plain leads to the Severn. It is peopled with heroes, larger than life, already beyond the grave. Certainly the young man who challenges him, with yellow curling hair and yellow horse, all tricked out in the green of the fir tree and the yellow of the broom-flower, knows already what he has to repent. He is Idawc, the Embroiler of Britain. This is the spirited young envoy who craved too much for battle. He falsified the message of Arthur to Modred. When the king would speak the kindest words he could to his son and nephew, to bring peace to the Island of Britain, then Idawc spoke them the ugliest way he knew and brought about the Battle of Camlann.

He has served seven years' penance at the Blue Stone for that, but he has more wonders to show. He conducts Rhonabwy to a warriors' camp beside the Severn. Here is Arthur the king, with his bishop Bytwini and the son of Cei decked out in black and white. Old names from story come and go across this scene, and as in dreams, these heroes are both here in camp beside the Severn and yet will be found fighting Osla Big-Knife at midday at the battle of Mount Badon.

Now Idawc sets the scene for Arthur and Owain.

Arthur's servant is called for, a rough, red, ugly man with a bristling moustache. He rides a red horse and carries a handsome pack.

Here on the riverbank he spreads out a fair white mantle of ribbed brocaded silk with an apple of red gold at each of its corners. If a man wrapped himself in it he would be invisible. On it, he sets a great golden chair.

Arthur seats himself, and says to Owain, son of Urien, standing beside him, 'Owain, will you play gwyddbwyll with me?'

My son accepts the challenge.

The gwyddbwyll set is laid before them, a silver board with golden pieces. The game is going well for Arthur. A messenger all in gold comes hasting up from a white and red pavilion that bears a red-eyed black serpent. His news is not to Arthur but to Owain.

'Lord, is it by your will that the emperor's men are molesting your Ravens?'

Owain lifts his eyes. 'Sire, you heard the boy. Call your men off my little Ravens.' He waits for Arthur's move.

'Play on.'

They start a second game. Another squire in yellow and red comes hot-foot from a yellow pavilion that sports a bright red lion.

'Lord, the emperor's young men have started killing your Ravens.'

Owain's voice is low and steady. 'Call them off, my uncle.'

'Continue the game.'

The third round is in progress when a furious lad in green comes

227

at a canter from a spotted yellow pavilion surmounted by a golden eagle. He carries a speckled yellow spear with a newly sharpened head and a conspicuous standard on it. He speaks with rage.

'My lord Owain, the most notable of your Ravens have already been slain. Others are so hurt they cannot lift their wings from the ground. How long will you let this continue?'

'I ask you once more,' says Owain to his king. 'Call off this slaughter.'

Does Arthur's hand hover above the board for a moment?

'Our game is not done yet. Your move, lad. See if you can get yourself out of that trap.'

Owain's hand reaches obediently to the board, but his head has turned to the lad with the spear. 'Be off with you. And where the battle is thickest, raise our standard. Let God decide.'

Still Arthur is winning. The two contestants address their attention to the fourth game. Now fortunes turn. The air is torn with the shrieks of men and the croaks of exultant birds. When the next messenger comes galloping up to the chiefs on the riverbank, riding a parti-coloured horse of dapple grey and red and yellow, he wears a yellow-red leopard on his helmet and his green and red spear is scarlet with the blood of ravens and black with their feathers. His voice trembles.

'Sire! Owain's Ravens have turned upon your warriors. They are swooping from the sky and tearing off the men's heads and eyes and ears and arms.'

Arthur angrily turns to the younger man.

'Stay your Ravens.'

Owain lifts his eyebrows.

'My move, I think.'

The next game zigzags across the squares. Valuable pieces fall and are lifted away. Into this calculating silence a new commotion erupts, screams of agony and caws of triumph. A pale horse is coming, and now there is heavy green armour with a surcoat of yellow on the rider and a flame-tongued yellow-red lion on his golden helm. He bears blood on the new head of his ashen spear.

'My king, the Ravens are carrying your men up into the air. They are tearing them apart between them and letting the pieces of flesh fall to the ground. If you do not end it, there will be no heroes left to defend the Island of Britain.'

Now it is Arthur's turn to plead, 'Stop them, damn you!'

'Let us play this game to the end,' says Owain, unsmiling.

When the sixth lad comes, on a white and red horse with yellow-speckled armour, himself wearing a black and white cloak with purple fringes and weeping with rage under the image of a griffin on his crystal-studded helm, the king is encircled.

'Great Arthur! It is too late. They are all dead!'

A lift of Owain's hand. His standard is lowered. The glutted birds wheel from the carnage and their shadow passes to leave a bloody peace. In the moment before his final defeat, Arthur snatches the last few pieces from the board and crushes them into powder in his mighty fist.

Horsemen arrive. The Battle of Badon is over, and Osla Big-Knife sues for truce. Bards sing the praises of Arthur. Twenty-four asses appear, loaded with tribute of gold and silver. The bards — a broad hint, this — are rewarded with the asses.

What does it mean?

Does Owain my son once seek revenge against Arthur? Does he take arms against him at Badon? Or at Camlann? Where does all the flower of Britain's manhood fall?

Owain is my child. No matter how he is goaded, no matter how much blood his Ravens shed in revenge, he cannot be allowed to win. Arthur must sweep the board, even though he smashes the golden king, himself, to get the victory.

Save your sympathy. Rhonabwy is waking on the yellow ox-hide. It was only a dream. It is too early to weep for Owain ap Urien yet. Owain is history. We know he dies three-quarters of a century after Arthur fell at Camlann. Taliesin sings his elegy.

> 'In the grave below is
> much-sung great renown,
> the wings of the dawn
> like shining javelins:
> for no equal will be found
> to a lord of dazzling joy,
> enemy-reaper, grasper.'

So whose were the Ravens which turned against Arthur?

Chapter Fifty-three

What purpose can there be in talking now?

They are like men who stand on opposite mountain-tops, bellowing at each other across an unbridgeable whirlpool.

There have been bridges over other chasms, painful and perilous. The edge of a sword, a narrow plank beneath the rushing torrent, and the abyss is crossed, the gatekeeper is overpowered, the prison falls, the Lady is restored.

How can that be done now?

The taunts have stung like horse-flies, and the swelling grows, hard and itching.

Modred has fulfilled his destiny, Merlyn's prophecy. This is the flaw in Arthur's life that has finally cracked the finest jewel apart. Few can know how Modred grieves in his shadowed heart that he was made only for this. Should I have kept the truth from him? Yet how could I not have told him? How could he be my love-gift to Arthur, how could I rejoice my brother's heart with the son he lacked, and the lad not knowing whose he was? I bred him up to be a king's son. Should I have guessed he would choose to be the king?

How could I know that every song I sang to the little boy to praise his father Arthur, every tale of his valiant deeds and battles won, all his fame for generosity, honour, justice, would add fresh wounds to the first vital one when Modred learned the truth? This is the Arthur who rejected you. This is the father whose son you are not fit to be. This is the light in which you cannot live. This glory is not for you.

Black night will not draw back its advance because it sees the majesty of the setting sun. Modred will not yield to Arthur.

Still, pity might yet work a miracle. Arthur has won himself fresh renown from the war in Gaul. He has thrown back Modred's attack on the beaches, hounded him out of

230

Winchester, sent those untried allies running back behind the crumbling frontiers of the east and north. He is winning, and success can make a great man magnanimous. He will agree to a truce, send Modred to Brittany, where there are kinsmen to watch him for further treason. Keep him from meddling in Britain with the chancy Saxons and Picts and Cornish. He can still be named Arthur's heir. The youth has diplomatic skills. Fill up the time that remains to the old king with face-saving occupation for the young. This is flesh of his flesh. Arthur would spare himself.

But the Angles and Saxons have crossed the divide that Arthur set after Badon.

Great Gawain and his brothers are dead.

And there is Gwenhyvar.

This is the wound that is slowly killing Arthur. Crowns are often got by the sword and may be won back so. Arthur Pendragon was our Emperor of Battles by that right arm alone, before I made Ygerne reveal that he was Uther's son. He claimed his right to rule as much by spilled Saxon blood as by his mother's. But gentle Gwenhyvar never needed to lift a sword to prove her royalty.

Warfare has taken Arthur away from Gwenhyvar. It cannot bring her back. Arthur may tell himself he does not want her now, that she was always false.

But was she? Is Gwenhyvach lying?

Did Modred force his queen to sin, or was she all too willing?

Arthur's heart aches with unanswered questions.

He cannot let Modred have what was once his.

In bitterness then, father and son walk towards each other, one down the sloping flower-strewn meadows, the other out from the darkness of the cliff.

Neither of them knows that they have both lost her. She, who was once the Sovereignty of Britain, has vowed herself to a solitary bed. She lies hidden from all men's eyes, husbandless now, in the house of religion where I left her. Without her, both these kings are widowers, and dispossessed.

Nimue knows now, standing in her chariot on the height, the sun catching her spear. This will be almost the last you see of her. She gave young Arthur his arms at the dawn of his manhood. She goaded Modred into this doomed battle. When they fall, she will disappear, and surface sometime later to inspire another young hero.

Is it hopeless then? But all humans will hope. These two approaching the ford of the Camel will become legends greater than all other heroes of Britain. This morning, they are both more and less than that. They have the limitations of mortal men, and the possibilities. One at least will not believe the inevitable.

Such a sunny morning for tragedy. The heather is purple on the distant heights of Bodmin Moor. Behind Modred the sky is brilliant with light thrown up from the sea. The little river Camel winks among cresses and bulrushes. Too close a valley this, for mighty armies. There are hundreds of men on Modred's side, a thousand and more on Arthur's. You may find it strange that in these ancient times such a handful of heroes could brand the names of battlefields on history. The warriors watching mistrustfully above Camlann know many of those facing them on the opposite bank. Without visors, the wilder of them unhelmeted, they recognise the men they are about to kill.

Like two lovers naked beneath their outer robes, then, Modred and Arthur come to their tryst. Yet magic has raised a hedge of mist between them. They must not be allowed to see each other truly. A dart of love might fell this ogre of bitterness and change the Dolorous Castle into the Joyous Keep.

They cannot approach each other alone. Each king comes guarded by a prickly mail-clad retinue. Blades have been sharpened for this meeting and hang loosely sheathed. Men, jealous of honour, ambitious for advancement, grieving for fallen friends. Warriors fiercely loyal to their leader, chiefs too proud to admit they may have chosen the wrong man.

This is not the blessed Isle of Apples. The worm is in the core already. The fruit is about to fall.

Do not judge them too harshly. These two men's tangled histories have been a tale of hurt and treachery from their conception. Why should it be different for them today at Camlann? Where were the good fays at their births to bestow a happy ending? I, Margawse, Elaine? Or Nimue? Could we have changed this?

Follow their paths, then, down to opposite banks of the river, through the long bright grass and the sun-warmed stones. Their war-bands watch from the high ground, alert, suspicious, in an uneasy silence. Bedwyr, Lucan, Custennin, Caradawc, Urien, Owain. These aristocratic men have been bred only for warfare. They distrust peace. The horses paw and snuffle, as restless as their riders. You could believe they were as eager for combat, as swift to strike with their hooves, as single-minded.

The slopes below them are bare of men and mounts on either side of the water. Once juicy pastures, from which the herds of cattle have been hurried away. Nothing to see now but tall red sorrel and gaudy buttercups. Yet the lush grass masks a secret, less intelligent animal life.

'King Arthur recognises Modred the Prince.'

'Modred, High King of Britain, gives good day to his father.'

How much the old king yearns to cast aside his dignity, the young one to retain his.

'It's over, boy. You thought I was dead before my time, did you? Your motley army is hacked to pieces. The brave few that are left to you are cornered here. The same host that defeated them at Winchester has come to finish the task. No need to condemn your men to die. We will accept your surrender.'

'Have you forgotten that I am your child? It was not in your dream that I should be given up to you, was it? Arthur's blood will not own himself bested, as Arthur would not.'

'Do you throw that old story back in my face again? I was younger than you are now, the year you were born. For the love of heaven, boy! I am not an ogre. I don't want to cut off your beard to trim my cloak-tail. Lay down your sword and you'll be honourably treated, as befits my son.'

But if we sisters had surrendered him as a baby, it would have cost him his life. And what treatment befits what Modred has done to Arthur?

'You presume a power you no longer have, venerable father. It is the victor who will dictate the terms after today. I am the May-King now. The Queen of Summer has blessed my cause. The Lady of the Lake fights on my side. Your own sister, Morgan the Wise . . .'

233

'She was always faithless!'

Yes, faithless to save this one surviving son of Arthur. Yes, faithless to bring these two together at last. Yes, faithless to think that I could give my heart to both of them and not be torn in two.

Which will I bless?

'I see my father fears the powers I can name.'

'Puppy! I'll show you how I despise your powers. Do you see King Urien on the heights with all his Northmen? Do you see Owain Enemy-Reaper? Your foster-father and your foster-brother, true men whom your rebellion shames! I have excused them from staining their swords with their household's blood. We will fight you, man for man. Two thirds of my victorious army against your tired tail-enders. And I will take from you the sword that is mine by sunset without loss of my honour.'

'You are old, my father, and your judgment fails you. I do not need mercy. I have my guarantee of victory: Gwenhyvar the High Queen.'

He must affirm her the true Gwenhyvar. Who knows what he believes? How could either of them tell that Modred has already lost her in his turn?

You cannot imagine the pain it costs Arthur to speak.

'That smiling adulteress! She has given neither of us what she promised. Give her up, son. Not to me, but to the fire. She was never worthy of Britain. Let not a mere woman stand between us. There are few enough of our young men left. For her sake, Gawain is dead, and Gareth and Agravain and Gaheris. Only you remain.'

But Owain, my own son, is not dead yet. He names my sister's children only. And doubt rises within me. Would he turn to Margawse, now, and make her his queen?

Blood hammers in my head.

Innocently the butterflies flutter from flower-heads, disclosing the tapestries of their wings. Small lacquered ladybirds climb dizzying grass stems. Ants march through the dusty soil.

High overhead men's voices boom. Summer heat warms their helmets and perhaps their hearts. Will there come a point when the kings have parleyed too long and the high tension of warfare slackens in their nerves and the sun has moved too far to mark the day of Camlann? The waiting armies fidget and begin to mutter. Sunlight dances on gilded trappings and on serviceable steel.

It could soon be over. The long book of Arthur's battles will be closed. The old warriors will hang up their shields, and only the bards will grow rich from the spoils of war. Arthur and Modred will come to a painful, damaged reconciliation. Pride will be patched up. If I could quell the red rage rising in my heart, I could help this healing.

Small fish swim in brown pools, deaf to the voices that call across the river. The bees are busy in the clover; Camlann to them means only honey. Through the sun-bright grass a sleepy adder coils towards a favourite stone.

And Idawc ap Mynio moves his weight from one restless leg to another. The shadow of his heel descends across the adder's path. So small a shift, to bring about annihilation.

Too quick those fangs to strike. Too sharp the pain to be forgiven. Territory has been invaded. Flesh has been violated. His sword is out of its sheath. Sunlight blazes on the blade. The serpent is severed with one blow. And a shout shatters the peace as the signal flashes up to the watching armies. Treachery! War!

The eager hosts descend like thunderclouds. The blood of innocent insects stains the soil, crushed beneath the onrushing hooves.

Chapter Fifty-four

The Morrigan. The Irish Raven-goddess of war.

Oh yes, if you know anything at all about Celtic mythology this is the one you have been waiting for, isn't it?

Morgan, the Morrigan. How avidly you seize upon their similar sounds. It is obvious, isn't it? This must be my true origin, long before the chronicles and romances were written down. This fits the malevolent character of Morgan the Fay.

Mor Rigan. The Great Queen.

The Goddess is three and she is one.

She appears as Ana, Badb, Macha. Or else as Macha, Badb and the Morrigan herself.

> *'Badb and Macha, rich their store,*
> *Morrigan, confusion and war.'*

They are ambiguous.

Ana. The Mother of Plenty. Twin mountain peaks are her paps In Britain we know her as the hag Black Annis, who devours children and hangs their skins on an oak tree to dry.

Badb, the 'Boiling'. Does she keep the life-giving cauldron? She is more usually the Scald-Crow of Battle. She foretells disaster. She plots the fight. In battle she darkens the sky. She perches upon a stone and exults in the slaughter. When her sister the Morrigan tries to keep the Ulster hero Cuchulainn from his last battle, Badb disguises herself as lovely Niam, the woman Cuchulainn can never refuse. She urges him on to fight.

Macha. Daughter of Strangeness, son of Ocean.

Two Otherworld horses rise from a lake in front of Cuchulainn. After a brief struggle they submit to his powerful hand. The pair are thereafter devoted to him for life. They are Black Sainglend and the Grey of Macha.

Her city is Emain Macha. One story makes her a war-goddess, protectress of Ulster. She forces their enemies to build her fortress.

In a different tale, she marries a farmer. Crunniuc is a widower with a household of sons. Macha simply arrives, a beautiful woman walking in off the hills and over the threshold. She makes herself at home and sets his house to rights. At the end of the day she comes to his bed. He's a lucky man. She brings him comfort and wealth.

Macha is fleet of foot, she is fertile, she is fearless. She bestows a blessing.

The Ulstermen are holding a fair. The world and his wife are there. Crunniuc is going, of course, dressed up in his holiday clothes. But Macha will stay at home. Her belly is swollen with child, and she is near her time. She bids him farewell and warns him not to say anything foolish.

At the end of the feast day, the king's own chariot and horses are brought on to the racetrack. They win the prize. All over the field people are exclaiming, 'Nothing in the world is so fast as those horses.'

Crunniuc brags, 'My wife is faster.'

A king's reputation is at stake. Crunniuc must make good his boast or die.

The summons comes to Macha. A great misfortune, the way she is today, but she will save her husband.

The labour pains come on her as she enters the fairground. She pleads with the men to wait, in the sacred name of the mothers who bore each one of them. There is no pity for her. The king asks her name. Macha, she tells him, and that name and those of her children will mark a curse upon this place for ever.

Now they are straining at the starting mark of the cursus. Macha is matched against the horses harnessed to the king's chariot. The race is on.

The track is long, the burden of her womb exceptionally heavy, the pace relentless.

Yet, since that is what the men demand of her, Macha exerts herself to the uttermost. These Ulstermen do not feel the anguish she is suffering. For them and their pride, she runs the race, hurling herself in front of the king's chariot at the finishing line, and wins. All horses own Macha their Queen.

For these men and their cruelty, her body splits in pain there on the track in front of the staring crowd. Twins are born, a son and a daughter.

For these men and their heartlessness, Macha dies. With her last breath she screams a curse on the Ulstermen listening. Four nights and five days, in the hour of their tribe's greatest need, the same pangs of childbirth she has suffered shall fall upon these warriors too, for nine generations.

Only Cuchulainn and his descendants are spared.

The place is called Emain Macha, the Twins of Macha, from that day.

The Morrigan. The Great Queen. The Queen of Ghosts.

Women and water are essential, changeable and dangerous. She is a shape-shifter.

At Samain the great god Dagda comes to the River Unius. He finds a woman with nine loosened tresses of hair down her back. The Morrigan is washing herself in the river, with one foot on the north bank and one on the south. The two of them fall to conversing. She mates with him. She brings him her magic aid.

It is dangerous to refuse her love.

She comes to the hero Cuchulainn as a woman of surprising form wrapped in a many-coloured mantle. She has loved him for the record of his deeds and she offers herself with all her goods and cattle. He is too busy with warfare to want a woman.

In warfare itself she will be his help, she tells him.

'It was not for putting my trust in a woman's aid that I took this job in hand,' he scoffs at her.

It will go harder with him if she fights against him.

Cuchulainn wakes in the night to hear a terrible cry from the north. He falls out of bed and rushes out of the house just as he is, with his wife chasing after him holding his clothes and weapons.

Across the plain he races until he catches up with a chariot drawn by a one-legged red horse with the pole passing clean through its body.

In the chariot is a woman in red, red herself, even to the eyebrows of her, and a great crimson mantle sweeping the ground behind her. A big ugly man is walking along beside her, wearing a crimson coat and carrying a forked stick on his back. He is driving a cow away.

The guardian hero of Ulster won't have that. He challenges the man, 'That cow is not pleased for you to be taking her.'

'What is that to you?' the woman replies. 'She doesn't belong to you or yours.'

238

'All the cows of Ulster are mine to keep,' Cuchulainn tells her.

He demands their names, but she answers him in riddles. So he leaps on the chariot and sets his feet on her two shoulders and his spear on the parting of her hair. She will tell him only she is a satirist and the cow is her reward for a poem she made. He has been warned, but he still demands to hear that poem.

'Get off me then,' and he jumps to stand between the two wheels.

It is, of course, a song of insult. A satirist's words can wound a man as sorely as any weapon. Cuchulainn is about to leap on her to avenge his hurt. In that instant, the woman, chariot, man, horse and cow all disappear.

And then he spies her, on a branch close by. She has turned into — wouldn't you expect? — a crow.

If he had known she was the vengeful Morrigan he would never have let her get away so easily. But still she taunts him. Whatever he had tried to do to her, it would only have brought him ill luck.

Now she has his fate in her keeping. The cow she was driving has come from the dreaded Otherworld cave of Cruachan. This cow is going to mate with the Brown Bull of Cuailgne. A calf will be born from the union. Until it is one year old, so long has Cuchulainn left to live. That calf will cause the fatal Cattle Raid of Cuailgne.

They taunt each other.

In the thick of battle, she'll hinder every movement of the hero. If he fights in the ford she will be an eel around his legs.

He will bruise her against the green stone of the ford.

She will become a ravening grey wolf, and take the flesh from his right hand as far as his left.

He will break her leg with a cast of his sling, and she shall never have help from him.

She will turn herself into a magical white heifer with red ears. Fifty pairs of heifers like her, linked together with bronze chains, shall be wading in the same pool of the river. They will stampede into the middle of the combat, bringing confusion, and Cuchulainn's head will be severed that day.

He will gouge out her eye with the point of his spear.

Yet the night before Cuchulainn's last battle, the Morrigan breaks his chariot in an effort to keep him at home.

When he persists in going, his faithful horse, the Grey of Macha, struggles to resist being harnessed to the war-chariot and weeps tears of blood.

A female satirist begs him not to go. Thrice fifty queens lament and beat their hands. His foster-mother's cup of milk turns to blood. He passes two beautiful maidens grief-stricken as they wash a bloody garment at the ford.

These women would save his life. But there are others.

On his way to the battle he meets three crones, each ritually blinded in one eye. They are cooking a dog with spells on spits of rowan. They invite him to eat. There are two 'geis' on him, two sacred prohibitions. To break either is death. He must never pass a cooking hearth without sharing the food. He must never eat the flesh of a dog, his namesake.

He tries to refuse the food. The crone who holds it out to him is insulted. Cuchulainn takes the dog's shoulder-blade from her left hand and eats. He is doomed.

The battle is bloody. Cuchulainn receives his death-wound.

With the last of his strength the hero straps himself to a standing stone. He will die on his feet, with his sword in his hand, facing his enemies. While his heart still beats, there is a crow perched on the top of a stone nearby, lamenting. She will not leave him while he has breath in his body. As Cuchulainn dies, the crow soars into the sky.

At his master's death, Black Sainglend gallops from the battlefield and plunges into the lake from which the horses once rose, making it seethe and boil. The Grey of Macha is wounded too. He bids his master farewell and follows his companion under the water.

Not till the smaller birds come to perch on the dead hero's shoulders does his enemy Lugaid dare to come forward to cut off his head. As he approaches, the sword falls from the lifeless grasp of Cuchulainn and severs Lugaid's hand with its last stroke.

You may ignore these ambiguities in the Morrigan's character. Her reputation is that she is bloody, vindictive, an implacable man-hater.

What does it matter if, in the beginning, she was a goddess of fertility and the protectress of warriors?

Mor Rigan. The Great Queen. The British Rigantona.

Is she Morgan?

The scholars still dispute. Some see Celtic mythology at every turn in the Arthurian path. Others are sceptical.

They say that by the time my story is written down in Britain, the language has softened. 'Mor Rigan' would mutate into 'Mor Rian'. I should be 'Morien', not 'Morgan'. Our British 'Rigantona' becomes 'Rhiannon', who is also forced to play the role of a horse.

Can the Morrigan really have been the pattern for Geoffrey's Morgen in Avalon? The Raven of Battle for his fairy healer?

Writers have seized upon the idea with relish.

She makes for a more exciting story, doesn't she?

Chapter Fifty-five

This is the day of death. We have come to our final flowering. Here is true tragedy, sprung from a central stem, rooted in character, fed by our origins. This is the name that will beat through history like the sound of the solemn drum.

Camlann, Camlann.

Look at them. Nimue galloping in her chariot along the hilltop, brandishing her spear, calling up valour from the army, calling down vengeance from the skies. The sunlight catches her golden breastplate. She is brave and wonderful. This is the Lady who has shielded the lovers. She is a dangerous woman. Changeable Nimue, who once armed Arthur, who protected and advised him when he was green and malleable. He was insufficiently grateful. He chose the Church.

She has not aged. She has turned from Arthur's grey hairs to Modred's black. She feeds on youth.

My ravens are black and hungry. But they will soon be glutted. Then the field will fall silent. It will be over.

Whose guardian will Nimue be next?

But now the men bellow and the horses scream and the weapons hack through armour to flesh.

On the opposite ridge, the Church's phalanx. Christ's white-robed druids lift their cross, like a sword reversed. 'Michael the Archangel, fight for us! Tread the pagan dragon under your heel.'

Does the Goddess who gave us birth also require these deaths?

We sprout and wither. Earth to earth. Life for life.

Arthur is a dangerous champion for the Christian cause. He has been a thief and a brigand in his youth, the Red Ravager. He tried to violate Saint Cadoc's Christian sanctuary; he killed the monk-historian Gildas's brother. But who else was there for them to turn to when the keels were grounding, when the Saxons and Angles were marching, when the Picts swarmed over the Wall, when the Irish came raiding? Priests and nuns fell at the altar, the church steps ran with martyred blood, the first precious centuries of faith and learning guttered like a candle-flame as the door opened on the night. Who could stop it?

Who but the strength, the laughter, the warlike zest, the ready sword of Arthur the soldier, Arthur our leader of battles, Arthur the Briton? It was not a chivalrous Arthur of the banqueting hall, presiding over Round Table and tournament, that they needed. It was a younger, a more ancient, Arthur. Never mind if the people believe he is half a god himself, with tales of his hounding Cat Palug into the sea or the boar Twrch Trywth across half Britain, and all the mighty hunters of legend at his heels. So much the better if these tales of him terrify the enemy.

Today the Church pays her debts.

Modred the pagan made an alliance with the strangers. Arthur the Christian slew them. Nothing is simple.

The rage is in his blood now; it is a fearsome sight. How could he fight this war otherwise?

No fury is visible in Modred's face. His is too vulnerable a soul to be exposed naked to the sun. A young man under an iron control. What wells of bitterness or grief chill his passion? How little have I known him? What is he thinking as he seeks out his father in the thickest of the fight?

What can any of these bawling men think as they heave their weapons in the heat of battle but, 'This is my death approaching. This is the blade that will finish me. This man is my slayer, unless I kill him first.'

Brother against brother. Fosterlings fighting. Father and son. Is this the Matter of Britain? Where is wisdom and justice? Where is chivalrous love?

It is waste; it is folly.

What else could they do?

It is glorious war.

Look down on this battlefield and see the human condition, bitterly acted out, the pattern of nobility fatally flawed, Arthur is brought to this reckoning by one youthful sin.

There is the horse, obedient between his knees. There is

the stabbing spear. There is Arthur drawing his sword to finish a man, to smite at splintering shields, to clear a circle round him.

Caliburn cannot be vanquished, can it? Why, then, am I sick with fear? Why am I screaming to them like Nimue? If Arthur cannot be brought down by force of arms, what is there left to dread but treachery? Would I want him to die in his bed, old, crippled and bitter, his sons dead before him, like King Llywarch Hen?

All day they struggle and bleed on the slippery sides of Camel's banks. The sea-mist creeps inland to cover this shame, this sorrow. The sun is dimmed. The shadows of horses gallop to aid the ghosts of warriors locked in death-holds. The blades ring hollowly on jagged shields and the javelins part the air with the whistle of expiring breath. The crows are gathering, silent, watchful, shuffling on the branches of the elm trees, waiting their time.

I wait my time.

No pity in either of them now. Two loves more cruel in their indignation, their disappointment, fuel the sparks that fly from steel. Cover it over. We will witness no quarter, no plea for mercy. Let them finish it here.

And the mist comes.

Nimue's curses and the Christian priests' prayers are lost in the cloud on the hilltops now. What shall we do when the long day ends, and the stars come out and our hope lies mutilated at the water's edge? What will be left of the Island of the Mighty?

And I? Come lower; stand under the trees with us. I kept vigil when Arthur and Modred were born. I must see them die. Margawse, Elaine and I, holding hands here, cold flesh to flesh, feeling the earth of Cornwall under our feet fed with fresh blood, tears on our cheeks like rain, chanting in broken voices, singing the dying home.

They have met. In a stillness of anger too deep for words. The blunted spears thrust. The broken shields are advanced. Their weary horses stagger and sidestep. What weight of sorrow drives their aching muscles on?

Aah!

Arthur's spear has gone in. The merciless shaft revolves, retracts, in a gush of too-bright blood. The old king is not so staled with battle that might has failed his arm. Modred is down. He kneels on the earth like a dutiful son, weeping for pity more than pain. Arthur is unhorsed beside him. The thin grey daylight shows horribly through the gaping javelin-wound. The father could stand and watch his son die. But Caliburn must strike the final stroke, clean to the neck.

Those lips, that once sucked my breast, bubble like a baby, but too darkly. You would not think Modred's lungs had breath enough for one more blow.

Now Arthur stands, staring down like a man amazed. No grief, no agony of pain, no tears on his face, only a dead-faced wonder. This was his child, and now he has no son. Who has robbed him?

His warrior's body has forgotten the cunning drilled in him since boyhood. His shield hangs useless at his side. And Modred's hilt quivers like a strange protuberance from Arthur's guts.

Blood has choked Modred's mouth. He has no last word for his father. Only that slow and feeble thrust below the rim of breastplate. This is his final statement. His hands leave his sword. His spirit leaves the world. It is over. We are finished.

Caliburn has got Arthur the victory. He will never need it again.

There will be pain soon.

Bedwyr and Lucan come, looming like giants out of the fog. Their shout of anguish now is louder than their king's. Arthur hides his fast-clouding eyes on his friend's shoulder.

'Take me away,' he begs. 'Let no one find me thus.'

These men are loyal. Bedwyr knows what must be done. Shriek now, to cover his drawing out of that sword, the humiliating moans of a royal hero hastily strapped and hoisted on his horse. Lucan bites his lips till the blood runs, as he heaves that weight up. He is wounded too. But he will put his king's need first, though it kills him. They lead the horse away slowly into the fog, supporting Arthur. And when we sisters unstop our ears the bird-headed trumpet is sounding the croaking call that ends even the bitterest battle.

The wind is rising. The mist is thinning into merciful dusk. The priests on either side come chanting down the hill to comfort the dying and to claim their dead.

The legends are done.

Who but the bards will inherit this bloodstained field, now Arthur and Modred are lost?

What is there left, that we should call Britain the Island of the Mighty?

Chapter Fifty-six

I am a pagan myth. I am a romantic fiction.

'537 The Battle of Camlann, in which Arthur and Modred fell; and there was plague in Britain and Ireland.'

This simple, grief-laden statement lies between two others:

'521 Saint Columba is born. The death of Saint Brigid.'

'544 The sleep of Ciaran.'

A voice out of history, of a sort. The Welsh Annals. Not wholly accurate, of course. The dates, at least, are unreliable. But names bulk on the page with the solidity of remembered truth. These men and women lived and died. Their inspiration and their suffering are not a fiction.

Columba and Brigid? Ciaran? An ecclesiastical history, then. Arthur and Modred are numbered between the saints.

The British Church mourns the passing of Arthur. It owns no knowledge of me.

Chapter Fifty-seven

Look, here he is. This is Arthur, the king of all the Britons. He has finished his thirteenth great battle. He has won. He has killed his son.

Study him well. Here is the pinnacle of chivalry. This is what kingship means.

Grieve with all of us.

A man larger than common. His broad chest lusty and loving. My head longed to rest there. Now his beard is matted with bright blood that keeps on welling, and the plates of his body-armour are clogged with a red more shocking than rust.

This little sanctuary is shadowed, far from the ravens' wings over Camlann. Even the pool is still, no tide to fret it. We wait for the pulse of Arthur's heart to die away.

One of these three is dead already, Lucan, brave warrior, whose own broken ribs supported the agony of Arthur to this place. Men do that for their king. The lesser bear great suffering so the great may suffer less. Too powerfully Arthur clutched his friend, driving the splintered bone-ends through Lucan's chest to choke his loyal breath with blood.

What of it? Soon they will all be dead. And those that linger the longest while will mourn they did not die at Camlann.

Not Bedwyr, though. Not yet, though half his heart was killed already when Cei fell in France.

Now he crouches, hunkered on the earthen floor. So the bright images show the gods of old, cross-legged and waiting. His hands are empty, but not for long. I have work for him.

'*Bedwyr!*'

The warrior's head rises, and he shivers, as one who hears an owl and fears she may be something else.

'*Bedwyr.*'

That troubled, loving glance at Arthur. But those blue eyes

are tight in the self-centred lock of pain. Arthur does not hear me cry. He has never heard me.

Strangeness has hold of Bedwyr. He is leaderless. Better the voice that calls him to terror than this silence. Strong-muscled yet, only a little stiff with middle-age and battle-weariness, his legs unfold and hoist him upright.

He lets tears fall. Arthur is lying a few steps from the altar, his sacrificed blood shed too early. It will not gladden any god. His son's wound burns in his belly. Modred he slew cleanly, but he is dying slowly at this same son's hand.

'*Bedwyr!*' Even this slow death may come too swiftly for what must still be done.

So, like a sleepwalker, Arthur's dearest remaining friend steps from the chapel into misty moonlight, and leaves the dying with only the dead for company.

A shining mere, cupped in the hills. The smallest sign may serve as token for infinity. I stand on the far, seaward side of it, where the brook spills out, and call to him. I must fight to hold back the heart that would surge over oceans, burst into that chapel, seize Arthur in my arms and sob out his salvation. There is an order in the universe. Its ways cannot be broken, or we break ourselves. I have learned the path of healing. I know its toll.

Will the wind carry my voice over the water?

'I bring a message for Arthur Pendragon.'

The heavy dew of summer trembles on the moonlit bulrushes like frost. He sees me, indistinctly, across the shimmering surface.

'Who . . . are you?'

There is more than query in the tremor of his voice.

Is it Nimue, Lady of the Lake, standing in front of the trees at the water's edge, or Morgan, Sea-Born? Or the shape of something Other, that never knew human flesh and blood, come for the Dragon's son?

And which of us would be more dangerous to the king now? Their warlike foster-mother, who brought up both these men and taught them arms, who all this time has been sheltering the love of his adulterous queen, a midwife nursing treachery to the inevitable birth of this last battle? Or Arthur's bitter sister, cheated rival, Modred's foster-mother, who hated Arthur for his father Uther's sake, loved him for his own?

Nothing is clear, no ground is sure, except this one certainty: Arthur is dying.

I move into the moonlight; let it fall upon my face.

'Morgan the Wise!'

Oh, yes, there's hope. I hear it. I am Morgan, the renowned physician. It is to me men bring their gravest wounded for healing.

He starts to run around the bank towards me, stumbling on the muddy grass. I stop him with one lifted finger. Merlyn would be proud of me.

'Not yet. Oh, I have healing far beyond the stars. My potions are powerful, my hands are sure.'

'Come round to the chapel, then! Quickly, he cannot have long. Morgan the Holy, I beg you. Undo this evil!'

What lies a man will babble in ecstasy or fear. And a woman too, when her barriers are down. I know why he needs me, why he speaks me fair. He believes I caused this war, that I dealt this wound, and so I, more than any other, am the one who can close it.

Let it pass. He is right in one respect. The time is short, and there is so much to teach him.

'There is a price to pay.'

'For the love of heaven, he is your brother!'

Hold back my tears. I would have given Arthur more than he ever dreamed of asking. This is no time for self-justification.

'Power is mine to work with. I cannot command it. The ways of Wisdom were carved in the first pattern of creation. Those who would wield it must become her humblest servants. Yes, I know how Arthur may be healed. I did not lay down the path.'

'You called me here. What do you want done?'

Bedwyr has never been humble. He is a warrior-aristocrat, chief of Arthur's personal war-band, his *teulu*, his fighting-family. He is a man who takes orders from one king alone. He is touchy, proud, jealous of insult. Look at him trembling now, trying to plead with me, fighting to keep that ready hand away from his sword and not compel the words of mercy from my throat at its battle-dinted edge. Across a watery space I smile at him. I am less sure of myself than he must think. Say rather, I am less sure of Bedwyr's good sense, and fearful

250

far more of Arthur's rebellion. I could lose him yet, and this time it would be for eternity.

'One thing only. My price is small, for immortality.'

'Name it, Lady.'

'Easy to say. Not easy to give. Caliburn.'

A puzzled stop. 'You want his battle-weapon?'

Not the rich jewelled sword of Britain's government? He could understand my seizing that, though we sisters once guarded the native Stone that allowed it to Arthur. I feel his mind racing with bewilderment, suspicion. He would play for time, but time is what Arthur no longer has. I want the fighting sword, his talisman of victory? The sword we sisters once stole, and in so doing nearly cost him his life? Caliburn, forged ages ago in Avalon. Caliburn, whose healing scabbard-mate I, with my own hands, sacrificed to the Goddess in another pool, and bear the wound that cost me upon my heart still?

'Not I. One greater than any of us requires it.'

His mind is too small, too practical, too human-sized, to sense the shape of the truth that stands behind me.

He knows what Nimue would do with Caliburn. The Lady of the Lake in her golden breastplate, riding in her battle-chariot. But Morgan the Wise? Have I some little king-in-waiting, another Accolon, who hopes to win through warfare, with Caliburn, what Modred failed to secure with the symbol of peace?

Abruptly, then, 'And if he lives? What would Arthur the warrior be without his battle-weapon? What good is his life if he surrenders Caliburn?'

I shrug, as though I do not care, as though it is nothing to me that Arthur is slipping from the world, for ever, and from all worlds of faeryland beyond.

The mere between us is wide enough for our voices to call thinly, like the scream of hawks.

'Do you condemn your king to die, and will not ask him?'

A hesitation, his balance swivelling on the ball of his foot. Loving fear wrestles with indignation. Then we hear a groan, wrenching the heart of both of us. The chapel seems to heave against the stars like a wounded bear, grieving with rage and pain and coming loss.

Bedwyr is running back into that mouth of darkness.

And only now Arthur's final battle begins.

Chapter Fifty-eight

I can give, and I can take away. I can hurt and I can heal.
Take Ogier the Dane.

From the twelfth century, our story is told. You may remember, I am the sixth fairy at his cradle. My gift exceeds all the rest. I promise that he shall never die by the hand of man, but that, after a long life of glory, he will come to live in joy in Avalon, as my lord and love.

Ogier does indeed become a great hero in France in the service of Charlemagne. He lives a hundred years. The time has come. I arrange for him to be shipwrecked on a lodestone rock, conveniently near my island, which itself lies just this side of Paradise.

The entrance must not be made too easy for him. This is a famous warrior. I have lions for him to encounter, King Kapalus for him to fight. He succeeds, of course.

What would you expect on such an island but an apple orchard? He eats the fruit and falls into a dangerous sickness. Expecting only death, he turns to face the east and sees a beautiful lady so magnificently attired he takes her for the Virgin Queen of Heaven. I modestly explain his error and reveal my name. I am Morgue the Fay. I have loved Ogier since the day he was born. It is I who have brought him here to enter my bliss.

Ogier protests that a man so sick is no fit companion for the fairest of fays and her maidens. That is easily remedied, since I have caused this sickness. A touch of my hand is all that is needed to restore him to perfect health.

I do more than that. I put a ring on his finger which restores his youth. I place a crown on his head which makes him forget all the past. I lead him to Avalon where he is greeted by all my maidens with mirth and songs and the best of entertainment. A son, Meurvin, is born to us.

Two hundred years pass as though they were twenty. But Christendom is now in danger again. With heavy heart I know the time has come to loose him. I lift the crown from his head, and memory returns. He cannot believe how long he has been in Avalon. His one desire is now to return to France. I urge him not to forget me, and never to speak of the wonders of my island. I give him two gifts: the ring he has worn since his arrival, which preserves his youth, and a magic firebrand. When the wood is entirely consumed by flames, Ogier will die.

Thus equipped, he is transported on a cloud back to the world of King Philip I. Much has changed, but Ogier is still a doughty warrior. He vanquishes the foes of Christianity and seeks more adventures, leaving his firebrand for safekeeping with the Abbot of St Faro.

King Philip dies. I have ensured that Ogier is still young, handsome and valiant. The widowed Queen of France now sets her eye on him as her next husband. Alarmed, Ogier remembers me. He rides to the Abbey of St Faro, demands the firebrand, and flings it on the flames. He pulls the ring from his finger and instantly becomes a man three hundred years old. I race to save him. I snatch the brand from the hearth and lift Ogier into my fiery chariot. We vanish from sight.

But others say Ogier is actually on his way to the altar to marry the Queen of France when a maiden in shining white appears, throws her arms around him and snatches him out of the church in a great cloud.

I am the original fairy mistress. I offer joys untold. I would not advise you to be unfaithful to me.

Renoart is less appreciative than Ogier. It nearly costs him his life.

In the Bataille Loquifer *I find the hero asleep by the sea. He is exhausted by weeping for his lost son Maillefer. I come flying down to land beside him, with my sister Marrion and another fay. I will have this hero for my love but my jealous sister designs him harm. We lift him, still asleep, ask God's blessing, change his club and hauberk into birds, his helmet into a harp, his sword into a boy, and enchant him away to Avalon. Arthur greets him and introduces me as the beautiful Morgue. Renoart falls passionately in love with me.*

But his ardour quickly fades. He sails off to seek his son.

Spurned, I persuade a youth Kapalu in the same fleet to sink his ship. Only at the last moment is Renoart saved from a watery grave by softly singing sirens who carry him to shore.

It is dangerous to reject me.

Chapter Fifty-nine

He cannot do it, can he?

Even now, in his extremity of pain, Caliburn still lies under his hand. Do the dragons on its hilt bite as his curled hand grips them with each spasm? Does their breath burn? He would rather their cruelty should turn on him, to drive out the pain of that other wound, the thrust of his son's sword.

A dreadful double agony. How could he not feel that?

He found it easier, once, to forget this son.

I remember that day, in the high open courtyard of my fort at Lyvennet. We were young then. I watched a golden-bearded general, with a boy's blue eyes, striding across the space to meet me and learn that he was the Pendragon's son and I was his sister. And then I showed him Margawse. I saw the hope in kingship vanish from his eyes, drowned deep in her blushing laughter. This was my sister, and therefore his. And she was big with his child. I understood what we had both lost. I would have gathered him on my shoulder and let him weep.

And so the Wheel of Fortune comes full circle. Merlyn contrives that Uther should trick Ygerne, steal her from Gorlois to get him Arthur. Margawse tricks Arthur, steals him from . . . me? . . . to make Modred. Now Arthur's own son, treacherously got, steals Arthur's queen. The old king must die, tumbling earthwards from his high revolution.

Earth, open your arms. Receive him gently. This is the Hero of Britain.

He cannot bear to die. It is more than physical fear. Who will inspire the war-host after him? For so he understands the call to kingship. Caliburn was always dearer to him than the sword of peace. His other sons are dead before him. Llacheu of Great Renown, his favourite bastard, heroically in battle. Anir, that poor pale stripling Gwenhyvar gave him,

255

gone early to his long home under the cairn trying to imitate Arthur's reckless folly. Then Modred his firstborn returns from the shades of the Otherworld, like a blossom in February, and Arthur welcomes the son he once tried to kill.

Modred the princely, so lately his well-beloved. Too lately loved. Modred is slain. We knew he must kill the baby. He still had his way to make, his kingdom to win, his reputation to guard. To a soldier it was simple. The baby was in the way. The baby must die.

Was I responsible? To this day I shall feel Arthur's hands on my wrists, hear the screaming of babies who do not yet know what they have to weep for, command the iron to armour my heart. He shall not have Modred! I will shut my ears to the howling of the mothers. I will not see the fearful indecision in the eyes of Arthur's young warriors as they seize their tiny enemies. I will not fall into Arthur's arms, though he supports my waist and smiles and coaxes and all my bones have melted to liquid fire.

I enraged him by my defiance. Saxons had surrendered to him. A British woman wounded his pride.

Might I have calmed the sea? I sent Teilo to bear witness for me. I did not follow the children myself to the coast. Could I have made the ebb-tide carry the ship safely in her bosom when all that freight of innocent babes was cast adrift upon the Solway? I stayed at home and, furious as Arthur, I devised a spell so that Modred, son of Arthur, should come sound to shore. I shudder now, remembering that act. Like Arthur, I was too singleminded. I worked magic only for one. I had my will. Modred was rescued by a fisherman. And all the rest were lost.

I wept then for the cruel profligacy of the Mothers who had robbed so many human hearts to leave us only Modred. Now I let the tears fall for my own heartlessness.

Arthur never knew. We were always adversaries. He avoided my court for shame and so he never saw my dark-browed foster-son growing. In secret, I guarded Arthur's child, taught Arthur's child, cherished Arthur's child. Margawse had given him flesh. I shaped his soul. It was never enough. I told him the truth, and kissed him on the forehead, and lost him. It was not my love Modred wanted then, but his lost father's. The son was acknowledged, that love was given, too late. Modred learned that Margawse was his mother, not me. He has followed her road to revenge, coldly where she went warm.

Forgive me, Arthur. My hands are round the sword that stabbed you as surely as Modred's. I reared him for this. I fed him my grief and bitterness.

Now Arthur rages. He will not die for this. He must not die. He groans for the failure of his hopes, the fouling of his love. Do not think it was Modred's neck only he was severing with that stroke; it was Gwenhyvar's too. A bigamous marriage! His wife to his son? Modred crowned! He'll wipe them both out, from the earth, from history, from his heart. He and Britain will live on. He will yet find his true mate.

I wait for his understanding. I am here, Arthur. I have always been here.

The king's clenched eyes open, reluctantly. He has too many pains to fight within. Bedwyr is shadowing the stars.

'Arthur! My lord. Morgan has come.'

There, I knew that would enrage him. A curse, a twist of the broken body that brings back physical pain howling to eclipse the other. A sharp, animal noise. It is mastered quickly. He is still a fighter, this Arthur.

'That faithless whore!'

No, I am the Faithful Whore. I, the Maiden, have given my body generously. Since my king would not admit he wanted it, what worth was it to me? If, opening it, I could feed the earth, if I could coax the sap to rise, the streams to flow, I would offer it freely. Only my supreme gift, the sovereignty of all Britain, I kept for him alone. Instead, he took it from Margawse. She cheated him. The land has never been made whole. Arthur has chosen to win a fractured kingship by another right, the sword. He has lost it so, and all our blood is passing into twilight with him.

'Morgan is the Healer.'

'She would not heal me, even if she could.'

His face turns from the door. He will not see the truth.

'She makes you an offer.'

Now there is stillness, like a blade of steel. The controlled force of Arthur tenses. The warrior, hard beset on every side, spies a tiny weakness in the ring of enemies, and all his manhood sharpens into one death-defying resolve to escape.

'What?'

'She will heal your wound if you will pay her price.'

'Have I not been a generous king? I've emptied a hundred treasure-houses in gifts. I've won fame for granting everyone whatever they asked me, so long as it was not my horse, my weapons, or my wife.' His voice trembles at the last.

Bedwyr kneels. I do not need to see his face. I can tell by the shaking of his shoulders the tears. This man loves Arthur. As we all must.

'Your sister asks that you surrender your sword to her.'

'Caliburn!'

He does not feel now how he grips the hilt, though his palm will bear the mark of it. Fury is what he knows, and it gives him strength. He tries to rise, and the blood spurts on the earthen floor dampening it more menacingly than the night dew. Bedwyr darts to catch, to cradle him, to lay him down.

I can do nothing but wait. I know the promise I offer may be the sentence that kills him. It must be his choice.

'She would still be queen, would she?' he gasps, when he can speak again. 'And with Caliburn? A warrior-queen, like Boudicca! Tell her she's too old.'

'You need not fear that. The people turned to Gwenhyvar, with her sword of government, and it brought them civil war. You came back with Caliburn. You have won the field. You have proved yourself the true king. They will not trust a queen again.'

I offer immortality. They talk of politics.

It is chill in the chapel. Arthur is stiffening before he is dead, to stop the shuddering of his weakened limbs.

'Tell her I will never give up Caliburn. Remind her she is my subject and my sister. Tell her, when her husband Urien put his sword and coronet under my hand, he pledged his wife's obedience too. *Command* her to heal me. I will be generous to her afterwards.'

Oh, little brother, did you play so at kings in Nimue's foster-house? Did you bind laurel leaves upon your golden brow and wave a wooden sword and order your playmates with your high-pitched shout? Has all the tutelage of the sage Merlyn come to this? Is this your notion of kingship? He might as well have left you to be brought up a warrior's whelp in Uther's court. Your mother and your sisters could have taught you more of the deep fitness of things.

Bedwyr is more afraid. He has seen my face by moonlight. Some little part of him has felt the Lady's power beneath the surface of the pool between us. His hand rests gently on the sword-hilt, over Arthur's.

'Arthur . . . sire, . . . your wound is grave. We have come too far in the mist. It is too late now to turn back and try to find the battlefield and the surgeons. This part of Cornwall is desolate. The people have fled us. I have no salves. I have done what I can, but the dressing I have strapped round you will not hold off death till morning.'

'Gawain might have healed me. He had some skill.'

'Gawain is dead.'

'And Morgan the Wise will watch me die.'

'She says the cure is costly.'

'A false surgeon! She would amputate the arm she wants for herself!'

'She speaks as though the sword is not for either of you now. Remember, she gave the scabbard up.'

'*My* scabbard! It was not hers to drown. But for that spite, I should not be bleeding to death now. She stole my healing. And now she wants to beggar me of my might as well. She has made all Britain a waste-land with her plots.'

Did I deal that wound to Modred, who brought us all to this?

'Will you not test her faith, at least?'

'Morgan is always faithless. Tell her no, no, no!'

I feel a cold wind fret the mist. Low waves lap the shore. I cannot keep it from the chapel door. It chills the sweat on Arthur's face. Within the stiff pride of his battledress he shivers. I can do nothing to stop it.

Chapter Sixty

I am the figure of evil.

We cannot put it off any longer. It is time at last to turn our attention to Sir Thomas Malory. Forget the Welsh legends, the early chronicles, the thirteenth-century romances, the Breton folktales. This is the book that really matters. It has become the definitive version.

Le Morte d'Arthur, *concluded in 1469, two years before Malory's death in Newgate.*

This is the one that has coloured all subsequent tellings. Malory's portrayal of me has left its indelible mark upon the twentieth century. It is not a pretty picture.

He writes a collection of eight epic tales about the court of King Arthur. There is certainly no shortage of material.

It is all here, everything the romantic heart could desire. Arthur's birth at Tintagel, the sword in the anvil, the establishment of the Round Table, Excalibur rising from the lake, Lancelot and Gwenhyvar, Trystan and Essylt, the Quest of the Holy Grail, Modred's treachery, Arthur's falling at Camlann, the queens who come to bear him away.

William Caxton, the printer, seizes the opportunity of the newly invented printing press. He arranges the tales into twenty-one books, containing the sum of five hundred and seven chapters, and publishes the collected work in 1485. For one so new to the printed word and the publishing trade, he certainly has an eye for a saleable manuscript.

Men clad in armour ride bravely into the forest and do battle with any knight they meet, without revealing their name. Foul enemies are slain in the process and sometimes, unfortunately, friends or brothers. Damsels lure knights into perilous castles, wronged ladies are rescued. The vision of the Grail inspires Arthur's knights. The quest is achieved. The Maimed King is healed. Galahad is transported to heaven.

But the fellowship of the Round Table has been weakened by the Grail quest, by the loss of Lancelot through banishment, by the death of Gawain and his brothers who oppose Lancelot. When Arthur dies, the romantic lovers remain separated and make a holy end as nun and monk.

Morgan le Fay is the villainess of this piece. I am Arthur's lifelong foe. Time and again I plot to bring about his death. I am the enemy of all true lovers and the bane of Arthur's knights.

Malory knows the sources. If there is an unpleasant story about me to be found he uses it.

Note what he does not choose to say.

He never shows me in my original role as healer. Instead he tells the story of the ointment I give to Alexander l'Orphelin, which causes him agony past bearing until he accedes to my will. He writes of my theft of the magic scabbard that prevents Arthur from losing blood. He tells of the mantle I send him which burns the wearer to death.

I have changed a great deal since Geoffrey and Chrétien de Troyes.

I no longer offer my lovers an island of enchantment and youth and the delights of faerie. Now I trick hapless knights away to my castle and imprison them because they will not give me their love.

Even at the end, I do not appear to bear Arthur away to my land of joy. True, I am one of three hooded queens who take the still-living king into their ship. True, Arthur himself believes he is bound for healing in the Vale of Avalon. True, Malory quotes the legend that Arthur is living still.

But we queens are dressed in black and shrieking for grief. Next morning Bedwyr arrives at Glastonbury to find a new-made grave. A hermit reports how at midnight ladies arrived bearing a corpse, begged that it be buried there in the chapel, and paid for the lighting of a hundred candles. Malory knows of the famous inscription on the tombstone:

HERE LIES ARTHUR, THE ONCE AND FUTURE KING

I am not suggesting that Malory invents these unflattering tales of me, though he sometimes gives them a twist of his own. But authorship is the art of selection, what to include, what to omit, what words to use. In the choices we make we give our own selves away. Of all the versions of the Arthurian story available to him in the fifteenth century he seems to be drawn in particular to those from the pens of Cistercian monks whose writings betray how much they fear women.

In Malory most women are supernaturally malignant or false to their husbands. They bring about the downfall of good knights. Courtly love of a hero for his unattainable mistress is still romantic, but it is no longer the high ideal inspiring gallant action. Women are dangerous to men. One of Arthur's knights even beheads the Lady of the Lake for slaying his mother.

Love is most tender between man and man. Arthur himself is made to say:

'I am sorrier for my good knights' loss than for the loss of my fair queen; for queens I might have enough.'

But I am the queen of evil.

Who is this man who has branded his image of me so searingly on the imagination of the twentieth century?

It is charged that on the fourth of January 1450 Sir Thomas Malory, with other malefactors, lay in ambush in the woods of Coombe Abbey for the purpose of murdering the Duke of Buckingham.

That on the 25th of May of the same year he broke into the house of Hugh Smyth at Monks Kirby and raped his wife Joan.

That ten weeks later he raped her again.

That the following year he engaged in sweeping cattle raids and twice extorted money by threats.

He is arrested and imprisoned by the Sheriff of Warwickshire. Five days later he escapes by swimming the moat, breaks into a Cistercian abbey, and steals money and valuables from the abbot's chests. Next day he repeats the crime with many accomplices, breaks eighteen doors, insults the abbot, steals more money. Months later he is rearrested and ends up in the Tower.

In 1454 he is released on bail but still he plots attacks, goes back to jail, seizes swords, daggers and halberds and escapes again.

He seems to spend the rest of his life in and out of prison. It is as a prisoner that he ends his story of Arthur with expressions of piety and hopes for release.

> *'I pray you all, gentlemen and gentlewomen that readeth this book of Arthur and his knights from the beginning to the ending, pray for me while I am alive, that God send me good deliverance, and when I am dead, I pray you all pray for my soul. For this book was ended the ninth year of the reign of King Edward the Fourth, by Sir Thomas Malory, knight, as Jesu help him for His great might, as he is the servant of Jesu both day and night.'*

A nice try. We must suppose it fails. He is buried at Greyfriars Church near Newgate Jail.

This is the man who writes the epic account of the deeds of gallant knights in shining armour. He has influenced all our imaginings.

A would-be murderer. A rapist.

Should you trust what he tells you about women?

Chapter Sixty-one

Keep back among the trees. Bedwyr is coming out. Arthur's answer will widen this distance between us into a grievous wound. He must close it before I can mend the lesser one. It will need high courage.

'Lady Morgan?'

Wait a little. The moonlight shimmers uncertainly across the mere. The air is cloudy. Let him doubt his eyes. This is the hour of faery. Give him time to fear. Now speak. Make the voice calm, cool. He must not guess how much this means to me.

'I am still here. I have always been here. I can wait more lifetimes yet. But Arthur's own hour is almost over. What is his answer?'

'He will not make this bargain for his sword. He calls you faithless, proud, ambitious.'

Is it faithlessness that has brought me here to keep tryst with Arthur now he has passed beyond all other help? Is it pride to hold out my healing hand to the brother who caused me such humiliation? Does he call it ambition, that I am offering immortal kingship to him?

Say none of this.

'Arthur has chosen his own way, then, and I mine. If he will not accept my help, let him turn to others. The Christian Church will ask its own renunciation from him, before it promises bliss.'

'I cannot tell where we are, but there is no priest near, or nun, or monk. He has no soul-friend but what I am, a plain soldier of Christ.'

'Need the Christian King Arthur fear to die unconfessed? He took the Great Offering before the battle. Will he not enter Christ's heaven?'

He bites his moustache. 'Why must you talk of death,

264

Lady? This is Arthur the Emperor! Would you have him live and love, fight and fall, take the sacrament and give up the ghost like any other lusty hero among us? He has no generation to carry on his name. There can be no second Arthur. This is a king like no Briton before or after him. This is our greatest chieftain, woman, robbed of the realm he saved! He embraced his son, only to have him steal his crown and stab him with a mortal wound. Would you see Arthur Pendragon die at Camlann in a cuckold's brawl and not go out in a blaze of triumph and glory against the Island's enemies?'

He calls me proud.

'Must not the grave have us all in the end, and after, Paradise?'

'But his name, woman! Arthur's passing must be worthy of the man.'

'His coming had a cloud upon it.'

'Still the jealous sister! Still bitter, after all these years?'

Oh, yes, I have been bitter. For my father Gorlois, for my mother Ygerne, for my own lost reputation. Yet I could forgive him everything, if he will only cross this perilous bridge.

'Does not the Church teach us that all crowns are nothing before the throne of Heaven, all swords surrendered in the realm of peace, all distinctions of rank lost in the great choir of praise, save for the shining coronets of saints and martyrs?'

'Traitor! Would you make the Pendragon equal in death with the lowest peasant?'

'Even with a slave, in the carpenter's kingdom, so the nuns taught me.'

The rip of his own sword then, half out of its sheath.

'This is Arthur we talk of! The Great Bear of the starry heavens. His like will not come again once he is dead. Can you not understand that? Cure him, woman!'

Not ready, then, to die in faith, and calls me faithless.

'Have Arthur's groans dulled his hearing? I have promised you I can, and will.'

A sigh, that seems to shiver the rushes on the mere. Bedwyr thinks I have played with him, only to demonstrate how much Arthur is in my power.

'Come then. He will reward you richly. Be quick, lady.

265

He has lost much blood and the wound has entered dangerous organs.'

He strides to the water's edge, holding out an eager hand over the waves. The water splashes round his knees. The bank is treacherous. Step swiftly back into the shadow of the trees by the mere's-foot. More wraith than woman now. Stand tall, warning, with lifted hand. He must recognise the authority I carry. Everything hangs on this.

The wind wars with my voice.

'Stop! Not yet. I named the price. You have brought nothing in your hands to pay his passage.'

An angry slap of boots as he struggles to regain the shore.

'You are his sister, curse you! Half the women of Britain would give their hearts' blood to see him live, though it cost them their own lives. But you, who know more of necromancy than any woman alive, must calculate, reckon the length of your brother's years upon an abacus, make him buy the restoration of his right with a hilt of gold and garnets and a blade of thrice-hammered steel! Have you no heart?'

No heart, who held my brother in my arms at one day old, and bit his neck to mix his life-blood with my own? No heart, who wept to see his light, lewd wife betray his bed, and for no goddess but herself? No heart, who tried by every means I could to warn him, though he damned me for it? I could not make him hear me then. Can I now?

'The laws I serve were written in the creation of the earth and stars and waters. I did not make them. I am called Morgan the Wise only because I have searched deep all my life to understand and obey them. I have learned with pain what makes for wholeness. Tell Arthur I know how to work no other way.'

Believe me, Bedwyr! Make him you love believe me. I will not plead. I have stated our terms. He must surrender it willingly. This is the only gate to life.

'But his weapon! Caliburn? You know what that means to him?'

Oh, yes. I know.

'I know we women gave him two swords, Arthur the Briton. The Sword in the Stone of the land, the sword of kingship, guarded by Uther's step-daughters, the blade in our hollowed flesh. It was handed to him again by the

Church at his coronation, a doubled blessing. This sword he entrusted to Modred when he went to fight abroad. This was the sword Modred delivered up to Gwenhyvar, kneeling, and hailed her Queen over all of us. This is the sword of peace Arthur has won back from him today on the bloody field of Camlann.

'But Caliburn is dearer to him than that. Caliburn he never lent to any other man or woman, nor ever would. When we sisters took it from him, he was like a man deranged until Nimue snatched it back for him without the scabbard.'

'That sword is his right.'

'The Sword in the Stone is as old as the Island of Britain. But Caliburn is older far than that. It was forged in Avalon, before countries, before kings and queens, when there was only a man and a woman. It came from the oldest Lady of all. By her authority, Nimue armed Arthur with it in his youth. It has served him truly. By that same authority, she calls it back to her tonight.'

'You stole it once. He will never let you cheat him again.'

'The night Arthur bedded Gwenhyvar, after both of them were crowned, my sisters and I took it into our safekeeping. Yes, it was vengeance. That marriage wounded us all. We would have done better to have taken back the other sword. Arthur never truly wanted to be king; that was Merlyn's doing.

'Caliburn is a weapon, not a symbol. It inflicts real wounds. In his heart Arthur is still that triumphant youth who first flourished it. He is still Arthur the Leader of Battles. It is not his kingship my brother clutches so fiercely to him on his deathbed, is it? It is his warrior's blade.'

'Why not? So we all rose to fame, Arthur and I and the rest, fighting the Saxons.'

'So you will let him end.'

'Like this? Shamefully killed by his own son? With that son's lifeblood staining the blade you ask for? Arthur the prince of honour and glory, sordidly falling victim to a traitor, who stabs him when he has dropped his shield?'

'I can wipe all of that nightmare away. His sins and shame will not be remembered. The bards shall sing him through all ages as the most valiant, just and chivalrous king that ever was. His fellowship of knights shall be renowned. But I must have the weapon first. Or rather, not I, but she who gave it him.'

'And if he did, would you heal him?'

I have waited a lifetime to say this, to have Arthur ask.

'There is no tear so bitter, but I can wipe it from his eye. No flow of blood, but I can staunch it. No ache so deep I cannot cure it with a kiss.'

My voice rings across the wide, dark water. I have not let it tremble. I am offering him hope.

Bedwyr does not trust me. Bedwyr loves his friend and king. His warrior's code wrestles against his breaking heart.

'I will try a second time. Wait!'

Arthur is blood of my blood. He calls me faithless, proud, ambitious. And so is he. It is himself he should most fear now.

Chapter Sixty-two

Who is Arthur's Healer?

In Chrétien de Troyes' Erec I am Morgan the Wise, the giver of marvellous ointments, which can cure any wound, of body or spirit. Erec comes back to Arthur's court badly wounded, with his much-abused wife Enid. It is my salve that heals him.

The Mabinogion has a remarkably similar story. Enid's husband appears here as Gereint son of Erbin.

Gwenhyvar has risen too late for the hunting, but she will go after the party all the same. There are only two horses left in the stable. She rides, imprudently, with one maiden. But behind her comes a young, auburn-haired, bare-legged knight of princely mien, with a gold-hilted sword on his thigh and a tunic and surcoat of brocaded silk about him, and two low boots of cordwain upon his feet, and over that a mantle of blue-purple, and an apple of gold at each of its corners. He is riding a high-mettled, brisk, lively, young, willow-grey charger of immense size. This apparition is Gereint son of Erbin. She accepts his escort.

They meet a knight on a huge horse, heavily armoured, accompanied by a lady and a dwarf. At Gwenhyvar's command her maiden rides forward to request the knight's name. The dwarf bars her way, and when the maiden persists he strikes her across the face with his whip and draws blood. She flees back weeping and Gereint indignantly takes her place and gets the same treatment. He cannot fight a dwarf, and dressed as he is, he can hardly challenge the fully armoured knight. He retreats.

Naturally, these men are destined to meet again. There is a tournament for a sparrowhawk, to be given to the victor's lady. Three wins, and she will have the right to a hawk every year for life. The knight who has won the sparrowhawk for the last two years is the same whose dwarf injured Gwenhyvar's maiden. He has also wronged Gereint's host. Gereint challenges him. The young man is hard pressed. It is the memory of that old insult that gives Gereint the final strength he needs to fell the knight. He wins both the sparrowhawk and the hand of his host's charming daughter Enid.

He spares his adversary's life. Now back to Gwenhyvar's court comes a sorry sight. A big bowed knight with his head hanging low, exceedingly sad, and broken worthless pieces of armour about him, and the colour of his blood upon them getting the better of their own colour, with a dwarf and a lady riding sadly beside him. This is the erstwhile Knight of the Sparrowhawk, Edern, son of Nudd, sent from the tournament by Gereint to surrender himself to Gwenhyvar's mercy.

And what does Arthur call for to take care of his wounds? Not the ointment of his sister, Morgan the Fay, as in Chrétien's Erec. *Here, the healer who is summoned to Edern's bedside is Arthur's Chief Physician, Morgan Tud.*

A man.

My principal power has been taken from me. Or have I, to keep that power, surrendered my gender?

As with Erec, so Gereint hears from his faithful Enid the whispers that married life is sapping his reputation for knightly valour. He takes his horse and arms. He orders Enid to put on her worst dress and ride ahead of him. He forbids her to speak to him. Time and again she disobeys and saves his life. He makes her suffer greatly on his many adventures. It is Gwalchmei, whom others call Gawain, who brings the wounded knight down at last and takes him against his will to Arthur's camp. Great the distress of the court to see both Gereint and Enid in this wretched state. A tent is pitched for Gereint, and Morgan Tud and his disciples are sent for again.

When I heal Erec in the French story, he is well enough to ignore my advice that he be treated for a week, and rides on his way next morning. In the Mabinogion *it takes Morgan Tud a whole month to make Gereint whole.*

So who is Morgan Tud?

The histories know of Margodud, whose father built the Castle of Maidens, where I am so often found in the romances, and Morgetiud, who had a son called Owain. Easy to see a confusion of names and attributes.

HERSELF

Or was there a mischievous Breton demon, Morgan Tuth?
Which of us is the original? Or were we always separate people:
Arthur's male court physician, Arthur's fairy sister?
Which should he call on for healing?
Which of us would you trust?

Chapter Sixty-three

There is a smell of blood. Here in the smothering, mothering darkness Arthur strains for life. Only I can give it to him.

This is the thickening, clotting blood of kin that sticks us to each other. He yearns to trust me, even now. I am his sister. I am Morgan the Fay, the wisest of the Wise. Above all I am pre-eminent in healing. As Arthur on the battlefield was always victor, so I in the dark struggle with death may win the day.

Well, so he argues. He is Arthur the soldier. War is his metaphor. Death is his enemy. He has not learned to hold out his hand in friendship to the darkness, to go willingly under the earth. That is not his rite.

Hope is not dying, even at this low hour. We are brother and sister. The children of Ygerne will not be beaten. Arthur Pendragon cannot, must not be allowed to die.

Look at him rising on his elbow. Even in the shadows his eyes sparkle with expectation.

'She is still there? What does she say? What will she have in place of Caliburn? Be quick, man!'

Bedwyr kneels, lowers him softly to the floor. Harness-hard hands are gentle now.

'Nothing.'

'Aah!' He sinks back satisfied. 'I knew it! I've seen the lust in her eyes. She will save me, only for myself.'

'She will take nothing except Caliburn.'

'*No!* She cannot mean it! She will take my weapon from me or else let me die?'

'Steady, Arthur! The wound is bleeding fast. I cannot hold it.'

Still he fights me. It is anger more than fear that drives him on.

'Bitch! Fool!'

Yes, I am a woman, and therefore devoid of reason, though I am called a scholar in astronomy. I must be made to see. He rages against my treachery, but that is not what he truly believes. In his own mind he still sees himself as Arthur the golden boy, Arthur of the winning smile, Arthur Pendragon who has broken as many British hearts as Saxon heads and claimed the rights of kingship over every blushing maid who gladdened his eye. How could I, a weak woman, refuse his glamour?

Has he forgotten already that he has lost Gwenhyvár's love?

I will be honest. He is right, in part. I own my weakness. Now Bedwyr is gone I can let the pent tears flow in the too-brilliant moonlight. These are all the treasure Arthur has allowed me.

But pity is not enough to buy his life. Do you think I would not run to that chapel, swifter than the magical horse that carries Queen Rhiannon, if that would save him? Would I not lay my cool hands on his burning wound? Would I not cradle his pain-crazed head on my breast and sing the rhymes of restoration? Harder for me to hold myself back from giving my love than for Arthur to give up what he loves most. We torment ourselves.

It can be done no other way.

Hold fast, my will. I am a gambler staking insignificant gains against the last great throw that will decide all. The Wise revere me as the wisest. I know how the foundations of the world are laid. I have shown him the hard truth. I have offered him the prize all heroes dream of. Will he believe me?

'She is offering you life. It is your only chance.' That break in Bedwyr's voice. Men love great Arthur with the same intensity as women, perhaps more. He has given meaning to manhood. What would the warrior's world, what would Britain be without Arthur? A waste-land. A desert of the heart. Whom should swords serve but him?

'How could I be Arthur Pendragon without Caliburn?'

'We are none of us young. The great battle of Badon was over long ago. We have held the Saxons back to keep half Britain free. We can make do with lesser swords for lesser battles.'

'And lesser men?'

Yes. In his bitterness he understands more than he knows.
Now, can he let go?

'What you have done will stand for ever. The name of
Arthur cannot be less than you have made it.'

'You would watch me crumble into a living death, like
Llywarch Hen?

> *I am old, I am lonely,*
> *I am decrepit and cold,*
> *after my sumptuous bed of honour;*
> *I am wretched, I am bent in three.*

'Would you leave me weaponless, wifeless, sonless? Shall
I have to plead with a reluctant people to crawl back to my
heel?'

Does he think that Caliburn can win him back Gwenhyvar?
Caliburn has murdered Modred. Will he always see in the
jewels and the rune-chased blade of this sword the magic and
the glamour of his youth? Did Nimue not teach him the
wisdom of the circle? Does he imagine Caliburn was his to
own? Does he believe it rose from the lake for Arthur the
man to possess and not for Arthur of Britain to wield? Even
after Camlann?

'You have won this day. The traitors are dead. The land
is at peace. Modred's remnant are fled, or have surrendered
their swords to Custennin of Dumnonia.'

'Will my war-host hail my successor already, before they
have found my body? And what of the greatest traitor of all?
Gwenhyvar?' This pains him more than his wound.

'Hidden in some convent, they say. She will not trouble
your land again. We will find the place. Our men will seek
her bastard child out, and destroy it.'

Not child, but children, Bedwyr, as once you sought and
found another baby boy. Gwenhyvar I have lodged with
Abbess Bryvyth. She, at least, I have protected in her
underground cell.

Gwenhyvar is the past. Her twin babies, grandsons of
Arthur, are a future that will never come. My time is passing
from this world too. I cannot shield Modred's infants, as once
I sheltered him.

Arthur groans. For what? For that moment of ecstasy in

which his son got new life upon Arthur's wife? For the last of his blood, innocent as blind kittens but damned from the womb to die? For a lonely life, espoused to Caliburn alone, his first, perhaps his only true love? For simple physical pain?

Dream, Arthur. See visions higher than any of these.

I will embrace my brother. I will offer a dream of such joy that a hundred years will pass as one brief day. His sunlit hours shall be glorious with races and fights, his evenings warm with fine wine and stirring song. Then night. Delight of body and touch, ecstasy of spirit and heart, close tender sleep. He shall lie down spent and laughing, he shall rise whole and eager to greet another brilliant morning. He shall have a crowd of beautiful women, in all their variety, to wait on him; he shall have bold men for companions, vigorous sport to make his days merry. There shall be skilful poets and storytellers. The blossom shall hang fresh as foam on the apple-boughs when he wakes at daybreak, and the red fruit fall ripe into his hand when he rides home at sunset. I shall invite an infinite multitude of stars to light our loving.

Just one thing is required. The hilt lies under his hand. One slender key of steel. Two dragon hasps of gold to open the lock of life.

His voice rasps.

'She has stolen everything from me, even Caliburn. She shall not get it a second time.'

Chapter Sixty-four

I am the wicked witch who promises healing falsely.

I tricked Alexander the Orphan.

We are in the dangerous territory of Cornwall again. King Mark is the villain. The Saxons are beaten, but now other heathen ships are invading Cornwall. Mark's brother, Boudwin, sends wild fire among their fleet. He kills their crews and Cornwall is saved.

It is all over before Mark hears about it. The glory is all Boudwin's. Mark quickly invites him to his castle, bidding him bring Anglides his wife and their infant son Alexander. Supper passes pleasantly. Then Mark reproaches his brother for not inviting him to share in the slaughter. Boudwin protests it was an emergency; there was no time. No time is left him now. Mark plunges a dagger into his heart.

Anglides swoons. But she recovers in time to find good sorrowful knights preparing her husband's corpse for burial. She takes his bloodstained shirt and tunic. Essyllt, Mark's queen, sends word to her to flee the castle with her son, lest young Alexander suffer the same fate. Anglides escapes with horse and child and a poor company.

Only just in time. Mark is searching the castle himself, sword in hand. Finding them gone, he orders the good knight Sadok to hunt them down. Mark warns him that if he values his life he must bring them back. Sadok catches up with them. But he too grieves for Boudwin. He lets them live, on condition that Anglides avenges this murder. Then he returns and tells Mark that Alexander has been drowned.

The boy comes to manhood. He is to be made knight along with twenty aristocratic lads of the neighbourhood. In church, at the solemn mass, Anglides shows him his father's clothes, stiff with old blood. The young man starts and pales. She tells him the truth of his uncle's treachery. The first charge of young Alexander's knighthood is revenge.

276

He jousts with all his knightly companions and overthrows them. One, in spite, runs to Mark and warns him Alexander is alive, and made a warrior now. Mark rushes to Sadok's chamber, brandishing his sword, and charges him with treachery. Sadok defends his honour and his life, slays four strong knights and escapes the castle.

Mark turns to means more to be feared than swords. He sends letters to Queen Morgan the Fay and to the Queen of Northgales. He prays us as great sorceresses to set the whole country on fire and engage dangerous knights so that by no means shall Alexander escape us.

But when I hear reports of this Alexander the Orphan, I have other ideas for him.

The young man sets out to ask the renowned Lancelot to train him for his grim destiny. He seems to have little need of tuition. He loses his way and fights at a tournament where he overthrows King Carados and twenty knights.

A damsel brings me news of him. I will see this young knight. I slip away from my friends in secret. Better to start my journey before I have rivals. I pitch my tent by the wayside where I encounter four more knights. They too have fallen to Alexander, who is now defending a castle. A damsel holds it. But her evil neighbour will permit her to marry no one but himself. Already he has killed twenty knights.

Alexander fights this monster more wildly than wittily. I arrive in time to witness the combat, along with the damsel for whose sake he is duelling. Naturally, the Orphan wins, and strikes off the evil knight's head. But the toll has been heavy. He has sixteen great wounds, and one in particular seems likely to lead to his death. He cannot stay upright.

I have him in my power now. He is laid on a horse-litter and borne into the castle. I search his wounds and smear them with an ointment of my own. Not kind, that salve. He spends the night in agony. In the morning he capitulates. He will do anything I say if I will soothe him. I release him from his pain. I will serve my own purposes now, not Mark's.

The damsel of the castle comes to me to ask my help. She would like to wed this young man who has fought so bravely for her. I tell her she shall see my answer presently. Then straight to Alexander's bedside. I forbid this marriage. He makes her a courteous excuse. She takes it philosophically and settles instead for her childhood sweetheart.

277

Then I drug Alexander so that he will feel nothing for three days and nights. He is laid in the horse-litter again. This time the journey is rough and long. We arrive at my castle, the Beautiful Keep, and he is put to bed. I shall keep him carefully. When he wakes, I ask if he would like to be well.

'Who would be sick, and he might be whole?'

Here is my condition. He must swear, by his knighthood, never to leave this castle for a year and a day. And with his oath, I restore him to health. At once he regrets his promise.

My cousin arrives at the Beautiful Keep. This castle is rightly hers, but I have taken it. She finds Alexander the Orphan low-spirited. He would rather be on his way to seek his revenge on Mark. She warns him he will be kept for the pleasure of Morgan the Fay. At that he swears he would sooner cut off his balls than pleasure me. They plot together. Her uncle will ride against the castle and set fire to it. She herself will help Alexander out by a secret postern. He need not break his oath. He will stay within the walls and keep the site for her for a year and a day. They kiss and pleasure each other. Her plan succeeds. Alexander goes no further than the castle garden.

My cousin sends me her triumphant message. I have lost. I disappear from his story. My plot has gone up in smoke.

But there is still an enemy lurking in the shadows.

Gratitude is not one of Alexander's chief characteristics. He challenges all comers to the Beautiful Keep. Alice the Fair Pilgrim hears of him. She promises her hand to any knight of Arthur's court who can overcome him. Alice is rich as well as beautiful. There is considerable interest. She has hardly pitched her pavilion to watch, when the first contestant arrives. He loses.

But the Fair Pilgrim is fickle also. Despite her offer, she falls for the young defender of the Beautiful Keep before she has even seen his face. He lifts his helmet. She removes her wimple. It is love at first sight.

Too bad for the lady of the castle, my clever cousin. She laughingly tells Alice how she helped Alexander escape from my toils and from the castle fire. Alice observes, correctly, that he is much beholden to this damsel.

Alexander continues to fight all comers, though he has now won Alice the Fair Pilgrim for himself. Then Modred appears.

At that moment, Alexander is standing so besotted with love at the sight of his Alice on horseback that he takes no notice. The ungallant Modred humiliates him, leading him helpless on his horse up and down. Alexander has not yet noticed how he is being shamed. My resourceful cousin arms herself. She sets a shield upon her shoulder, grasps a naked sword and mounts a horse. She has more sense than to attack Modred. Instead she strikes Alexander such a blow on the head that sparks fly from his eyes. It does the trick. Alexander returns to his senses and draws his sword. Prudently, the damsel flees to the pavilion and Modred in the opposite direction.

Alexander the Orphan and Alice the Fair Pilgrim tease the damsel for the sad stroke she hit him. The three will not be separated. They make for Benwick, Lancelot's country, and live together in great joy.

My evil plots have always been thwarted by another woman.

Chapter Sixty-five

Bedwyr is on his knees. He is weeping without shame.

'My lord! Arthur! It is our only chance.'

'Would you trust any of my sisters? Am I so weak even in death I must let them take what they want, and leave me nothing? They would steal Caliburn from me and let me die.'

'If you trust Morgan and she proves false, yes, you will die. But if you do not trust Morgan's healing you will still die. Fight, man! Here is an opening; seize it. Will you surrender to your last enemy while there's a chance?'

'Which is my worst enemy, death or that woman?'

'I believe Morgan loves you!'

There, the words are out. What all the world has known yet will write centuries of romances to deny. It wasn't difficult, was it? Three short words. So we might carve them with a knife in bark, trace them in sand, scratch them upon rock. MORGAN LOVES ARTHUR.

Why could I never say it? Why could Arthur never admit this truth? Why this conspiracy on every side to make us mortal enemies?

'Morgan loves me? Is that why she fostered Modred in her family? So his shadow could foul my sunny court of Camelot? So all the bitterness she's taught him would take its revenge upon my wife and queen? My Gwenhyvar opens her legs for Morgan's boy!'

'Women, Arthur! Margawse was Lot's wife and queen when she opened her legs for you, and got Modred.'

Another day he would have struck Bedwyr for that reminder. King Arthur has saved Britain from Saxon conquest. King Arthur can be forgiven. What have Modred and I achieved? But it is long past time for indignation. The ebbing blood has left him weak. Self-pity closes in to gnaw at his pride. He is sobbing now.

280

'I did heavy penance for that sin. Where's the priest? Am I going to die without the sacrament?'

'No need for that. We started this day with clean swords, clean souls. So we may depart. Be easy.'

'A clean sword? Look at it! Stained with my own son's blood! Oh, Modred, Modred! Say he was still alive, only drenched in blood from this slaughterhouse of Camlann. Say I did not kill my son!'

He writhes, and his hand grips the fouled blade beside him in his agony. If he had left to him but a token of the strength he possessed when he buckled it on this morning, that grip would do him much hurt. Bedwyr takes it like a dangerous toy from a baby, mothers him, weeps over him.

And I can only watch and wait, knowing that with each moment Arthur's heart beats more faintly, and the choice has still not been made.

The whisper comes after long silence.

'Could she heal this?'

My feet have moved a dozen swift paces towards the brink before I check them.

His wound is deep. Was I the mother of this pain? Did I raise Modred to do this? Certainly I meant no good to Gwenhyvar. They called her the Giant's Daughter. She claimed the blood of kings. But she was never wise. In her, Arthur thought he had wedded the sovereignty of Britain. We had given him that. He told her he served his High Queen best when war took him away to fight for freedom. She did not see it so. Too shallow, vain and selfish, she called his destiny desertion. Arthur was holding the high-water mark of British story, of Christian faith, of Roman law against the encroaching waves of Saxon barbarism. And she was bored.

I never meant the son I restored to his arms to serve him so. To steal his queen, usurp his kingdom, win over the fickle love of Britain's people. When I walked through the woods telling the little boy old tales of hate and saw him stab the bramble bush with a rotting stick, I did not imagine him today defying Arthur, sword in hand, running his father through, destroying his love, his life, his dream, bringing him to this sobbing wreck of all he was. Have I done this?

Pain has always bred pain, since that bright Easter Day when Gorlois took my beautiful mother to Uther's feast, and

I was left at home in Cornwall, lonely and bitter. I wove a childish spell of anger. Lust, pride, revenge have howled about us ever since.

How can I end it?

I have shown you a path to peace, Arthur, my brother. I sacrificed the healing scabbard, the easy magic of a talisman that makes us falsely proud of our power. I kept only my woman's wisdom, hardly got. I have learned it in a long initiation of humility to her I serve. I use her ways, rooted in the earth, not high sorcery. From that come all the salves I know. It has been enough.

Can you make an equal sacrifice, my brother? Trust what you are? Be only Arthur, warrior, emperor, winning battles by your own effort without the prop of magic? Has Nimue trained and armed you skilfully enough for this, to make you victorious in history as well as in romance?

'Take it,' he pleads through choking tears. 'I never want to see it again.'

A thrill like unspent lightning prickling in the air makes the roots of my hair tingle on my scalp. Can it be this easy, after all? Can all the snarls and tangles of our conjoined lives fall into one looping rope of life, strong, long and surely spun?

Bedwyr is coming down to the shore, the precious gift unsteady in his hands. His is the swift step of a true friend who fears the time is short. He knows this line must be made fast before it can be stretched out towards eternity. Only I can tie the knot. Shut out all doubts. Forget the history of animosity. Hope speeds him on. His eyes are on this harbour. All shipwrecks before this must be ignored.

My heart is hammering faster than his steps. My hands are reaching out across the width of moon-chased water. I would close the gap as nearly as I may. But there is still this mere between us.

'Halt!'

He is on the opposite shore, and Caliburn is in his grasp. He would run to me now around the grassy margin, but I must not let him. If Arthur is too weak to rise, then Bedwyr must do this in his stead.

'I have brought the sword, Lady! Take it. Hurry! He is in the chapel, and weaker than the hour in which he was born.'

Oh, yes, I remember well that hour, the storm, Ygerne's cry. I hated my brother then. Through Arthur's coming, I had lost my beloved father to Uther's sword and my mother to his softer weapon. I was unwanted.

That was before I saw him, a tiny, soft-skinned boy and held him to my heart. Merlyn parted us.

Tonight, let us lay down the cover on that time, and shut the first painful page for ever as I close this final wound.

'I do not want it.'

'We have no time for riddles, Lady. You demanded it.'

'I asked for its abandonment.'

'Do not play cat and mouse with us. Speak plainly!'

'How did it come to him?'

'It was the first morning of his manhood. Midwinter. A mist upon the lake. The night before, the priest Bytwini had given him the sacrament in the chapel. Then Arthur kept the vigil apart while we feasted. Before dawn, he came to meet Merlyn at the lakeside . . . Why do you ask this?'

'Who gave the sword?'

'You have heard the tale told many times.'

'Tell it to me for the last time.'

'For pity's sake! Arthur is alone and dying.'

'And you alone hold in your hands the means by which he may live. How came that sword?'

'He says he saw fays dancing on the water. And in their midst an arm rose from the lake holding up the sword. At Merlyn's bidding, Arthur rowed out and took it. Then Nimue bound his swordbelt on him, and handed him shield and spear and knife. He was armed with the blessing of the Lady of the Lake.'

'But it was not Nimue's gift. She has demanded her reward in blood and slaughter. The hand that offered Caliburn was older far than Nimue. Now she must take it back.'

'Here? In this pool? But it is not the same lake.'

'The earth is one. The waters are one. There is one Lady.'

He has spilled the wind before the final anchorage. He hesitates. One thing to trust this treasure to a sister's keeping. To know, however jealously, it still lies somewhere safe on earth. To dream that there may one day be an Arthur restored to grasp that dragon hilt again, greasing its rune-rich blade with the blood of Britain's enemies. But drown it? Still now,

283

in brilliant moonshine this little lake is black, cold,
immeasurably deep, and even shallow wells may hide the
entrances to wide realms of faerie. What falls in this will be
lost past all recovering. The water sighs amongst stiff reeds
and nameless reptiles plop and croak, and the wind troubles
the trees. What is once given to the Goddess can never be
taken back.

But Bedwyr is the king's man. He accepts orders.

Unwillingly, and with an unsteady arm, he raises the great
blade of Caliburn above his shoulder. It seems to both of us
a weight too heavy for the boy Arthur to have hacked his
way to glory with. I feel relief draining the blood from my
heart. We are all weak now, Arthur from wounds, Bedwyr
from reluctance, I from this achievement, almost too late,
of my life's hope.

The blue blade trembles against the stars, cold as the water.
It is not long for the light now. Do not veil your eyes. You
must watch it go.

'No! Do not destroy it!'

A mourning bellow, like a cow that fears she is losing her
calf. We both spin like eddying leaves and the blade spills
the moonlight to fall back at Bedwyr's side.

Arthur's voice laments hollowly inside the chapel.

'If she takes back the sword, then I am done. You hold
my manhood in your hands.'

Chapter Sixty-six

I am the fay of the volcano.

Mongibel. You call it Mount Etna.

My original realm was Avalon, the ultimate Otherworld island. Now I am invading territory closer to you.

The Normans cede me part of their empire, in Sicily. Morgan lives now in a dazzling white palace high up on Mongibel. It is set in a delightful plain that can be reached only by climbing the roughest slope.

Like Avalon, it is a place of joy, an unending paradise. Here I welcome all the heroes: Arthur, Cei, Bedwyr and a host of others. I give them health, youth, sport, feasting, love.

Mongibello, 'the Beautiful Mountain'. Etna, 'I Burn'.

There are three regions on this mountain. The first is cultivated, an area of luxuriant fertility. The slope is gentle. Vines, olives, fruit, vegetables, corn abound. It supports a grateful people.

The second is wooded and wilder. Pine, broom, chestnut, beech and ferns offer welcome shade. The gradient is steeper now. It becomes harder to see the way ahead.

You climb out through the trees into the last and highest region. Your reward is . . . desert, a wilderness of lava, ash and snow. Nothing before you but the peaks and abysses of dangerous upheavals. There is no trace of animal life.

My volcano is active now, as always. Its lava flow enriches the land below with wonderful fertility.

It also kills.

There are more than two hundred craters. With each new eruption the face of my mountain changes.

Step carefully.

Chapter Sixty-seven

Bedwyr and Caliburn have gone from view. Darkness is humped within the chapel. The moon is going, as the clouds sweep in.

The sea is calling me. I have retreated beyond the limit of the trees now, to where the heather arches over the tumbling brook. They will hardly see me here.

I can only wait.

I cannot bear to wait.

And yet I must. I, that as a nimble, reckless child ran and rode and scrambled over rocks. Exulting in the wind and fearless among horses, I chased the flying vision of my father in the hunt. I climbed the cliffs, scornful of Gwennol's warnings or the nun Luned's pleadings. I thought then I should have been a boy. My father would rather have had me so. So would they all: my mother, kinsfolk, tribe. But if I had been Gorlois's son, Uther Pendragon would have killed me to protect his Arthur. I discovered that femaleness meant life. So I began to learn from others – Gwennol, Ygerne, the nuns – slowly and unwillingly, the glory, power and grief of womanhood.

My boyish freedom ended at Dimiliock, where Gorlois retreated to draw Uther Pendragon to him and lure him away, while we women sought fragile sanctuary on Tintagel. Fragile, because I doubted my mother Ygerne wished the high gate of the convent on the cliffs securely barred. A king would soon be outside, calling for her. Fragile, because we did not know how much respect the nuns might have from that barbaric chief who nonetheless claimed the old authority of Rome. Fragile, because Merlyn was on Uther's side.

Men's bodies are fragile too, beneath their armour.

I have been to Dimiliock since. The ground was cleaned of corpses and the fattened crows had returned to their scraggy shape. The wind moaned there, as it does here tonight. It was all that my iron will could do to hold down my fear-crazed body and stop my feet from fleeing. So many unwilling spirits had found their portal to the Otherworld there. How should my slight and tenuous mortality hold on to this present life and not be swept into the ship of souls with all those others? So after Camlann, too many are dead and we survivors seem like blasphemers.

It is time to go. My ship will soon be here. Must it still end in failure? Shall we leave without him?

I yearn to run around the pool in my distress. Almost, I have broken the Lady's stern command. What now if I pressed forward to the chapel door, offered him my covenant in person, challenged him, pleaded with him, face to face?

No!

Wait still, though this is harder than a lifetime's waiting. My brother and I have met face to face too often, only to part in anger. He made his choice. Gwenhyvar was his queen, Nimue was his counsellor, and what he felt for me, and what he sensed in me, could only anger him. We tormented each other with what could never be. Our physical closeness grated upon our spiritual unlikeness, like steel and flint to spark a catastrophic fire.

Yet Gwenhyvar has gone. Nimue is overthrown. I am still here.

Only be patient. I must summon through distance, waiting, fear, his impossible hope. There is no other way. He must come to me.

But will he? What is that murmur of argument from the chapel now? Oh, how can love be strong enough for this, to wait for the final weakness in Arthur, my brother, my king, my dear? Must his proud body break before his stiff spirit bends? I have so much stored up to give him, and he could die with nothing.

'*Caliburn!*'

Nothing?

He clutches Caliburn back to him, his first, perhaps his truest love. They came together the day he got his manhood. All his life, through doubt of his sisters and disillusionment with his wife, through rivalry of chieftains and treachery of son, Caliburn has stayed faithful. He thought the sword had failed him once when he began to lose, but the weapon he wielded was counterfeit. This blade is his fame, this is his authentication. Can he bring himself to let it go; lay down his weapon to win a greater victory?

'*Why, Bedwyr, why this?*'

Do not imagine I cannot understand your cry, Arthur. Believe I feel how great the darkness into which I am inviting you to step. Do not think I cannot hear you whimper on the poor thin bed of bracken Bedwyr has laid for you. This is a dreadful day, a desolate place, a fearsome hour. Be quick! The gate of the garden I am showing you is narrowing to its final closure. Yet if you break through, will you find yourself its lord or my prisoner?

'Tell her to come and show her face. Let me see for myself if there can be any honesty in those eyes.'

'She will not move beyond the far side of the lake. She sets the terms. My lord, you have no time left to parley.'

'*I will not die!*'

'Arthur, my sword-brother. I am no surgeon. But I have seen enough of wounds to tell that this one cannot be closed by ordinary skill. If you will not take Morgan's risk, well then . . . I have been your soul-friend since boyhood, companion at your side in every fight. I can do you one last service. If you want to unburden to me whatever is heavy on your soul tonight, I think I am Christian enough to hear my king's confession and say the prayer that will send you on your path to peace.'

'You traitor, who call yourself my friend! Are you so sick of Arthur Pendragon, like the rest? You'd send me skywards and leave the land of Britain to Custennin?'

'Not I, my lord! If I had any skill to keep your precious life, if I could guard it safe in the hollow of my hand . . .'

'Morgan is a braver warrior than you are. She comes here to fight for my life with all her armoury. She will not let death have me, will she?'

'So I said, my lord. And yet she has asked too high a price for you.'

'Too high a price? What earthly fee can be more valuable than Arthur's life? I say she honours me, to name a treasure beyond all else I have and tell me the gods will be content with nothing less. Have I an equal? Shall I not buy a second lifetime with an honour-price of my own worth?'

'A second half of life without your greatest talisman?'

Oh, cunning love in Bedwyr that has stopped him arguing longer for my side. Arthur the soldier will do battle even in his dying hour with his closest friend. While Bedwyr counselled submission to me, Arthur jealously raged against it. But if Bedwyr now smooths the path to death, then Arthur will grab the last chance of life. The Lady is wise. If I had rushed to kneel in Bedwyr's place, I should have been thus fiercely opposed.

Caliburn was a two-edged gift. It made a hero of the boy, won him that other sword of kingship, kept for us Britons our partial freedom. Now it sticks to his stiffening hand and will not give us peace.

'*Take it.*'

He is giving it up.

Wait for that sword to cry out, with a shout like the stone of truth. There is a hollow in the highest rock of Tintagel, like the print of a foot. They say that when the true king stands there, a cry goes up from the island itself: '*This is the chief! Follow him!*' Will Caliburn scream like that as it leaves his hand: '*Morgan is taking away his power! Stop her!*' Do either of them realise what it means?

How will it feel to meet at last, just our bare, scarred selves, without the magic of the scabbard, without an enchanted sword? Not quite; we are marked for all time by what we have handled. My miracles of healing have restored whole families' lives; his battles have altered the landscape of history. How could we two sit out the rest of our years in the inglenook of normality?

The Pendragon's weapon of war is in Bedwyr's hand now. A shaft of moonlight from the door shows the eagerness in Arthur's face. He is raised on one elbow, a desperate effort. He wants Bedwyr to run with it. He is making his sally. He is dashing out through the postern of hope, leaving the ramparts of doubt and caution behind him. My brother is taking a great risk. Let its outcome be swift, let it be certain, let it be now. He catches a vision of victory.

And so do I. There is so much Arthur would never let me tell him. All depends on his faith now.

Bedwyr is racing towards the water again with the sword.

All creation waits wide-eyed to see this. The full-faced moon looks down into the pool's bright circle. Hares stretch curious necks, old badgers peer. Shadowed deer stand with poised hoof, their antlers still as branches. Even the moths hang motionless on the stems of trees.

Only Bedwyr moves, more carefully now, his steps crunching on stone, soft on wetter earth, down to the water's edge. His hands bear that wonderful blade, resting across them like a baby. And I find I am gazing at its nakedness with all my being. So I felt once, when I saw my hated brother for the first time, and found I loved him. So I felt, joyful beyond all reasonable hope, when I discovered Arthur's son was still alive and reached out my arms to take him.

I will not touch Caliburn. These hands that warm and heal must not be chilled by this stained steel. I know whose blood shadows the cutting edge. That same small baby, rescued from his father's wrath, saved from the sea, cradled at my breast. Modred is dead. His blood was the last that glutted Caliburn, or ever shall.

I have shed Arthur's blood, as though I had wounded him with my own hands. While he kept the scabbard no weapon could weaken him. I ended that. I made him mortal. I caused this mortal wound. Now I shall give him immortality. We will both have cast away the power that bound us to this world.

Scabbard and sword.

We shall be free and joined.

Chapter Sixty-eight

I am the Land of Joy.

When Hartmann von Aue writes his German version of Erec *around 1190, he calls me Famurgan.*

I am a dangerous goddess.

From the time when I first begin to display my magic art, I can go round the world in the twinkling of an eye and return at once.

I walk the earth, I can silently fly, I can live upon or beneath the wave.

As I desire, I transform a man into a bird or animal.

I can work wonders.

I compel dragons to bring me from the air a contribution for my work, and the fish theirs from the water.

The earth bears no herb whose virtue is not known to me as well as his hand to the author.

I can raise the dead.

And most wonderful of all, the evil spirits called devils are all under my control.

Since Sybil died, the earth has produced, you may be sure of this, never a better mistress of magic skill than Famurgan.

Some ten years later, another German, Wolfram von Eschenbach, writes his own wonderfully colourful version of the Arthurian story, Parzival. *He mocks his predecessors like Hartmann, while telling a rattling good yarn and scattering literary jokes.*

I have transformed myself in a curious shape-shifting. The fay is here named Terdelaschoye, the 'Land of Joy'. It is her magic mountain that Wolfram calls 'Feimurgan'.

In this guise of Terdelaschoye, I cast a spell of love over the fairy ancestor of heroes, Mazadan. I lure him to Feimurgan, and from our union descend Uther Pendragon, Arthur, Gawain, Parzival.

Is this witty German, who claims to be a shrewd judge of

291

*women, really unable to distinguish between the lady and her
land? Or am I another of his jokes?*

*Well, let it stand. In my place, the earth herself has become
a living being, opening arms of welcome.*

And I am his Country of Bliss.

Chapter Sixty-nine

The moon is reaching her zenith. The clouds are tearing apart. Have we waited too long?

Darkness lurches from the chapel. I start with fear. Arthur lies slumped in the shadow of the doorway. He clutches Modred's wound. The strength is ebbing fast between his faltering fingers. He has let the talisman of his victory out of his hands.

Youth is gone. Modred is cold.

Do not change your mind! You killed him, Arthur. You could not nurse that stained blade like a second child.

If only I could run to him! I would throw my arms round his bowed shoulders, hold him in my life-giving embrace, kiss his pain-wracked face, his crouched, exhausted chest.

No. Hold agonisedly still. Listen. Will he fetch it back?

His voice bellows with astonishing strength, startling unseen creatures that slop the surface of the mere, making Bedwyr spin round.

'MORGAN!'

Never till now. For the first time, powerless, he cries my name as though he truly desired me. I have known the truth when our eyes have met, when our hands have touched. Yet he could never admit his need of me till now.

Bedwyr is hesitating between us. The moon hovers uncertainly over the swaying Caliburn, paling the dragons, darkening the slick steel blade.

Draw further back yet, following the stream that slips through the low lip of hills behind me, out of sight.

My steely will astonishes me, I will save him yet though it tortures me.

'Where is the trickstress gone? Has she left me to die in the dark in a Cornish bog after all? Give me Caliburn.'

No, Arthur, no!

Bedwyr is running back to help him. He knows that love requires he casts away the sword. Loyalty demands obedience to Arthur. I cannot hear his muttered chiding, though every gasp that Arthur draws is tearing me apart, as though I sucked it through gashes in my own body.

'What can you see, Bedwyr?'

'Only the stars in the water and the dark shore. But she was there a moment ago, a flicker of white in front of the woods.'

'I can see nothing but moonshine and shadows. Is that a phantom? I cannot make her out. She was always shifty.'

I am here, Arthur. I have always been near you. You could never see.

'*Morgan!*' That plaintive cry, broken now.

So small the circle of water that separates us. I almost think my sandals are bewitched. I feel I could fly to him. I would easily leave this clinging ground, part the night air like a javelin, fill him with my own sweet breath.

Yet I must stay.

Bedwyr's voice is urgent. 'Arthur, I beg you! She will not come while you still keep Caliburn. Pay her what she asks. Let me give her the sword.'

No, Bedwyr. Do not give it to me. I never asked that.

But can he really yield?

Silence, like a rope between us. I take the strain. Walk backwards now, beyond the trees, beyond the lake, towards the sea. My face is fading out of their dimmed sight to a last pale blur, like the flutter of an owl's wing. The tension heightens intolerably.

Which of us will prove more faithless?

I have halted by the farthest boundary of this hollow now, where the stream is hurrying westward. Behind me, a solitary pine, and then a limitless darkness arched by stars. A vast possibility. My land of promise. Can he trust me?

That agonised cry.

'Give it to me, Bedwyr! I will do it myself. I must live!'

You will live. Oh, my brother Arthur, you shall live!

He staggers upright with Bedwyr's help, fighting his anguish, slipping in the clotted blood of his own shedding. He leans gasping on the doorpost of the chapel. I am wracked with his pain.

The moonlight is grey on his matted hair.

Caliburn is grasped between his hands now. He leans on it like a pilgrim staff.

'I cannot see her. Will she not come and take it from me?'

Arthur totters out into the open, dragging the weighty weapon. His loyal friend supports him. Desperately halting now, they shuffle down the uneven slope towards the lake. Bedwyr's arms surround him swiftly as Arthur's legs give way. Still he forces himself to struggle on.

They have come to the mere's edge. A gust of wind troubles the water, sending white-capped waves lapping to his feet. We all wait.

'Will she mock me yet? Rob me of victory and leave me to die here?'

'Sire, you have no other hope.'

No hope, except in the plain shroud of a burial beneath the sign of his weaponless Christ. No swords in heaven. He is not ready for that yet.

Caliburn is alive in his hand once more. The dragons of all his victories are half-upraised. Still he jealously grasps their magic.

The moonlight glints on patterned steel. From the skies, the sparkle of ruby, emerald, sapphire stars leap like lightning to catch their images on the hilt of Caliburn.

Now, Arthur, now! Our moon is turning.

It is too difficult. The great weapon sags into the shadow by his side. The golden dragon-guard of Caliburn's glory has not taken wing. We are gambling for the highest stake of all. What if he were to let go and win nothing from me?

'What can you see?' he demands again.

'Only waves breaking on dark water, and the wind bending the trees.'

Terrible dilemma.

'Yet I will live!'

The shining blade swings high over Arthur's head now, urgently brandished at last. Where does he find such strength?

'Is she there now?'

Sweat glistens on his poor pale face between the encrusted blood. Let me kiss it clean!

'The stars confuse my eyes, sire. There is a white shadow on the farther shore. It may be may-blossom.'

'*Morgan!*'

So small a shout for such a victory. There is a moment in our lives that arrives almost without decision, when the arms swing and stop, when the fingers loose their grasp, and the hands open. When the thing is done. We have let go.

So short a vault into eternity. Caliburn's magnificence flashes across the stars. Great Arthur Pendragon's sword is going home. Swift as a lifespan, it reaches its apogee and falls spinning along Arianrhod's Way, on down into darkness. Our eyes are locked on its descent, our heartbeats seem to catch. We await its final plunge into the nether waters.

Our end is written in our beginning. The circle closes. The serpent's mouth swallows its tail. The sword blade sends a white wave leaping, and we see in this moment a white arm strike up from the depth to catch and flourish the hilt. The Lady draws it under. He has done her bidding. She has given Arthur this blade, blessed its warfare, now she calls it home to her. The rugged half of Britain Arthur has saved. Too late to weep for the fertile part we have lost. I, Morgan the Healer, could have taught him the magic of the scabbard.

Let time stand still, while I give him that long sweet lesson. He is disarmed, and I am empowered at last.

Chapter Seventy

I am a mirage.

Fata Morgana. An atmospheric phenomenon seen across the Straits of Messina.

Yes, I am still to be found in Sicily.

By a trick of the Mediterranean light, objects on the opposite coast appear to be supernaturally tall. Towers soar high in the clouds, and are doubled mysteriously underwater. I show you a fisherman's cottage, and you think you have seen a fairy castle.

Beware what you are trusting yourself to, Arthur. I may be an illusion.

Wait, though. Not all mirages are totally false. The traveller in the desert is maddened by a vision of shimmering water always just beyond reach as he stumbles towards it. Death, not the wished-for oasis, lies that way. Yet others show the near reflections of far-off solid substance.

There is no fairy castle over the water, but the pinnacled images of my mirage are grounded in a smaller, homely reality.

I am Fata Morgana, giver of visions. I enchant the truth of that distant shore you have not yet reached. By the wonderful extravagance of my promise I fire your desire to seek and find me. Will I disappoint you at your voyage's end?

You must take ship and sail out across the strait before you know the answer.

Chapter Seventy-one

And so we come. Morgan Sea-Born, Margawse the Red, Elaine the Fair. Ranked round us are all the wisest of the Wise. We bring with us, night-hooded and crowned in moon-silver, the shadow behind all our authority, the Lady. Our ship is swan-prowed and hung with golden chains, its sides draped with purple silk that we have marvellously embroidered. And we three stand, black-robed, keening the laments, but our hearts high with joy, our faces beautiful beyond believing, our hands eager to welcome, our eyes immortally young.

And in our wake, the small shores part and waves wash glittering far behind us. A long, moon-bathed river is opening before our prow. Dark-heathered moors give way as the silver brightens past seeing. We sail the river of life.

'What is it, man? My eyes are swimming in a sea of silver. What is happening? What is that shadow swooping on me like a raven?'

'A ship, my lord. I see a long white-painted neck upon its prow, a swan's head circled with gold. There are no oarsmen, but the mast flies a great sail that blots out the stars.'

'The brook was shallow, Bedwyr.'

'This keel is deep.'

The river flowing from this mere broadens beyond imagination over our stern, an endless sea-road. This night is not melancholy, for all our wailing. Heaven dances in the crest of every surge. Arthur and his sisters are coming together.

We are three, and we are one. Elaine, who was once the Lily Maid, and now the Ancient Sybil. Margawse, full-bodied, gloriously mature, Mother and Whore. And I, Morgan, the youngest and the most senior of us, I am both Crone and Virgin tonight. We have been all things to you,

Arthur. Kore, Demeter, Hecate. Parvati, Derga, Kali. Take us in the fullness of our diversity. Embrace our wholeness.

'Who sails this ship, Bedwyr? What is this wailing in my ears?'

'Three great Ladies with royal crowns, weeping and holding out their hands to you.'

Three sisters, Arthur's sisters. We are more than this. In other races we have been the three Fates, the three Norns, the three Graces, that can make each man a king and all women queens. We are the fays who croon over cradles, crown heroes in their heyday, gather them to the Fortunate Isles at last. Your warfare is finished, Arthur. Your work is over.

'Morgan is coming, after all! I knew she could not refuse me. She has ointments more precious than the wisdom of all the physicians in the world. She has healed dying men before, when all other hope was lost. She will save my life!'

Yes, Arthur, my brother. I will heal you.

We glide towards the shore, and the mere widens in a vast dark sigh to let us pass.

Three queens are coming. We were royal women before we took our earthly husbands' coronets. Power was born in our blood. We hold authority, over life, over death, over loving, over hating. We come to hail our brother. This is King Arthur. Praise him! This is more than the Imperator, Duke of Battles, clad in Roman leather and steel, rallying Christianised chieftains to defend the Island. He is more than a courageous Celt, victorious against Saxons for a while. More than the myth of an almost-forgotten god, whom no one worships now, leading his preposterous war-band through the wild hunts of folk-tales. We come for King Arthur of Britain. And in our empty hands we hold his immortality. This night we shall give him that lasting life for which he always craved. No dubious battle-site shall confine him to a page of history. No spurious grave shall hold him, crumbling to dust. Our advent this night shall crown him with an unforgettable name. In his departure he shall endure for ever.

The ship slows, and the sail unbidden spills the breeze. Still we glide forward, and a tension grips us now for we are coming into the moment of greatest danger. Is he weakened enough? Is he weaponless, powerless, lost enough to accept the gift that only we can offer? Creep on, my ship, through the soft sibilance of wavelets to the muddied earthly shore and the bloodied man with hope still in his eyes.

'My sight is clouding, Bedwyr. What colour is the sail?'

'Black, my lord.'

Keep courage, Arthur. For letting go of the land you shall have Paradise, the Fortunate Isles, the Realm of the Ever-Young. Palaces of coral and crystal, golden apples on every silver-branched tree. Swift-racing, dappled horses, lovely women, strong, fair-limbed heroes, who once fell gashed with wounds. Feasting and wine and dancing and song, song, song!

'No, Bedwyr, no! Say it is not that dreaded barge of souls!'

Sing, sisters! Call down magic from the moon. Weave harmonies of healing, lullabies of love. Drown out his cries. Faster, my ship. He may slip from us yet in this last foot of water.

'Morgan has betrayed me! The murdering, lying bitch! I asked for life and she has raised the black sail of my death!'

Gently grounding now. A shudder runs through the ship. Reach out my arms.

'Come.'

For you, little brother, there will be the greatest myth of all. Where is the grave of Arthur? A mystery! He is not dead, but sleeping somewhere. In Britain's darkest hour someone will blow the horn and he will leap to his feet with a hundred knights at his side and his white mare Llamrei pawing the ground.

Arthur cannot die. I will not let him.

He is weeping like a baby. Bedwyr is cradling him on his shoulder. Does he understand? My hands touch the stiffening shirt of leather, the chilly arms.

'Brother.'

Sobbing in helpless rage and furious disappointment.

'*Arthur!*'

He has nothing left to fight me with. He has thrown away his wife, son, sword.

'My dearest heart.'

'You have cheated me!'

He is in my arms now, held close to my breast. He shudders

like a frightened hound as we lift him lightly into our barge. Be easy, my love.

His head is resting now in Elaine's wide, soft lap as she strokes his temples. Margawse's fragrant hair tumbles over his chest as she kneels by his side. I hug his feet against my heart.

The silver night in the west is ablaze with exultation. The heavens are dancing. The land is going. Over our bows the ocean tosses jewelled manes, and to the far horizon all the stars are singing the great king home.

The breeze is fresh on the tears of my cheeks, scented with may-blossom.

Chapter Seventy-two

I am the woman of your fantasies.

We need our fictions.

I have been given many roles, benevolent, ambiguous, wicked. I am indeed the Shape-Shifter, as my tale is transmuted down the centuries.

No, not my tale. Never till now my own story. I am the immortal fay, the faery mistress, the wicked witch. But it is the deeds of the human hero you would rather hear, a myth in which you seek to find yourself. Morgan is required only to serve the author's purpose.

It is Arthur's story you want to read, not mine. Or the love-affair of Lancelot and Gwenhyvar. Or the Quest of the Holy Grail.

For each telling, I become what you need me to be. Lover, mother, enemy.

In a tale of kings and warriors, I am the goddess who invites Arthur to my island of bliss, the hero's just reward.

As the story of the Sovereignty of Britain develops, someone must betray King Arthur. After all, he has Caliburn now. He cannot be defeated in fair fight, can he? Very well, I am that traitor, working by treacherous magic to bring his kingdom down. I plot against his life. I steal his scabbard. I cause his death.

When the Norman French become jealous of British heroes and their own knight, Lancelot of the Lake, takes the centre stage, I shift my attention from Arthur. In these courtly romances I am now the jealous temptress spurned by Lancelot, wreaking my vengeance on the lovers. I betray them to Arthur. I destroy the fellowship of the Round Table. Arthur loses the knights who could have saved him. I am responsible for the final tragedy.

Do more spiritual writers turn to the Quest for the Holy Grail? I play little part in their story. Even Arthur gives place to the saintly Galahad. Safer to shun me. Pagan, female, I am a dangerous, beautiful woman who turns foul and ugly when I take up the devil's arts.

Malory fixes the most powerful image of me. I am the vicious villainess. The evidence is there in his sources. It is partly true. But even he suggests at the end it may not be the whole truth.

The original fairy tradition lives on, in Brittany, Sicily. I am overwhelmingly generous to men who please me, alluring, autocratic, ambiguous.

The Victorians, like Tennyson, prefer to draw a modest veil over me. Uther, Ygerne, Margawse, Modred, Morgan: best not explore our relationships with the noble King Arthur too closely. Between us, blood and semen have mixed more nearly than the prudish might wish to know. Better a baby washed in from the Otherworld with choirs of angels. Better to say that Modred is

'my sister's son — no kin of mine',

and opposes Arthur from pure wickedness. Better not even mention Arthur has other sisters. Merlyn the sorcerer may fall to the wiles of Vivian. Arthur the king must be stainless.

The twentieth-century writers have no such inhibitions. I am, I must be, the bloodthirsty Morrigan. They seize upon this portrayal of my character with gusto. Malory's version is triumphant. I am the vindictive witch, the figure of evil, the arch-enemy. Arthur is always the goodie. Forget the Lives of Saint Cadoc *and* St Padarn, *which paint him as a free-booting, lustful brigand at odds with the Church. Any evidence that points to ambivalence in either of us is rejected.*

In countless children's stories, fantasy novels, television romps and second-rate films I am the unthinking stereotype of the satanic. I may appear beautiful but malevolent, or ugly in face and warped in character. I am a terrifying sorceress, but in the end I am ever thwarted, always the baddie, always the loser.

So, in John Boorman's film Excalibur, *you see Merlin tempt me to use once too often the magic I wheedled out of him. Before your eyes I shrivel from a sensuous beauty to a hideous old crone, and die. When the ship comes for the wounded Arthur after Camlann, it cannot be I who carries him to Avalon.*

So, in Stephen Lawhead's Pendragon Cycle, *I become the poison, the viper, the black-clad embodiment of the powers of darkness. I am entirely possessed by evil. Again, I cannot heal*

Arthur. I am killed before the final battle. Arthur is wholly good. There is no fault in him. This is the Christ-figure.

In Nikolai Tolstoy's The Coming of the King, *women are almost invisible. But Morgan is here, the malevolent hag, the Washer at the Ford, the attacking shape-shifter. Wholly wicked.*

This is the standard picture. What makes these men seize upon this polarity so avidly? Is it so difficult for them to recognise ambivalence? Why do they find it essential to whiten Arthur's or Merlyn's name and blacken mine? Why must they so select or distort the evidence to deify the man and demonise the woman? Does this tell you more about them than about me?

One struggles to admit a tiny ray of truth.

In T.H. White's The Once and Future King, *Morgan is queen over the fairies.*

> *'They have no hearts. It is not so much that they wish to do evil, but that if you were to catch one and cut it open, you would find no heart inside. They are cold-blooded, like fish.'*

Margawse is boiling a cat:

> *'She was not a serious witch like her sister Morgan le Fay. She was doing it because the little magics ran in her blood — as they did with all the women of her race.'*

When young Arthur finds me, I am in my magical house in a lake of milk. It is made of butter and cheese and tripe and chitterlings. My prisoners are lashed to columns of pork. I am stretched on a bed of glorious lard. At the approach of an iron knife I writhe in agony like a slug before my castle collapses.

This is standard stuff. But when Arthur becomes king he observes,

> *'If my father killed the Queen of Orkney's father, then I think she has a good reason for wanting her husband to rebel against me.'*

To which Merlin replies,

> *'It is only a personal reason. Personal reasons are no excuse for war.'*

*Even in the more thoughtful treatments of Morgan the trap
awaits us all to vilify Margawse.*

The women writers struggle with our sisterhood.

Rosemary Sutcliffe's Sword at Sunset, *finds a down-to-earth
explanation for Arthur's success in the introduction of heavy
cavalry. Little place for an enchantress here. But Ygerne is
Arthur's unknown sister by Uther Pendragon. She lures him to
become the father of Medraut in revenge for her mother.*

> *'I saw a woman and a child, a woman and a girl, beside
> the peat fire in this place, the one teaching and the other
> absorbing that corroding, soul-destroying lesson of hate. All
> at once I saw that what I had taken for the ruins of beauty
> in Ygerne's face was the promise of beauty that had been
> cankered before ever it could come to flowering and for one
> instant pity mingled with the horror that was rising like vomit
> in my throat. What had I let loose? What had my father let
> loose before me, into the world?'*

To Mary Stewart, then: The Wicked Day. *In earlier books,
I am the wronged younger daughter, betrothed to Lot of Orkney,
but then palmed off on Urbgen so that Margawse can marry Lot.
But now:*

> *'Morgan's natural aptitude for sorcery had already led her
> to surpass the witch of Orkney, with her sex potions and
> poisonous spells by almost as much as Merlin in his day
> surpassed them both. And none of it was used for good.'*

*Margawse's motives are personal, mine political. I plot against
Urbgen and Arthur to achieve greater power for myself. So at
the end I can be trusted to tend the wounded Arthur, because*

> *'without him she was, and would be, nothing.'*

And so at last to Marion Bradley's The Mists of Avalon. *The
feminist version. A novel for the late twentieth century. Here is
indeed my story, not Arthur's. See it fresh through my woman's
eyes. It looks very different. I am the heroine, much misunderstood.
Bradley extols my paganism as much as Lawhead curses it. She
rails against the Church as passionately as he praises it. Only*

at the end we sense a partial reconciliation with the nuns, the converse of Malory's with the hooded queens.

We are all trapped by the metaphors of warfare, opposing sides, the Either/Or.

Morgan is rooted in circularity, in ambiguity. I am Both/And.

Well, you may do with me what you will. I am the shape-shifter. I can assume whatever form you wish me to take. Each author alters my myth to serve their particular purpose.

No doubt Fay Sampson is using me here for her own ends. This will not be the last you hear of me.

Epilogue

How could you understand?

He is not your lover.

You do not wail to see his blood staining your dress.

He is not your brother.

You did not hear your father's wife cry out in the treacherous, shape-shifting, face-changing moonlight as Uther Pendragon twined himself upon her.

He was not your king, though in him you find your definition of kingship.

He is not your dead.

Shield him gently as our ship begins to rock. He cannot shrink from me now as my tender hands caress his face. This gold-bearded, white-lipped, blood-crusted face pillowed in the lap of Elaine.

Close his eyes. The blue, fierce, staring, kingly eyes that will scan no more British battlefields.

Margawse weeps as her trembling fingers unlatch the clotted buckles of his armour.

You do not know what you have to thank him for.

You have nothing to forgive him.

Nimue has left him.

He was never Gwenhyvar's, that was not worth a broken fingernail to him.

He has slain Modred.

But first and last and always he was ours.

Sleep, Arthur. My golden bed awaits you. One night will cancel out a lifetime's pain. When you wake, all will be well.

Night arches over us. Caliburn has blazed for the last time between the stars.

This mere is dark. Glide on, my boat. The king is sleeping soundly.

307

The river is wide. His breath grows faint. Sail swift, my ship.

Dream well, my love. Morgan Sea-Born is singing the lay of healing.

The sky is brightening. The ocean is dancing. Glory is all about us.

Fly on, my ship. Beyond the Island of the Mighty, beyond the western sea, out past the farthest reach of sunset.

In Avalon the sword will meet its scabbard.

Welcome to my bed, Arthur.